The Good Mother

SINÉAD MORIARTY

PENGUIN BOOKS

PENGUIN BOOKS

UK | USA | Canada | Ireland | Australia
India | New Zealand | South Africa

Penguin Books is part of the Penguin Random House group of companies
whose addresses can be found at global.penguinrandomhouse.com

First published by Penguin Ireland 2017
Published in Penguin Books 2017

001

Set in 12.01/14.27 pt Garamond MT Std
Typeset in India by Thomson Digital Pvt Ltd, Noida, Delhi
Printed in Great Britain by Clays Ltd, St Ives plc

A CIP catalogue record for this book is available from the British Library

ISBN: 978-0-241-97074-4

www.greenpenguin.co.uk

MIX
Paper from
responsible sources
FSC® C018179

The Good Mother

For Dad, we miss you

'Motherhood: All love begins and ends there'

Robert Browning

Summer

I

Kate stood in the empty hall and looked around. Nothing left but memories. She remembered moving in around ten years ago. Nick had carried her over the threshold, even though it was a long time since she'd been a blushing bride. He'd been like an excited little kid, running around, showing her the fancy fridge that churned out ice cubes, the Jacuzzi and the big garden where the kids could play football.

It was his dream house. Nick felt as if he'd 'arrived'. Big house, big garden, fancy car. Things were good, really good. Nick was doing well and finally able to have the life he'd always dreamed of living.

They'd been happy then. Luke was eight and Jess was two when they'd moved in. Jess had taken her time to arrive. After three miscarriages and years of disappointment they had almost given up, but then Kate had got pregnant and gone full-term. The longed-for and beloved Jess had arrived, like a ray of sunshine, in their lives. She had been worth the wait. Gazing at her adoringly in the hospital, Nick said they now had the perfect family.

The house had been full of laughter and fun. They'd had lots of birthday celebrations and good times there. Kate had enjoyed it all, every minute.

She knew buying the house had been a stretch for them financially. She just hadn't realized how much of a stretch. Nick had been vague about the deposit and repayments, and she'd been too wrapped up in the kids and the daily chores, and too naive to ask questions.

Or maybe she hadn't wanted to know. The truth was, she'd stuck her head in the sand on purpose. Life was good, and Kate hadn't wanted to know the details. Nick had said he had it under control and she'd gladly left him to it.

When the economic downturn had badly affected the big estate agent Nick worked for, Kate had just hoped for the best. She'd redoubled her efforts to create the perfect home, always having a meal prepared for Nick when he came in at the end of the day. She'd become a regular domestic goddess, trying to smooth over the cracks.

She'd wanted to make their home a haven for Nick, but it hadn't been enough. And then, instead of bringing them closer, Bobby's birth had pushed Nick even further away. When Nick had started to work late all the time and come home smelling of someone else's perfume, Kate had ignored it . . . until it was too late.

She looked around at her home and bit her lip to prevent herself crying. Everything was so messed up. What the hell would her life be like from now on?

'*Muuuuuuum!*' Bobby shouted from the front door, hands on his hips. 'I want to go now. It's hot and sweaty in the car.'

Kate went over and kissed his hot little face. 'I just need to get Jess. She's upstairs.'

She found Jess in her bedroom. Her daughter had her back to her. Kate knew by the hunch of her shoulders and the quiet sniffles that she was crying. She went over and put her arms around her. Jess stiffened. 'I'm sorry, pet.'

'I'm fine, Mum.'

Kate turned her daughter to face her. Jess wiped away her tears roughly with the sleeve of her shirt. 'I know this is hard, Jess, but I think living with Granddad will be fun.' She tried to sound convincing.

Jess nodded. 'It's just . . . it's just all so final. I thought that maybe Dad would come home, but now I guess I know he won't. Will he?'

Kate hugged her. Poor Jess. She was the optimist in the family. The boys knew Nick was never coming back. Even at seven years old, Bobby knew. But here was Jess, the middle child, still hoping for the happy ending that could never be. 'Your dad's with Jenny now, pet. They have a new baby and a new life, and that's not going to change. But he still loves you all very much,' she added hastily.

'Yeah, which is why he never comes to see us,' Luke drawled from the doorway.

'Luke,' Kate said, in a warning voice. 'Your sister's upset.'

Luke came in and put a big muscly arm around his little sister's shoulders. 'Come on, Jess. I know Granddad's house is a lot smaller and he's a bit mad, but we'll be fine.'

'You don't have to share a room with Bobby,' Jess reminded him.

Luke grinned. 'Yeah, it sucks for you. But I have to study for my Leaving Cert so I can't have Bobby droning on about his facts all day long. Besides, I'll probably move out next year and live close to whatever university I end up going to, so you can have my room then.'

'But I don't want you to move out. I'd miss you.'

Luke kissed the top of her head. 'You're too soft, Jess. You need to toughen up.'

'She's perfect just the way she is.' Kate smiled at them.

They both rolled their eyes.

'You always say that, Mum,' Jess said, grinning at her brother.

'It's true. You three kids are my proudest achievement. And I know the last few months have been awful and I wish . . . well, I just wish that . . .' Kate was choking up.

Luke put his hand on her arm. 'It's okay, Mum. You did everything you could. Dad's just a selfish dickhead.'

'Luke, don't speak about your father like that.'

'Daddy's a dickhead,' Bobby shouted from the door, giggling.

Kate glared at Luke.

He shrugged. 'I speak the truth.'

'You're eighteen, Luke. You should know when to zip it. And as for you, Bobby, you're supposed to be waiting in the car.'

Luke flung his arm around her and pulled her in for a hug. 'Chill, Mum.' To Bobby he said, 'Don't use bad words. It's not cool.'

'But you said it and you're cool.' Bobby frowned, trying to make sense of these conflicting statements.

Kate bent down to look her youngest in the eye. 'Bad language is not okay. You know that and so does Luke. Now, come on, all of you, Granddad's waiting for us.' She ushered them downstairs and out of the front door, telling them to get into the car and buckle up.

Once they'd left, she allowed herself a few minutes for a final walkabout. It was stupid: she should just walk out of the door and not look back, but it was so hard to leave the place. You spent all your time creating a home, but you never really knew just how much it meant to you until it was taken away. This had been her sanctuary from the world, the place she most enjoyed being, an extension of herself and her hopes for the future. Now, it wasn't hers any more, and she had no idea what her future held – stress, loneliness and financial worry, probably. Nick had taken everything from her, home, security and, most of all, her self-esteem. Leaving her for a younger model was so cliché it should make her laugh. But it wasn't funny. It hurt like hell. The pain of it kept looping out and around her, drowning her sense of self and self-worth.

Slowly, she forced herself to walk towards the front door. She didn't want to go. She had a brief, crazy thought of staging a sit-in protest and forcing the bank to let her keep it, but she knew that was daft. Besides, this home and that future were gone now: the place was stripped bare, back to how it was when they'd first bought it. Just like me, Kate thought sadly. Right back to square one.

Her phone pinged and she pulled it out of her pocket. A message from Maggie. She opened it and smiled. Trust Maggie and her perfect timing! *Today must be hell for you. Chin up! I'll be over at the weekend to help you unpack and put manners on George! I'll bring wine. Lots and lots of wine! You'll be okay. Love you. M.*

She pushed back her shoulders, took a deep breath and stepped outside onto the step. As she pulled the front door shut behind her, the finality of the lock's click almost made her sink to her knees and cry. Instead, she waved to her waiting children, swallowed her grief and took her place in the driver's seat.

Kate eased her battered old car down the driveway. She saw Jess's lip quivering in the rear-view mirror and her heart ached. This was not the life she'd planned for her children. She'd never wanted them to come from a broken home. How had everything gone so wrong?

I'm a forty-two-year-old woman with three kids moving back in with my dad because I'm broke and homeless, she thought. She gripped the steering-wheel and tried to control her breathing. Now that Nick was preoccupied with Jenny and Jaden, the baby, Kate had to be even more mindful of the kids. She had to be more loving and patient and giving . . . but she was exhausted. All she wanted to do was lie down, pull the duvet over her head and cry.

*

George was standing at the gate when they arrived, wearing his navy apron with 'The Village Café' on it. His cheeks were flushed.

'Uh-oh, Granddad has a cross face,' Bobby said.

They climbed out of the car.

'Lookit, Kate, I'm happy for you to move in, you know I am, but your removal men have left boxes all over the kitchen and I'm trying to run a business here. Besides, Sarah just called to say she's not coming in today and that she's found another job. The new French girl, Nathalie, is useless, so I'm pretty much on my own. I need a hand.'

Kate took charge. 'Right. Luke, you and the others tidy up the boxes while I help Granddad in the café. Put all the boxes upstairs in my bedroom. Pile them up in the corner out of the way and I'll sort them out later. When you've finished, come down and help. We'll be busy for lunch.'

Kate followed her father through the hall into the big kitchen that served the café.

'I'll sort these out if you go and serve coffees,' George said, as he began firing homemade quiches into the big oven.

Kate went through the kitchen door that led to the café. There were two tables waiting to be served. At the other three occupied tables, people were busy drinking coffee and eating scones. Five tables were empty, but not for long. The lunchtime rush would start soon.

Kate took the orders for the two tables and went back into the kitchen. She inhaled the scent of the fresh coffee beans and closed her eyes. The familiar scent of her childhood always calmed her. Kate knew the place like the back of her hand. She'd grown up behind the counter. As far back as she could remember she'd helped her mum and dad run the Village Café. Her mum had always been more front-of-house while her dad did a lot of the cooking. But after her

8

mother's death six years ago, that had changed. George had had to engage more with the customers and he had grown used to it. It didn't come naturally to him, but he was much better at it than he had been.

Throughout her married life Kate had often received urgent calls whenever a staff member had called in sick or a big party was booked in. She liked helping her parents – as an only child she was close to both and the café was her home from home.

After her mother died, she had called in every day to make sure her father was coping. He had been utterly shattered by Nancy's death, but with Kate's help and the café needing to be run, he had muddled through. Having to get up and open it every day had kept him going, given him a purpose. Kate often wondered what he would have done if he hadn't had the business. It had been a life-saver and kept him active and busy.

Her dad had been a rock to Kate when Nick had left her two years ago. He'd stepped in and given her money to get her through, and when the bank had repossessed the house, he had immediately suggested they all move in with him. Kate had wanted to weep with relief.

She knew it wasn't going to be easy, given that her father was used to living alone, but they'd get through somehow. She'd make it work. She had to – she had nowhere else to go and the kids needed stability. As a new customer came to the counter, Kate put a smile on her face. She willed herself to be positive and hopeful for the future. Things would get better – for sure they couldn't get worse. This was the lowest she had ever fallen. The only way was up. It was a new beginning.

Autumn

2

Jess swung back and forth on the little black gate. She was bored and wanted to go back inside the house, but she didn't want to leave Luke alone.

He was leaning against the wall, looking up and down the road. Jess watched him check his phone. No message.

Maybe Dad's just late, she thought. He was always late. In fact, he had never been on time in his life. Jess was always on time. She hated being late because she knew how it made the other person feel – like they didn't matter.

Luke raised his face to the sun. He was so handsome, Jess thought. He'd got a lovely tan over the summer, even though they hadn't gone on a sun holiday this year. There was no way Mum could afford it, and Dad had said he couldn't either. But Luke had spent so much time training outside, he looked as if he'd been in Spain for a month. He was super-fit, like the professional rugby players on TV.

'I bet when you go back to school tomorrow you'll be the fittest guy on your team,' she said, trying to distract him. She wanted to make him feel better. She had a horrible feeling their dad wasn't coming and she knew it would hurt him.

Luke gave her one of his crooked smiles. 'I doubt it. I'd say Harry's been working out in Italy.'

Jess stopped swinging and leant against the gate. 'Maybe not. Maybe Harry got really fat and lazy in Italy. Maybe he spent all summer eating pizza and ice cream and lying about by the pool.'

Luke laughed. 'I hope so, but it's very unlikely. Knowing Harry's dad, he probably hired him a personal trainer to make sure he stayed in top condition.'

Unlike our dad, who doesn't give a damn, Jess knew Luke was thinking.

'How come Harry's dad is so into rugby?' she asked.

Luke put his phone down on the wall. 'He played senior cup rugby when he was in school and he's obsessed with Harry making the team. I know he's hoping I'll get injured so Harry will get picked.'

'You won't, though, will you, Luke? Get injured?'

Luke shook his head. 'No. I'm going to get on that team if it kills me.'

Jess knew that rugby was the only thing Luke really enjoyed . . . well, that and being with Piper.

Jess glanced down at her brother's trainers. Piper had handed him a box yesterday covered with shiny paper. When he'd unwrapped it and held up the trainers, he'd been over the moon. He was so happy. Jess wanted to kiss Piper for making Luke's face light up like that.

'Jesus, Piper, they're way too much,' he'd said.

'Hey, babe, it's not every day you turn eighteen.'

'I know, but seriously . . .'

'I got paid last week and wanted to treat you.'

'They're awesome.' He'd leant over and kissed her.

Jess had looked away then because her eyes had filled with tears. She was so happy that Luke had Piper for his girl-friend – she was amazing.

Jess reckoned Luke was in love with Piper. She often caught him staring at Instagram photos of her when he thought no one was looking. She prayed that Piper was as into Luke as Luke was into her. She thought she was, but it was hard to tell with Piper because she was super-nice to everyone.

But when Jess saw the trainers yesterday, she'd felt really good. If Piper had spent that much money on Luke, she must be really crazy about him.

Bobby came up behind them on the path.

'Hey, little guy,' Luke said, high-fiving him.

Jess loved it when Luke was nice to Bobby. Poor Bobby worshipped him and sometimes Luke kind of ignored him. Jess knew Luke didn't mean it, but when he gave Bobby attention, Bobby was the happiest kid ever. It was a bit annoying because Jess always tried to be nice to Bobby but he didn't seem to care about her. He really only wanted Luke.

'Whatcha doing?' Bobby asked.

'Waiting for Dad to pick me up and take me out.' Luke sighed.

'For your birthday?'

'Yep.'

'But it was yesterday.' Bobby frowned.

'I know, but he was busy then.'

'Dad's *always* busy.' Bobby took Jess's place on the gate and swung back and forth.

Luke checked his phone again. Still no message. It was six thirty. Their father was half an hour late.

'He's probably with stupid Jaden and his pooey nappies,' Bobby said.

Oh, God, not Jaden again, Jess thought. All Bobby ever did was bang on about poor Jaden. It wasn't his fault he was born. He was only a baby. Bobby was so mean about him. He hated him. Like, really hated him. Jess sometimes worried that he might pinch the poor baby or hurt him if he was ever left alone with him. On the rare times they saw Jaden, Jess watched Bobby like a hawk.

'Dad's probably having his balls squeezed by his stupid girlfriend,' Luke muttered.

Thankfully, Bobby didn't hear him say that. Jess felt her stomach turn over. Even she hated Jenny. Well, 'hate' was probably too strong a word. You weren't supposed to hate anyone. But Jess certainly didn't like her. Jenny had caused this whole mess. Jenny had made her parents split up and then her dad leave, and now baby Jaden had made him not even be around any more. Jess wished he had never met Jenny.

'I heard Mummy on the phone yesterday calling Daddy a prick.' Bobby grinned.

'Bobby! Mind your language,' Jess said.

'I'm just saying what Mummy said.'

Luke's phone beeped.

'Is it Dad?' Jess asked.

'Nope. It's Harry.'

Jess leant in and read the message. *See you tomorrow, bro, hope the summer was good. I hear you and Piper are serious now – niiiiiiice.*

Luke typed back: *Not bad ☺ See you 2mrw.*

'Do you think Harry will be the winger on the team or you?' Bobby asked.

'Me.'

'I hope so. You're brilliant at rugby. I know Daddy thinks soccer is the best game because he was good at it, but I think rugby is. I want to be like you, Luke.'

Luke smiled down at him and ruffled his hair. 'I bet you'll be brilliant at rugby too.'

'I don't think so. I heard Daddy say, "Bobby can't kick snow off a rope."' Bobby looked down at his bare feet.

Luke cursed under his breath. 'He was only joking.'

'You're great, Bobby. I'm sure Dad didn't mean it,' Jess added.

'Can I tell you both a secret?' Bobby asked.

'Sure,' they said, exchanging a look.

'I hate Chelsea Football Club and I only pretend to like them cos of Daddy. I think they suck.'

Luke laughed. 'So do I, but we'd better not tell Dad that – we don't want to wind him up.'

Jess smiled. It was nice being together, just the three of them, chatting. Luke spent so much time with Piper or training that they didn't see much of him.

They heard the front door opening and their mother's voice calling, 'Luke?'

They turned around. She was standing in a flour-covered apron holding her phone. She looked upset. Oh, God, Jess knew that face. She was wearing her your-father's-let-you-down-again expression.

'He's not coming, is he?' Luke said, pushing himself away from the wall and standing up straight.

'I'm sorry, love, no. He said Jaden has a temperature and Jenny's panicking so they're taking him to the doctor.'

'Why can't she take Pooey Pants to the doctor on her own, like you take us on your own?' Bobby asked.

Jess heard her mother mutter, 'Because she's a child herself,' but out loud she said, 'I don't know, Bobby. She's obviously worried.'

Bobby wandered back into the house as Kate came down the path towards them. Luke was staring at the ground. Kate put her hand on his shoulder, and Jess watched as he moved away from her touch. She knew he was struggling not to crack.

In a strangled voice he said, 'I thought this once, this one bloody time, my useless fucker of a father would actually be here. Turning eighteen is kind of a big deal.'

Jess wanted to reach over and hug him, but she knew not to. Luke's fists were clenched, and he was trying hard not to cry.

'Oh, Luke, it *is* a big deal. I'm sure he'll make it up to you,' Kate said.

Luke's eyes were full of rage. 'No, he won't, Mum, because he's a loser. When Killian turned eighteen his dad bought him a car and threw a huge party for him. My dad can't even turn up a day late with a card.' He kicked the wall. 'How could I have been so stupid, waiting at the gate like a little kid? Even Bobby knew he wouldn't show. This is it, Mum. It's over. I'm never letting him disappoint me again. If you expect nothing, you can't get hurt.'

'Don't say that.' Kate looked like she might start crying. 'Why don't you call some pals and go to the movies or something? My treat.'

Luke shook his head. 'You did enough yesterday, Mum. It's fine. Forget it.'

'Luke, your dad loves you, he's just . . . a bit overwhelmed and not very good at juggling things.'

Jess flinched as Luke gazed straight into their mother's eyes. 'Dad has let me down for the last time.' He pushed past them, walked into the house and went up the stairs.

Kate's shoulders dropped and she looked defeated. Jess reached out and held her hand. Kate pulled her into her arms and hugged her tightly. 'What would I do without my little angel?' she whispered into Jess's hair.

'It's okay,' Jess said. 'Luke'll be all right soon. He's just disappointed.'

Kate straightened. 'I'd better get back before Granddad fires me,' she said, smiling weakly.

Jess watched her mother walk up the path and back inside. She worked from morning till night now, and still there wasn't really enough money to go around. As Jess went slowly into the house, she wondered how long Kate could carry on without getting sick. If anything happened to their mother, she and her brothers would be shattered. She was the centre of the circle, the point around which they all lived their lives. They needed her.

Jess went upstairs and stood outside Luke's bedroom door, listening to the music blaring. She knew he was in there, probably crying or punching the wall. She had to do something. She couldn't let his birthday weekend end like this.

Yesterday had been so nice. Mum had made Luke's favourite dinner and bought him a lovely hoodie. Jess knew that August was a really bad month for her because it was 'back to school' and she had to pay for books and uniforms, and money was tight. But you'd never have guessed it yesterday. She'd gone all out for Luke.

Jess had helped her make a cake and they'd blown up balloons and put up a banner so the kitchen looked really nice, and her mum had said how proud she was of Luke, the 'fantastic young man you've turned into', and she'd cried a bit then and Luke had allowed her to hug him. Granddad had gone all mushy too, which wasn't like him. He'd told Luke he was a 'wonderful young man and grandson' and that he had high hopes for his future. Then he'd given him a voucher for his favourite clothes shop. Jess was delighted. Luke didn't get new stuff very often. It had been a really lovely day, but now it had been ruined.

She went back downstairs to the hall, picked up the house phone and dialled Piper's mobile.

'Hello?'

'Piper, it's Jess, Luke's sister.'

'Hi, hon, what's up?'

'It's about Luke . . .' Jess explained what had happened and how unhappy Luke was, that he was in his room on his own and it wasn't a good birthday any more.

'Oh, no, poor Luke.' Piper sounded upset for him. 'I'll be finished work in about an hour and I'll come straight over. Don't worry, sweetie, we'll cheer him up.'

An hour later, Jess opened the front door to Piper and grinned. 'Thanks for coming,' she said, as Piper kissed her forehead.

'Where is he?' Piper asked.

Jess brought her upstairs and Piper knocked on Luke's bedroom door.

'Go away, Jess.'

'It's me, babe,' Piper called.

'Just a sec.'

Jess and Piper could hear Luke scrambling around, opening and closing drawers.

'He's tidying up for you,' Jess said.

'That's kind of sweet,' Piper said, with a smile.

Jess walked away as the bedroom door opened.

'Hey, what are you doing here?'

'I came straight from work. Jess called me about your dad standing you up. Sucks.'

'She shouldn't have told you.'

Piper put her arms around his neck. 'Hey, I want to know when you've had a bad day. I'm here for you. I'm Team Luke.'

As Jess went down the stairs, she saw Luke pull Piper into his bedroom. While kissing her, he kicked the door closed.

Happy with herself, Jess headed into the café to see if she could help. Kate still looked worried, so Jess went over to her and told her that Piper had arrived.

'Thank goodness for that,' Kate said, clearly relieved. 'That'll put a smile back on his face. Why don't you go and ask if she'd like to stay for dinner? I'll make something nice and we'll all cheer him up.'

Jess nodded. 'Sounds good. I'll just tidy those tables over there first.'

Jess worked for the next hour, helping her mother and granddad by clearing tables and putting on the dishwasher. As the café started to empty, she went back into the house and mixed up a batch of Rocky Roads, her speciality, then ran back upstairs and knocked gently on Luke's door.

'Luke?'

'What do you want?'

'Would Piper like to stay for dinner?'

Luke opened his bedroom door. 'Yes.'

'Cool.' Jess grinned. 'Hey, Piper.'

'Thanks for the call. I think I've cheered him up.' She winked.

Luke grabbed his sister's nose and squeezed it. 'You're an interfering little mouse but I forgive you.'

'I didn't want you to be unhappy on your birthday weekend.'

'Don't give out to her. She's a sweetie,' Piper said.

Jess gazed adoringly at her. Piper was so cool and nice and pretty and just . . . fabulous. Jess hoped for the thousandth time that she'd look just like Piper when she was eighteen.

'So, are you coming?'

'We'll be there in a minute. Go on.' Luke nudged Jess towards the door.

'I made Rocky Roads for dessert. I know you like them and I thought it would cheer you up,' Jess said.

'Awww, you are too cute. My sisters would never do something so nice for me,' Piper said.

'Wouldn't they?' Jess asked. 'I wish I had sisters.'

'Never! All we do is fight over make-up and clothes and who ate whose food. Yesterday Penny came into the shop I'm working in and actually tried to pull my boots off.'

Jess giggled.

'Seriously, in front of everyone, including my manager. She said they were hers, I hadn't asked to borrow them and she wanted them back. My manager had to peel her off me and ask her to leave. I nearly got fired. You're lucky not to have sisters.'

Jess shrugged. 'I guess the boys are okay.'

Luke kissed the top of Jess's head. 'I hope we're a bit more than just okay. Come on, enough talking, I'm starving.' He led the way downstairs.

Granddad was sitting at the table, reading the paper and trying to ignore Bobby.

'How high is the tallest man ever?'

'Eight foot two.'

Jess smiled. Granddad hadn't looked up from the paper when he answered. Eye contact with Bobby was dangerous: it indicated that you were interested in talking to him, and if you showed interest, he was relentless.

'Nope, eight foot eleven point one inches. How small is the smallest woman ever?'

'Three foot.'

'Two foot. How long is the longest tongue?'

'For the love of Jesus, this is the twentieth question,' Granddad said wearily.

Kate placed a roast chicken on the table. 'Bobby has a curious mind, Dad. It's important not to discourage him.'

'How long *is* the longest tongue? *I* want to know,' Jess said.

'Three point nine seven inches.'

'It's so cool that you know all this stuff,' Piper said.

'That's one word for it,' Granddad grumbled.

'How wide is the –'

Kate cut across him. 'That's enough facts for now, Bobby. Let's eat.'

'Thank God for that.'

'Don't mind Granddad,' Kate said to Bobby. 'He's just a bit grumpy.'

Jess sat beside Piper. 'Which sister are you closest to?'

Piper sat back. 'Probably Posy.'

'Do all your sisters have names that start with P?' Bobby asked.

'Yes.'

'Why?'

'Because, for some crazy reason, my parents thought it was a good idea.'

'What are they all called?' Bobby asked.

'I'm Piper, the twins are Poppy and Penny, and then there's Pauline and Posy.'

'Five girls!' Granddad said. 'Your poor father must be demented.'

Piper laughed. 'He is. He spends most of his time in the shed at the end of the garden.'

'I need one of those, these days,' Granddad said.

'I think it's lovely to have a big family,' Kate said. 'I was an only child and I always envied people with brothers and sisters.'

'One perfect child is plenty,' Granddad said.

Kate squeezed his hand.

Even though Granddad could be a bit grumpy, Jess could see how much he loved her mum. It was good to see how a normal father behaved, she thought.

Kate kept telling them all that their granddad was an example of what a great father should be – kind, caring and generous. Jess knew she was afraid that their own dad being so selfish was setting a bad example for them, especially for the boys. But she didn't need to worry. Luke and Bobby would never be like that. They were kind and not selfish at all.

Piper was telling Mum and Granddad a funny story about work. Luke was sitting back, staring lovingly at her. He was happy. Jess smiled. Everything was better again. They had each other and that was all that mattered.

3

Kate listened to her father chatting to the customers. She heard him say in a loud whisper, 'It was a big adjustment, but I'm used to it now and we're all getting along well.'

She continued unpacking the wine cases and thanked God for her father and the security of his house.

When she'd married Nick, she'd imagined a life full of happiness and fun and children and love . . . It had been, for a while.

Nick had begun pulling away after Bobby was born. He was home less often, working more often, distracted, disengaged. Kate knew she was losing him, but she didn't know how to fix it. She'd been overwhelmed with a third baby and didn't have the energy to put into their relationship. Nick had checked out, first emotionally and then physically. Jenny was the inevitable final straw. Nick's mid-life crisis had started at thirty-five and ended up with him shagging a twenty-two-year-old. He was a walking cliché, the estate agent who sleeps with the client.

Kate pulled a bottle of Bordeaux out of the case and wiped it down. She tried to quiet her mind, but it was always turning over the same questions. How was she ever going to afford her own house? Was she going to end up living with her father for ever? Would she be alone for ever? Would the kids be emotionally scarred for life? Would they not believe in marriage, having seen their parents fail at it?

Kate knew that Bobby was the most affected. Luke had had good years with his dad and so had Jess – as the only girl,

Nick had doted on her. But Bobby had drawn the short straw. That was why he was angry all the time. He felt let down by the father who wasn't interested in him. George said she indulged Bobby too much, but Kate felt she had to compensate for Nick's lack of interest.

Nick and Bobby just grated on each other. Kate had begged Nick to make more of an effort, and when he tried, Bobby ended up driving him crazy. Bobby drove everyone crazy, but he was so sweet underneath it. Kate wished more people could see that. He was a bundle of loveliness underneath his prickly exterior.

Kate sighed. Was she enough for her kids? Everyone said boys needed a strong male presence. Since Jenny had given birth to Jaden five months ago, Nick had barely seen Luke, Jess and Bobby. Kate was glad that her father was in their lives so much now. At least he was a positive male influence, even if he had got a bit impatient in his old age. He was a good granddad and a good man, and she knew Luke and Bobby would benefit from being around him.

'Kate?' George called. 'I need you.'

She moved over from the wine section, in the corner of the café, to the counter.

'I have an order for two of those green juices you put on the menu.'

Kate smiled. 'Really? The juices you said no one would want?'

Her father put his hands up. 'Okay, you were right. I think they look, smell and taste awful, but it seems people like them. Why anyone would want to drink kale and spinach and God knows what else is beyond me.'

Kate began to make up the juices. 'They're healthy, Dad. People are into health and nutrition, these days. Even Luke drinks them.'

'Do you think he'll get picked for the team?' George asked. 'He seems awfully nervous about it.'

Kate was nervous, too. Luke was so wound up about it. When he hadn't been helping in the café he had spent every spare hour of the summer working out and training – it was almost an obsession. Kate worried about the fallout if he wasn't picked or got injured or something. After three weeks back in school he seemed even more het-up. Through a series of questions, which Luke answered with grunts, Kate was able to surmise that Harry was playing well and Luke feared his friend would replace him on the team.

'I hope so. It'd be so good for his confidence and self-esteem.'

Her father raised an eyebrow. 'That little Piper seems to have done wonders for his self-esteem.'

Kate grinned. 'She's nice, isn't she?'

'She seems like a grand girl.'

'I like her. She makes Luke happy and she's very sweet with Jess.'

'Sure how could you not be sweet to Jess? She's a dote,' George said.

Kate added wheatgrass powder to the juicer. She loved that her father was so fond of Jess. Kate didn't know what she'd do without her daughter. During the break-up and Nick's departure, Jess had been so helpful. Kate had found her crying in her bedroom a few times but Jess had never complained about anything. Luke had raged against the world and got into trouble at school. Bobby had gone around kicking everything, including Kate, but Jess had been supportive. She was twelve going on sixty.

'She has an old soul,' George had said, when Jess was little, and he was right. Jess did have an old soul, and a very big heart to go with it.

Kate sometimes worried that Jess bottled up her emotions. Over the last year she'd tried to talk to her, but Jess had just said, 'It's okay, Mum. I know you and Dad love me. I'm sad because we're not a family any more, but don't worry, I'm not going to get drunk or kick things.'

Kate had hugged her and tried not to cry all over her daughter's hair. Jess didn't even seem angry with Nick. She'd come home from spending time with him and say, 'I feel sorry for Daddy. Jenny hates being pregnant. She's always complaining. He seems very stressed.'

Kate loved hearing how much of a pain in the arse Jenny was and that Nick was stressed. It made her feel considerably better. She wanted him to be miserable. She was thrilled to hear that bouncy, sexy, fit Jenny wasn't so much fun, after all. Serves the snake right, she thought. I hope their baby never sleeps.

Kate finished the juices and brought them to the table. 'Enjoy,' she said, with a smile, then went back to the counter.

'You look tired, Kate, will I make you a coffee?'

'Thanks, Dad. That'd be lovely.'

'Did you sleep badly, pet?' he asked, and Kate suddenly wanted to weep.

She had been up half the night working out her finances. Back to school had used up all of her wages, and Luke had given her a chunk of his earnings to help with his books. But Nick hadn't paid his child support again this month. When she'd called him yesterday, he'd said he didn't have it because, unknown to him, Jenny had spent a fortune on his credit card doing up Jaden's nursery.

'Jesus, Nick, I need that money. Your three children need books and uniforms. You know back to school is a really expensive time.'

'Don't start, Kate. I've had Jenny in my ear all day. Look, I just don't have it. I'll get it to you next month.'

'I need it now!'

'Ask your father for a loan.'

Kate had felt the blood rushing to her head and thought she might explode. 'My father is housing your children, feeding your children and helping to raise your children. I will not ask him for any more. Find me the money and send it or I'll contact my lawyer.'

'You don't have to be a bitch about it.'

'Go to Hell.' She'd slammed the phone down on him, then stood there, trembling with fury. She hated talking to him — any conversation ended in an argument.

She'd spent the rest of the evening trying to figure out how to pay for Jess's horse-riding lessons. She'd paid for all of their books, but had nothing left over for riding. It was Jess's one treat. Piano lessons and dance lessons had had to go as there was simply no money, but horse-riding was Jess's favourite thing in the world. She adored animals, and was happiest when she was at the stables, riding and grooming. Kate couldn't bear to tell her she couldn't go back. She'd called the stables yesterday and they'd agreed to give her a discount, but she still had to come up with two hundred euros to pay for Jess's lessons.

'Just my mind working overtime,' Kate said.

Her father laid his hand on her arm. 'Is it money?'

Kate was afraid to speak — there was a lump in her throat. This wasn't fair. She shouldn't be living on top of her elderly father with three kids, and she shouldn't be asking him for money. She felt such a failure. 'Nick didn't pay this month,' she muttered, her face bright red with shame.

'For Christ's sake,' George cursed. 'It's not your fault. I'll help you out.'

'I just need two hundred euros for Jess's riding. I know it's expensive, but she loves it and never asks for anything.'

'Of course we can sort that out. Jess deserves a treat.' George patted Kate's hand. He opened the cash register and took out four fifty-euro notes and handed them to her. 'I'll never see you short, Katie.'

It was the use of her childhood nickname that set her off. She turned to walk out so her father wouldn't see her sobbing into her sleeve.

At twenty to three Kate hung up her apron, pulled on her coat and left to walk the short distance to Bobby's school. She stood alone at the gate, not wanting to engage in small-talk with the other parents. She was still feeling raw after borrowing the money from her father and didn't think she could fake a good day in front of the others.

As the children poured out, Kate waved at Bobby, who ran straight to her and threw his arms around her. 'Good day?' she asked, hustling him along and studiously avoiding eye contact with the teacher.

'It was okay,' Bobby said. 'But guess where the most shark attacks happen?'

'Mrs Higgins,' the teacher called. 'May I have a word?'

Kate froze. Turning, she put on her I'm-not-worried-about-where-this-conversation-is-going face and followed the other woman into the school.

'Bobby, will you be a good boy and help put those books away?' Mrs Lorgan asked.

'In alphabetical order?' Bobby enquired.

'Mmm, yes, perfect.'

While Bobby was busy sorting out the little class library, Mrs Lorgan faced Kate. She was a woman in her fifties and had the authority of a teacher who had been around a while and took no nonsense.

'Mrs Higgins –'

'Call me Kate, please.'

'Fine. Kate. Bobby is a very energetic boy with a very keen interest in facts and figures, information he's always impatient to share with his classmates. While we always try to encourage enthusiasm for learning, with a class of twenty-five I can't allow him to monopolize the time.'

'Yes, I understand. He can be a bit relentless with his facts, but it's his passion and he hasn't had the easiest of years at home. Learning facts seems to keep him calm.'

'He mentioned his father's new baby in Show and Tell. I think some of the children were alarmed to hear him describe him as an evil devil baby.'

'He's having some problems adjusting.' Kate watched Bobby through the classroom window, carefully arranging the books, a frown on his serious little face. She just wanted to go in, put her arms around him, tell him not to worry and hug all his anger out.

'There was some bad language too, I'm afraid. He described his father's girlfriend as a tart. Thankfully, the children thought of apple tart rather than . . . well, the other kind. But I did take Bobby aside and we had a word about it.'

It's lucky he didn't say 'whore' or 'slut', Kate thought, which were names Luke had called Jenny when Nick had told the kids he was leaving them to go and live with her. 'I'll talk to him,' she said, 'but please don't be too hard on him in class. I know he can take over a bit with his facts and figures, but he's very insecure and he needs attention and praise. Honestly, underneath his bluster he's an anxious little boy.'

Mrs Lorgan nodded. 'I can see that, and I'll do my best to work with him and encourage him along.'

'Thank you.'

Kate called Bobby and they headed home.

'Mummy?'

'Yes?'

'Does Mrs Lorgan not like me?'

Kate stopped and crouched down. 'Hey, now, she was actually telling me how great you are and how clever, and she wondered where you got all your amazing facts. So I told her about *Guinness World Records* being your favourite book.'

'Mummy?'

'Yes.'

'Do you think Daddy will hate stinky Jaden and come back home and love us again?'

Kate put her arms around her son and drew him in. 'Oh, Bobby, Daddy loves you, Luke and Jess. No new baby is ever going to change that.'

'What if he has more babies? He'll never have time to see us.'

'I'm not sure he's going to have any more, but even if he does, he'll still love you the same. Besides, you have me and Granddad, who love you too.'

Bobby nodded and they started walking again. As they reached the gate, Bobby threw his arms around Kate's legs. Muttering into her left thigh, he said, 'If there was a world record for best mummy, you'd win it.'

Kate's heart lifted. It was moments like these that made all the pain and worry disappear.

4

He was in a deep sleep, the kind you can have only when your body and mind are completely exhausted. When he had crawled into bed earlier, his body had felt as if it had folded itself into the mattress. They were one and the same. Sleep, these days, was Nick's favourite thing to do. It was his only switch-off.

'Waaaaaah . . . waaaaaah . . . waaaaah . . .'

In his sleep he could hear something. Ignore it, his brain said.

'Waaaah . . . waaaaah . . .'

He scrunched his eyes closed and tried to block out the sound.

'Nick!'

He felt a thump on his arm. He rolled over.

'*Nick!*' This time she walloped him.

Jesus Christ, could a man not get one decent night's sleep? He opened his eyes and prayed it was after five a.m. Please God, let it not be the middle of the night. The alarm clock said it was two thirty. *Fuuuuuck!*

'It's your turn,' Jenny whined.

'I have an early viewing. Can you do it? Please?'

'No bloody way. I've been with him all day *and* I did the ten o'clock feed. Get up.'

Nick wanted to tell her to sod off. He was tempted to remind her that she wasn't working. She got to sit on her arse all day, watching TV.

He, on the other hand, was trying to sell houses to people who had no money. Thankfully, the housing market had turned a bit of a corner, but it was still a bloody hard slog trying to get people to commit to a sale. He had to get some sales in soon. He owed the bank and he owed Kate, too.

He'd spent weeks trying to get that couple to buy the big house on Jacobson Road, but they'd pulled out at the last minute. The commission on it would have paid the rent on the apartment and the childcare costs for four months, but no such luck. The wife had decided the kitchen was too dark. He'd explained to her that with a lighter colour on the walls and cream tiles on the floor it would be transformed, but the stupid cow had had no imagination.

The stress of trying to pay everyone was killing him. He needed a few drinks after work to take the edge off, but he couldn't even do that without Jenny ringing every fifteen minutes to find out when he was coming home.

Between Jenny and Kate and the kids, he felt suffocated. Sometimes lately he'd felt like running away. Just getting on a plane to South America and never coming back. He'd live in a beach hut, spend all day lying on white sand, drinking cold beers, and not have six people depending on him all the time.

He wouldn't do it, though. He wouldn't leave his kids. Even though they hated him. Well, Jess didn't, but Luke did and Bobby was hard-going. Nick had always felt Bobby could see through him. Even when he was only four years old, he'd catch Bobby looking at him, and it was as if he knew Nick was having an affair. It had freaked him out.

He hadn't wanted another child. Kate had tricked him into it. They were just getting their lives back: Jess was in school, and she was easy anyway, and Luke was eleven and they were starting to go out again, getting their mojo back, until Kate had said she wanted another baby.

He'd told her no way. She said she'd hated being an only child and wanted three kids at least. He'd said no, one boy and one girl was perfect. Why push it? They were happy, life was good. They didn't need another baby.

'We're finally getting lie-ins,' he'd argued again and again, 'and we're able to go out, have a few drinks and stay late without having to worry about bottles and night feeds and nappies and early mornings. Come on, Kate, let's just enjoy it.'

But Kate wouldn't let it go. She'd kept banging on and on about how she wanted a big family and how two wasn't enough, until eventually he gave in and said they could try for six months, and if it didn't happen, that was it.

Of course she'd got bloody pregnant in the fifth month and their lives had gone back to her being pregnant and wanting to stay in all the time. Then Bobby had arrived, and it was night feeds, no sleep, shitty nappies, early mornings and early nights. All the fun and freedom were gone.

If he was honest, Nick had been angry since the day Kate announced she was pregnant. He'd known it would change everything and he was right: it had. Bobby was just too much. Three kids was too much.

The Kate he'd married was funny and kind. She'd asked him about work, drunk wine with him and chatted about the day. This Kate went to bed with the kids at eight p.m. and never wanted to have sex . . . ever.

After Bobby was born, she'd barely acknowledged him when he came home from work. She was always feeding someone or doing homework or washing clothes or tidying up or cooking or sewing . . . The old Kate would have laughed at his stories about annoying clients and actually have been interested in him.

He hadn't meant to cheat on Kate, but when Jenny had come to view that apartment for the second time, he'd given in to lust. The first time she'd viewed it she'd flirted with him and he'd been flattered, very flattered. She was hot and young and she was definitely giving him the eye. He'd been on a high, so he'd flirted back a bit, and it had been fun, really good fun.

When she rang to say she wanted to see the apartment again, he'd worn his favourite shirt and suit. When he saw her in her tight black dress he'd had to walk away to hide his hard-on. He'd wanted her then and there.

He'd used all of his charm and she'd responded to his flirting, making it pretty obvious she found him attractive. So he'd asked her out for a drink. One drink had led to five and they'd ended up back at her place having great sex. Nick had become completely addicted to her and the sex. He couldn't have stopped even if he'd tried. She was like a drug. He hadn't felt so alive in years. He saw her at every opportunity he could.

To be honest, Nick was surprised Jenny had gone for him. He was twenty years older than her. But she'd said she liked older guys, that he was sexy and confident. He knew what he wanted and where he was going. She'd said a lot of guys her own age were still behaving like teenagers.

'I feel protected and safe with you,' she'd said, after a few months of seeing him. 'My dad left before I was born so I never knew him. My mum was a drinker, so my home life was always difficult. I guess I've always craved security. You're so sure of who you are that I know you'll look after me and never let me down. I know you won't "borrow" money from me, like my last boyfriend, who fleeced me, or the one before that, who got so drunk that he puked on me. I'm sick of immature man-boys. I want a real man, like you, Nick.'

Nick had eaten up her adoration. It felt so good to be needed and wanted. He couldn't get enough of it.

When he was with Jenny, he felt powerful and invincible – the opposite of everything he felt in his other life, the half-life he had with Kate. Jenny thought he was wonderful. She laughed at his jokes and told him he was the best estate agent in the world. Nick felt as if he mattered again, as if he was someone's number one, rather than always coming last, after the kids.

He only felt guilty when he was at home, so he avoided being there as much as possible. But he was careless. In a way he wanted to get caught.

Kate found texts on his phone. She hadn't freaked out or screamed or broken plates. She'd just cried and cried and cried. It was as if there was a river inside her.

'I want the kids to come from a happy home, not a broken one,' she'd said, making it clear that the kids came first, even in something as personal as an extra-marital affair. She'd offered to forgive him and to give it another go, but he didn't want to. He didn't love her any more – they were like strangers. He wanted out. He wanted a new start. He wanted Jenny. He wanted sex and freedom.

He looked down at Jaden's red face. What freedom? What sex? Jenny had told him she was on the pill, but somehow she'd got pregnant. He wondered sometimes if she'd tricked him. She'd always said she wanted security: was Jaden her way of making sure Nick stayed with her and looked after her? What was it with women and babies? Why did they have to have kids and ruin everything?

Nick felt his chest contract. He gripped the side of the cot. Breathe, he ordered himself. In and out, in and out. He was beginning to panic, and his head was spinning. He needed to make more money. He needed to spend more time with his kids. He needed to sort things out with Jenny because they were arguing non-stop, these days.

He felt guilty about losing touch with Luke. He missed him. They used to play football together and joke around, but now Luke just glared at him or rolled his eyes whenever Nick tried to be funny. Jess was still her sweet self, but he knew he should go and see her horse-riding and make more of an effort with her. As for Bobby . . . He had a lot of making up to do. Bobby had had the worst of him. Nick had resented the poor kid for the first few years of his life, then he'd been tied up with Jenny and then he'd left. He'd never really got to know Bobby. He felt bad about it. He didn't know his own son. But Bobby was always angry and all he seemed to do was talk about his world records, which drove Nick mad. He'd tried to play football with him but Bobby had two left feet and he'd ended up kicking Nick's leg, hard, because it was 'a stupid game'.

Nick had to try to figure out a way to communicate with Bobby before it was too late. He was already seven years old and they had no relationship. He needed to find some kind of common ground. But since Jaden had been born, Jenny barely let him out of her sight. She panicked all the time and cried a lot and kept thinking Jaden was going to die. Nick had Googled it, and she had symptoms of postnatal depression. When he'd suggested she might have it and she should talk to her GP, Jenny had gone absolutely mad and accused him of trying to leave her. But he was only trying to help.

How the hell had he ended up in this mess? He had only ever wanted a nice life, a few quid in the bank, a wife, two kids and some drinks on a Saturday night. But somehow, he'd ended up with four kids, two families, no money and stress everywhere he looked.

Jaden let out a roar. Nick picked him up and held him against his chest. He walked up and down the bedroom singing quietly. It was the same song he'd sung to all of his kids to calm them down – Frank Sinatra's 'Fly Me To The Moon'. It had even worked on Bobby.

Jaden stopped crying and soon fell into a deep sleep on Nick's shoulder. Looking down at his baby son's peaceful little face, Nick promised him he'd be a better dad. He wouldn't mess this up. He'd help Jenny more with Jaden so she wasn't so overwhelmed. He had to make this relationship work. He wanted to – he needed to.

5

Jess looked at Chloë's many photos of her trip to Australia.

'And there's me with a koala, and there's me surfing, and look at how cute that guy is! And here's me drinking a mocktail . . .'

The holiday looked amazing. White sandy beaches, posh hotels, and Chloë had got loads of new clothes as well. Jess felt a pang of jealousy. She'd spent her summer helping to move all of their belongings into her granddad's house, then helping in the café. She'd had just one week of sports camp because her mum and dad had no money for more than that.

Being poor sucked. Her dad said he was sorry but that he had two families to support now and they all had to 'make sacrifices'. But why did they? Why did he have to leave? They used to be happy. Jess remembered their holiday in France. She was only about five, but her parents had been laughing together and going down slides in the water park. They had been a family, a real family.

Bobby said he couldn't remember anything but Mum and Dad shouting at each other and Dad never being around. Luke just said Dad was 'a selfish prick' and didn't want to discuss it further. Jess wished she had a sister she could talk to.

Her dad had messed up and it was Jenny who had got the best of the whole rotten deal. She had Jess's dad and they lived together in their own place and now they had a new baby. It felt like they'd lost everything and Jenny had won. She had taken Dad away from them, with her short skirts and her red lipstick and her fake laugh. She'd tried to be all friendly with Jess when they'd first met her two years ago, after Dad had left them to move in with her. Luke had ignored her and Bobby had kicked her, so Jess knew she was just trying to go for the easiest kid. She'd been polite for Dad's sake, but she could see through Jenny.

The weird thing was, Jenny was only seven years older than Luke and she was twenty years younger than Dad. It was creepy. At first Dad was all bouncy and happy around Jenny. He called her 'babe', held her hand and rubbed her leg. It made Jess want to puke. Jenny kept saying, 'Your dad's so amazing. He's so good to me.'

Jess had wanted to shout, 'Well, he isn't good to our mum, you horrible cow,' but she didn't.

But then Jenny had got pregnant and stopped wearing short skirts and lipstick of any colour. She was grumpy and didn't laugh any more, not even fake laughs. She snapped at Dad and he stopped rubbing her legs.

The baby was really ugly. It was mean to say babies were ugly because it wasn't their fault that they didn't have any hair and dribbled all the time, but Jess couldn't help it because Jaden really was ugly. Jenny dressed him up in dorky outfits, with ripped jeans and leather jackets, and he just looked even worse.

Jess was glad she had only seen Jenny and Jaden twice since he was born. She much preferred seeing Dad on her own. The last time she'd seen Jenny, she was on her own. Luke said he had to work and Bobby had a meltdown so Mum had given in and let him stay home. Jess ended up going alone: she didn't want to let Dad down.

When she got to the apartment, Jenny was trying to breastfeed. It was disgusting – she just pulled her boob out right in front of Jess and tried to stick her nipple into the

41

baby's mouth. Jess didn't know where to look. It was mortifying.

When she'd told Chloë about it later, Chloë had almost vomited in shock and disgust.

Jenny kept trying to get Jaden to suck but he wouldn't, and they both started crying. Jess's dad had ended up grabbing the baby and stuffing a bottle into his mouth. Jaden had stopped crying but Jenny had cried louder. She kept saying, 'But Gisele, the supermodel, says mothers should breastfeed their babies for six months.'

'For Christ's sake, will you stop banging on about Gisele? The baby needs food. Look, he's happy now,' Dad had snapped.

Jess made an excuse to leave the room then and hung about in the small hallway, watching the clock and trying not to listen to the argument Jenny and her dad were having. After twenty-two minutes her dad had come out and asked if maybe she wouldn't mind if he dropped her home early. Jess was never so happy to leave somewhere in her life.

'OMG,' said Chloë, pointing at the next picture. 'Here's me learning to surf. Check out my pink wetsuit. Dad bought it for me.' She swiped her phone screen to show Jess more photos.

'It must have been an amazing holiday,' Jess said wistfully.

Chloë wrinkled her nose. 'You know, it was in one way but, honestly, being an only child sucks. I have to do every-thing with my parents and they focus all of their attention on me. I know I'm spoilt, but sometimes I wish I was like your family.'

Poor and broken up? Was Chloë mad?

Chloë put up her hands. 'I don't mean that you haven't had a terrible time with your parents separating and your dad running off with that, like, OMG, total ho. I just mean that at least you have fun with Luke and Bobby.'

'But I don't really. Since we've had to sell the house and Jaden was born, Luke is all moody. All he does is train and spend time with Piper. And Jaden being born has pushed Bobby over the edge. He was bad anyway, but he definitely has anger-management issues now.'

'Poor Bobby. He was the baby of the family and now he isn't.'

'I know but he needs to stop freaking out all the time. It's a total pain.'

'Have you seen the ho lately?'

Jess shook her head. 'No, and I haven't seen Dad much either. He's busy with work and the baby.'

Chloë applied lip-gloss to her already over-glossed lips and offered some to Jess. 'Well, my mum said she saw Jenny in House of Fraser and she looked terrible, like totally wrecked. Mum said she had big bags under her eyes and she was wheeling the buggy around looking miserable. Serves her right.'

Jess knew this was supposed to cheer her up, and she certainly didn't care if Jenny was miserable, but then again, if everyone was miserable, the whole nightmare would have been for nothing.

If Dad and Jenny broke up, there would be two broken families and four kids sharing a bit of a dad. In the beginning Jess had prayed that her dad would change his mind and come home to them. But after nearly three years apart, she didn't want him to do that. She knew Mum and Dad could never live together again. All they did was argue, so there was no point in dreaming about becoming a perfect family again: they never would be.

But if Jenny and Dad were happy, then Dad might be a better dad again. He might have more time for them if Jenny was able to look after the baby without crying or phoning him all the time. Maybe if they were happy, Dad would make more of an effort with Luke and Bobby and not seem so awkward around them, like he did now.

'*Sooooo* what will we do? Do you want to play tennis?'

Chloë had a tennis court and a swimming pool at her house. Her father was a builder, and Jess's mum said, 'He prints money.' They were the richest people in the school. When Chloë had joined two years ago, everyone had tried to be her friend because they all wanted to hang out at her house. Jess's dad had just said he was leaving them to live with Jenny, so Jess couldn't have cared less about Chloë's swimming pool.

Jess often thought it was because she hadn't tried to be Chloë's friend that Chloë had sought her out. They'd clicked pretty much instantly. Chloë was fun and funny, and she never worried about anything. Jess spent her life worrying about everything. Chloë said she had to stop or she'd end up with really bad lines on her forehead, but Chloë's mum, Hazel, said she didn't have to worry about that because Botox would sort it out.

'Shouldn't we do our homework first, though?' Jess asked.

'Seriously, Jess, live a little. It's only week three back at school, we can do it later or I'll forge a note from Mum. I can do one for you too, if you like. I've got really good at copying handwriting.'

Jess grinned. 'No, thanks.'

'I knew you'd say no. I bet you end up being, like, a doctor or a scientist and finding cures to all the awful diseases of the world.'

Jess laughed. 'Are you still planning to be a professional tennis player?'

'No. That got canned this summer. I went to see this top coach in Australia and he said I'm just not good enough. I knew I wasn't anyway. When I didn't even get picked for the club's first team, I told Mum that the dream was over. Besides, I'm sick of playing two hours every day after school. It's a pain and it's boring. I'm so over competitive tennis. Dad was a bit grumpy, though, seeing as he'd built the tennis court because Mum told him she thought I'd end up playing in Wimbledon.'

'Did he go mad?'

Chloë tied the laces on her sparkling white runners. 'He huffed and puffed a bit, but then I told him he was the best dad ever for building me a tennis court and I was sorry I wasn't good enough – I laid that on very thick and even squeezed out a tear – and then he was all, "Don't worry. You're a star in my eyes . . . blah blah blah."'

Jess shook her head. 'Your poor dad. You're unbelievable.'

Chloë giggled. 'I know! Mum said I should be an actress. But I've actually decided to invent a pill where you can eat anything you want – jars of Starbursts, big boxes of chocolates – and never get fat. I'll be a zillionaire, like my dad.'

They ran downstairs and went into the vast kitchen, which was bigger than the entire Village Café.

'Hey, Jess.' Chloë's mum looked up from her magazine.

'Hi, Hazel.'

'My God, you've grown! You look lovely. How was your summer?'

'Oh, Mum!' Chloë broke in. 'Don't start asking her loads of questions – we're going to play tennis.'

Hazel arched an eyebrow. 'Really? I thought tennis was "so over".'

'Competitions and training are. We're playing for fun.'

'Did Chloë tell you my dream of watching her win Wimbledon is over?'

Jess nodded.

'She's so selfish. I even had my outfit planned, right down to the fabulous hat.' Hazel grinned.

'The scary thing is, she's not joking.'

'Well, I do have a lovely cream Roland Mouret dress that would have been perfect. Oh, well, never mind. How's your mum?'

'Good, thanks,' Jess said.

'Have you all settled in at your granddad's now?'

'We've been there nearly four months, so it feels like home.'

'Good. I'm glad to hear it. You know you're always welcome to stay here if you want a change of scenery, and if your mum needs anything, she isn't to hesitate to ask. I mean that now. I said it to her myself, but if you feel she needs help, please tell me.'

Jess smiled. Underneath her make-up, overly coiffed hair and OTT clothes, Hazel had a huge heart. 'Thanks.'

Chloë tugged at her sleeve. 'Come on, let's play.'

They knocked up a bit, then decided to play one set before doing their homework.

It was when she ran for a drop shot that Jess's nose began to bleed.

6

Piper's father, Seamus, glared at her. 'Where have you been?'

'Luke's.'

'Who's Luke?'

'My boyfriend.'

Seamus's eyebrows flew up. 'What in the name of God? Boyfriend? You're only twelve.'

Piper grinned. 'I'm eighteen.'

'When did that happen?'

'Over the past six years.'

'What age is Luke?'

'Forty-three.'

'WHAT?'

Piper laughed. 'I'm kidding. He's just turned eighteen.'

'Is he a nice lad?'

'Very.'

'How long have you been together?'

'Five months.'

'Does he know how lucky he is to be going out with the only sensible daughter I have?'

'I think so.'

'Good. Well, thank God you're home.'

'What's up?'

'Your sister has locked herself in the bathroom.'

'Which one?'

'How the hell should I know? Poppy or Penny.'

'Why did she lock herself in?'

'Because the other twin wore her top and then she pulled it off her in front of someone and she was "mortified" so she took scissors to the top and cut the sleeve off and now the other one has threatened to kill her.'

'I bet it was Penny. Poppy probably borrowed her new Superdry top.'

'Now that you mention it, there was screaming about Superdry.'

'Where's Mum?' Piper asked.

Her dad frowned. 'Olivia is at one of her lectures. I'm all for your mother having her own life, but she's never home.'

Last year, the day Posy had gone into senior school, their mother had decided to do something for herself. She'd signed up for a course in equality and human rights.

They could hear screaming from upstairs. 'Come out of there or I'll kick this door down,' Penny shrieked.

'Help! She's a lunatic! Help!' Poppy shouted.

'Hello! Can someone please tell them to shut up? I'm trying to study here,' Pauline roared. 'Someone in this house actually cares about more than stupid clothes.'

'Shut up, Pauline. You're a bore who's going to die alone because all you do is study,' Penny yelled.

'At least I'm not one half of ridiculous twins who can barely spell and will end up stacking shelves in Tesco because no one else will hire them.'

'Oh, yeah? Well, I'd rather work in Tesco than be a nerdy, weirdo scientist freak,' Penny retorted.

'I'm studying medicine, not science, you moron.'

'Same difference. You'll end up with big glasses and a white coat, living on your own with cats.'

Seamus sighed. 'I can't handle them. They're like wild animals. I've an article to write. I'm off to the shed.'

Of course you are, Piper thought. It's your hideout. She wished she had a shed. There was nowhere to get any peace in this house.

As her dad scurried off to the shed to compose his piece for the newspaper, Piper went to see if there was anything for dinner. She opened the fridge. Empty. Damn. There was a note, though, sitting on the empty middle shelf – *It starts when you sink into his arms and ends with your arms in his sink!*

Piper sighed. She missed her mother, the one who used to be waiting for them when they got home from school, with scones in the oven and hot chocolate on the hob. Now it was all about lectures and essays, study groups and equality. Piper was fine about equality. Yes, men and women were equal and should be treated that way. But her dad had always treated her mother as an equal. He discussed everything with her, shared everything he had with her and always told her she was great. Besides, her mother had chosen to give up her job in the bank to have five kids, so why was she behaving now as if her husband had chained her to the kitchen sink?

Maybe he had taken Mum's cooking for granted and the fact that she ran the house and did most of the childcare, but he was working to support them. Wasn't that the deal? Her friend Vanessa's mum was a lawyer and Vanessa's dad stayed at home and did the cooking and childminding. Maybe it was best if you both worked. Maybe then everyone was happy. But Frannie's parents both worked and they always seemed to be in a bad mood. Piper didn't know what the answer was, but she wished her mum would stop writing silly notes and start cooking again.

Crash . . . bang . . .

Piper closed the fridge and ran upstairs. It sounded as if Penny had kicked in the bathroom door.

'Aaaaargh!' Penny screamed.

'What the hell?' Piper found Penny with her foot stuck in the door. 'Are you insane?' she shouted at her sister. 'You've made a hole in the door. Dad's going to go mad.'

'I don't care. I want to kill her.'

Piper pulled her sister's foot out. She had a cut down one side, which was bleeding slightly.

'You see what you've done, you stupid cow? You've scarred me for life,' Penny shouted through the hole at her twin.

'Is it bad?' Poppy asked, peeping out from the other side of the hole.

'Look.' Penny showed her. 'Actual blood.'

'Does she need stitches?' Poppy seemed worried.

Piper wiped the blood away with a tissue. 'No. It's just a small cut.'

'Small but deep. I'll have a scar for life,' Penny wailed.

'Scars can be cool,' Poppy said.

'No, they can not.' Piper was annoyed. The twins were maddening.

'Let's Google maddest scars ever,' Poppy suggested.

'Cool.' Penny struggled to her feet. 'I need help walking.'

'Hang on.' Poppy unlocked the bathroom door and went to help her twin hop back to their bedroom.

Behind them lay the top with no sleeves and splinters of wood from the bathroom door.

'I'll just clean up, then, shall I?' Piper snapped.

The twins turned. 'Well, I'm injured,' Penny said.

'And I'm nursing her,' Poppy added.

A bedroom door swung open. A red-faced Pauline stormed out. 'That's it! I've had it with this family. I cannot stay here another minute. I'm going to the library.'

'Your favourite place.' The twins giggled. 'Where all your friends hang out.'

'At least I have a brain. You clearly only got half of one each, which is why you're so inane.'

'We're not insane,' Poppy said.

'Inane, you idiot! *In-ane.*'

'Pauline, you need to lie down. You're not making any sense. Maybe your brain exploded from too much studying,' Penny said, and the twins fell about laughing.

'Boom!' Poppy cackled.

Pauline held her laptop to her chest. 'Why was I born into this ridiculous family? There must have been a mix-up at the hospital.'

While Pauline stormed off to the college library and the twins looked up scars on the internet, Piper got out the Hoover and cleared up the mess. As she was putting the Hoover away, Posy came home and flung down her schoolbag.

'Bad day?'

'I got a detention.'

'Why?'

'Mrs Pender said I was far more interested in putting on lip-gloss than reading Shakespeare, and I said she was right because lip-gloss is way more interesting than boring old Shakespeare and stupid Romeo and Juliet and their lame relationship – and that Juliet was a really bad role model for women because no self-respecting feminist would kill herself over a guy.'

Piper groaned. 'Why did you say that? You know you're not supposed to answer back. It's always going to get you into trouble.'

'Mum agrees. She thinks it's a dumb play too. She said we should be studying Gloria Steinem and Simone de Beauvoir.'

Why did their mother have to fill Posy's twelve-year-old head with all of her college stuff? She was too young and it was getting her into trouble. Piper was going to have to talk to her mother when she got home.

'Look, Posy, if you want to make your life easy in school, just follow the curriculum and say nothing. You can read what you want in your spare time.'

Posy plonked herself down at the kitchen table. 'Fine. I'm starving. What's for dinner?'

Before Piper could tell her there was nothing, the back door opened and their father walked in.

'Hello, Poppy.'

'It's Posy.'

'Right, what's for dinner?'

Why did everyone ask Piper? Why did everyone assume she was the one in charge when their mother was out? 'I don't know. There's nothing in the fridge except a quote.'

Seamus opened the fridge and slammed it shut. 'Apparently your mother thinks we can live on notes and quotes. I'll nip down to the shops and pick something up. You can come with me.' He pointed to Posy.

'Not until you say my name and date of birth.'

Seamus narrowed his eyes. 'Posy Barbara, born October 2003 in the middle of the rugby world cup, which was very inconvenient. You're the cheeky, lippy one. The youngest. The one who gets into trouble in school. Mind you, the twins do a fair bit of that too. You have your mother's hair, my eyes and your grandmother Doran's determination. God help us all.'

Posy smiled. 'Okay, I'll come.'

While they went to buy food, Piper tidied up the kitchen. As she was emptying the dishwasher, her mother sailed in, carrying a large pile of books.

'Hello, Piper, how was school?'

'Fine, but there's been a lot of drama here. The twins have kicked a huge hole in the bathroom door.' Piper scowled.

Her mother plonked the books on the kitchen table. She pushed her fringe off her face and waved her hand. 'It's just a door. There are real problems in the world,' she said, shaking a leaflet at Piper. 'Did you know that up to a hundred and forty million women and girls are thought to be living with the consequences of female genital mutilation? In Somalia, ninety-eight per cent of young girls are cut. Can you imagine?'

Piper knew she should feel desperately sorry for the girls who were suffering in Somalia, but right now she just wanted her mother to cook a bloody meal.

The twins bounded into the kitchen.

'Hi, Mum.'

'Hi, girls. Here, read this.' Olivia handed her daughters a piece of paper. 'I want you all to be aware of how lucky you are.'

'Uhm, what is it?' Penny asked.

'Female genital mutilation,' her mother replied.

'Yeah, I can read but, like, what does it mean?'

'It's when young girls have their clitoris cut in order to curb their sexual desire and preserve their "honour" before marriage.'

The twins squealed. 'OMG, did you just say "clitoris"?' Poppy was horrified.

'Yes. It's nothing to be embarrassed about,' Olivia said calmly.

'It's mortifying,' Penny said. 'You have officially gone mad. Please do not *ever* say that word again.'

'These poor girls are being mutilated because –'

'Stop,' Poppy said, putting her hands over her ears.

'You need to be aware of what's going on in the world.'

Penny shook her head. 'We're fifteen! We do not need to know about that. You're supposed to protect us, not shove all this crazy stuff in our faces.'

Piper silently cheered her sisters on.

'You can't live in a bubble. I want my girls to be strong, independent women, who help other women.'

'Can you please go back to being a normal mum?' Poppy begged. 'I much preferred you when you were cooking and ironing and watching *I'm a Celebrity* with us. You're so boring now.'

'I'm trying to teach you to be strong, independent women,' Olivia persisted.

'Stop banging on about it. Go and save the girls with the cut fannies and leave us alone,' Penny snapped.

Piper felt exactly the same but would never have had the guts to say it to her mother's face.

Olivia sat down at the table. 'I'm disappointed in you, girls. I thought that as young women growing up in a safe, peaceful Western society you would reach out to your fellow women and support them –'

Seamus and Posy came through the back door. 'Chipper chips for tea,' Seamus called out.

The twins ran over to grab the food.

'Thank God you're back, Dad. Mum's been going on about girls having their vaginas cut,' Poppy said.

Seamus dropped his bag of chips. 'What in the name of Jesus?'

'*Aaaaah!* Don't say the V-word! It's so embarrassing.' Posy blushed bright red.

Olivia picked up her husband's chips and popped one into her mouth. 'I'm just telling them what I learnt about in college today.'

'For the love of God, Olivia, stick to equal pay and subsidized childcare and leave off the genital mutilation.'

The girls clapped. 'Yes, listen to Dad.'

'I'm just interested in my subjects, that's all.'

'I know, love, but seriously?'

Olivia shrugged. 'It's happening out there. We can't ignore it.'

Piper felt a bit sorry for her mother. She was enjoying this new chapter in her life after all of the years she had devoted to raising her kids. Some of what she told them about her college course was interesting, but sometimes it was a bit too much – like today.

Olivia stood up. 'I'm a bit sticky from cycling home. I think I'll have a quick shower.'

'FYI, Mum, when you take those clothes off, put them in the bin. You're too old for jeans,' Penny said, stuffing chips into her mouth.

'What's wrong with my jeans?' Olivia looked down at herself.

'Your legs are too short,' Poppy told her.

'Are they?'

'The jeans are way too tight. They look ridiculous,' Penny said.

'Oh.' Olivia's face fell.

Piper didn't like to agree, but the twins were right. Her mother did look weird. She'd bought skinny jeans to 'blend in' with the other students, but she just looked like an older woman trying too hard. 'Your legs are fine, but your normal clothes suit you better,' she said.

'I feel so old in skirts and black trousers with all the students around me wearing jeans,' Olivia said.

'You *are* old,' Poppy reminded her.

'You're nearly fifty. You're not fooling anyone by wearing jeans,' Penny added.

'Your other clothes are just more flattering,' Seamus said.

Olivia tugged at her jeans. 'Okay. Well, thanks for telling me. I think.'

While Olivia went to have a shower and throw out her jeans, the twins breathlessly filled in their father on why they thought Zayn *soooo* hot.

7

Jess and Chloë sat on the edge of the playing fields, watching Luke's team's training session.

'That bruise really is massive. Donna must have whacked you in hockey. Cow.'

Jess looked down at the big bruise on her leg. 'It looks worse than it is. I seem to bruise easily at the moment.'

'Get a move on!' the coach roared at the players.

Luke staggered forward with one of his teammates, a big burly guy, hanging onto his back.

'OMG, Jess! That guy Luke's carrying is huge. This isn't training, it's torture.'

'Right, suitcase carries – move it!' the coach bellowed.

There was a communal groan. Luke made his way over and lifted the handle of the 'suitcase' of huge weights.

'Let's go!' the coach shouted.

Luke closed his eyes and forced himself on. Jess felt sorry for him. This was mad. The players all looked as if they were either going to pass out or vomit.

'I'm so glad I'm not a boy. Imagine having to do this all the time!' Chloë was incredulous. 'Can we go now?'

'In a minute.' Jess knew that the coach was naming the team today and she wanted to see if Luke was picked. She'd told Mum she'd try to find out after school and that she'd text her as soon as she knew.

After the suitcase exercise half the team fell to the ground. Others bent over and tried to suck air into their lungs, while two threw up.

Luke moved away from those who were vomiting and lay on the grass, close to where Jess and Chloë were sitting. He didn't notice them as he was too wrapped up in catching his breath.

'I know Jenson wants to prove himself in his first year as head coach, but he's going to kill us,' Lorcan said, lying beside Luke and gasping for air.

'I know. It's insane.'

'Did you hear he's naming the team today?'

Luke nodded.

'I reckon you're safe, man.'

'I dunno. Harry's playing well.'

'You've got the pace, though. You're class in attack.'

The coach came over to them. 'I'd like a word, Luke,' he said. Lorcan left them to it. Jess held her breath.

Mr Jenson put his hand on Luke's shoulder. 'I've seen how much work you've put in over the last few months, and I'm pleased with your progress. I want you to know that I'm starting you on Saturday. Play well and you'll be number-one choice. But I've said it before, you need to be more aggressive in the tackle.'

Luke nodded. 'Yes, Coach. I've been working on that. Thanks for the opportunity. I won't let you down.'

'Good, because if you do, Harry will get the place. Don't mess it up.'

As the coach walked ahead of him, Luke punched the air with his fist. *Yeeees!*

Jess jumped up and whooped. Luke turned, surprised to see her. 'What the hell?'

'I was passing.' She grinned.

'Spying on me, more like.' Luke picked her up and swung her around. 'Come on. I told Granddad I'd help in the café and I'm late.'

*

58

Luke told George his good news as he and Jess helped him clean up. George clapped him on the back with a soapy hand. 'I knew you'd do it. You deserve it after all those hours of training you put in over the summer. Good to see they've paid off. If the café's not too busy, I'll be out to see you. And I'll make sure your mum's free to go.'

Luke smiled. 'Thanks, Granddad. I sent Dad a text, but I haven't heard back yet.'

George fell silent. Jess had noticed that every time her dad's name came up, he said very little.

As they put away the clean crockery, Bobby came in and kicked one of the kitchen chairs.

'Hey, what's up?' Luke asked.

'Stupid, stinky Tommy said I was a know-it-all in class and that I sound like an incyclopedian when I talk.'

George stifled a laugh.

Luke turned to his brother. 'Tommy's an idiot,' he said.

'He's probably just jealous of all of your knowledge, Bobby,' Jess said, keen to make Bobby feel better.

Bobby perked up. 'Yeah, he probably is cos he's not very clever. He actually thought that an okapi was something to do with going to the toilet, like an "okay pee"!'

George and Luke looked at each other and laughed.

'Imagine that, a boy who doesn't know what an okapi is.' George winked at Luke.

'What a dork.' Luke grinned.

'I know.' Bobby giggled.

'Remind me again of the details,' George said. 'My old mind keeps forgetting things. The okapi is the one with the –'

'Stripy legs like a zebra but is related to the giraffe,' Bobby said.

'Yes, of course. I remember now.' George patted Bobby's head.

'It lives in the Congo and is about four feet nine inches tall. It –'

'I'd better check inside, but Luke and Jess would love to hear the details about the oki-thing.' George disappeared into the café.

Bobby watched him go. 'Luke?'

'Yes?'

'Sometimes I think Granddad's mind *is* a bit old. He doesn't seem to want to know a lot of new stuff. He forgets everything I tell him, and sometimes when I tell him things, he says his head hurts from too much information. Do you think your brain shrinks when you get old?'

Luke paused. 'I think Granddad is just really busy with the café and the wine shop and looking after us. Maybe you should stick to telling me and Jess and Mum about your facts.'

'Okay.'

Jess decided now was a good time to tell them about the dinner. They were both in a good mood. 'Did you hear Dad's coming to take us out for tea?' she said.

'What?' Bobby said.

Luke's head jerked up. 'Tonight?'

'He's taking us to Arturo's for a treat.'

'I'm supposed to be seeing Piper later.'

'Is stinky Jaden coming?' Bobby asked.

'Nope, just us. It'll be great. We'll have Dad to ourselves. Come on, guys, we haven't been out just the four of us in months.'

Their mother came into the room. 'Did Jess tell you about your dad?'

'Yes. It would have been nice to get some notice. When did he call?' Luke asked.

'Only about two hours ago. He said he had a gap in his schedule and wanted to see you.'

'I don't want to go, Mummy.' Bobby's face reddened. 'I don't like Daddy.'

She crouched down. 'Hey, now, he's your dad and he loves you. Don't say things like that. I know he's been busy with Jenny and the baby and work, but he really misses you and he wants to see you.'

'He either feels guilty for being a deadbeat dad or Jenny's up the duff again,' Luke said.

'Luke!' Kate snapped.

'Does this dress look nice, Mum?' Jess interrupted.

'Gorgeous.'

The doorbell rang. Jess raced out. She flung open the door and Nick bent down and kissed her. 'Hey, Jessie – wow, you look great! All the boys are going to be chasing you.'

Bobby stood in the doorway, peeping out. Luke grabbed his jacket and, taking Bobby's hand, led him towards the front door.

'Evening, you two,' Nick said cheerfully.

His sons went by him silently, walking straight out to the car. Nick's face dropped and Jess smiled as widely as she could at him, trying to make things okay.

Kate came to the door. 'I know they might not seem it, but they're glad to get time with you.'

Nick looked towards his car, where the boys were sitting side by side on the back seat. 'They really don't seem it.'

Kate found herself feeling sorry for him. 'Honestly, they do want to spend time with you,' she said. 'Just give them time to come round.'

'I'll help,' Jess said, slipping her hand into Nick's. 'We'll get them talking about rugby and world records.'

Kate loved her daughter for trying so hard, even though at the same time she was sad that she had to shoulder all the responsibility. 'Good luck,' she murmured, as she watched Nick and Jess get into the car. 'You'll need it,' she added, under her breath, as the car pulled away.

Bobby pushed aside his plate. 'It's yucky. I'm not eating it.'

Nick's jaw set. 'You said you wanted pepperoni pizza.'

'Well, I don't like this pepperoni. It's too spicy.'

'Here, take some of mine.' Nick cut a slice and handed it to Bobby.

'I don't want your stinky pizza. It has peppers on it.'

Jess watched nervously as her father tried not to lose his temper.

'You need to eat something, Bobby. How about some plain pasta? Shall I order that?'

Bobby shook his head.

'Here, he can have some of my Margarita.' Jess handed Bobby a slice, which he accepted.

'How's your chicken, Luke?' Nick asked.

'Fine.'

'How's school and rugby and all that?'

'Fine.'

Luke wasn't going to make it easy for him. Jess knew he was still furious about being stood up on his birthday.

'He's been picked for the senior cup team,' Jess said, trying to smooth things over.

Nick was obviously impressed. 'Well done! That's great. You look very fit – I can see you've been working out.'

'Daddy, do you know what an okapi is?' Bobby asked.

'What?'

'An okapi.'

'Uhm, no –'

His phone rang. Jess saw Jenny's name come up on the screen. He ignored it.

'Guess,' Bobby said.

The phone rang again.

'I dunno, what?' Nick put the phone on silent.

'What do you think it is?' Bobby persisted.

'I . . . uhm . . .' The phone flashed. Nick cursed under his breath.

Jess touched her father's sleeve. 'Maybe you should answer it, Dad. Maybe Jaden's sick.'

Nick rubbed his eyes. 'There's always some drama with Jenny.'

The phone flashed again. He sighed and answered it.

'WHAT IS AN OKAPI?' Bobby shouted.

'Jesus, I don't bloody know,' Nick snapped. Pressing his phone to his ear, he hissed, 'What is it? I'm with my kids.'

'I TOLD YOU TO GUESS,' Bobby roared.

'Your kids!' Jess heard Jenny screech down the phone. 'What about Jaden? He's your kid too and he's got a temperature.'

'Daddy, you have to guess.' Bobby was not letting it go.

'I'm here all by myself, Nick, and I'm freaking out because I think he needs to go to hospital.'

Jess could hear Jenny crying. She actually felt a bit sorry for her.

'He's fine, Jenny. You always overreact,' Nick said gruffly.

'GUESS!' Bobby bellowed.

Nick glared at him. 'Jesus Christ, Bobby, will you shut up?'

'Don't speak to him like that!' Luke yelled.

'Come home now or I'm calling an ambulance,' Jenny sobbed down the phone.

'Jenny, will you calm down?'

'I'm frightened, Nick. Come home.'

His shoulders slumped.

'Maybe you should just go. She sounds really upset,' Jess said.

'I'm on my way.' Nick shut the phone.

They all looked down at their food. Jess could see Bobby's hands clenched into little fists. His face was red, and she could see he was trying hard not to cry.

Luke was twisting his napkin around his hands tightly. He wanted to punch the wall, she thought . . . or probably Dad.

Nick asked for the bill. 'I'm really sorry, guys, but I have to go. I had hoped I'd get a couple of hours with you without Jenny calling every five seconds, but apparently I was wrong.'

'What if Jaden's really sick?' Jess worried.

Nick ran his hand over his face. 'I don't think he is. Jenny overreacts every time he gets a bit hot.'

'I hope he is sick. I hope he's really sick and he dies,' Bobby blurted out.

'What the hell?' Nick glared at Bobby.

'He's upset! Give him a break,' Luke said tersely.

'Look, guys, I really wanted tonight to be good. I wanted to spend some time with you on my own, uninterrupted. I'm sorry. I really am. It's just . . . not easy at the moment. I'll make it up to you, I promise.' Nick paid the bill.

Jess and Luke held Bobby's hot hands in theirs. As they walked out, Jess's leg began to throb.

Bobby's Diary

I HATE Daddy. He shouted at me and I was just trying to tell him about okapis. He didn't even care. All he cares about is stupid Jaden. Jess said it was a teribel thing to say that I hope Jaden dies but I don't care. Jess said God was waching and lisening and that made me a bit scared. She said you should be nice to every one and not ever say you want some one to die. But I do.

Mummy said she was sorry the dinner with Daddy was rooined and she gave us all yummy brownees to eat and I felt better then. Granddad came in and when he hearded about the dinner his face went all red and he said 'Tipical.' But Mummy did squinty eyes at him so he stopped talking and put on a pretend smile and said he was sure Daddy was very sorry to have to go home in the midel of dinner. Then he hugged me and Jess and gave Luke a pat on the sholder.

I like living here with Granddad. He is super-nice and always gives us hugs and treets and never shouts. He is super-nice to Mummy and she is waaaaaaaaaaaaay happier now. She has a real happy face and not a pretend happy face like she used to with Daddy.

Even if I have to share a bedroom with Jess, I don't mind. Jess is a nice sister and she lets me talk about facts and actualy lisens and remembers stuff.

There is something wrong with her leg. Mummy is taking her to the doctor tomorrow. She is limping like a dog with glass in his paw.

Mrs Lorgan was cross with me today. She said I need to control my temper and that calling Sammy a 'dickhead' for knoking over the green paint onto my copybook is unaxeptabel. I told her that Luke said that word about Dad all the time. She asked how old Luke is and I said eighteen and she said that he was old enuff to know better. She said it was a very bad word and not ever to use it.

Then she asked about Jaden and was I growing to love my baby brother. I said no, that I wanted him to die, and her face went all red and her eyes were all big and she said that wasn't a nice thing to say and that I'd grow to love him.

I decided not to speak. She doesn't understand, no one does. Jenny took my daddy out of the house but Jaden took my daddy out of our hearts. That's why I hate him.

8

George stood behind Kate as they watched the women stream through the café door and up the stairs. Each one had a big bag of colourful balls of wool and long needles.

'Are they really called the Stitch 'n' Bitch Club?' he muttered.

'Yes, Dad.'

'What do they do – knit and give out?' He clicked his tongue. 'I never liked all those groups of women getting together and giving out and gossiping. Sure, half of them don't even like each other. The minute you put your knitting down to go to the toilet they'll be sticking a needle in your back.'

'I'm sure they support each other too, Dad,' Kate said, smiling.

'Nonsense. Your good friends support you, not a big group like that. Sure, Dorothy Chambers hates Nuala King. All she ever does is complain about her.'

'Dorothy wouldn't know what to do if she wasn't criticizing someone.' Kate chuckled.

'I'm not sure I like it, a bunch of women up there giving out,' George grumbled, eyeing the ceiling suspiciously.

'They're paying for the privilege,' Kate reminded him.

'You're right.' He grinned. 'They can knit and bitch and scratch each other's eyes out as long as they pay.'

Kate welcomed the women with a warm smile and directed them to the stairs that led to the room above the café.

'Hello there, Kate,' Dorothy said. 'You look well, dear. Much better than when I last saw you. You were very pale and old-looking back in the spring. I said to my Gerry, that poor girl has aged twenty years because of that awful husband of hers.'

Kate gritted her teeth and plastered on a smile. 'Well, enjoy your night. Straight on up the stairs there.'

But Dorothy was going nowhere. She heaved her balls of wool over her vast chest. 'Of course, your father always said that that Nick of yours was a bad egg. Rotten to the core.'

Kate could hear her father spluttering in the kitchen behind her, out of sight but perfectly well able to hear. 'Well, Nick is my children's father so I prefer not to speak ill of him,' she said evenly.

'A skirt-chaser. That was what George always said about your Nick. Full of his own importance, he said, and all flash with no cash.'

Kate could feel her temperature rising. 'Well, as I said, he is the father of my children, so I prefer not to speak ill of him.'

'Of course, Janice upstairs married one of those. Oh, sure he rode half the town, that fella. A philanderer, as my mother would have said. Poor Janice hadn't a clue. She was being made a holy show of, so I took it upon myself to tell her.'

'Did you? How . . .' Kate paused '. . . considerate of you.'

Dorothy placed a wrinkled hand on Kate's arm. 'I always think of others.'

Yes, I imagine you do, Kate thought, all day bloody long, peeking out from behind your twitching curtain, you nasty woman. Smiling, she said, 'Well, I mustn't keep you from your knitting.'

Dorothy dragged her large frame up the stairs while Kate turned to go back into the kitchen.

George moved quickly from behind the door and pretended to read the paper.

'I've just had a very interesting chat with Dorothy.'

'Oh, yes?' He feigned disinterest.

'She told me you've been slating Nick to everyone.'

'I wouldn't believe a word out of that woman's mouth. She's pure poison, your mother always said.'

Kate stood in front of her father, hands on hips. 'Seriously, Dad, don't criticize Nick in public, for the kids' sake. You can rip him apart in front of me, but not other people. Okay?'

George rustled his newspaper. 'Sure I barely mentioned him. Dorothy exaggerates everything. I'd never do anything to upset those kids.'

Kate ruffled his hair and kissed his forehead. 'I know you wouldn't.'

When Kate went to check on Jess and Bobby, she found Bobby fast asleep with his face stuck to the pages of *Guinness World Records*. Jess was still awake, reading.

Kate gently moved Bobby's face from the page to his pillow. Even in his sleep he frowned. She hoped he'd become less angry now that they'd moved in with George and things were calmer. But the poor little fellow still seemed full of rage, especially towards Jaden, who was an innocent victim in all this. Kate needed to spend more time with Bobby. She'd have to find it somehow.

'Mum,' Jess whispered.

'Yes, pet?'

'Am I going to be sharing a room with Bobby for ever?'

'For a while anyway.'

Jess sighed. 'Okay. It's just he's kind of annoying. I was trying to read my book and he kept going on and on about his facts.'

Kate moved over to sit on the edge of Jess's bed and hugged her.

'What's that for?'

'You're just great, and I don't tell you enough. You're so good with Bobby. I know it's not easy sharing a room with him. I'll tell you what, I'll let him sleep with me three nights a week. How does that sound?'

'Amazing!' Jess beamed.

'Was the dinner with Dad awful?' Kate asked. The kids hadn't said much about it in the two days since it had happened.

Jess nodded. 'Pretty awful. Jenny was stalking Dad on the phone and freaking out about Jaden, and Dad was getting really stressed, and Bobby kept on about the okapis, and Dad ended up shouting at him.'

'God, it sounds like a mess. I'm sorry for all of you. It would have been nice for you to spend time with your dad without any drama.'

Jess snuggled down under her covers. 'To be honest, Mum, I think there's always going to be drama with Jenny and Dad. She worries a lot about Jaden. Dad seemed kind of fed up.'

Did he indeed? Kate tried not to smile. So hot, sexy Jenny wasn't so great, after all. She actually had weak spots. Fancy that!

Jess fiddled with her hair. 'Do you think Dad will ever be able to be a proper dad again?'

Suddenly Kate felt bad for being happy that Jenny was turning into a nightmare. This wasn't about her: it was about her kids.

She pulled Jess's hands gently out of her hair. 'Yes. New babies always take up a lot of time and energy, and it's Jenny's first child, so naturally she's nervous. She'll calm down soon and Dad will have more time for you guys. This is only temporary. Don't worry. You know he loves you.'

'I suppose you're right.' Jess rolled over, yawning. 'I just hope it's soon. I miss him.'

Kate leant over and kissed her cheek. 'Sleep well. We have that doctor's appointment tomorrow. I don't like the look of those bruises. I'm worried you might be a bit anaemic. You'll be going to school late.'

Jess smiled. 'Yes! I'm missing double maths.'

Kate switched off the bedside lamp and tiptoed out of the room. When she went back down to the kitchen, Luke was tucking into a large steak.

'What are you doing? We had steak for dinner,' Kate said.

Chewing, he said, 'We were told to eat as much protein as possible.'

'You're going to bankrupt me.'

'I need it, Mum. I have to be in peak condition.'

'What's this?' She picked up a half-empty carton.

'Protein milk,' Luke said, chugging down half a glass in one go.

Kate gazed at her son. He was a man now. Tall, strong, very muscular, with a shadow of facial hair. Where had the chubby blond toddler in red shorts gone? It felt as if she'd blinked and he'd grown up. She wanted to reach out and smooth down his hair and kiss his lovely face, but she knew not to.

She sat down opposite him. 'I want you to do your best at rugby but don't overdo it, Luke. Too much protein isn't healthy. You need a balanced diet, love.'

Luke polished off the steak. 'Chill, Mum. It's all under control. I know what I need to do.'

'I worry about you getting injured. Did you see the Leinster winger got a terrible concussion in the last match?'

Luke snorted. 'He can't tackle. He goes in with his head.'

'Well, you just mind yours.'

Luke rolled his eyes.

'Did you tell Dad about the match on Saturday?' she asked.

Luke shook his head.

'Ah, Luke, call him and tell him. He'll want to come.'

Luke stared into her eyes, something he very rarely did these days. 'Mum, Dad couldn't give a flying fuck about rugby or about me. I texted him when I made the team and he didn't reply. Then at the restaurant it was like he'd never fucking heard about it before.'

'Language!'

'I'm serious. He's a tosser, and I'm not putting myself out there any more. If he wants to know what's going on, he can bloody well ask. I'm over it.' Luke stood up and slammed his plate into the dishwasher.

He was so clearly not 'over it'. Every muscle in his body was tense with rage and frustration. Kate would have to call Nick and make sure he went to the game.

George came in, looking flustered. 'For the love of God, Kate, save me.'

'What's wrong?'

'Rosemary Jacobs just pretended she couldn't find the toilet. She came into the wine shop, grabbed my backside and squeezed it!'

'Way to go, Granddad.' Luke grinned.

Kate laughed. 'What's the problem, Dad?'

'The problem is, I don't want to be assaulted by the Stitch and Bitchers. They must have brought their own wine with them – she smelt of alcohol.'

'There's no law against having wine while you knit.'

George crossed his arms. 'If I was a woman, you'd all be up in arms if someone pinched me. Because I'm a man I'm supposed not to care.'

'You should be flattered, Granddad. If some bird pinched my arse, I'd be cool with it,' Luke said, and drank the last of the protein milk.

'I'm seventy-three, too old for all that.'

'Charlie Chaplin became a father again at seventy-three. It's never too late,' Kate said.

'No way!' Luke held up his hands. 'No more babies. Jaden is enough.'

'I don't think Rosemary is in any fit state to be having children. She's seventy years old and has had two hip replacements.'

'You could be one of Bobby's facts in *Guinness World Records* – the oldest couple ever to have a child.' Kate giggled.

'You could just shag her,' Luke said. 'Treat her mean, keep her keen, you know.'

'Luke!' Kate cried.

'What? I'm just saying, if he wanted a bit of action . . .'

George tapped the kitchen table for attention. 'Thank you for your advice, but I think I'll steer clear of Rosemary. If I want "a bit of action", I'll choose my own partner.'

'That Caroline who comes into the café isn't bad. She's in good shape for an auld one,' Luke suggested.

'She is attractive, all right.'

'Not too wrinkly,' Luke said.

'She's fifty-three!' Kate exclaimed. 'She's only eleven years older than me.'

'So?' The two men turned to her.

Kate was incredulous. 'So? So she's too young for you and, no offence, Dad, you look good for your age but I doubt she wants a man twenty years older than her.'

'Loads of old dudes go out with younger chicks,' Luke informed her. 'Jenny's twenty years younger than Dad.'

'Thanks for reminding me,' Kate retorted. 'It's a man's world. Right, well, I'd better see the Stitch 'n' Bitch Club out. Maybe one of them will have a brother in his sixties or seventies who might be interested in a single forty-two-year-old woman with three kids.'

She left her father and son laughing. It might be funny for them, but was this really her future? Would only men in their sixties be interested in her from now on? It was depressing.

After showing the knitting ladies out and collecting the money – a hundred and fifty euros – Kate locked the doors and went to sit in the café, where it was quiet. She made herself a cup of frothy cappuccino and called Maggie.

'Hey!'

'Hey.'

'How are you?'

'Are the only men who'll be interested in me going to be in their sixties?'

'Hell, no,' Maggie growled. 'What gave you that idea? I was with a thirty-year-old last week. Younger guys love older women. We're not needy, we don't want to have kids with them and we're not after commitment.'

Kate took a sip of her coffee. The problem was, if she was to meet another man she would want commitment. She didn't want to sleep with random strangers. She wanted a man to love her and be nice to her. Maybe it was naive, but she liked being in a relationship. She liked sitting in the cinema with someone sharing popcorn or curling up on the sofa together and talking about your day.

Maggie had always hated the idea of commitment. Even when they were at school, she had never dated anyone for more than two weeks. She was on a mission to get the hell out of Ireland and make it big in the world, and no one was going to stop her, least of all a boy. It was as if boys could smell her indifference and it drove them wild. Kate could remember the queues of boys who had chased Maggie all over town.

But the girl was not for turning. As soon as she'd finished her business degree, Maggie had been on the first plane to London, where she'd made success happen.

'How are the kids? How's my goddaughter? Beautiful and lovely as ever?'

Kate smiled. 'Yes.'

'Actually, I know more about Jess than ever now that she's allowed me to be her friend on Facebook.'

'Good. You can keep an eye on her and let me know what's going on. She refused to let me be her friend, needless to say.'

'That's normal, Kate. No kid wants their mother spying on them on Facebook. How are the boys?'

'Good. Luke got picked for the senior cup team so he's thrilled and eating every animal he can get his hands on, alive or dead. The whole diet thing is crazy. Honestly, Maggie, he consumes cows and chickens daily.'

Kate could hear Maggie lighting a cigarette. 'He has to, Kate. All those rugby guys have to build up as much muscle as they can. It's to protect themselves from the opposition who, you can be sure, are also going around eating steaks for breakfast. How's Bobby?'

'Bobby is Bobby.'

'Still spouting facts and kicking things?'

'Yes. He's kicked a lot of furniture in the last two days.' Kate filled her in on the disastrous dinner with Nick.

'Oh, for the love of Jesus, would Nick grow a pair of balls and stand up to that moany cow? She's obviously sitting in that apartment, alone all day, with leaky boobs and a sore fanny, and wondering what the hell she's got herself into. Serves her right for shagging your husband. It's always the same. These men have their pathetic midlife crises, start screwing some young slapper, think it's all going to be sex on the kitchen table and blow-jobs, until the woman decides she wants a kid and it all goes tits-up. Then they realize that the wife they had was actually fantastic.'

Kate laughed. She loved Maggie. She always made her feel better about things. It was a gift. 'That about sums it up. I was feeling a bit gloaty about it all, but the kids are upset so I'm hoping Jenny will get herself together and let Nick see them more than once every six weeks.'

'He's their father! It's up to him to stand up to her. Poor Bobby, though. Not nice to be shouted at.'

'No, and he's so sensitive when it comes to Nick.'

'I'll send him something to cheer him up. How's George?'

'He's great. It hasn't been easy for him. Mum's been gone six years and he was used to living on his own when we landed on him. I think he finds us all a bit much at times, but he's really good with the kids, particularly with Luke, and God knows he needs a positive male influence. He loves Jess, but I think he finds Bobby a bit trying, and patience was never Dad's strong point. Poor Bobby, no one really understands him.'

'Except you.'

'That's true.'

'Is George still being chatted up by the local widows and singletons?'

Kate laughed. 'Yes, but he doesn't seem interested. Anyway, enough about me, how are you?'

'Good. Crazy busy. Travelling to the States a lot since I last saw you, having good casual sex with younger guys, and spending a lot of money on Botox and fillers.'

'You don't need it. You're lovely the way you are.'

Maggie exhaled her cigarette smoke. 'No way! Kate, a woman breaking glass ceilings has to keep herself looking good. If I walk into meetings with men of my age looking old and wrinkled with black bags under my eyes, I'm on the back foot. I know it sounds ridiculous, but that's the reality. If I walk in fit, fresh-faced and ready to go, they sit up and take notice.'

'Come on! What about Angela Merkel? She's not having work done on her face.'

Maggie snorted. 'She looks like a bloke. I'm going for the Christine Lagarde vibe.'

Kate was ashamed to admit she wasn't quite sure who Christine Lagarde was. That was the problem with kids and working: there was never enough time to read the papers. Even when she did have a second to herself, she was usually so tired that she'd pick up a magazine or skim the headlines in the paper but never actually read the articles. She'd Google Christine Lagarde later. 'Well, I still think you're lovely without all that stuff.'

To be honest, Maggie's face seemed a bit pulled. Her forehead was frozen. She was like one of those presenters on American TV, glittering white teeth and flawless face. She looked fabulous but, close up, it was a little fake.

Then again, what did Kate know about anything? She hadn't even had a bikini wax in almost a year. What was the point? They couldn't afford to go on holidays so she didn't need to wear swimming togs and no man was looking at her. Half the time she didn't even bother to shave her legs. She'd only plucked her eyebrows the other day when Jess said the way they were 'meeting in the middle' was a bit strange. It was only when she'd seen herself in the mirror that she'd noticed the very obvious monobrow.

That was the problem. She never looked at herself now. Not really, not closely. She climbed out of bed in the morning, got everyone fed and off to school, then helped her dad in the café, did homework with the kids, had dinner and went to bed. She avoided mirrors when she came within their range, basically ignoring herself entirely. She just didn't want to see. She had enough going on without owning up to how terrible she looked.

When she'd been with Nick, she'd made more of an effort with her appearance, her clothes and her weight. She peered down at her stomach: too many late-night comfort muffins. She'd have to start walking again and watch what she ate. Things were better now – the kids were happier, settled into the house and set-up. It was time for Kate to find herself again.

'So, do you think you're ready to date again?' Maggie asked.

'I'm not sure. Not yet. Maybe. No. Besides, who'd be interested? I'm a broke, boring mother of three who lives and works with her dad.'

'Kate. You're a gorgeous, interesting, kind, lovely woman. Any man would be lucky to have you . . . young or old.' She laughed her husky smoker's laugh.

'How old do you think I should consider?' Kate said, curiosity now taking hold of her.

'The oldest man I've ever slept with was ten years older than I am, but he was very fit – he had a Liam Neeson vibe.'

'There aren't any Liam Neeson lookalikes in our area, I can tell you.'

'Keep an open mind – you could go younger. My youngest was twenty-eight.'

Kate giggled. 'I'll be eyeing up Luke's friends soon.'

'Why not?' Maggie chuckled. 'Oh, shoot, my plane's boarding. I'd better go. Big hi to the kids, especially Jess. By the way, she said on Facebook she's had a couple of nose bleeds. Is she all right?'

'I'm a bit worried. I think she might be anaemic. She's very pale. I reckon she needs iron. I'm taking her to the doctor tomorrow.'

'Good idea. Keep me posted.'

They said goodbye and hung up. Kate finished her now lukewarm coffee and headed upstairs to shave her legs. Tomorrow she'd book a bikini wax. It was time to move on. She needed to take control of her life and shake herself up. She wasn't past her sell-by date. She was still relatively young and, with a bit of effort, could be attractive again, maybe even meet someone. Why not? Why was she writing herself off? Maybe this was one of the blessings in disguise that her mother used to talk about, a new chapter in her life, a happier one.

9

Jess was glad they were going to the doctor because she felt awful. She knew Mum was worried – she kept asking Jess if she was all right, then got that worried line between her eyes when Jess said no.

She was fed up herself: the bruises on her legs were big and ugly and the nose bleeds were a pain. Her gym teacher said she probably needed iron. She said Jess was probably going through a growth spurt and her body needed more vitamins. Jess actually hoped that what she had was growing pains – she'd like to be taller. Chloë was five foot five already, like a supermodel. Jess was still only four foot eleven.

'Now, pet, there you go.' George put a plate of homemade pancakes in front of Jess.

'Wow, thanks, Granddad.'

'Only the best for my favourite granddaughter.'

Jess grinned. He always said that, even though she was his only granddaughter. Jess loved her granddad. He could be a bit grumpy sometimes, but most of the time he was lovely and kind, generous and funny. But, most of all, Jess loved the way he minded her mum. You could see that he adored her. Jess supposed it was because she was his only child, and the way he looked at her made Jess's tummy all squidgy inside.

It was how her mum looked at her, Luke and Bobby – as if they were the sun, the moon and the stars. It was unconditional love. Her mum had told her about it one night. Jess had been upset about her dad leaving and she'd shouted at her mum that she hated her. She'd said, 'It's all your fault! You're always nagging him! He hates being nagged. He said so. You made him leave.'

Jess had felt awful after shouting. She was sick to her stomach. When she'd gone downstairs later to apologize, Mum had put her arms around her and said, 'It's okay.'

Jess had asked her if she hated her now for being so mean and her mum had laughed and said, 'Don't be ridiculous. Nothing you can do will make me stop loving you. It's called unconditional love.'

After that Jess had felt all warm inside. But she also understood that unconditional love was only between parents and kids, not mums and dads. They did not love each other unconditionally at all.

Jess had decided to stop wishing for her parents to get back together. It was a waste of time, Chloë said. 'Your dad's had a kid with another woman. He's not coming back, Jess. I'm sorry, but it's just not going to happen and, besides, would your mum even take him back? Unlikely. My mum said that if Dad ever had an affair she'd kick him out so fast his head would spin off, and then she'd smash his sports cars with a baseball bat. She said women have to be strong and show men that they can't be messed around.'

Jess thought this was good advice, but Chloë's mum was a bit scary. She was super-nice to Jess, but Jess had heard her on the phone one day to someone who had forgotten to deliver something on time and, OMG, she'd ripped their head off. Jess decided then and there never to do anything to annoy her.

Leaving their old house and moving in with her granddad had been a good thing, after all. She felt it sort of made things clearer in her life and everyone was happier – well, everyone except Bobby, but he was never really happy.

Jess ate some of her pancakes, while her mum and granddad bustled in and out of the café. Nathalie arrived through the back door into the kitchen for her morning shift. Jess loved Nathalie – she was so cool and dramatic in a fabulous French way. Chloë thought she was like a French version of Emma Watson.

Nathalie threw her bag down, plonked herself opposite Jess and began picking at her pancakes. Jess didn't mind – she wasn't all that hungry.

'How are you?' Jess asked.

Nathalie pouted in the coolest way. Jess and Chloë had practised in the mirror but they couldn't do it like her. 'Life ees sheet,' she said, chewing a tiny piece of pancake.

'Sorry to hear that. Did something happen?'

Nathalie shrugged. 'Men. Irish men are ridiculous. They are so stupid and immature, like leetle kids. They don't want to 'ave a beautiful connection, to talk about poetry and the meaning of life, they just want to get drunk and 'ave sex.'

'That about sums it up.' Kate bustled in. 'Right, Nathalie, when you're ready you might get up and go in to help my dad. Also, please try to remember that Jess is twelve. Tone down the sex chat.'

'In France we talk about sex from a young age. There is nothing to be embarrassed about.'

Jess was bright red and utterly mortified by the whole conversation. She liked Nathalie treating her as an equal, but she did find the word 'sex' really cringey and she was totally embarrassed by her mother coming in at that exact moment. She put her hands up to her face to try to cool her cheeks.

'Well, in Ireland we're less free and easy with the sex chat – hence the fact that men can't talk to women without ten pints on them,' said Kate. 'So, if you don't mind, I'd appreciate it if you kept that conversation for people older than Jess.'

Nathalie picked up her bag. 'Fine, but you should not 'ide your children from the conversation of the beauty of sex and the satisfaction of the body.'

'Thank you, Nathalie. Off you go now. You can tell my dad all about it.' Kate grinned.

'All about what?' George stuck his head around the door.

'Sex,' Nathalie said.

'Mother of Holy God, will you keep that chat to yourself! The average age of the customers in here this morning is seventy – you'll give them heart attacks.'

'Or maybe I will wake them up from the coma they are living in.' Nathalie half smiled.

'With that bit of a skirt on you, they'll be wide awake in no time,' George grumbled. 'Didn't I tell you to wear something that reached your knees? Here, put this apron on or I'll have to invest in a defibrillator.'

Nathalie sighed dramatically. 'Once again the Irish men and the body. You are afraid of the woman's form. You are all totally suppressed.'

George held up his hand. 'I'll have to stop you there. Much as I enjoy these conversations about the uselessness of Irish men and their many failures, I've a business to run and people to serve. Now, hop it.'

Jess and Kate giggled as Nathalie and George went into the café. Jess tidied her plate into the dishwasher, while Kate rushed around looking for keys and money.

'Come on,' she said, smiling at Jess. 'Let's get going while the going's good.'

Jess watched her mother's face darken.

'What do you mean, blood tests? Why?'

Dr Willis smiled reassuringly. 'It's just a precaution. I'm a little concerned about the bruising and the nose bleeds. She might be anaemic or have a low-lying infection. I think it's worth checking out her bloods.'

Jess felt her mother relax. 'Okay. She probably is a bit low on iron.'

Dr Willis rolled up Jess's sleeve and gently inserted the needle, chatting to Jess to distract her. He was a really nice man. Jess trusted him. He was the only doctor she'd ever been to – they'd always come to him when they were sick. He was nearly as old as Granddad and very kind. Mum had been seeing him since she was a little girl, too.

The needle didn't hurt as much as Jess had thought it would. It was all over quickly and they were able to leave. Her mum asked if she should give Jess iron straight away, but Dr Willis said it was best to wait and that he'd get the results as quickly as possible.

Jess felt there was something he wasn't saying. She couldn't explain it exactly but she sensed that he was worried. She felt very tired, like super-tired. She wanted to go home and lie down. She hoped the blood tests would show what was wrong and that they could give her some pills and make her better.

Kate paid and they left the surgery. Dr Willis promised to call as soon as he had some news.

'Would you like to go for a hot chocolate before I bring you to school?' Kate asked.

Jess shook her head. 'Actually, Mum, I feel really tired. Can I just go home and rest?'

Kate frowned. 'You're very pale. You poor thing. I've been so distracted I haven't paid enough attention to you. I hope you don't have an infection, but it'll be good to find out whatever's wrong and get you better.' She put her arm around Jess's shoulders. 'Come on, let's get you home and into your pyjamas and cosy you up. It'll be nice and peaceful with no Bobby to annoy you.'

Jess leant her head into her mother's shoulder. It was nice just being the two of them. Kate kissed her. They walked home across the village green and went through the back door. Kate went to check if George needed any help in the café while Jess went up to change into her pyjamas and dressing-gown. When she came back to the kitchen, her mum handed her a mug of hot chocolate, which she gratefully drank.

'It's quiet now, the lull before lunch. Can I get you anything else, pet?'

'I'm fine, thanks. I might go up and read or watch Netflix.'

'Good idea.'

George popped his head in. 'How did you get on?'

'She had blood tests done and now she's tired so I've let her off school.'

'Good idea. You're as pale as a ghost, Jess. A good rest will help. Would you like something to eat?'

'No, thanks. I'm going to bed to read.'

Nathalie slunk in. 'I am reading a fantastic book of poetry all about love and 'ow it can drive you crazy. I read one this morning on my way 'ere about a man who sets himself on fire because the woman he loves is a lesbian. If you would like to borrow it, I can lend it.'

George threw his arms into the air. 'Just what a twelve-year-old needs to cheer her up, a book about a fella frying himself over a lesbian. I tell you what, Nathalie, you're going to make one hell of a psychologist when you finish that degree of yours. They'll be queuing round the block to listen to your words of comfort and joy.'

Jess tried not to giggle as Nathalie wagged a finger at George. 'Irish people drink all this alcohol because they are so sad inside.'

George put his hand on her arm. 'This may come as a shock to you, but some people drink for a bit of fun. Not everyone who has a pint or a glass of wine is an emotional cripple.'

Jess looked at her mum, who was smiling. It was lovely to be here with them all, listening to the funny conversations and feeling like she was a grown-up.

Nathalie shrugged. 'I prefer to talk rather than drink.'

'I noticed that. I also noticed that you prefer to talk rather than work. Now come on.'

'I am entitled to a break.'

'You haven't exactly been run off your feet, and after the double espresso you just had, I'd have thought you'd be buzzing.'

Nathalie pulled her hair into a bun and anchored it with a pen. Jess thought it looked so cool – she'd try it when she was on her own.

'You are like a . . . 'ow do you say it? Driver of the slaves,' Nathalie said.

George hooted. 'Slave driver? I'm the best boss you'll ever have. You spend most of your time drinking coffee and sighing. You need a rocket under your feet to get you moving. Now, come on, I've a business to run here.'

Nathalie shuffled in behind him, pulling a face at Jess over her shoulder as she went.

'I'm not sure how long Nathalie's going to last. She's the laziest waitress we've ever had,' Kate said, as she began to make wraps and rolls for the lunchtime rush.

Jess hoped Nathalie would work a bit harder so she wouldn't get fired. She'd miss her crazy talk so much if she had to leave. And, anyway, she had a feeling that, underneath all the giving out, Granddad liked having Nathalie around too.

Jess headed upstairs, her legs heavy and uncooperative. They felt like they were made of iron already, but if everyone thought she needed more, she'd happily take it – anything to get rid of this worn-out feeling.

10

Piper watched Poppy and Penny doing their homework while, at the same time, trying to eat Weetabix. A lump of the milky cereal landed on Poppy's copybook.

'For God's sake, Penny! Look what you just did!'

'It's not my fault! You nudged my arm.'

Poppy tried to wipe it off, but made the stain worse.

'Great! Now Mr Keane will think I didn't bother trying.'

Pauline clicked her tongue. 'He'd be correct, then, wouldn't he? Doing your homework over breakfast doesn't qualify as much of an effort.'

Poppy glared at her eldest sister. 'Oh, go and qualify yourself, you bore.'

Penny giggled. 'I bet you always did your homework the night before and never handed anything in late.'

'Yes, actually, I did, which is why I got in to do medicine.'

Penny snorted. 'Who wants to do boring medicine and wear a horrible white coat . . . Zzzzzzzz.'

The twins pretended to fall asleep.

Olivia, who had been concentrating on reading her college notes and not listening to any of them, suddenly looked up. 'I think you'll find that studying is extremely important and valuable. Pauline could end up finding the cure for cancer or Parkinson's.'

Pauline smiled. 'That's my plan.'

'She could end up being an adviser on *Grey's Anatomy*,' Posy said, suddenly joining in the conversation.

'I have no intention of advising some ridiculous TV show,' Pauline snapped.

Posy frowned. 'I was just saying.'

'Did you know,' Olivia said, 'that it was a woman who –'

'Mum!' Piper had sensed that their mother was about to launch into one of her long lectures about women.

'What?' Olivia said impatiently.

'Don't forget you have to help out at the cake sale this morning.'

'What cake sale?'

'The one for the St Vincent de Paul. I told you last week.'

Olivia had clearly forgotten all about it. She never forgot about her lectures, Piper thought grumpily, but she did forget about everything else.

'Well, I can only stay an hour. I have a lecture at half ten. We're covering transgender this week.'

'Oh, like Caitlin Jenner,' Poppy said. 'OMG! Is he – I mean she – going to be talking?'

'Duh! Caitlin Jenner is way too busy to come to some crappy college in Ireland,' Penny said.

'Is transgender when a man wants to be a woman?' Posy asked.

Olivia put down her book. 'It means someone whose gender differs from the one they were given when they were born,' she explained to her youngest child.

'Like you,' Poppy said to Posy. 'You're going to have to be a boy because Dad wants a son.'

Posy's eyes widened. 'I am not,' she shouted.

Seamus walked into the chaos. 'What's going on? Why is Posy shouting?'

Posy rounded on her father. 'I don't care how much you want a son, I'm not going to be it. No way. I'm a girl and that's it.' She stormed out to howls of laughter from the twins.

'Would someone like to explain?' Seamus asked.

'I'm going to college. This family is insane.' Pauline picked up her laptop and left.

'The twins were winding Posy up,' Olivia said. Turning to the twins, she added, 'It's not nice. You're always tormenting her. Besides, being transgender is not a joke. It's a very serious issue.'

Penny put her cereal bowl into the dishwasher. 'We know, Mum. We've watched *I Am Cait*. God, can no one have a joke around here any more?' The twins left to get ready for school.

'Transgender at eight a.m.' Seamus sat down. 'You've outdone yourself, Olivia.'

Olivia poured herself and Piper another cup of tea. 'I just said I had a lecture on the subject. Besides, kids need to be informed.'

'Not at twelve years of age and not before breakfast is even over. Can you please tone it down?'

Olivia bristled. 'Men telling women to "tone it down" is what got us into this mess in the first place.'

'What mess is that?'

'Men thinking they're superior and putting women down.'

'When have I ever put you down?'

'Well, obviously you haven't, but I'm talking about other men.'

Seamus folded his arms over his chest. 'What – like Muslim men?'

Olivia nodded. 'Well, some, and others.'

'Like who?'

Piper saw her mother waver.

'Like other men, ones who feel insecure and put women down to make themselves feel better.'

'In my humble male opinion, women are pretty good at putting each other down.'

Go, Dad! Piper cheered silently.

Olivia put her mug down. 'You have a point there.'

'What? Me? A mere man saying something you agree with? My God, Olivia, your equality lecturer might not like that.'

Piper watched as a smile spread across her mother's face. It was nice to see – she could be a bit serious about her studies.

Seamus spread a thick layer of butter on his toast. 'So, let me get this straight. Posy thinks I want her to be a boy?'

'Yes.'

'Excellent. With her already raging hormones, it'll make her even more difficult to live with.' To Piper, he added, 'Thank God one of my daughters is sensible.'

Olivia reached out and patted Piper's shoulder. 'You're right there.'

Piper smiled. With four loud sisters, it was rare that she got any time alone with her parents. Maybe now was the time to tell them. No, she had to tell Luke first. Oh, God. Her stomach twisted into a tight knot.

The door burst open. Posy stormed in wearing her uniform, her face plastered in make-up, with big hoop earrings and bracelets jangling from her wrists. The twins followed her, laughing.

'See?' Posy threw her hands into the air. 'I'm a girl. Not a girl who wants to be a boy. Not a girl who is a lesbian. Not a girl who doesn't want to be a girl. Not a girl who wants a willy. Just a bloody girl, okay?'

'To be honest, with all that make-up on your face, you look like a transvestite,' Penny said.

They all laughed, even Olivia.

Posy's face went bright red. 'What did you say?'

91

Olivia jumped up and went over to her. 'Calm down. She's only joking.'

'Transvestite!' she shrieked. 'One minute I'm a transsexual and now you're saying I'm a transvestite. I hate this family. I'm going to get a lawyer and divorce you all. Yeah, I saw it on TV. Kids can divorce their families.'

'On what grounds are you going to divorce us?' Seamus asked, trying not to laugh.

'On the grounds of you being mean and calling me names and . . . What's that word? Oh, yeah, racists and bigerts.'

'Bigots?' Seamus suggested.

'Yeah, that's it.' Posy pointed a finger at her father. 'You're all worse than the Nazis.'

'I'm not sure you can compare genocide to a bit of joking around,' Seamus said drily.

'Okay. Well, you're worse than – than – Paul Potts.'

'Who?' Olivia and Seamus looked confused.

Piper couldn't help it. She burst out laughing. 'Paul Potts was the singer from *Britain's Got Talent*. I think you mean Pol Pot.'

The twins cracked up.

'Pot, Potts, whatever. You're all just mean and cruel.'

Olivia laid a hand on Posy's tense shoulder. 'Take a deep breath, darling. You're going to have a heart attack. You must learn to handle teasing.'

'It's not teasing, it's abuse.' Posy began to cry and her mascara streamed down her face in black lines, reminding Piper of a sad clown, the red lipstick making her mouth seem droopy.

'Come on. I'll help you take the make-up off so Mrs Kinsella doesn't freak when she sees you.'

Piper took her little sister upstairs and used wet wipes to remove the thick layer of foundation. When she'd finished,

Posy, who had now calmed down, grunted thanks and went to get her schoolbag.

Piper went into her bedroom and unplugged her phone from the charger. She cursed: it was already five to nine. Posy's drama meant they were going to be late. She slid the package from under her pillow into her bag. She'd dump it in the bin outside the Spar shop on the way to school. No one would find it there. Her hands shook as she tried to zip up her backpack. She had to tell him today. No more pretending, he had to know. She couldn't keep it in any longer. The last three days had been hell. She wanted to tell him, to share the news, to have him comfort her. She wanted him to tell her what to do.

Today was the day she would tell Luke that she was pregnant.

Winter

Bobby's Diary

Mrs Lorgan was super-cross with me today. She was talking about Jesus being born in a mainger and that Mary was his mother and God was his father. But I didn't understand cos Joseph was the Dad. But Mrs Lorgan said no, God was the Dad.

So I asked her how come God gets to be Jesus father when Mary is married to Joseph? She must have had an afair like my dad did with Jenny. And so how come Joseph doesn't mind about God and the afair? How come he doesn't go over to God and punch him in the face?

Mrs Lorgan said it wasn't an afair and that God got the baby in Mary's stomach by ima-coolate konsepshun — but I don't understand that. So she said it was like God magiked the baby into Mary's tummy.

But you can't magik babies. That's just rubbish. Mrs Lorgan made that up to try to pretend that God was good and not a bad man who had an afair with Joseph's wife.

When I said that Mary was a slapper for going off with God when she was married to Joseph, Mrs Lorgan went mad. She shouted at me for using bad words and for blasfeeming. I don't know what that is but it must be bad.

I said Luke used that word for Jenny all the time. Mrs Lorgan said it was a very bad word and Mary was a saintly woman who never did anything wrong in her life. But I don't care what Mrs Lorgan says. Mary must be a slapper cos she went off with another man when she was married.

In the yard, Tommy said Mary must have sexed with God to have a baby. I asked him what that means, and he said when a man and woman go in the same bed and roll around babies are made.

I know that's true cos that's what Dad and Jenny did, they rolled around in the same bed and then Jaden was in her tummy. When we went to stay with them I could hear them rolling around and Jenny was saying, 'O, O Nick. Yes, yes,' and Dad was saying 'O, O, Jenny.'

But Mummy was foorious when Dad rolled around with Jenny so I know Joseph was not happy about it. I think Mrs Lorgan is just pretending that God is a good person cos she is very religos. She goes to mass all the time. We only go on Christmas and some times Easter.

I'm surprised about God cos he is suposed to be a great man who made us and the world. I heard Mum say to Maggie on the phone that all men are week and can't keep it in there pants.

I think she means money cos Dad never seems to have enuff money to give to Mum. Dad is

always stressed about money. He says kids
and wimen are too expensif. If he thinks
that then he should never have married Mum
or rolled around with Jenny.

Luke came to get me from school wich was
brilliant cos he never does. But then I saw
his eyes were all red and he seemed sad. He
kept huging me, which he never does, like
never.

I thought maybe he got dumped from the
rugby team but when I asked him he said no
and then he hugged me again and said that
there was bad news.

11

After the meeting Nick checked his phone. Two missed calls from Jenny and three from Kate. He knew Jenny was just calling to tell him that something was wrong with Jaden, like she did every day. Her panicking about his health was getting worse. If he had a runny nose, she thought it was pneumonia. He'd have to make an appointment with the GP and take her there himself. She needed pills. She was freaking out over every little thing and crying all the time. He couldn't cope with much more of it.

Sometimes at night he lay awake, wondering if he'd made a huge mistake. But it was too late now. He was stuck. Stuck with a new baby and a depressed girlfriend. What a bloody mess he'd made of things.

He knew Kate was calling about money. She was probably going to shout at him for not giving her enough last month. Thank God that house sale had gone through yesterday – at least he'd be able to pay her next month. He hated not being able to support his family properly, but with the debts and the rent on his apartment with Jenny, everything was just going out faster than it was coming in. He felt bad about Kate, but he had been honest when he'd told her he just didn't have it to spare.

He'd call them both later, he decided. Give himself a breather before facing the music. But then he saw a text from Kate: *Call me. Urgent, it's Jess.*

Nick's heart sank. Unlike Jenny, Kate did not panic about the kids unless it was serious. Damn, what was wrong? Nick's hand shook as he dialled.

'Kate?'

'Nick . . . oh, God, Nick . . .' Kate was sobbing so much he couldn't understand what she was saying.

'What? Jesus, Kate, what is it?'

'Jess has . . . They think it's leukaemia.'

What the fuck? Nick's heart stopped. 'Kate, did you say leukaemia?'

'Yes, the blood tests came back, and . . . It's bad, Nick. Oh, God, Jess, our beautiful Jess . . .'

Nick fell against the wall of his office. Blood was rushing to his ears. He couldn't hear. He couldn't think. When he could finally speak, his voice was faint. 'But how . . . I mean, what the hell? They must be mistaken. She's fine. I know she wasn't feeling great but it was no big deal. It's a mistake, Kate. It has to be. There is no way she has cancer. No fucking way.' He was shouting now, fists clenched, body tight.

'They think it is.' Kate was bawling. 'I don't understand either, Nick. I'm freaking out here. Come to the hospital. I need you – Jess needs you.'

'I'm on my way. I'll sort this out.' Nick hung up but his legs wouldn't move. He was frozen. His mouth felt dry and his head too heavy for his body. He dragged one leg forward, then the other.

As he was stumbling through the office a colleague approached him. 'Are you okay, mate? You look like you've seen a ghost.'

'Fine. Just have to pop out – problem with my kid,' Nick rasped. He didn't want to get into it. He didn't want everyone talking about Jess. And, anyway, it was a mistake. It had to be. This was bullshit. Kate must have misunderstood. There was no way his daughter had cancer. No way.

Nick didn't remember driving to the hospital. The journey was a blur. He threw his car into a wheelchair-user's parking spot, then sprinted through the door and up the stairs. Level three, Haematology and Oncology, Kate had texted.

He burst through the doors and saw Kate on the phone, crying. He strode straight over to her.

'I know, Maggie, thanks. I haven't said anything to Dad or the boys yet. I want to find out more first. I'll call you as soon as I know more.' She hung up, turned to rest her head on Nick's shoulder and sobbed into it.

'Where's Jess?' he asked.

'She just went to the toilet,' Kate said.

'Who's in charge here?'

'I don't know. There are lots of people involved. I've spoken to a Dr Kennedy.'

Nick went over to the nurses' station. 'I want to speak to Dr Kennedy now. Right now.'

'I'm afraid he's with a patient.'

'I don't give a fuck if he's with the president, I want to speak to him *now*.'

The nurse recoiled.

Kate grabbed Nick's arm. 'Stop it. Don't shout at everyone.'

He shook off her hand. 'GET HIM!' he roared at the nurse. He could feel the veins in his neck bulging.

A door opened and a well-dressed man came towards him. 'Is there a problem here?'

'I'm sorry, Doctor. This is Jess's father – he's just arrived,' Kate said.

'Don't apologize for me,' Nick snapped. 'Are you Kennedy?'

'Yes.'

'I want to know what the hell is going on. You've clearly misdiagnosed my daughter.'

Dr Kennedy nodded. 'I'm very sorry, Mr . . .'

'Higgins.'

'Mr Higgins, I understand this has come as a shock to you. I can assure you that we're going to run every test we can to get an accurate diagnosis of your daughter's condition. From the initial test results, she does appear to have leukaemia. We need to narrow down which type she has so we can treat it accordingly.'

'She can't have it,' Nick snarled. 'She's perfectly healthy.'

'I'm afraid it looks as though she does, but please be reassured, the rates of success with the correct treatment are extremely high.'

'She's only twelve.' Nick felt his throat closing. 'How can she . . .'

Kate reached over and held his hand.

'I'm very sorry,' Dr Kennedy said again, 'and I know it must be a terrible shock but please don't be disheartened. As I said, the recovery rates are very high. I'll be back to you later with some updates.'

Dr Kennedy went to leave, but Nick grabbed his arm. 'I want results now. Why the hell do we have to wait? I want my daughter seen to first. She's your priority. No one else. Jess is number one, okay?'

'I'll speak to you later.' Dr Kennedy firmly removed his arm from Nick's grip and walked down the corridor.

'Stop it, Nick. You're going to alienate the staff,' Kate said.

'I want answers. I'm not going to sit around being patient. I'm going to rattle the bloody cage and make sure these people know they're not dealing with doormats. I want the best for Jess.'

'So do I, but shouting at everyone isn't helping, you moron. Stop behaving like a bloody caveman. You're upsetting everyone, and if Jess hears you, you'll upset her too.'

Nick frowned. 'I'd never upset Jess.'

'Well, you will if you carry on like that.'

He looked away. 'Why the hell is this happening? Jess is . . . she's . . . Why, Kate? Leukaemia? I just don't . . .' He brushed away the tears that were welling in his eyes.

'I know,' Kate said. 'I don't understand it either. But we have to be strong for Jess and show a united front. I need you to calm down and help me figure this out. We have to listen to what the doctors say and help them make Jess better.'

Nick nodded. 'You're right, I just . . . I can't sit around doing nothing.'

'I feel the same. Here she is now. Be strong.'

Nick took a deep breath and turned to see Jess walking towards him. She was in a hospital gown. She looked so young and pale. His little girl, his only daughter, his favourite child. He knew it was wrong to have a favourite, but Jess had always been so easy to love. He'd always thought he'd bond more with his sons, but the minute he'd set eyes on Jess, he'd fallen head over heels in love. He pulled her in to his chest and held her tight.

'Ouch, Dad! You're crushing me,' she said.

'Oh, God, I'm sorry.' He let go. 'Are you okay?'

'Well, I'm a bit freaked out, but Dr Kennedy said not to worry, that I was in the best place and they'd all help make me better.'

Nick could see Jess was trying not to cry. His little girl was being so strong. He felt physically sick. He had to protect her. That was his job. He'd shout the place down, if it helped get her the best care or to the top of a queue. Whatever it took. He wasn't going to sit around doing nothing. He knew how the health system worked: you had to demand to be seen and heard. You had to make sure they knew you weren't going to wait patiently for results and treatment. It was the squeaky hinge that got oiled, and Nick wasn't going to take this lying down. He was going to save Jess, no matter what it took.

He hugged her again. 'I love you, Jess, and you're going to be fine, okay? I promise. I'm going to fix this. It's just a little blip. They'll give you some medicine and we'll all go home.'

'Well, she's going to have to stay here overnight for tests, but then hopefully we'll go home,' Kate said.

Nick frowned. He didn't want Jess in here. What if she got one of those hospital bugs? This wasn't good. He'd have to talk to that doctor and get her out of here. She could come in for tests – surely she didn't need to stay the night. Kate was way too weak: she had obviously said yes to everything. Well, Nick wasn't going to. He would question everything and make damn sure that his daughter didn't get misdiagnosed or pick up some crappy bug. Those consultants thought they knew everything – well, they weren't going to push him around. He was going to research leukaemia and tell them what to do.

He felt himself beginning to calm down. He'd take charge and it would be okay. He looked around to see if he could spot Dr Kennedy, and as he did so, a boy hooked up to a drip wheeled himself out of a room. He had no hair and his eyes seemed huge in his small head.

'Welcome, newbie. I'm Larry,' he said to Jess.

Nick grabbed Jess and pulled her away from him. He didn't want her near sick kids. Jesus Christ, they didn't need to see that – bald head, emaciated body. Nick felt fear rising in his throat. That was not going to happen to Jess. No way. Not while he had breath in his body.

Kate left Bobby eating his pasta and went upstairs to Jess's room to pack a bag. She put in Jess's pyjamas, tracksuit bottoms, her Kindle and her favourite cuddly toy – Whiskey. She still slept with him every night. Kate's mother, Nancy, had given him to Jess when she was born, and Jess had curled her tiny fingers around his soft paw and never let go.

Kate held the yellow-and-black striped cat in her hands and squeezed him. She mustn't cry. She'd managed to hide her tears from Bobby by turning when he'd pulled out of a hug. She could hear Luke listening to music in his room next door. She didn't want him to see her falling apart. She had to be strong.

Her father popped his head around the door. He came towards her but she put her arm out. 'Don't. Don't hug me or say anything nice. I'm hanging on by a thread here, Dad.'

George nodded. 'I understand, pet. How's Jess?'

Kate looked at Whiskey's ridiculous face and shook her head. 'She's confused and frightened. They're doing all these tests on her tomorrow to find out more but they're pretty sure she has leukaemia. Now it's a question of finding out which type and how bad it is. Cancer, Dad? How the hell can Jess have cancer? I know she was feeling tired and she had those bruises, but I thought it was from playing sport. How can she just have developed cancer? I can't get my head around it.'

George sat beside her on the bed and took her hand. 'Listen to me, there is no "why" in cancer. It just is. The good news is that the survival rate is ninety per cent. Our Jess is going to be fine.'

'Ninety per cent?'

'Yes. Piper Googled it and rang Luke to tell him. I'd said he wasn't allowed to Google it as all you find on that old internet is bad news. So Piper did it and called him.'

'Good old Piper.' Kate gave a small smile. It was great news. Ninety per cent was okay. Ninety per cent gave Jess great odds. 'The nurse told me not to look it up. She said all you get is misinformation. She said to ask her and the consultants any questions I had. But I didn't have any. I couldn't think straight. All I want to know is – is Jess going to be okay? They can't answer that.'

'The tests will give them the information they need and then they can tell you what the treatment will be and how soon she'll be better.' George patted her hand.

Kate held Whiskey to her face. 'It was bad enough, but Nick kept shouting at everyone that he wanted results *now*, why the hell did we have to wait and he wanted his daughter seen to first. He was making the whole thing worse and freaking Jess out.'

George stood up and began pacing the bedroom. 'I'll have a word with him for you.'

'No, Dad, it's fine. He calmed down after I spoke to him. In fairness, he was just upset and worried. You know how he dotes on Jess – she's always been his favourite, and he isn't subtle about it.'

'He isn't subtle about anything,' George said.

Luke came in. 'Hey, you should have told me you were back. What's going on?'

Kate looked up at him and almost broke down. 'Well, they have to run some tests tomorrow and then we'll know more.

I'm going back now with a bag for Jess and I'll be staying the night with her.'

'Can I come and see her?' Luke asked.

'Sure – she'd like that.'

'Is she freaking out?'

'She's definitely worried and frightened, but the doctors and nurses have been very kind and reassuring so she's okay.'

'Did Granddad tell you about the ninety per cent?'

Kate smiled. 'He did. Tell Piper thanks.'

Luke went over to Kate and gave her an awkward hug. 'It'll be okay, Mum.'

She held him tightly. 'I know, Luke, I know.'

'Hey!' a grumpy seven-year-old voice shouted. 'You all left me by my own downstairs. I want to know what's going on too.'

Kate put her arms out and Bobby came to her and allowed her to hug him again. 'We're just talking about Jess and how she has to stay in hospital for a bit. I'm packing a bag for her.'

'Luke told me she has lukeemia. It's kind of weird – "Luke-eemia". She has a sickness called Luke.'

Kate half smiled.

Bobby shuffled his feet. 'I know about cancer cos Kerry in my class, her mum had it and her hair all felled out and she looked weird, but then it grew back and she looked nice again.'

Kate bent down to him. 'Jess might be given a medicine called chemotherapy and it will probably make her a bit sick and her hair may fall out. But it's going to make her better after that.'

'I don't understand. Why does she have to have medicine that will make her sick? Isn't it supposed to make you better? Maybe chemotherapy is the wrong stuff. Maybe the doctor got mixed up.'

'Dude, stop annoying Mum with questions,' Luke said.

Bobby tugged at Kate's sleeve. 'Mummy, I looked up cancer in *Guinness World Records* and there was information. The highest cancer death rate is in Hungary, which is good cos we live in Ireland. So you can tell Jess that she's lucky we don't live in Hungary. Right? Right, Mummy?'

'Bobby, leave your mother be,' George said.

Kate held up a hand. 'It's okay. Yes, Bobby, it is good news. Now, don't worry, pet, the doctors will make Jess better.'

'Don't forget to pack Whiskey,' Bobby said.

Kate held up the cat. 'I have him here.'

Bobby went over and picked up his *Guinness World Records* book. 'Give her this too. I always read it when I can't sleep or if I'm scared and it really helps.'

Kate took the book and turned to put it into the bag so he wouldn't see she was crying.

George stood up. 'Right, Bobby. It's time for you to go to bed – we've all lost track of time.'

'Come on, little dude. I'll give you a piggyback in to brush your teeth.' Luke picked Bobby up and carried him off to the bathroom.

George put his arm around Kate. 'Tell Jess I'll be in tomorrow morning. I'll have my phone beside me all night so call if you need anything – anything at all.'

'I will, Dad, thanks.'

Kate put Jess's favourite hoodie into the bag, then her little washbag, her One Direction towel, her iPod, her sparkly slippers and pink hairbrush. She was looking around the small bedroom for anything else she might need when her phone beeped.

It was a text from Nick: *Can u come back asap. Jenny wrecking my head, Jaden's sick. I have 2 go home.*

He really was under her thumb, Kate thought. Who would have thought it? Nick was being pushed around by his girlfriend. But he'd have to stand up to her. He needed to be there for Jess now: she was their focus. He'd have to tell Jenny to back off. If he didn't, Kate bloody well would. It was all about Jess now and she needed her dad. No one was going to stand in the way of that. No one.

13

Jess stared up at the ceiling. Haematology and Oncology. She rolled the words around her mouth. It didn't sound awful, but she knew what it meant now. It meant cancer. It meant leukaemia. It meant tests. Many, many tests.

Jess watched as a young boy was pushed past her room in a wheelchair. He was bald and hooked up to a drip. She turned her head to look at the ceiling. It was safer, less frightening. She didn't want to see bald kids. She didn't want to hear the crying parents, the screaming children and the soothing nurses. She wanted to close the door, lock it and put ear plugs in to block out the noise. Her head ached.

How could your life change so much in just a week? She'd had millions of blood tests and then they said she needed blood transfusions ASAP. Apparently she was very low on red blood cells so they'd pumped her full of 'good blood'. She felt cold and scared. The nurses covered her with warming blankets and Mum had held her hand.

As the week went on she had lots more tests – blood tests, bone-marrow aspirate, a lumbar puncture, chest X-rays – and there were lots of hushed conversations.

A few days ago, after yet another test, Jess had pretended to be asleep and listened as the doctor told Mum and Dad that she had a rare subtype of AML.

'Acute myeloid leukaemia. We call it AML . . . high-risk category . . . based on cytogenetic and molecular features . . . unfortunate . . . chemotherapy . . . activating mutations . . . haematopoietic cell transplantation, more commonly known as bone-marrow transplant...' Dr Kennedy spoke quietly and Jess strained to hear what he was saying and take it in.

She didn't understand it all, but she heard Mum gasp and Dad say a really bad word. She dug her nails into the palms of her hands to stop herself crying. Chemotherapy? She knew that was bad. She'd seen the movie *My Sister's Keeper*: the girl in it had chemotherapy and she was bald and sick and . . . God, it was so scary.

Why was this happening? How did she get it? Where did cancer come from? In the first few days Luke had kept telling her that she was ninety per cent okay, and so did Piper, but when they heard it was AML they stopped saying that.

Jess wasn't supposed to Google anything. Mum and Dad had banned her from using the internet, but Jess knew from everyone's reaction that AML was bad. She also knew that 'acute' was not good. She was terrified. She wanted to know but she didn't want to know. She knew there was one person who would tell her straight. She texted Nathalie and asked her to come on Sunday night, when she hoped she could see her alone.

Bobby, who didn't understand that AML was bad, just kept going on and on about the fact that it was great they didn't live in Hungary. Granddad squeezed her hand, kissed her head and coughed loudly into his handkerchief.

Jess loved her family, but sometimes they were too much. Their worry sort of passed over into her and she felt a big weight on her chest. She preferred when it was just her and Mum, sitting quietly, watching movies, or when Mum read to her. That was when Jess felt safest.

When Dad came to see her in hospital it was always kind of stressful. He'd hug her really tightly and then he'd go out and shout at the nurses and doctors, telling them his daughter needed more attention. His phone would ring and beep all the time and he'd go in and out of the room to talk to work or to Jenny – he usually argued with her – and then he'd be back all stressed. When Dad came to visit, Mum usually left them alone. Jess would have preferred her to stay.

Dad would try to cheer her up by telling her stories about when he was a kid, the goals he'd scored and the 'funny things' he'd done in school. But Jess found it all kind of boring. She knew he was doing his best, but every time he left she always felt exhausted.

Tomorrow was D-Day. They'd put the Hickman line in yesterday and tomorrow she'd be starting chemotherapy. Dr Kennedy told her that the Hickman was 'an intravenous line that facilitated drawing blood and administering medications, including chemo'. She had nodded as if she got it, then watched as they inserted it under the skin on her chest, and the attached tube went into a vein near her heart.

They had told her that getting it in wouldn't hurt, but it did and it felt weird. Jess wanted to pull it out. It felt like an alien in her chest. When she looked in the mirror, she could see the bump under her skin. She looked like a freak. She hated it.

Her mum had squeezed Jess's hand really hard when the doctor said chemotherapy. Jess knew she was freaking out but pretending she wasn't. It was silly, really. Jess could see her red eyes and she'd heard her crying on the phone to Granddad and to Maggie when she'd thought Jess was asleep. She was getting very good at pretending to be asleep – it was the only way she could hear people talk honestly and escape from Dad's stress and noise.

On Sunday, Granddad, Bobby and Luke came to visit while her mother went home to shower and catch up on some paperwork. Granddad brought her a holy medal for luck. 'It's the medal of St Raphael, the archangel and the saint of sickness.'

'Why is he the saint of sickness?' Jess asked. She was happy to get the medal – she wanted all the help she could get. She had to beat the cancer. She had to get better. She wanted to get out of this stupid hospital and go home. She wanted it all to be a bad dream. She wanted to wake up and be normal.

'Because in Hebrew the name Raphael means "It is God who heals".'

'Thanks, Granddad.' Jess held the medal to her chest, touching it against the Hickman line.

'It'll protect you, my little pet, and keep you safe.'

'Is all your hair going to fall out?' Bobby asked. 'Mrs Lorgan said that chemotherapy makes your hair fall out but that it grows back again. She said you'll look weird for a bit but that I'm not to say anything about it and pretend that it's just normal that you have no hair. She said it's worser for girls to lose their hair cos girls have long hair. She said –'

'Thank you, Bobby, I think Mrs Lorgan has said quite enough,' Granddad said.

'It's okay, Granddad. Yes, Bobby, I will probably lose my hair but the doctor and the nurses said it grows back quickly.' Jess was amazed that her voice sounded casual when inside she was panicking about losing her hair.

'I'll love you just the same whether you look like an alien or not,' Bobby said.

Luke turned his back on them and Jess saw him wipe his eyes.

'Thanks, Bobby.'

'I miss you, Jess. I've no one to talk to at night, and when I try to tell Mummy my new facts she says, "Not now, Bobby," all the time.'

'Your mother has enough going on, Bobby,' Granddad said. 'You need to be helpful and leave her in peace.'

'You can tell me your facts,' Luke said.

'You're always in your room with your earphones in or on the phone to Piper or else training or studying or helping Granddad in the café. I've no one to talk to now Jess is stuck in here with stinky cancer.'

'Tell me something now. I'm listening,' Jess said.

Bobby went over and stood beside her. 'Well, in 2013 Belgium had 1,714 robberies for every one hundred thousand people, so it's a good thing we don't live there.'

'Yes, it is.' Jess smiled at him.

'I always knew that the Belgians were a strange people.' Nathalie walked in, holding a book.

Damn. Jess had wanted her to come when everyone else was gone.

'I brought you a book of poems.'

'Cheerful ones, I hope,' Granddad muttered.

'Yes, George. They are poems of love. When Jess is sitting 'ere she can look out of the window at the blue sky and read a beautiful poem about love and it will make her less . . . How you say? Sorrowful.'

'She's not sorrowful, she's fine,' Luke insisted.

Nathalie rolled her eyes. 'She 'as cancer. Of course she is sorrowful. Everybody is a bit sorrowful. It's part of the 'uman nature.'

She was right. Jess did feel sorrowful, very sorrowful. But, most of all, she was tired and frightened.

'Bullshit,' Luke said. 'Not everyone is sorrowful. I'm not, Granddad isn't, Bobby isn't.'

'I am, actually,' Bobby said. 'And you are too, Luke. I heard you crying in your room last night and Granddad pretends to blow his nose all the time but he's really crying into his hanky.'

Luke and Granddad glared at him.

Nathalie patted Bobby's head. 'It's okay. It's normal. Why do men always pretend everything is fine? Of course you are worried about Jess. You love 'er and you want 'er to be well. It's good to cry. It's bad to block the emotions.'

'Mrs Lorgan said I need to control mine,' Bobby said. 'She said I have *waaaaaay* too much anger inside. She said I should ask Mummy to take me to kickboxing or karate so I can channel it.'

'Mrs Lorgan needs to keep her opinions to herself,' Granddad muttered.

'Tell 'er she is wrong,' Nathalie told Bobby. 'It is very important to let the emotions out. If you want to scream, scream. Cry? Cry. Be depressed? Be depressed. Always 'aving the 'appy face like a clown is ridiculous. Nobody is 'appy all the time.'

Granddad got up from the chair beside Jess's bed. 'Well, thank you, Nathalie. It's always fascinating hearing your cheerful thoughts on life.' He raised an eyebrow at Jess, who grinned. 'However, I think that's enough French philosophy for one evening. Jess needs her rest.'

He bent down and hugged her, careful not to squeeze the port. 'Best of luck tomorrow. I'll be praying for you, my little pet.'

Then Luke hugged her. 'Hang in there, sis, you're going to be fine. Love ya.'

Bobby reached up. 'I love you, Jess. Come home soon.'

Jess tried really hard not to cry. She wanted to cling to them all. She wanted to tell them how scared she was, but she didn't. She put a clown smile on her face and pretended she was stronger than she was.

As they turned to leave, Nathalie sat down beside her.

'Come on, Nathalie, out you come,' Granddad said.

'I will stay a little bit longer.'

'No, you won't.' Granddad made his way over to her.

'It's okay, Granddad. I want her to stay,' Jess said.

'Are you sure? She's not known for making people feel better, ever.'

Jess smiled, a real smile. 'Let her stay five minutes.'

Granddad didn't look happy about leaving Nathalie with her but, thankfully, he didn't argue and the boys all left.

As soon as they were out of sight, Jess turned to Nathalie. 'Well, did you Google it?'

Nathalie hesitated. 'Yes. Are you sure you want to know this?'

Jess sighed. 'Yes. Everyone's blocking me from getting information, but that's freaking me out. The doctors have tried to explain it to me. They said that AML is where too many immature white blood cells are made. The cells are not right and can't grow into normal white blood cells. So the chemotherapy I have to have is to kill the leukaemia cells and allow normal blood cells to come back. I think that's what they said anyway, but my head hurts and I find it really hard to concentrate. But I want to know more. I want to know what the percentage chance is of me getting better. Not knowing is making me think the worst.'

Nathalie fished around in her handbag and pulled out a sheet of paper. 'Okay. So I look up the cancer websites for AML. It says . . . "As with many cancers, the AML leukaemia survival rate has increased in the last decades due to advances in medical knowledge and technology. The general survival rate for children under fifteen years of age is sixty point nine per cent" – so it's good news, basically you have a sixty-one per cent chance to be better.'

Jess gripped Whiskey's soft paw tighter. Her heart was pounding. Sixty-one per cent. It was closer to fifty than one hundred. Oh, my God, I could die. I really could die. Why had she asked Nathalie to look it up? She shouldn't have. Mum was right: she was better off not knowing. She began to cry.

Nathalie took Jess's hand in hers. 'Jess, you could die in a car crash. You could get 'it by the lightning. No one knows what is in the future. You at least understand what is wrong with your body and you 'ave the best doctors looking after you. You will get the strong medicine tomorrow and you will be well again. You will fight the cancer because you are a brave girl with a beautiful spirit. You are lucky because you 'ave a family who love you very much.'

Nathalie handed Jess a tissue to wipe her tears. It was the first time Jess had really broken down in front of someone. She sobbed and let all her fears and worries out. For some reason, she didn't mind crying in front of Nathalie. She knew Nathalie wouldn't try to cheer her up or distract her with silly stories. Nathalie was comfortable around sorrow so it wasn't awkward to be upset in front of her.

Nathalie dabbed Jess's left cheek with a tissue. 'My mother loves 'er stupid dog more than me and my father is only interested in 'is son, who is only seven but is an incredible player of the violin. So even though you 'ave the bad luck with the cancer, you 'ave the good luck with the family.'

'What about your grandparents?' Jess asked.

'Dead.'

'Sorry.'

Nathalie shrugged. 'This is life. Sometimes it ees sheet.'

Yes, Jess thought, sometimes it is 'sheet'. She cuddled into Whiskey's soft comforting face, closed her eyes and, before Nathalie had even left the room, she was fast asleep.

14

Piper watched in silence as Luke added more weights to the bar bell. He lay back on the bench, took a deep breath, lifted it and pushed upwards with his arms. His whole body trembled. His eyes seemed about to pop out of their sockets.

Piper tried not to say anything. She knew he needed this. He needed to hurt physically because it distracted him from his emotional pain. He let the bar down and pushed up again. His arms shook violently and sweat dripped down his face. He gritted his teeth and kept going.

Piper put her hand on her stomach. How could she tell Luke about the baby now? Ever since he'd called her, crying about Jess, she'd known that her news would have to wait. But for how long? She couldn't bear to add to Luke's stress, but the doctor said she was about six weeks gone. She'd have to hold off for as long as possible: she couldn't land this bombshell on the poor family – they had enough to deal with at the moment. No one knew that when Piper cried about Jess she was also crying about the baby.

Luke's whole body shook.

'Stop, Luke. Please stop. You're pushing yourself too hard.'

Luke put the bar back on the stand and gulped to catch his breath.

'You'll hurt yourself,' Piper added.

Luke wiped his face with a towel. 'Every time I close my eyes I see the word "cancer",' he said, in a strangled voice.

Piper leant down and held him tightly. 'It's just awful, babe. I wish I could do or say something to make you feel better.'

'Will you come with me to visit her today?' Luke asked. 'I want to give Mum a couple of hours off. She's not sleeping at all in the hospital and she's wrecked.'

'Of course. I'd love to,' Piper said, glad to be able to help in any way.

They walked into Jess's room and her bed was empty. Luke was just going out to ask a nurse where she was when Piper caught his arm. She pointed at the bathroom door and then at her own ear, indicating he was to listen. They both went still. They could hear someone crying behind the door.

Luke went over and knocked lightly. They heard Jess putting on the taps to drown her crying. Luke kept knocking. 'Jess, it's me, Luke. Open up.'

'Go away. I need some privacy.'

'No. Open the door.'

'Please, Luke, go away.'

'I'll break the door down if you don't open it.' Luke's hand was trembling. Piper laid a hand on his arm and whispered, 'Go easy.' Then, 'Jess, sweetie, it's Piper. Can you let us in? We just want to say hi and see that you're okay. I know chemo is awful and you must be so upset and feeling terrible, but can you please open the door just for one second so we can say hello?'

They heard the lock click and Luke pushed the door open. Jess was sitting on the side of the bath, staring at the floor. Her left hand was covering the side of her head. Long strands of brown hair lay on the bathroom floor.

'Oh, Jesus,' Luke said.

Jess's tear-stained face turned to them. 'Yeah, that's exactly how I feel.'

Piper went over and put her arm around her. 'Oh, Jess, this really sucks.'

'I knew that your hair fell out after chemo, but I didn't think it would happen so soon,' Jess sobbed. 'I went to brush my hair and big lumps fell out.'

Piper held her tight. She didn't know what to say. How do you console a twelve-year-old girl when she's going bald? What were the 'appropriate' words of comfort? *I'm sorry about the hair loss. Bald can be cool. I'll buy you a great hat.* Piper scrambled around for the right thing to say.

'This shouldn't be happening. It's just not fair,' Luke raged.

Jess gulped back tears. 'I know, but it has happened. It's real, Luke. It feels really real now. I'm going to be a bald freak.'

'No. You'll –' Luke was at a loss for words to comfort his sister.

Piper knew she had to take control. Jess needed help, practical help. 'Right. We need to give you a haircut and get you some cool headgear or maybe a wig, whatever looks best. We'll look up some websites when I've sorted out your hair.'

Luke's hand squeezed her shoulder. She patted it.

'Luke, you need to go to the nurse and ask for an electric head-shaver – someone around here has to have one. Half the kids in this unit are bald.'

Piper got Jess onto her feet and turned her away from the mirror. 'I'm going to use these scissors,' she pointed at the nail scissors in Jess's washbag, 'to cut your hair short so it'll be easier to shave. All right? It's best if you look at me and not in the mirror so you don't get too freaked out. The good news is that your hair will grow back thicker and stronger, so don't worry.'

Piper turned her back to them to pick up the nail scissors. Her hands were shaking, and she didn't want Jess to see how nervous she was.

Luke rushed off to find a head-shaver, and by the time he returned, Piper had hacked off most of Jess's hair. Piper was glad Jess couldn't see herself in the mirror. Despite her best efforts, Jess's hair was short and uneven – awful. She looked so young and helpless and . . . well . . . sick.

'Right.' Piper turned to Luke. 'You can do the shaving. I've no idea how to use those.' Piper couldn't do the shaving: there was a limit. She felt sick about cutting Jess's hair off – there was no way she could shave off the rest. Besides, her morning sickness was bad today and she was afraid she might throw up.

Luke stared at her. 'What?'

'You've used those on your own hair so you know what to do. If Jess's hair is gone, it can't upset her by falling out.' Piper was using a bright voice, but her eyes were filling with tears. She was upset, exhausted and feeling sick. It was all too much. 'Come on, Luke,' she pleaded.

He nodded. 'Don't blame me if it isn't perfect, sis.'

Piper held Jess's hand while Luke gently shaved his sister's head. Piper dug her nails into her leg to stop herself crying as the last strands of Jess's hair floated to the floor. Seeing the girl's bare scalp made her want to weep.

'It looks kind of cool, very edgy. Very kick-ass-girl.' Piper was determined to make Jess feel better.

'No one's going to mess with you now, sis.' Luke tried to sound cheerful.

'Can I see?' Jess asked.

Piper hesitated. 'Are you sure you're ready? It's a big change. Maybe take a minute.'

Jess inhaled, but as she was about to turn around, Luke shouted, 'Stop. Hold on.'

Without thinking, he took the shaver and ran it over his hair.

'What are you doing?' Jess was shocked. 'You've spent ages growing your hair long on top.'

Luke kept going. He quickly finished off and put the head-shaver down. Piper's heart swelled with pride. This was the guy she loved. Her Luke. The kind of person who would shave his head for his sister. He wouldn't let her down either: he wouldn't run away when he found out she was pregnant. It was going to be fine. All three of them were now crying and smiling.

Piper clapped her hands. 'You both look amazing.'

Jess slid her small hand into Luke's big one. 'Thanks, Lukey,' she said.

'We're in this together.' His voice quivered.

'I'm not so scared to look now,' Jess said.

Piper nodded. 'One, two, three . . .'

Luke held his sister's hand tightly as they turned to the mirror.

Piper heard the little 'Oh' that fell out of Jess's mouth. Her lip trembled as she took in her bald head.

Luke put his arm around his sister's shoulders. 'We're two bad-asses now. You and me against the world.'

Jess gave him a watery smile. 'Yeah.'

Piper came over and threw her arms around them both. 'You guys are amazing. None of my sisters would ever shave their heads for me. The twins would probably scoop up my hair and make extensions for themselves out of it.'

Jess giggled, and Luke whispered, 'I love you,' into Piper's neck. She felt her legs shake. Would he love her when she told him about the baby?

15

Kate finished the chapter and looked at Jess's drooping eyelids. 'Time for you to sleep now,' she said, kissing her cheek.

'I don't want to, Mum. I want to enjoy every second of being home. It's so good to be back. The last few weeks have felt like a year.'

'I know, pet, and you've been so brave and wonderful.'

'I don't want to go back for more,' Jess said, and Kate felt her shaking. 'I hate the chemo.'

'Jess, I know you do, and it's just horrible, but it's going to kill the cancer so in a way it's a good thing, even though I know it's rotten for you. I hate seeing you so unwell, pet.'

'I'm sorry, Mum,' Jess whispered.

'For what?'

'For being sick. I know it's terrible for you and I promise to try my best to get better quickly.'

Kate couldn't even pretend not to cry. She hugged Jess to her and sobbed. 'None of this is your fault. It's just awful luck, but we're all going to help you get better. Don't ever apologize again. You're the best thing that ever happened to me, the light of my life. I'm so sorry this has happened to you, but I will do everything in my power to help you.'

Jess nodded into Kate's shoulder. Kate gently laid her back on the pillow and kissed her sweet face. 'Love you, Jess.'

'Love you, Mum.'

'Sleep now, pet. It'll help.'

Jess turned her head, pulled Whiskey close and shut her eyes. Within minutes she was sound asleep.

The first round of chemo had made her very ill. She could barely hold down any food and was weak and exhausted. Kate hated seeing her like that. To feel so helpless was torture. All she could do was tilt the bowl for Jess to vomit into and hold her when she cried. They knew she'd be allowed home after the first round, and that had been some tiny consolation, but chemo took so much out of Jess, and Kate admired her daughter's stamina in getting through each day.

Kate kept asking questions, but although the haematologists and nurses were kind and caring, they wouldn't give false hope. They kept saying they had to wait and see if the chemo was working. It was all about waiting . . . waiting for test results, waiting for treatment to work, waiting for information. Kate hated the waiting.

She went over to her laptop and started Googling. After an hour her eyes were throbbing and her heart was pounding from information overload. The internet was a blessing and a curse. She'd always thought 'information is power', but it wasn't. Sometimes you were better off not knowing what was coming down the line. Sometimes ignorance was bliss. And yet she found herself Googling every single symptom and test result Jess had received, and it often led to frightening outcomes and stories.

She glanced at Jess, who was still asleep. She looked so peaceful when she slept. The worried frown she'd developed between her eyebrows was smooth and her frightened eyes were closed.

It was wonderful to have her home for two weeks before she had more chemo. Jess was so tired that she slept most of the time, but Kate could see that being at home was cheering her up. She had put Jess into her double bed with her so she could keep an eye on her. She also liked to hold her at night, imagining that if she put her arms around her she could hug away the cancer. She could protect her daughter with her magical mother's love. If only . . .

A mother's job was to make her child better, but Kate couldn't fix this. Neither could Nick. He was so angry. Every time he'd come to the hospital, he'd shouted at some member of staff, and usually ended up accusing them of not doing enough. He looked wretched, almost as bad as Kate. She knew he was suffering too, but he really wasn't helping with his aggressive attitude and she'd come to dread his visits.

Kate chewed her lip and tried to think of the best way to word what she had to ask Luke to do. The doctors were quite clear that it would help enormously, which meant it had to be done, but she knew she would be asking a huge amount of him. She hated to do it, wished more than anything she could do it herself, but she wasn't a match. Instead, it might fall on Luke's young shoulders. It was just unbearable.

Kate felt a panic attack coming on. She was getting them regularly now. Maggie had suggested a mindfulness course, and she was thinking about doing one. She needed to stop the terror that came over her at night and crippled her, dark thoughts consuming her.

She kissed Jess's cheek and inhaled her lovely Jess smell. Then she went to get a cup of herbal tea. She tried to control her breathing to keep the panic at bay. As she reached the kitchen she saw the light was on. She could hear voices: her dad's and Luke's. She stopped and listened.

'This is crazy,' George said. 'No one can eat this much food.'

'The coach said I'm not getting enough protein. I should be eating four to five full meals a day. The problem is, I don't feel hungry. Since Jess's diagnosis, I've lost my appetite.'

'Does your coach know about Jess?'

'Yeah, and he cut me a bit of slack at training, but I can't fall behind or I'll get dropped.'

'How about I make you breakfast in the mornings? It says porridge, eggs, nuts and/or smoothies loaded up with protein powder. We can do something different each morning.'

'Thanks, Granddad.'

'Sure I'm happy to help, Luke. You need your rugby. I'd say it's a good switch-off for you.'

'It's the one and only place where I don't think about Jess. I don't want to get dropped. I need it, Granddad. I feel good when I'm playing.'

'I understand, son, and I'll help you. We'll feed you up but you might need to exaggerate a bit on your diet sheet for the coach. As I said, no one could eat this much.'

Kate pushed open the kitchen door.

'Is she asleep?' George asked, as she came into the room.

Kate nodded. 'Peacefully.'

'Ah, good. Poor little thing is wiped out.'

Kate sat down at the table. 'So, how are things here? Are you managing in the café, Dad?'

George patted her hand. 'Absolutely. Nathalie's doing more hours for me and continuing to charm and frighten away customers in equal measure. She told Brenda Kent last week that she was an ugly-handsome woman. Apparently this is a compliment in France, but Brenda didn't see it that way.'

Kate and Luke laughed.

'She's kind of mad, but Jess loves her,' Luke said. 'She always cheers her up.'

'For that I love her too.' Kate smiled.

There was silence. Then Kate took a deep breath. No point in waiting: he was here now and she might as well bring it up. 'Luke, there's something I need to ask you.'

He looked at her warily. 'What?'

'Jess may need a bone-marrow transplant and I need you to get tested, to see if you're a match. Your dad and I have been tested already and unfortunately we aren't.'

'Sure. What is it? What does it mean?'

'Well, you'll have a blood test and they'll use it for tissue typing to evaluate how close a match you are with Jess. Siblings tend to be the best matches.'

'If I'm a match, what happens then?' Luke asked, spinning his cup around on the table, avoiding Kate's eyes.

Kate hated having to ask him to do this, mainly because the bone-marrow aspiration was supposed to be painful. But at the same time, another part of her was praying he would be a match. 'Well, I have the information here.' She handed Luke a leaflet.

He took it from her and read aloud, '"You begin by having a peripheral blood stem cell (PBSC) collection. For five days before PBSC collection, a donor receives injections of a white blood cell growth hormone called G-CSF (Neupogen). These injections last five minutes. On the fifth day, a needle is placed in each of the donor's arms. The person's blood is circulated through a machine that collects the stem cells. Then the rest of the blood is returned to the donor. This collection takes about three hours and may be repeated on a second donation day. There is very little blood loss. Side-effects may include headaches, bone soreness, and the discomfort of needles in the arms during the process."' Luke stopped reading and dropped the leaflet onto the table.

'It's a lot to take in and you might not be a match, but I think it makes it out to be worse than it is.' Kate tried to hide the desperation in her voice. 'The boy in the room next to Jess had his sister do it and she said it was okay.'

Luke gripped the table. 'If I'm a match I'll do it, of course I will, but will it interfere with rugby, Mum? I can't get dropped.'

Kate nodded. 'We'll work around it, I promise.'

'Please, God, you will be a match. It'd be the best thing you could ever do,' George said, patting Luke's arm. 'With your healthy bone marrow, Jess would definitely get better. No doubt about it.'

Luke's shoulders relaxed a little and he gave his granddad a small smile. Kate exhaled. Her dad was right. Luke's brilliant bone marrow would heal Jess and get rid of the goddamn leukaemia.

16

Chloë marched up and down at the end of Jess's bed in a gown and mask. 'OMG, I feel like I'm in an actual TV show and I'm a surgeon about to do a serious, lifesaving operation.'

Jess smiled. It was nice having Chloë visit. She'd only seen family in the last week because she'd been told to keep visits to a minimum, but Chloë had begged to come and see her so they'd said she could, but only if she wore protective clothing. Jess's blood count was so low that her risk of infection was very high so she'd been isolated to protect her.

The second round of chemo was even worse. Jess felt totally wiped out and, again, could hardly eat. She felt as if she was being blasted with poison, which was just making her sicker and sicker. It didn't seem possible she could ever feel well again. The doctors said things were going well and that the cancer cells were being destroyed, but that the 'good' white cells were being affected by the chemo too, which was why she felt so ill.

All Jess knew was that she was sick of being sick. She wanted to go back to school, to sit in class listening to Mrs Fingleton talking about wars and books and maps. She wanted to be normal again. She wanted to sit beside Chloë at lunchbreak, giggle about boys, look up cool Instagram photos, play tennis and hockey, and just be the old Jess.

She wanted her life back, the good one, the one where she didn't vomit every ten minutes and she had energy and everyone didn't treat her differently.

Chloë stopped prancing, went over to Jess and held her hand in her gloved one. 'Hey, I know this sucks for you.' Her voice was slightly muffled because of the mask over her mouth. 'But I promised my mum that if she let me see you, I'd cheer you up. She said I had to make you laugh and distract you so you forget about cancer for a little bit. She said when she was in hospital after giving birth to me, she was feeling awful, so she had a team of people come in and do her nails and hair and make-up, and she felt *waaaay* better after. Obviously I can't do your hair,' Chloë said, as Jess grinned, 'but I did bring you loads of clothes for when you get out, and some cool hats.'

She bent down and heaved a large bag onto the chair beside the bed. 'This is from Mum. She is, like, totally freaking out that you have cancer so we both went shopping and bought loads of stuff for you. You should have seen her, Jess, she was like a crazy woman. She was charging from shop to shop and kept telling me to buy more. I hope you like the stuff. If you don't, I can take it back. We kept all the receipts.'

Jess sat up. This was fun! Lots of new clothes – cool ones, too. She felt excited for the first time in ages.

Chloë reached into the bag and pulled out a pair of pink jeans. She looked at the jeans and then at Jess's spindly legs. 'My God, Jess, I didn't realize how skinny you'd got, but hopefully they'll fit you.'

Chloë spent the next half an hour pulling clothes out of the bag and holding them up. 'Now all you have to do is put your thumb up if you like it or down if you don't,' she said. 'That way you won't use up too much energy.'

Jess gave a thumbs-up to everything, even the clothes she knew were too big or that she wasn't crazy about. There was no way she'd send any of it back. Chloë had got her three gorgeous beanie hats with diamanté across the front. Jess put one on.

'Amazing!' Chloë clapped her hands. 'It's fab on you. The blue one is the nicest.'

Jess lay back on her pillows, exhausted from the visit but happy. 'Thanks, Chloë, and please say thanks to your mum. This is just so kind. I can't believe it.'

'Hold on, there's a couple of pairs of pyjamas too – Mum wanted you to have these. Apparently she got them online and they're, like, super-soft cotton or something. Anyway, I'll leave them here for you.'

Jess smiled, then a wave of nausea hit her and she threw up into the bowl beside the bed. 'Sorry,' she said, wiping her mouth with a tissue.

Chloë sat on the chair beside the bed and handed her another. 'Don't be sorry. Is it awful?'

Jess nodded. 'I just don't understand it. Where did it come from? Did I do something to make it happen? Should I have eaten more vegetables?'

'Don't be mad. If it was cos you didn't eat vegetables, I'd have it too. I hate vegetables. There's nothing you did wrong, Jess. Cancer is just . . . well . . . cancer and it hits people for no reason. Sure if they knew why you got it they could cure it.' Chloë blushed. 'I mean cure it for everyone. Obviously you'll be cured. I know you will.'

'What if I'm not?'

Chloë jumped back in her chair. 'Jeepers, Jess, don't even say that.'

'It's possible.'

'No way. Kids hardly ever die from cancer – Mum said so and so did Mrs Fingleton.'

'Did she?' Jess thought Mrs Fingleton would be a very reliable and well-informed source.

'Yeah, totally. She said she expected you to be back in school after Christmas. I hope you are – I miss you. I have to hang out with Denise and Judy now.'

Jess smiled. 'They're not that bad.'

'They're *sooooo* annoying. All they talk about is Judy's neighbour, Jack, and how hot he is. I've seen him. He's a dork.'

Jess wished she could be sitting with them, talking about Jack. She'd gladly talk about anything, just to be out of this hospital and back to actually living.

She'd never complain about school again, ever. She'd skip in and do her homework without a grumble. Mrs Fingleton had been sending in work for her, but a lot of the time she was too sick to do it. The best part of her day was when Mum read to her. She loved that. She didn't have to talk or think, just lay back, listened and let herself be transported by the stories. She was reading *Pride and Prejudice* and even though some of the words were olde-worlde, she loved the sisters – they reminded her of Piper and hers – and she adored Lizzie Bennet and the way she stood up to Mr Darcy.

When it was just her and Mum and the stories, Jess could forget . . . for a while.

Chloë tucked her legs under her on the chair. 'What's the story with the guy who was leaving when I arrived?' She giggled. 'He was kind of cute.'

Jess grinned. Trust Chloë to spot him. 'That's Larry. He's been here some of the time I have. He's really nice. When we're allowed, we play cards together and sometimes watch a movie.'

'*Oooooooooh*.' Chloë's eyes widened. 'Love in a cancer ward. Maybe I don't feel so sorry for you, after all.'

Jess laughed. 'He's just a friend. He feels like a brother. He gets it, you know. He understands. With Larry I don't have to explain how I feel because he feels the same. We're just buddies.'

'Well, if you don't want him, will you introduce me to him?' Chloë batted her eyelids.

'When he's feeling better I will.'

'Okay.' Chloë's phone buzzed. 'Oh, my God, look at these.' She sat up on the bed beside Jess and they scrolled through hundreds of Instagram pictures. After a while there was a knock on the window. It was Chloë's mum, Hazel. She waved cheerily and held up a sign: 'We love you, Jess. Get well soon.' Jess waved back and smiled. She was glad Chloë was going – she was exhausted. She could feel her eyelids closing. It had been wonderful to see her, but she needed to sleep now.

Chloë groaned, then gave Jess a big hug. 'I love you, Jess. Focus on getting better, then come back to school and save me.'

'I will.'

'Bye for now. I'll text you later.'

Jess watched her friend leave, envying her the freedom to walk out and go back to the real world. Hazel helped Chloë out of the protective gear, then with one last wave, they were gone. Back outside, into fresh air, walking on their strong legs, safe inside their not-sick bodies. Jess curled up tighter and cried herself to sleep.

The following morning, she was getting ready for her chemo session when she heard Larry in the room next door, screaming. He was shouting and roaring at his parents, yelling that he hated them. They were to get out and leave him alone. Jess listened, her heart beating faster. It sounded so horrible, like Larry was possessed by a demon. She couldn't understand it because he was really nice and his parents were too. They talked to Kate all the time and reassured her. Larry had had two relapses, but he was still alive and seemed to be reacting well to his latest bone marrow. Jess tried to ignore his crazy shouting, feeling sorry for his parents.

Now that she was in isolation, she couldn't play cards with him on long, boring afternoons, and she missed it. Now they just chatted on the phone and sent each other goofy photos. She decided to send him one now. Maybe it would cheer him up a bit. She found a video on YouTube of a bear dancing to some funky music and forwarded the link to him. It wasn't much help, but it might just make him smile.

Later in the afternoon, when she was back from chemo and had had a nap, she phoned him.

'Hey, you, what's going on?'

'Infection,' he said shortly.

'Oh, no. I'm sorry. Did it come on last night?'

'Yep. I'm in isolation too now.'

'Sucks.'

'Sure does.'

'I'm really sorry.'

'Yeah, me too. It's back, Jess, I know it is.'

'It's just an infection, not the cancer.'

'Jess, it's not just an infection. I know it's back.'

'How?'

'Fingernails. If the bone marrow works, the dark ridges on your fingernails disappear. Mine haven't. We get the results tomorrow, but I already know.'

Jess swallowed the bile rising in her throat. This time it wasn't the chemo making her nauseous: it was fear and sorrow. 'But you can't be sure,' she said, although she knew she didn't sound convincing.

Larry sighed. 'Jess, I've been through this three times. It's not working.'

'Maybe they just need to try something new. You're young and strong, you can fight this. The infection is making you feel low.' Jess couldn't let it go: she wanted him to say there was hope.

'I need everyone to stop saying that,' Larry snapped. 'I can't pretend any more. It's over, Jess. That's why I shouted at my parents. I want them to hate me. They have to really hate me so when I die it won't hurt so much.'

Jess could taste the salty tears running down her face onto her lips. 'Larry, they could never hate you. They adore you.'

'That's the problem.' His voice was quiet and sad, so sad. 'I need them to stop. I need them to stop hoping and trying and praying and wishing . . . I need them to stop looking as if their hearts are breaking. I can't take it. It's too much.'

Jess stayed quiet while Larry cried. Sometimes there was nothing to say. In six weeks she had learnt a lot about pain, suffering, fear, death and heartbreak. She had learnt that listening silently was often the very best thing you could do.

When she heard his sobs subside she said, 'No matter what you do, no matter how much you push them away, they'll love you just the same. Don't make your time with them awful. There's no point. Make it special.'

'I don't want to die, Jess,' Larry whispered. 'I want to grow up and be a pilot. I want to fly all over the world. I'm not ready to die – I'm thirteen. It's not fair.'

'It's just . . . cruel, that's what it is. Look, I know you don't want false hope but maybe –'

'Don't, Jess, please. I need to be honest with someone.'

'Well, then, it sucks, it really sucks.' Jess wiped tears from her eyes. 'How can there be a God who lets kids suffer like this?'

'I stopped believing in God after my first relapse. I don't believe in Heaven either. I think this is it.'

'Why us?'

'You can't ask why, Jess. It'll melt your head. We can't change the fact of having cancer, we can only fight the cancer. But I think I'm coming to the end of fighting. I want to live, but I don't think I can. I keep thinking about . . . after, you know?'

'You mean, like, the afterlife?' Jess said quietly.

'Kind of. I don't think there's a Heaven, but some people say that our energy lives on. I was thinking, you know, if I die, I'd like to send a sign to my mum and dad.'

'What kind of a sign?' This conversation was making her head throb, but she knew Larry needed to be able to say this stuff out loud.

'Well, that's just it. I can't make up my mind. It has to be something not too unusual, like an eagle landing at the kitchen table, but not something really common either, like a blackbird in the back garden. It has to be something in between.'

Jess had never thought about signs. But she knew exactly what hers would be.

'Any suggestions?' Larry asked.

'My sign would be a white butterfly,' Jess said. 'I've always loved them. They're so pure and beautiful and . . . well, white.'

'Damn, I wish I'd thought of that.'

'How about a robin on your parents' windowsill or something?'

'Nah, too boring. We'll have to think up something better. Hopefully I'll live until we figure one out.'

Jess shuddered. She hadn't really allowed herself to think about death. She'd pushed it far down in her stomach. She was sick and she was going to get better. No one ever mentioned death, except Larry and Nathalie. The first time Jess had actually spoken to Larry, she'd been throwing up into a bowl. He'd stopped at her door and introduced himself, then asked her if she was scared of dying. Just like that. After only exchanging names. Jess had lied and said no because she wasn't planning on dying.

Larry had smiled. 'New and full of hope. I need to hang out with you. Maybe your optimism will rub off on me.'

But it hadn't. Cancer had rubbed off on him, more of it, aggressive, unstoppable. Still Jess did not, would not, believe Larry was going to die. He couldn't. It just wasn't possible. Like he'd said, he was only thirteen, one year older than her. She would continue to hope that he'd come out the other side. But she knew not to say that to him now.

'I wish I could come over and hang out,' she said.

'Me, too . . . I know! How about we watch the same movie at the same time and stay on the phone so we can give out about it? I don't want to be alone, and I've chased the only visitors I've had out of the hospital.'

'You'll have to apologize to them tomorrow,' Jess said. 'Now, what will we watch?'

'How about *The Fault In Our Stars*?'

Jess giggled. 'Or *My Sister's Keeper*? That'll cheer us up.'

Larry laughed. 'Seriously, how about *The Hunger Games*?'

'Again!'

'Humour me.'

'Okay.' Jess reached for the iPad Kate had lent her and clicked on the movie. 'Ready?'

'Yes. One, two, three, play.'

Jess nestled into her pillows and welcomed the distraction of the film. For now, she wanted to be anywhere but where she was.

17

Piper studied her calendar. Nine weeks. She was nine weeks pregnant. You could have an abortion in the UK up to twenty-four weeks. But that was six months. She couldn't imagine having an abortion at six months. If she was being honest, she couldn't imagine having an abortion at all.

At first she'd thought she'd definitely get rid of it. Who the hell wanted a baby at eighteen years of age? She'd even looked up cheap flights for her and Luke to go over to London. But then Jess had got cancer and everything had gone crazy.

Meanwhile, the baby was growing. Piper put her hand to her still flat stomach. She knew she had to tell Luke, but there was never a good time, these days.

She'd tried to tell him last week, but he'd been put on the subs bench and Harry had got to play the whole match. Luke had been so upset that she just couldn't do it. The time before that was when his mum told him that he needed to get his bone marrow tested. Luke had been upset about that, too. They'd spent the whole evening Googling it and talking about it.

Piper lay back on her bed and put an arm over her face. She had to tell him, but what if he wanted to get rid of it? He probably would. How could he cope with a baby on top of everything else? How could she cope with a baby? She wanted to go to college and travel the world, not be tied down with a screaming kid. The weird thing was, in the last few weeks she'd felt love growing inside her for her baby. She knew it was dumb, it was only a foetus, but she felt protective of it now.

She pictured her dad's face when she told him. Piper, the sensible one – not so sensible now. She wasn't sure how her mum would react. Disappointed obviously, but probably calmer than her dad.

And the girls? Pauline would probably think she was a slut – a stupid slut. She'd be right: Piper *was* stupid – unprotected sex, how could she? They were drunk and Luke had had a bad fight with his dad and he'd kept saying, 'I need you, babe,' and he didn't have any condoms and . . . Well, she'd given in. He'd pulled out early and she'd thought it would be okay. Stupid, really stupid.

She knew the twins, who pretended to be so worldly wise, would be shocked and that Posy wouldn't look up to her any more. Who'd look up to an idiot who gets pregnant?

Piper let the tears flow. It was a mess. Everything was a huge mess. Jess, the baby, Luke . . . everything. She needed to tell Luke, she needed him to support her, but she was scared. He was so fragile right now and had so much on his plate. Could he take any more? She was afraid he'd crumble under the pressure.

Piper wiped her tears. No matter what, she had to tell him tonight. He had to know and they had to make a decision together – soon.

She sat up and fixed her make-up. She was applying concealer under her tired eyes when the doorbell rang. Piper heard the twins charging down the stairs. She ran after them, but they got to the door first. 'Hi, Luke,' they gushed.

'Penny and Poppy?' he asked, grinning.

'Shove off, Poppy.' Penny pushed her sister out of the way. 'Hi, Luke, I'm Penny, the good-looking twin.'

Poppy elbowed her sister out of the way. 'I'm Poppy, the one who hasn't had a lobotomy.'

'Scoot!' Piper ordered, pushing them both aside. 'You'll scare him off.' The twins scattered.

Piper kissed Luke and ushered him in. 'Mum got stuck in a tutorial and has only just arrived home, so Dad ended up cooking. We're having steak and mash.'

'Sounds good. I brought wine – is that okay? I wasn't sure what to bring. I'm a bit nervous about meeting your parents, to be honest.'

Not as nervous as you would be if you knew I was pregnant, Piper thought grimly. She said, 'Don't be nervous. Dad's a bit mad but nice underneath.'

'It was good of them to invite me.'

'They said I spend so much time in your house and talk about your family so much they were afraid I was going to leave home and move in. And also obviously because they know about Jess.'

Luke pulled her in for another quick kiss. 'I wish you would move in. You'd brighten things up.'

They heard a cough and Luke moved away from Piper.

'Luke, I presume.' Seamus held out a hand.

'Yes, sir, nice to meet you.'

Seamus raised an eyebrow. 'Probably better if I'd met you before I saw you with your tongue down my daughter's throat. Still, you're here now.'

Luke went bright red.

'Behave, Dad,' Piper warned him.

'I'll say what I want in my own house. Now, come on, the dinner's just ready.' Waving a spatula in Luke's direction, Seamus said, 'Piper tells me you need to eat loads of meat for the rugby.'

Luke was still standing, unsure when he should sit down. 'Yes, sir. We're encouraged to load up on protein.'

'In my day we just ate what our mother stuck in front of us, put on our boots and played. It's all protein and weights and statistics, these days. Load of nonsense.'

Piper rolled her eyes. 'Dad played rugby like a hundred years ago and claims he could have played for Ireland.'

Seamus went over and flipped a steak in the pan. 'I was a shoo-in until I broke my ankle. It was never the same again.'

'What position did you play?' Luke asked.

Piper could see him eyeing up her dad, who didn't look like he'd ever played any sport. He was quite tall and relatively slim, but he had a big belly that hung over his trousers and no muscles whatsoever.

'Fullback. I had great pace back in the day.'

Luke nodded politely, then handed Seamus the bottle of wine.

'Nice Bordeaux, thank you.'

'My granddad recommended it.'

'Ah, yes. He runs the café and wine shop up on the main street?'

'That's right.'

'Take a weight off, Luke,' Seamus said.

Luke sat down beside Piper. They held hands under the table.

Posy stormed through the door, her face red with rage. 'DO I HAVE A MOUSTACHE?'

Seamus shook his head. 'For the love of God.'

'Answer me!'

'No.'

'What's wrong, Posy?' Piper asked.

'Penny and Poppy told me I had a moustache and that I'd have to start shaving and that it was proof I was actually a boy in a girl's body and my testosterone was coming out now.' Posy was getting upset.

'When are you going to learn that they're evil twins who love nothing more than to wind you up?' Piper said.

'They said I'm gender fluid.'

Luke coughed to hide a laugh.

'You're a girl, Posy,' Piper reassured her. 'One hundred per cent.'

Posy sat down and picked up a piece of bread from the basket in the middle of the table. 'Are you Luke?' she asked.

'Yes, and I guess you're Posy, the youngest, right?'

Posy nodded. 'Yes. Being the youngest sucks. Who's the youngest in your house?'

'Bobby, and he'd say he gets a hard time too. He's quite angry and kicks things.'

'I bet you're not as mean to him as my sisters are to me.' Posy took a bite of the bread.

'I've definitely never told him he was gender fluid,' Luke said. 'And if it's any help, you definitely don't have a moustache.'

Posy touched her upper lip with her index finger. 'Good.'

'You're like a mini Piper, which is a very good thing.'

Posy grinned. 'I hope I am. I think Piper's so pretty.'

Luke leant in to whisper, 'So do I, and she's really nice too. How lucky am I?'

Piper felt her heart fill. She really loved Luke.

The back door opened and Olivia bustled in. 'Sorry I'm late. I brought wine as an apology.' She placed a bottle on the table. 'The tutorial just went on and on. It was so interesting. They had a refugee from Malawi talking about –'

Piper tried to catch her mother's attention. 'Mum, this is Luke.'

Olivia stopped talking and noticed him for the first time. She looked him up and down and proffered a hand. 'Sorry. I get a bit carried away with my new college life. Nice to finally meet you, Luke.'

'You, too, Mrs King.'

'Oh, God, call me Olivia. "Mrs King" makes me think of Seamus's mother, who was a total battleaxe.'

Seamus turned back from the cooker. 'Ah, now, she wasn't that bad.'

Olivia hung up her coat and sat down at the table. 'The first time I met her, I was probably Piper's age, and I was invited for dinner. After dessert she said, "You might think about your portion sizes. It's very easy to put on weight and not so easy to lose it. With your curvy figure, you'd need to be careful."'

'Oh, God.' Luke was grinning. 'What did you say back?'

'I smiled and said that a healthy appetite was usually considered a good thing, and that Seamus was very fond of my curves.'

Luke and Piper laughed. Piper loved that story and the way her mum had stood up for herself and answered back. Piper didn't really remember her granny – she'd died when Piper was five – but by all accounts she had not been a very nice person.

'That's enough stories about my mother and her sharp tongue. Call the lunatics down for dinner, please, Penny.'

'It's Posy!' she huffed, then poked her head out of the kitchen door and shouted, 'GRUB'S UP!'

The twins thundered down the stairs and threw themselves into their chairs. 'So, Luke, I hear you're on the senior cup team in St James,' Penny said.

'Well, yes, I'm on the squad,' Luke said modestly.

Piper put a hand on his shoulder. 'He's the winger and he's brilliant.'

'I always think it's good for kids to be into sports. It keeps them out of trouble,' Seamus said.

Not always, Piper thought.

'Sport is so boring.' Poppy groaned. 'I hate having to play stupid hockey in the rain. What's the point?'

'It keeps you fit and healthy.' Seamus popped a large piece of steak into his mouth.

'I like hockey,' Posy said.

'Good girl, keep it up. Don't turn out like these two reprobates.'

Penny rolled her eyes. 'Posy's a square.'

'Total dork,' Poppy agreed.

'Besides, girls who are into sports are lesbians,' Penny said.

'Stop that,' Olivia warned.

'What did you say? Are you calling me a lesbian now?' Posy's face was red.

'Calm down, darling. They're only joking.' Olivia placed a hand on Posy's arm.

'Big butch lesbians,' Poppy taunted her.

'I am not a bitch lesbian,' Posy roared.

'I said butch, you dork.'

'What is that? A lesbian word?'

'It means –'

'Enough!' Seamus cut across Penny. 'We have a guest here tonight and it would be nice if for once we could have a civilized family meal, without shouting and tears.' Turning to Luke, he said, 'This is why I have my shed. A man cannot live with six women without somewhere to escape to.'

Luke smiled. 'It's certainly lively.'

'"Lively" is a very polite way of putting it. Bloody mayhem, I'd say.' Seamus shook his head.

'How is your sister?' Olivia asked. 'Piper told us the poor girl has leukaemia.'

Piper watched as Luke's face darkened. 'Yes, it's been hard for her. But she seems to be reacting well to the chemo, although it's making her really sick.'

'Chemo's a blessing disguised as a curse. How's your mother coping?' Olivia asked.

Luke paused. 'She's . . . Well, she's just getting on with it, I guess. She's great. She keeps everything together.'

'Mum used to be like that for us, but now all she does is go to college and read books and talk about vaginas being cut,' Penny said.

Luke choked on his food.

'Shut up, Penny,' Piper hissed.

'For the love of God, Penny, be quiet,' Seamus barked.

Penny folded her arms. 'Fine, I'm just saying.'

'I'm sorry you feel that way, darling,' Olivia said, keeping her voice even, but Piper could tell she was annoyed. 'I spent nineteen years devoting my life to raising you all. I don't think a two-year course in university is too much to ask. Do you?'

Penny shrugged. 'I'm not going to boring college.'

'Really?' Seamus said. 'And what are you planning on doing?'

'Me and Poppy are going to start a vlog, like Zoella.'

'Who?'

Poppy squealed. 'OMG, Dad, you are *such* a loser. Zoella is the biggest thing ever. Her YouTube channel has over nine point nine million subscribers and over six hundred and sixty-three million video views.'

'She is amazing,' Posy agreed.

'Even I've heard of her,' Olivia said.

'How does she make money?' Seamus asked.

'Duh, she writes books, sells her own beauty products and people pay her to try their make-up brands.'

'She's worth millions and she does most of it from her bedroom. It's so easy,' Poppy said.

Seamus sat back in his chair. 'So you're telling me that some girl called Zooella –'

'Zoella.'

'Whatever. This lassie is sitting in her bedroom trying on lipsticks and over six hundred million people are watching?'

'Yes,' Penny said. 'And then she wrote a book – well, she didn't exactly write it all by herself. She got help to write it and it sold zillions of copies.'

'And it's all about make-up?' Seamus asked.

'And hair and clothes and stuff,' Penny added.

Seamus thumped the table. 'Well, then, what in the hell are you waiting for? We've a house full of bloody make-up and clothes lying around everywhere and two foolish girls who are obsessed with it all. Get up to that bedroom and start videoing yourselves. We'll be millionaires in no time.'

Poppy and Penny looked at each other. 'But, like, what would we say?'

'Say?' Seamus was incredulous. 'You never stop talking.'

'Yeah, but it's different when you think people are actually watching,' Penny said.

'Totally. You don't want to say anything you could get slagged about,' Poppy agreed.

'Or say a lipstick colour is cool when everyone else thinks it's lame,' Penny added.

'Besides, we don't have a cool boyfriend like Zoella,' Poppy said.

'We could use Luke.' Penny eyed Luke across the table.

'Totally.' Poppy was excited. 'He's cool and hot.'

Piper put her arm around Luke. 'Back off, witches. Luke is not going to be in any of your stupid videos. He's my boy-friend. Get your own.'

'You're so selfish, Piper. We could make zillions of euros and we'd pay Luke, obviously.'

'So you're going to pretend to the world that you share a boyfriend? Is that your genius plan?' Piper asked.

'I'm sure he has a friend who could pretend too.'

'You're being ridiculous,' Piper said.

Luke shook his head. 'Much as I'd like to help you on this mission to make millions, I'm afraid I'm out.'

Penny glared at Piper. 'Thanks a lot. You're so selfish.'

'That's enough nonsense, girls. You'd be much better off spending your time on things that matter, like equality and human rights, rather than the colour of lipstick,' Olivia said.

Penny and Poppy rolled their eyes.

'If we went on about what you go on about we'd have no friends. It's boring, Mum,' Penny told her.

'Boring and depressing,' Poppy added.

'Maybe we could ask Gavin and Roger to be our pretend boyfriends,' Penny said.

'Ewww, Roger has zits, no way,' Poppy said.

'Oh, yeah, good point.'

Seamus stood up and began clearing the plates. 'Enough of this nonsense. What the two of you need is to go running about in the fresh air. I'm signing you up for the athletics club tomorrow morning.'

The twins jumped up and shouted at him.

'Dad's right.' Olivia scraped a plate and stacked it in the dishwasher. 'You need a proper focus. You're becoming vacuous.'

'I don't know what that means,' Penny said.

'It's probably some weird feminist thing to do with vaginas,' Poppy huffed.

Luke leant in to whisper in Piper's ear, 'Your family talk a lot about vaginas.'

Piper grinned. 'Not normally. I'm sorry about this. I told you the twins were mad.'

'Speaking of vaginas, any chance I could see yours later?' Luke said, very quietly, into her ear.

Piper giggled. 'Maybe.'

Luke squeezed her hand under the table. Piper felt that tonight was the best time to tell him. He was in a good mood. After dessert, they'd go for a walk and she'd tell him then.

When dinner was over and Luke had thanked Olivia and Seamus profusely, Piper suggested a walk.

'Couldn't we just go up to your bedroom and have silent sex?' he muttered into her hair.

'Not with my parents downstairs.'

'Okay. Well, come back to my place, then. Mum will be at the hospital and Granddad will be working.'

'Can we go for a walk first? I want to talk to you about something.'

Luke shrugged. 'Okay, babe. You look serious – you're not going to dump me, are you?' He grinned, but she could see fear in his eyes.

She hugged him tight. 'Never. I love you.'

She felt his body relax into her. 'I love you too.'

They kissed, but just then Luke's phone buzzed in his coat pocket. He pulled it out. Since Jess had been sick he no longer ignored any calls – just in case.

'Mum?'

Piper could hear Kate's voice. She sounded excited. 'Hi, Luke, can you come home straight away? Maggie's here! She's dying to see you all.'

'Sure. I'm on my way.'

Luke hung up and turned to Piper. 'My mum's best friend Maggie's in Dublin. I have to go. Sorry. Call you later.'

Piper watched him stride down the path.

He turned. 'What was it you wanted to talk about?'

She waved her hand. 'Nothing. Don't worry.'

'Call you later.'

Piper closed the door. She leant against it and sighed. Another opportunity missed. Tears prickled her eyes. Damn it. At this rate she'd be giving birth before he knew.

18

When Kate answered the door, she wasn't expecting to see her best friend standing there. Maggie hadn't said a word about coming over to visit. Kate had thought she was in Dubai at a trade fair, so when the bell rang and she was greeted by the smiling face of her oldest friend, she crumbled. All pretence of bravery left her. She fell into her friend's arms and sobbed.

'Oh, Kate, you poor, poor thing,' Maggie said softly, stroking her hair. 'What a bloody awful time you're having. I'm sorry I couldn't come sooner.'

Kate took a deep breath and pulled back from Maggie's soft cashmere-covered shoulder. 'Sorry. Long few weeks.'

'Long few sodding years.'

Kate wiped her eyes with a tissue. She always had tissues in her pockets, these days. Crying was a daily, if not hourly, occurrence now.

'Right, let's get inside and crack open a bottle of vodka. I stocked up in Duty Free.' Maggie gathered up her bags and suitcase and followed Kate inside. 'This kitchen always brings me back to our childhood,' she said, glancing around. 'The amount of time we spent in here drinking coffee and smoking out of the window.'

Kate smiled. 'It's strange being back home, but nice too. Especially now. Dad's such a brilliant support.'

'Sure George was always great.' Maggie pulled the bottle of vodka from one of her bags. 'Right, let's get stuck in. I have tonic here too. We just need ice.'

Kate went to the freezer, took out an ice tray and plonked two cubes in each glass. Maggie poured the vodka.

'Jesus, Maggie, go easy! We'll be hammered after one glass.'

'You need it. It's medicinal.' Maggie shrugged off her coat. 'Cheers.' She raised her glass. 'To you, Kate, to the future being bright, and most of all to Jess getting better.'

Kate swallowed the lump in her throat and drank deeply. The vodka went straight to her toes. Oh, it was a lovely feeling. Apart from the odd glass of wine, she'd been steering clear of alcohol. She was afraid of the effects. She knew if she started drinking, she might never stop. Part of her wanted oblivion. Part of her wanted to disappear into a bottle of booze and block out all the worry and heartache, but she knew she had to be clear-headed and together for Jess, and for Luke and Bobby.

But tonight she'd allow herself to enjoy a few drinks. Maggie leant over and held her hand. 'Tomorrow, you and I are going to a fancy hotel and spa. My treat. We're going to get dressed up and go dancing.'

Kate put down her glass. 'I can't, Maggie. I have to be with Jess.'

'It's all sorted. George is going to look after her and he's getting Luke and his girlfriend to help out as well. It's one night, Kate. Give yourself a break.'

Kate picked up her glass and clinked Maggie's. 'Actually, that sounds wonderful.'

George came in. 'Ah, there she is.' Maggie stood up and hugged him. 'Good to see you, Maggie.'

'Good to be here.'

Kate wagged a finger at her father. 'I hear you and Maggie have been plotting.'

George put his hand on her shoulder. 'You deserve a night off. Besides, no one can say no to Maggie.'

Luke arrived.

'*Aaaah!*' Maggie squealed. 'Lukey! You're even more gorgeous than the last time, and that wasn't long ago!' She threw her arms around him. 'I know teenagers hate hugs, but you have to give me one.'

Luke laughed and hugged her back.

'What's going on?' Bobby came into the room holding his Nintendo. 'Why is everyone shouting?'

Maggie bent down and kissed him. 'Hi, Bobby.'

'Yuck, Maggie! You know I hate kisses.'

'Sorry, I forgot. Do you hate presents as well?' Maggie wiped her lipstick off his cheek.

Bobby shrugged. 'Not really, no. In fact, I quite like them.'

Kate watched as Maggie handed Bobby a big bag. He looked inside. 'Wow! This is so cool.' His beautiful brown eyes lit up, the way they hadn't in a long time. Kate loved Maggie just a little more.

Bobby held up a book. '*Five Thousand Awesome Facts*, cool, and . . .' He looked at Kate in shock. 'Mum, it's the Omano OM117L monocular microscope and the OptixCam Summit Series SK2 1.3MP digital microscope camera that Santa couldn't bring last year.'

Kate couldn't speak.

Bobby, forgetting his hatred of hugging, ran to Maggie and threw his arms around her tightly. '*Thank* you.'

Kate saw Maggie brush away a tear. 'I'm so happy you like it. Sure a genius like you needs to be kept busy.'

'Well, Maggie, you've outdone yourself. A book with five thousand facts for Bobby to share with us is just what we needed.' George shook his head.

'I thought of you when I bought it.' Maggie grinned. 'Now, this is for Luke.' She handed him a box. He opened it and a huge smile spread across his face.

'You legend.' He held up a black rugby boot.

'They look great,' Kate said.

'Mum, these are the Under Armour Speedform leather boots. They're the best.' Luke kissed Maggie's cheek. 'Thanks.'

'I hope they fit. I asked George for your shoe size so they should be okay. Check out the back.'

Luke's smile widened. 'No way!' He turned to show Kate that his initials, LH, were on the back in gold lettering.

'Amazing.' Kate smiled and mouthed, 'Thank you,' to Maggie.

'Now, George, don't think I forgot about you. This is your gift.' Maggie handed him a box wrapped in shiny red paper.

George opened it and frowned. 'Earphones?'

Maggie shook her finger. 'Not just earphones. These are noise-cancelling headphones, so when you want some peace, you just pop them on and the world will be quiet.'

George laughed. 'Well, now, that's about the most perfect gift I've ever received.'

'And for you, Kate.' Maggie handed her a beautifully wrapped parcel. It was heavy.

Kate opened it and under the gold wrapping paper was a box, inside which she found a bottle of pink champagne. 'Oh, Maggie.'

Maggie leant over and said quietly, 'It's to open when Jess gets the all-clear. I'll come and share it with you.'

Kate hugged her, willing herself not to cry. Having Maggie there made everything better, brighter and more hopeful.

'Now, before I have another drink, I need to see my goddaughter.'

Maggie drove Kate's car to the hospital. Even after only half a drink, Kate felt a bit lightheaded.

When they got there, Kate stopped Maggie in Reception. 'You need to prepare yourself. She's totally bald and she's lost a lot of weight. She doesn't look like the old Jess.'

Maggie nodded. 'Okay.'

'You'll have to be gowned, gloved and masked.'

'I understand.'

As they approached the room, Kate saw Maggie hesitate. With the mask on, her eyes looked huge, and Kate could see fear in them. 'Deep breath and smile. Right?'

Maggie smiled behind the mask, her eyes crinkling. 'I'm ready.'

Kate watched as Maggie put her shoulders back and marched into the room, exuding energy. 'Hello, my darling girl,' she said, throwing her arms around Jess but being gentle with the hug.

Jess's face lit up. 'Maggie! I'm so happy to see you.'

'Me too,' Maggie said, and Kate noticed her friend clasp her hands together to stop them shaking.

'Do I look awful?'

'You're the same beautiful Jess to me. What's hair? It comes, it goes. Yours will grow back even thicker and more stunning. Don't you worry. And you're lucky because you have your mother's beautiful brown eyes, which dazzle everyone.'

Jess beamed.

'So, this is shit.'

'Yes, it is,' Jess said.

'But you will get out of here and live a long and amazing life. You're a very special girl, Jess, and you'll get better. I really believe that.' Maggie tapped her forehead. 'Try and be as positive as you can, it'll help.'

Jess nodded. 'I'm trying.'

Maggie patted her arm. 'I know you are, pet. Now, in the meantime, because you're stuck here, I've got you some things to make the days pass a bit quicker.' She lifted the big bag she had brought with her and handed it to Jess.

Jess peered in and began to pull things out. A laptop. Ten box-set series. Twenty movies. A book on mindfulness. Jo Malone creams and shower gels. A neck support. Three cashmere wraps in different colours. A Mac make-up bag filled with beauty products, and a pair of noise-cancelling headphones, just like George's.

'Maggie!' Kate exclaimed. 'It's so much – too much.'

Maggie raised her hand. 'I'm allowed to spoil my gorgeous goddaughter and I will. Not another word out of you, Kate, or I'll evict you from the room.'

Jess's eyes shone. 'Oh, Maggie, it's just . . . I don't know what to say . . . Thank you. It's so generous. I'm so happy.'

Maggie blinked furiously. 'Don't say any more or you'll set me off.'

Jess held up her skinny arms and Maggie leant in for another hug. Kate knew she'd never forget this moment. She couldn't have loved her best friend more.

19

The following day, before they set off for the hotel, Kate left long lists of instructions for everyone. She ran around packing and unpacking bags until Maggie grabbed her arm and dragged her into the waiting taxi.

'I forgot to –' Kate was trying to climb out.

Maggie locked the door. 'Stop, Kate. Please, stop. Sit back and breathe. It's one night. Your dad and Luke can look after things.'

'I'm just worried about –'

'Everything and everyone?'

Kate smiled. 'Yes.'

'You always were. But you need to take care of yourself, too. That's what I'm here for. Now sit back and let me look after you.'

They started with a glass of wine. Then Maggie took Kate to a swanky hair salon to have her hair cut, coloured and blow-dried and to have her make-up done.

They added honey highlights to her light brown hair, cut layers into the shapeless style and a fringe, which made her look ten years younger. The make-up artist brought out her brown eyes with shadow, liner and false lashes. When the hairdresser and make-up artist had finished, and Kate looked at herself in the mirror, she began to cry.

'Don't cry, you'll ruin your eye make-up and you look fantastic!' Maggie said.

'I can't believe it.' Kate sobbed. 'I'd forgotten I could.'

Maggie hugged her. 'You're stunning.'

Then there was shopping. Maggie insisted on buying Kate a black dress that really flattered her figure. Kate tried to stop her, but Maggie was not taking no for an answer.

Then they went back to the hotel for more drinks, lots more. As the alcohol took effect, Kate felt her whole body begin to relax. The frown line between her eyes softened and she began to smile and laugh. 'Thank you for all of this. What a wonderful day.' She sipped her cocktail. 'I feel like a person again.'

'I'm glad. You deserve it.'

'I never thought it would be this hard,' Kate said.

'Parenting?' Maggie asked.

Kate nodded. 'I love them so much and, let's face it, they're all I have. No career, no husband, no life, really. It's just the kids. I'm a mum. That's my identity. So to have Jess so sick and not be able to fix it is . . . Well, it makes me feel like I've failed her. I've failed in my only job, to protect her from harm.'

'Kate, you can't control cancer. No one can. Your kids are amazing and it's ninety per cent down to your brilliant parenting. You're a fantastic mother. You're devoted to them. There's nothing more you could have done or can do. You're wearing yourself out looking after Jess. Give yourself a break.'

Kate put down her glass. 'I just want her to get better. I thought life was tough before this happened, but it wasn't. Money and houses don't matter. The only things that do are health and happiness. I really know that now. I don't care about Nick's affair or living with Dad. I just want Jess to be well.'

Maggie put a hand on her friend's arm. 'We all do. And she will get better. She's a fighter, just like her mum. I honestly don't know how you do it. You manage to juggle all your kids and their needs. It must be exhausting.'

'You run a successful recruitment business with twenty employees. That sounds terrifying to me. I couldn't do it.'

Maggie smiled. 'Some days at work I feel as if I'm dealing with children. But I know I couldn't be a real mother. I like my freedom too much. I guess I'm too selfish.'

Kate sat up straight. 'Don't say that. You're the least selfish person I know. Not having children isn't selfish. It's just a choice you made.'

Maggie sighed. 'That's not how society sees it. Men especially are always telling me how I've missed out and how I'll regret it. They're married fathers, who are usually trying to have sex with me. What a joke! And I don't regret it – I know full well I'd be a bad mother. I'd hate it.'

'Well, you're a brilliant "auntie". The best. My kids adore you.'

'And I love them, but after seeing them I do love to go home to my clean, tidy, quiet apartment. It's just who I am.'

Kate smiled at her friend.

They were so different. The idea of going home to an empty apartment filled Kate with dread. Although the chaos at home was sometimes overwhelming, she loved it. She loved the coming and going of the kids, hearing about their day, watching their school plays, Luke's rugby matches, Jess's tennis games, helping them with homework, minding them, caring for them . . . being their mum. Well, she had loved it until Jess had got sick. Now things were out of her control and she was terrified.

Maggie interrupted her thoughts. 'It's really important, when you're dealing with so much stress, that you carve out a bit of time for yourself. If you get too run down, you won't be able to help Jess.'

Kate knew Maggie was being kind and considerate, but where the hell would she find time for herself? She spent most of her time in hospital, reading to Jess, holding the bowl when she threw up, cuddling her when she was upset, persuading her to eat, watching movies with her – just being with her. When she got home she had to give Bobby time: he was upset by Jess being in hospital and needed reassurance.

Luke was the one who was missing out on her attention. She'd barely seen him lately. Thank goodness he had a nice girlfriend, whom Kate trusted. Piper wasn't the type of girl to get Luke into trouble. She didn't seem to be a drinker or a messer, and she was keen to go to college. She seemed to adore Luke, too, which was exactly what he needed.

'I know what you're thinking,' Maggie said. 'Where am I going to find the time? But you have to, Kate. Otherwise you'll get sick yourself from exhaustion and worry. How about a yoga class once a week for an hour? Or did you ever sign up for a mindfulness class like we discussed? It's supposed to be amazing. There must be one in the area.'

Kate drank more wine. 'Actually, there's one starting in the room upstairs from the café next week.'

Maggie clapped her hands. 'Perfect timing. Sign yourself up and go. It's just one tiny hour a week. You need it.'

She could manage one hour a week, she thought, and everyone kept telling her how brilliant mindfulness was for 'switching off your mind' and calming you down. She'd welcome any kind of help with her mind. It raced all day and most of the night, too. Funnily enough, the only time she felt calm was at night in hospital when things were quiet and she was holding Jess in her hospital bed, watching movies or reading to her or, if Jess was too tired, just lying there as her daughter slept in her arms. Those quiet times were when her mind briefly stopped whirring. She cherished them. With her arms around Jess, she felt as if she was protecting her a little – as if she was being a mother instead of a useless bystander, watching her child being poked and prodded and pumped full of drugs.

Maggie nudged her. 'Those guys over there are checking you out.'

Kate snorted. 'They're obviously looking at you. I'm hardly a catch – a cash-strapped, separated mother of three, one child in hospital with leukaemia. How could they resist?'

'Listen to me. Tonight you're Kate, a gorgeous, sexy, thirty-seven-year-old woman.'

'But I'm forty-two.'

'Not tonight.'

Maggie waved the two men over to join them. They sat down and introduced themselves, Henk and Ewoud. They were from Amsterdam and were in Ireland for a technology conference. Kate reckoned they were in their mid-thirties. Neither was wearing a wedding ring, and while they weren't particularly handsome, they were attractive enough.

Maggie bought drinks, the men bought drinks, and soon everyone was smashed, especially Kate.

One of the men suggested they go to a club. Maggie was all for it, of course. They piled into a cab and within twenty minutes they were all dancing to Taylor Swift.

Kate came over to Maggie. 'Oh, my God! He just tried to kiss me!'

'So?'

'So I can't do that.'

'Why not?'

'Well, I . . . I . . .'

'You're single, you can do whatever the hell you want. Now will you just go for it!' Maggie shouted in her friend's ear.

'What about Jess?'

'Jess is in hospital. How is you not kissing him going to make her better?'

Kate's eyes filled with tears. 'I shouldn't be enjoying myself while she's having a terrible time.'

Maggie grabbed her by the shoulders and shook her. 'Jesus, Kate, it's one lousy night. Stop feeling guilty.'

Henk came up and pulled Kate back to dance. Maggie pushed her forward. 'Let go, Kate, just let go.'

Kate felt an arm land on her back. What the hell? She opened her eyes. On the floor beside her were the new black dress, her tights, shoes and bra. She slowly turned over.

'Morning.' Henk gave her a sleepy smile and his hand reached down between her legs.

Kate leapt out of the bed. She was stark naked. Oh, God. She ran into the bathroom and locked the door.

'Hey, what's going on?' Henk called after her.

'Go away. Please just go away.'

'Come on, Kate, we had the great time. Let's finish with one more sex.'

One more sex? Oh, Jesus, she'd slept with him! Kate began to have little flashes of the previous night. Drinking, dancing, kissing and, oh, God, sex. Yes, definitely sex. She was a slut. How could she sleep with a total stranger?

There was a knock on the bathroom door. 'How about we shower together? We can have sex in there.'

Kate pulled the towelling robe around her and sank down on the bathmat. 'Please stop talking and leave.'

'You were a lot of fun last night, now not so much.'

Kate decided not to say anything. She closed her eyes as memories flooded back. She blushed as she remembered crying out when she came. It had been a long time since

162

she'd had sex. It was good sex, great sex. But, still, how could she?

He could have been a murderer or a weirdo or anything. And where was Maggie? Hang on, she was sharing the room with Maggie, so where was she now? Kate vaguely remembered leaving the nightclub and Maggie waving her off, telling her to have a great time. Maggie was with Henk's friend – what was his name? Ewoud. Kate began to laugh. She and Maggie had kept saying, 'He would. Would you?' while falling about laughing. Henk and Ewoud had just shrugged.

Had Maggie ended up with Ewoud in his room? Probably. She glanced around the bathroom. Her bag was there. She fished for her phone. No messages from home, good. Two from Maggie, one from last night: *Hope he was worth it!!!!! Had to book another room. Ewoud not my type. Am in room 234.*

There was another from this morning at ten o'clock. What time was it? Kate looked at her phone again. *Half past ten!* She never slept in late. Maggie's text said: *Gone for breakfast. Call when you wake up u slut!!!*

Kate could hear Henk moving around the room and prayed he was getting dressed.

He knocked on the bathroom door. 'I am going now. It was a pity that you were not so nice today. I had the good time last night. Goodbye.'

Had they used a condom? Kate thought wildly. Jesus, did I have unprotected sex? Kate opened the bathroom door and called, 'Wait, did we . . . did we use protection?'

Henk turned and nodded. 'Yes, I did. You were not asking me to, but of course I did.'

'Thank you. Thank you very much. Bye.'

Kate shut and locked the door. Thank God for that. How could she have almost had unprotected sex with a stranger? She was a disgrace.

Kate waited until she heard the bedroom door close, then exhaled deeply. Phew, he was gone. She texted Maggie, asking her to bring up some croissants and anything else portable from the breakfast buffet. Then she climbed into the shower and washed off Henk and the night before. She scrubbed and scrubbed. What was she like? A forty-two-year-old mother, with a sick child, out drunk, sleeping with strange men.

Mind you, it had been a good night. It had been fun. The sex had been pretty great, from what she could remember. Was it so terrible of her to have let go? She hoped no one had seen her. Imagine if one of the other mothers in Jess's class had spotted her falling around in the nightclub while her daughter lay in hospital. The shame! Kate closed her eyes and let the water wash away her embarrassment and her tears.

As she was drying herself, she caught her reflection in the mirror. A middle-aged woman with a thick midriff stared back at her. Who was she kidding? No amount of haircuts and make-up could change the fact that she was average-looking, with a saggy stomach and more baggage than any man would ever want.

Henk might have been the last man she'd have sex with in years, possibly decades, maybe ever. God, she might never have sex again. It was frightening but possible. She wasn't like Maggie: she couldn't just meet men and sleep with them. Well, not unless she poured eight cocktails down her neck. Could this be it? Yes, Kate thought, it could be.

There was a loud banging on the door and a shout: 'I want details!'

Kate grinned, unlocked the bathroom door and went to let Maggie in. She was holding a large napkin filled with mini croissants, *pains au chocolat* and muffins.

'I love you,' Kate said, as she began to eat one after another.

164

'Well well well! Let's hear it, then. Gory details, please.'
Maggie lay back in the chair and folded her arms.

Kate stuffed a mini muffin into her mouth. 'Nothing to tell, really.'

'Liar.'

Kate giggled. 'Okay, yes, I did bring him back and, yes, we had sex.'

Maggie whooped. 'I'm delighted. Was it good?'

'Yes. Although, if I'm honest, it's a bit hazy.'

'You were throwing back mojitos as if they were lemonade. I'm so glad you had a blow-out. You needed that.'

Kate picked up a mini croissant and took a bite. 'Thank you so much for organizing the day. I'm afraid your makeover is ruined. I look about a hundred and ninety today.'

Maggie rubbed her eyes. 'I don't feel too young myself.'

'What happened with Ewoud?'

'He was boring and had no sex appeal. I'm not that desperate. So I waved him off and booked myself another room.'

Kate winced. 'Sorry. Our whole night must have cost you a fortune.'

Maggie sat up and patted her arm. 'I work twenty-hour days to make money and that money needs to be enjoyed. I had a great time last night and, more importantly, you got to let your hair down for once. And, boy, did you let it down!' She winked.

Kate was blushing. 'God, was I in a state in the nightclub?'

'It was kind of hilarious when you were trying to twerk.'

Kate covered her face with her hands. 'Stop.'

'I'm kidding. You were absolutely fine.'

Kate drank thirstily from a glass of water. 'My head is throbbing. I'd forgotten what hangovers feel like.'

'I can book us in for another night, if you want to flake out, watch movies and order room service?'

Kate smiled. 'That sounds like heaven, but I want to go and see Jess and spend some time with Bobby.'

'Back to mother-mode. I get it. Well, I've changed my flight. I'm not going to London until Tuesday, so I'll pop in to see Jess later this afternoon.'

Kate scoffed the last croissant. To hell with her weight, she had much bigger concerns. 'I'd better get dressed.' She stood up and began to pull on her clothes.

'I'm sorry, Kate.'

Kate looked up. 'For what?'

'That you have to deal with cancer on top of everything else. It's not fair.'

Kate sighed. 'What's fair? If I let myself think, Why me? I'd crumble. Besides, nothing that's happened so far, Nick's affair and our money problems, matters even the tiniest bit compared to this. I'm so over it. It's all about Jess now. I have to believe she'll be okay. The alternative is unspeakable and unthinkable.'

Maggie went over to her and hugged her. 'She will be.'

Kate's phone rang.

It was her father. 'I'm so sorry, Kate, I need you to come to the hospital. There's been a setback.'

Bobby's Diary

Things are terribel. Last week everyone went all crazy. Jess gotted an infection and she was really sick, like bad sick. Mummy had red and sad eyes all the time and Daddy came to the hospital and shouted and punched the wall and he had red eyes too.

Granddad had sad eyes and so did Luke and so did Maggie. It made me feel really sick in my stomak. I told Mummy my stomak hurt but she said, 'Not now, Bobby.' I told Luke my stomak hurt and he said, 'For f-word sake, Bobby, Jess is really sick.' No one cares about me or how I feel.

At home Luke is grumpy and just goes into his room with Granddad's big headphones and lissens to music or else he is with Piper. I like Piper. She gave me sweets yesterday when she sawed me in the kitchen by myself. She took them out of her poket and said they were for me becos I'm a good boy and she nows it must be hard for me with Jess being sick.

It IS hard for me and now it's worser. Jess can't have visitors except Mummy and Daddy. We have to wave at her from a window and she looks really skinny and she's tired all the time and sleeps a lot.

Yesterday I heard Mummy say to Granddad, 'Jesus, Dad, we nearly lost her.'

Granddad hugged Mummy. I cried then becos I love Jess even tho I'm cross she got sick and everyone just talks about her all the time and nothing else. I don't want her to die. I don't like sleeping in my bedroom by myself. I used to go into Mummy some nights. She put her arms around me and we sleeped cuddled up. But Mummy sleeps in the hospital a lot now so I can't.

Mrs Lorgan tried to be nice to me when Luke took me to school and told her that Jess was 'not good'. She said I could play Joseph in the Christmas play. But Tommy said that it wasn't fair and he wanted to be Joseph and he should be becos his brother has special needs and my sister was just a bit sick. He said that you can get better from cancer but you can't get better from Down Sindrum.

I got foorious then and shouted that I didn't care about his stupid brother with Down Sindrum, whatever that means, and said that cancer is really bad and really serious and all my family had red eyes and I have to talk to Jess through the telephone and wave at her through a window and he can see his brother all the time.

He said Down Sindrum is way worser than cancer and I shouted, 'NO WAY, cancer is the worst,' and then I said a bad word that Luke uses. I called Tommy a 'dickhead'. I know it's a bad word but I was very angry.

Mrs Lorgan went all red in the face and said that I wasn't going to be Joseph becos Joseph would NEVER use such shoking words. She said Tommy wasn't going to be Joseph either.

She said she was making Declan be Joseph which is so dum. Declan has a stuter and he can't even say words properly. It takes him ages to say any word that starts with M, C, F, P, S or D — which is terribel because his name is Declan! His parents should change his name to Adam or something.

Anyway he is now Joseph and his wife is Mary and he can't even say her name properly which is just stupid. When he tried to say, 'Don't worry, Mary. I'll find a place for us to stay', it took him like about a hundred minits to say don't. So then Mrs Lorgan changed the words in the play to 'It's okay, I'll find a hotel.'

Declan should be a donkey or a shepherd. I should be Joseph. But now because I said the bad word I'm a stupid inn-keeper and I only have two lines and Declan has loads of lines and he can't even speak.

The play is going to go on for hours and hours with Declan in the main part.

When I told Mummy about Declans stuter in the beginning of the year when he arrived in the school and took ages to say his name, Mummy said that I shud be especially nice to him becos it was hard to have a stuter and I shud try to imagine what it's like not to be able to just say what you want.

I did feel sorry for him in the beginning but now my problem is worser than his. Jess has stinky cancer and she's not getting better.

The only good thing that happened was when Mrs Lorgan asked Tommy to be a donkey and he said no way and he said he didn't want to be in the stupid play and anyway his mum and dad said God and Jesus were just made up and only stupid people believed in all that nonsense. Mrs Lorgan put him in the bold corner.

But then a brilliant thing happened. Maggie came to collect me and I told her about the play and everything and she stopped walking and said, 'Hang on a bloody minit' and she turned around and went storming back into the school and asked Mrs Lorgan in a loud voice if she could have a word.

They told me to wait outside the classroom but I could hear them because they were kind of shouting, but not shouting. The way grown-ups talk loudly when they are angry but trying not to be rude. They talked and talked and then Maggie said, 'This is ridikulos. Bobby is having a very hard time, give the kid a break. Let him be Joseph.'

Mrs Lorgan said, 'My desishun is final.'

'Nothing is final.'

'I will not be changing my mind. I'm very sorry about his sister, but lots of families in the class have troubles at home. He is lucky to be an inn-keeper after his behavyer and cursing.'

'So you're giving a kid with a stuter who takes ten minits to say his own name the lead part? Isn't that just a little ambishus? Aren't you just putting him under huge presure? You give the kid who stuters two lines, not the main part. It's too much presure. What kind of techer are you?'

Mrs Lorgan opened the door then and she said, 'I am a techer with 37 years experience and I will not be spoken to like this or have my desishuns questioned. Good day.'

'Somewhere along those 37 years you lost your compashun you cold cow,' Maggie said and grabbed my hand and we marched out of the school.

Maggie called Mrs Lorgan a cow!!!!!!!!!!! I can't beleeve it.

Maggie did deep breathing out her nose and then she turned to me and said, 'Stuff Joseph, he's just a doormat anyway. The inn-keeper is a good part and you get to tell Joseph to go away. Now how about we go and get a hot chocolate and a huge bun?'

I love Maggie. I asked her if she could stay with us forever. She gave me a hug and I let her and then she said she had to go to other places a lot for work but that she was going to come home as much as she could to help us. That made the ake in my stomak go away and I felt better.

20

Kate sat on the mat and peeped out from under her eyelids. There were six other people in the room, three men and three women. Thank God she didn't recognize any of them. She was surprised to see men there. Then again, men had stress in their lives, too. Maybe she should suggest to Nick that he go to a class. He was certainly stressed enough to need help.

Kate could see how hard he was working to come up with the money to look after everyone and she appreciated it, but it was making him even more difficult.

Between Jenny, the kids and now Jess being sick, Nick was like a pot about to boil over. Kate tried to avoid him as much as possible. The only time she saw him relax was when he was with Jess. She'd arrived at the hospital not long ago to find the two of them laughing together over some silly game Nick had downloaded on his phone. Kate had sat outside to give them that time together. It was so good for Jess to have her dad's undivided attention and Kate hadn't wanted to break the spell.

The lady running the mindfulness class asked everyone if they were comfortable. Kate wasn't. She moved about on her mat but couldn't find a position that felt right. She hoped the class would help her to stop panicking and allow her mind to switch off even for five minutes.

Seeing Jess almost die when the infection ripped through her body had been unbearable. Kate was waking up every night with a panic attack, gasping for breath, her whole chest rigid with fear. Sometimes she thought she was having mini heart attacks. She'd never had headaches before, but now they were a permanent part of her life. Not a throbbing in her head, but a piercing, searing pain that made her want to throw up.

Dr Willis had been so kind, calling to the house and visiting Jess in hospital. When he'd asked Kate how she was, she'd told him about the headaches. He suggested she take something but she was afraid to resort to medicine: she had to be clear-headed and keep on top of things. He had told her to call him any time, day or night, if she or Jess was in need of anything. He said Kate needed to look after herself because having a sick child was such a huge strain. She told him about the mindfulness class and he thought it was an excellent idea. Everyone seemed to think it was – but Kate knew that an hour lying on a mat wasn't going to solve anything.

At night she lay in bed, her head spinning with dark thoughts about Jess and the ever-present what-if. Before the infection, she'd kept out of her mind the possibility of Jess dying. But now that she had seen her daughter so sick and so close to the edge, she couldn't block it out. It was possible: Jess could die, and it could happen in an instant.

Panic rose in her throat. She tried to concentrate on what the mindfulness lady was saying. Maggie had made her swear she'd go to the class: 'It's upstairs from the café so you have no excuse. It'll do you good,' her friend had insisted.

It wasn't worth not going and having to explain herself to Maggie, so Kate had promised she'd give it a go. What the hell? If it helped even a tiny bit, she'd be grateful.

The lights in the room were dimmed and there were candles lit along the windowsill. It was restful, she had to admit.

The mindfulness teacher sat with her legs crossed and her back straight. Kate tried to copy her but her lower back ached. She slumped against the wall, her legs bent in front of her.

'Welcome, everyone. My name is Marie. We'll go around the room and perhaps you can tell me why you're here and what you hope to achieve from the classes.'

A woman of about Kate's age said she was doing the course because she had some health issues. Next, a man said he was going through a difficult break-up . . . Then it was just Kate and a man with a beard to her left.

'Uhm . . . well, I'm Kate and I'm here because my daughter is sick and I was hoping to get some tools to help me stop panicking.'

'Welcome, Kate. I certainly hope I can help you with that,' Marie said.

It was the bearded man's turn. He looked about sixty, with dark hair, and the beard needed a trim. Looking at the floor, he said quietly, 'I'm Liam and I'm here because my wife died almost three years ago. I'm stuck. I can't seem to get past it.'

Marie nodded sympathetically. 'Mindfulness and living in the moment will hopefully help you with that.'

'And because my daughter forced me to come,' he muttered under his breath.

'My friend forced me,' Kate whispered.

Liam glanced sideways and gave Kate a little smile. 'I've never done anything like this before. I feel like a twat,' he said.

'I tried yoga once, but I found it really boring,' Kate admitted. 'Still, at this stage I'll try anything.'

'What's wrong with your daughter?'

'Cancer.'

Liam winced.

'What did your wife die of?' Kate asked.

He looked away. 'Cancer.'

Kate bit her lip. She wished he'd said a car crash or a brain haemorrhage – anything but cancer.

'Okay.' Marie raised her voice to get everyone's attention. 'Let's start by breathing. Inflate your stomach on the inhale, pull it in on the exhale.'

Kate had to concentrate hard on the breathing as it seemed to be the opposite of the way her body wanted to behave. They lay down and did more breathing, and then they did a sort of swaying to music that Kate found a bit embarrassing. They had to stand up and shake different body parts, concentrating on each one to focus their minds. Marie said if they felt awkward in front of the others, they could do it with their eyes closed. Kate kept hers open because she was afraid of falling, but Liam closed his.

She was shaking her left leg about when Liam landed on top of her, squashing her into her mat. 'God, sorry,' he said, scrambling up hastily. 'I shut my eyes and lost my balance. I'm such an idiot. I hope I didn't hurt you.'

Kate was winded but not hurt. She waved her hand. 'No damage done.'

Liam held out his hand to help her up. 'I really am so sorry. I'm such a klutz. Dancing was never my thing. I should probably go before I injure someone. So much for calm and tranquillity.'

Kate grinned. 'Don't be silly, I'm fine, and at least you distracted me from my thoughts, which is more than I can say for the breathing.'

Liam smiled back. 'I can't get that right either. I'm not sure this is for me. I think I might be better off taking my dog for a walk.'

'I think I need a vat of wine,' Kate said, and laughed.

Marie came over to them. 'We must try to remain quiet and focus on our breathing.' She inhaled and exhaled deeply to demonstrate. 'Now if we could all lie down on our mats in a comfortable position, we're going to do a body scan.'

There was something strangely intimate about lying on a mat next to a man you'd never met before, Kate mused. But she didn't feel awkward now that they'd broken the ice. Liam reminded her a bit of her dad – he had a kind face. She closed her eyes and tried to concentrate on feeling her toes, but images of Jess's beautiful brown eyes so full of fear kept flashing in front of her.

Beside her she could hear Liam rustling about and sighing. He clearly wasn't thinking about his toes either.

Half an hour later Kate held the door as everyone streamed out onto the footpath.

'Did you enjoy it?' Marie asked.

'Yes, it was definitely nice to lie down and do nothing for a little bit, but I found it very difficult to switch my mind off.'

'Don't worry. It takes a lot of practice but keep trying. It'll really help you.'

'I will, thanks.'

Liam pulled on his coat. He was the last to leave. 'After you,' he said.

'Oh, no, you go ahead. I live here.'

'What? Here?'

Kate nodded. 'Yes, my dad owns the café and wine shop and I live with him.'

'Oh, I see. To be honest, I'm rarely down this way, but the café looks lovely. I must come and check it out.'

'You should. We do the best coffee and scones in town.'

'I love scones, as you can probably tell.' Liam patted his midriff, although it certainly wasn't big, Kate thought. Probably less obvious than hers.

'Do you think you'll give this mindfulness another go?'

Liam wrinkled his nose. 'Not sure it's for me, but my daughter's paid for the six sessions so I'd feel guilty if I didn't come to one or two more.'

'I know what you mean. My friend Maggie bought them for me. I guess one or two more can't do any harm.'

Liam had a nice smile, warm and open. 'No harm as long as some oaf doesn't fall on top of you.'

'In the scheme of my life's catastrophes,' Kate said, with a half-smile, 'that was very minor.'

Liam held out his hand and they shook. 'I'll let you go. It was very nice to meet you.'

'You, too. See you next week, maybe.'

Liam waved and walked off into the cold night.

Kate locked up and turned off the lights. When she went into the house, she went to check on Bobby. He was fast asleep. Kate bent to kiss his forehead. George was beside the bed, snoring in an armchair, his glasses halfway down his nose, his book upside-down on his lap. Kate left him undisturbed and went to get something to eat. She'd wake him later if he was still asleep.

In the kitchen she heated up some of the pea and chicken soup she'd made earlier for the café. As she was sitting down to eat it, the back door opened and Luke came in.

Kate looked at the clock – it was after ten. 'Hi. Were you in Piper's?'

'Yeah,' Luke said, walking quickly across the kitchen to the other door.

As he swept past, Kate got a strong whiff of alcohol. What the hell? 'Hold on there.' She stood up.

Luke pulled the door open. 'I'm going to bed.' He made to leave, but Kate pulled him back.

'Have you been drinking?'

'No.' Luke's eyelids drooped.

'Luke, you reek of booze. Where were you?'

Where the hell had he been and with whom? Kate wasn't delusional: she knew some of Luke's friends drank. She also knew he had the odd beer on a Saturday night at a party, but that was rare because he was so obsessed with sport and health. But this was Tuesday, a school night, and judging by Luke's eyes, he'd had a lot more than one or two beers.

Kate was getting angry. Why was he risking everything he cared about by getting drunk? She budged him forward into a chair.

He sat down heavily. 'What?'

'I want to know where you were.'

'I was with a few of the guys.'

'Which guys?'

'Gus and . . . well . . . Gus.'

Gus was the kind of boy you wanted your son to stay away from. He was wild and always getting into trouble. Luke was always saying what an idiot Gus was and how he was going nowhere fast. So why on earth was he getting drunk with him?

'Were you in a pub?'

Luke shook his head. 'Gus's house.'

'Were his parents there?'

'No, they're away.'

'What did you drink?'

Luke shrugged. 'I dunno, vodka, beer, whatever.'

'Whatever? Are you kidding me? Jesus, Luke, I've enough on my bloody plate without you going out and getting drunk. What were you thinking? How is this helpful to anyone?'

Luke banged the table with his hands. 'Oh, for Christ's sake, Mum, I wasn't trying to be helpful. I was trying to forget. I was trying to get away from all this shit. I'm sick of it.

Everything's so . . . so . . .' He put his head into his hands and began to cry.

Kate stopped being angry. She was so wrapped up in Jess that she was forgetting how hard this was for everyone else. She put her arm around Luke. 'I'm sorry, sweetheart, I know it's awful for you.'

'She nearly died, Mum.' Luke looked up. 'We nearly lost her.'

Kate felt her eyes welling up. She needed to be strong. 'I know we did, but she's okay now. The thing about cancer is that it's going to have ups and downs, but as long as Jess keeps recovering and getting better, she'll be all right.'

Luke rubbed his eyes. 'Do you want to know why I really went drinking?'

'Why?'

'Because I didn't want to give her my bone marrow. I was pissed off about it because it means I'll miss training and probably a game or two. I'm such a selfish prick that I was resenting having to donate to Jess. And then when she nearly died I felt sick for even thinking like that. What kind of person am I? Jess, my little sister, the nicest kid in the world, needs my help and I don't want to give it.'

Kate hugged him. 'Luke, what matters is that you never said you wouldn't do it. You stood up and said yes when the doctors said you were a match. Whatever you were thinking privately doesn't matter. It's what you do that counts. Of course you're not happy about having to donate bone marrow. It's a big deal. No one would be thrilled about it. Don't beat yourself up for how you feel. You can't help that.' Kate held Luke's hand. 'You should be proud of yourself for agreeing to donate. I'm proud of you. More proud than I've ever been.'

Luke sniffed. 'As proud as you are of me getting drunk?'

Kate smiled. 'No.'

Luke pushed his hair out of his face. 'It's all so . . . shit. I wish Jess wasn't sick. I wish Dad wasn't such a dickhead. I wish we had loads of money and that you didn't have to worry about anything. I wish . . .'

Kate stood up and tipped her now cold soup down the sink's plughole. 'If there's one thing I've learnt over the last few years, it's that wishing is a waste of time.'

21

Jess sat up, fully clothed, on the edge of the bed and listened to Dr Kennedy. She was excited and desperate to get out of the room, but she knew she had to listen.

Mum was sitting beside her on the bed, fiddling with her handbag strap.

'Now, Jess,' Dr Kennedy said, 'I want you to listen carefully. We're allowing you to go home because the infection has cleared up and the tests have shown you're in partial remission. We'll be going ahead with the bone-marrow transplant to try to get you into complete remission, which is our goal. I think it's important that you get home for a few weeks' break before we do the transplant. However,' he raised his hands, 'I need you to be very careful to protect yourself from any further infection while you're at home. This is a list of helpful hints regarding how to avoid it.'

Jess glanced at the list the doctor handed her. It was very long, and the ones that stood out to her were: 'Tell your doctor or specialist nurse immediately if you get a temperature over 38° centigrade (100° Fahrenheit). Tell your doctor or nurse straight away if you notice any bleeding or bruising. Keep as clean as you can — for instance, wash your hands before preparing food or eating. Keep away from animals to avoid infection, especially cat-litter trays and bird cages. Put pressure on cuts for longer than usual to stop bleeding. Rest when you feel tired.'

She looked up. 'Can I go horse-riding?'

'I don't think it's advisable this time, but if the transplant goes well, then we'll have you back on a horse in no time.'

'Should we wear masks at home?' her mother asked. 'Would it help protect her?'

'Unless someone has a cold or a temperature, you don't really need masks. Keep visitors to a minimum, and anyone not feeling well is best to stay away for the moment.'

Jess stood up. She'd had enough. Weeks of talking and explaining and tests and drugs and feeling better and feeling worse – she was sick of it all. She just wanted to go home and be normal for a while. They were wasting time talking.

'Can we go now?'

Her mother put her hand on Jess's arm. 'Hold on, Jess, just one more question.'

'*No!*' Jess shouted. 'No more questions! I've had enough! I want to go home.'

Her mother looked shocked. 'Okay, calm down. We're going.'

Dr Kennedy took off his glasses and smiled at Jess. 'You've been wonderfully patient and I understand how particularly difficult the last few weeks have been. Go home and have a lovely time.'

Jess felt bad for shouting. 'Thank you so much.'

Mum picked up her bag and Jess walked slowly, much more slowly than she'd have liked, out of the door and down the corridor. Her energy was non-existent, and she hated being tired all the time.

The nurses waved her off. Aideen, her favourite, hugged her. 'Have a great time. You deserve it.'

Jess grinned. 'Thanks, I will.'

She stopped outside Larry's door and went in to hug him.

'*Whoooooaa!* I don't want your infection!' he said, grinning.

'Sod off! I'm clear and you know it.' Jess laughed.

'Enjoy your time out, you lucky thing.'

'I will. Call me anytime, day or night.'

Larry winked. 'I'll leave you in peace. You don't need me moaning down the phone when you finally get out of here for a bit.'

Jess smiled and tried to remain cheerful. Now that she was dressed in 'normal' clothes, it was as if she could see Larry from a different perspective. Instead of a fellow cancer victim, she was looking at him as an outsider would and saw how utterly wretched he was. She willed herself to see past his grey, sunken face into his lovely blue eyes. 'I'm here for you.'

He held her hand in his shrivelled dry one. 'I know. I promise I'll try not to die while you're out. I'll wait until you come back.'

She shook her head. 'Don't, Larry, please.'

His blue eyes gazed into her brown ones. 'Sorry, can't help myself. You look good, Jess. Enjoy freedom.'

She squeezed his hand. 'I will and I'll send you photos to make you jealous.'

'Why would I be jealous? I have a kingdom here.' Larry waved his arm around the hospital room. They laughed.

Just before she left, Jess turned to hug him again. 'I'll see you soon. You're not allowed to die, promise?'

'Promise.' He hugged her back.

Jess was glad her mother didn't talk or ask her any questions as they walked to the car. She was upset at leaving Larry, upset and worried. It was the only fly in the ointment of getting out of hospital. She knew Larry would miss her, just like she'd miss him. They were in it together and made each other's days so much more bearable.

She vowed to send him funny pics and texts to cheer him up and so that he'd know she hadn't forgotten him.

Hospital days were so endless and any bit of distraction was welcome.

Jess expected the house to be quiet when she got home, because the boys would be in school and Granddad would be working in the café. But when she opened the back door into the kitchen, she heard a cheer. Everyone was there – Luke, Bobby, Granddad, Piper, even Nathalie.

Bobby and Luke were holding up a poster that Bobby had painted. It said, WELCOM BAK JESS. The table was full of all her favourite food, and even though she didn't feel like eating, she was touched by all the effort that had gone into it.

Jess wanted to laugh and cry. Everything felt normal and weird at the same time. The kitchen seemed so safe and warm and full of love, and she was so happy. She tried really hard not to, but she began to cry. She turned her head and buried it in her mother's stomach.

'It's okay, pet, you're home now. Safe and sound with all the people who love you,' Mum whispered into her ear. Jess heard the catch in her voice. 'We're so happy.'

Jess took a deep breath and turned. Luke picked her up gently and swung her around. 'Good to have you back, sis. I never realized how patient you are with Mr Zillion Questions here.'

'And I never realized how good you are with Mr – Mr Big Hairy Muscles,' Bobby said.

They all laughed, which broke the tension and made everything more normal.

Granddad came over and hugged her. 'So glad to have you home, my little pet. You're the sunshine in this house.' He turned away to wipe his eyes.

Piper kissed her and Jess felt more tears on her cheeks. She noticed the black circles under Piper's eyes.

Then Nathalie came over to her. She was wearing a mask over her mouth. 'I am wearing it in case of the germs. I have the leetle cold.'

'You don't have a cold, Nathalie. Nor do you have allergies or sinus or headaches or back problems. You're just a hypochondriac,' Granddad muttered.

'Another problem with the Irish men is they are afraid of the doctor. In France when a man is sick, he goes to the doctor and takes medication. In Ireland the men pretend they are "grand" and then, *poof!*, they are dead on the road of the attack of the 'eart.'

'Seriously?' Luke glared at her.

Nathalie shrugged. 'It's true. I 'ope you will not be so stupid and stubborn as the older Irish men, Luke.'

'For the love of Jesus, Nathalie,' Granddad snapped, 'will you stop barking on about death and illness?'

'I am not afraid to talk about death. It is a fact of life. We are born and we die. *Voilà.*'

'Dude, zip it!' Luke demanded.

Nathalie looked at Jess. 'Do you want everyone never to say the word "sick" or "dead" in front of you? Does that not make it like pretending? Sticking the 'ead in the sand? Of course we all pray you will be better, but you 'ave cancer, *non?* It is a fact.'

It annoyed Jess that everyone avoided words like 'ill', 'sick', 'death' and even 'cancer'. Her family never used it. They said 'condition' or 'leukaemia' but the word 'cancer' was never uttered. Jess knew they were trying to protect her and themselves, but it bugged her.

Mum took charge. 'Nathalie, I think that's enough chat about death for now. This is a celebration.'

'Do you have celebrations in France or do you just sit around reading depressing poetry and staring at your navels?' Granddad grumbled.

'We are very good at the celebrations. We know 'ow to 'ave a good time.'

'Really?' Luke looked doubtful.

'When?' Granddad asked.

Nathalie was affronted. 'All the time. We don't need to wear a green 'at and drink ten pints and fall down to 'ave fun. We drink good wine and eat good food and talk and laugh.'

'Laugh about what?' Granddad asked.

'*Jeux de lettres.*'

'What?' they asked.

'You 'ave the sentence or the word and then you twist them around and make funny phrases. It is very amusing and good for the mental gymnastics.'

Granddad slapped his forehead. 'Mother of God, save me now. Nathalie, you need to lighten up. Maybe you should try the green hat and the few drinks. You might actually enjoy yourself.'

'Green does not flatter my skin,' Nathalie huffed.

Bobby kicked the table. 'Can we stop talking about boring stuff and eat?'

'Yes!' Kate smiled at him.

Nathalie left the room to look after the café.

'Take your mask off! You'll scare away the customers,' Granddad called after her.

Jess and the others sat down. Piper put her coat on.

'Babe, where are you going?' Luke asked.

'It's your family time, Luke. I'll call you later. Welcome home, Jess.' She blew her a kiss and left.

Jess ate little bites of everything, but she really wasn't hungry. She did manage a small bowl of strawberry shortcake ice cream and saw her mum smiling as she finished the last spoonful.

They chatted about the café, Luke's upcoming match and Bobby's Christmas play, which Jess was surprised that Mum didn't seem to know about.

'Oh, Bobby, that's awful, you should be Joseph. Maybe I could talk to Mrs Lorgan.'

Bobby rolled his eyes. 'It's way too late, Mummy. Anyway, Maggie already did and she won't change her mind.'

'Oh. Well, I'm sorry about that.'

Bobby ate a piece of scone. 'You never listen to me anyway. It's only ever about Jess.'

'Bobby!' Luke snapped. 'Mum's doing her best.'

'Be nice to your mother,' Granddad said. 'She's got a lot on her plate.'

Jess suddenly felt tired. 'I think I'll lie down for a bit. Thanks for the lovely welcome.' To Bobby, she said, 'Will you come up with me and tell me some new facts while I'm putting on my pyjamas?'

Bobby's face lit up. 'Yes!' He ran to get the book Maggie had given him.

'Are you sure about that, Jess?' Kate asked. 'You look very tired. Maybe he could read the facts later.'

'No, it's fine, Mum. Let him tell me a few. I reckon I'll be asleep in two minutes anyway.'

Luke brought Jess's bag upstairs and put it into Kate's room.

'What are you doing?' Jess asked.

'Mum said you're to sleep here while you're at home. She'll sleep with Bobby.'

'She doesn't have to do that.'

Luke put the case on the double bed. 'She wants to. We all want to help, Jess.'

Jess busied herself unpacking. With her back to Luke, she said, 'I never thanked you properly for saying you'll give me your bone marrow.'

'It's cool. No big deal.'

Jess put her pyjamas on the bed. 'It *is* a big deal and I'm sorry you have to do it, but thank you.'

Luke said quietly, 'I'd do anything to help you, Jess, you know I would. All we want is for you to get better.'

Jess didn't trust herself to speak. She was so grateful to Luke. The infection had terrified her, but it was gone now. She had to look forward. She really believed that, with Luke's strong, healthy bone marrow, she would get better, just like her mum said.

As she lay in bed listening to Bobby spouting facts, Jess tried to visualize Luke's vital bone marrow knocking down and destroying her cancer cells. It was a nice image: it made her feel strong and hopeful . . .

'As well as having unique fingerprints, humans also have unique tongue prints. Isn't that amazing, Jess? Our tongues are all different. Look at mine and then let me look at yours. Jess . . . Jess?'

As usual, Bobby found he was talking to himself. Jess had drifted off into the oblivion of sleep.

22

Piper sat beside Luke and held his hand. He was pretending to be nonchalant about the bone-marrow aspiration, but his right leg was bouncing up and down. Kate sat on Luke's other side, chewing her lip, which made Piper feel a bit panicky.

Dr Kennedy explained it all to them in a calm and reassuring voice. Luke had to have a general anaesthetic, and while he was asleep, they'd take out the bone marrow. A needle would be put through his skin into the hip bone. Then they would suck the bone marrow out through the needle and into the syringe. That part didn't sound too bad, but when Dr Kennedy said they usually had to put the needle into several different parts of the pelvis and, occasionally, the chest bone in order to get the one full litre of bone marrow they needed, Piper saw the blood drain from Luke's face.

Dr Kennedy must have noticed, too, because he patted Luke's arm and told him not to worry, that his body would replace all of the bone marrow within a few weeks.

'How long will the procedure take?' Kate asked.

'No more than two hours. After the bone marrow is harvested, Luke will be taken to the recovery room while the anaesthesia wears off. All going well, he'll be free to leave the hospital within a few hours or by the next morning.'

'I've got an important rugby game four days later. Can I play?' Luke found his voice.

'I'd advise against it. You may have soreness, bruising and aching at the back of the hips and lower back for a few days.'

'Fuck,' Luke muttered.

'Luke!' Kate said.

Fuck your stupid rugby match, Piper wanted to scream. What if you bloody die? What if something goes wrong and the operation is a disaster and you die on the operating table without knowing we're going to have a baby?

Piper let go of Luke's hand and gripped her own hands together tightly to try to control her panic.

'I'm sorry about that,' Kate said to Dr Kennedy. 'We're all under a lot of pressure.'

'That's quite all right. It's a very difficult time for you all.'

'Will Jess be in isolation after the transplant?' Kate asked.

Dr Kennedy nodded. 'Yes. Until her bone marrow starts making enough blood cells, she's at risk of picking up infections. She'll have to stay in a single room with minimal visitors until her blood count improves.'

'Poor Jess.' Kate's voice shook.

Kate looked so worn out and sad. That's a mother's love, thought Piper. When you have a child, you love it more than anything in the world. She touched her stomach. Would she feel that for her baby? Would Luke? Or would he resent her and hate the baby for ruining his life? Would Luke be a good dad? Would he be like his mum, devoted to her kids, or like his dad and leave Piper for a younger woman?

Piper desperately wanted to tell someone. She felt so lonely. Walking around with this huge secret all the time was wearing her down. She needed Jess to get better soon. If Jess got better, everyone would be happy, and maybe Luke wouldn't go mad when she told him. She prayed Luke's bone marrow would make Jess better. It had to, surely.

Dr Kennedy stood up and saw them out of the room. Patting Luke on the back, he said, 'We'll see you in two days' time. Don't worry, it'll all be over in no time and we'll have you back on the rugby pitch soon.'

As they walked towards the car, Piper saw Luke's dad coming running towards them. Luke froze.

'Sorry I'm late,' Nick panted, sweat running down the sides of his face. 'I had to show a house and they were late and . . . Anyway, it was worth it because I closed the deal and it's a big one, so it'll really help with the bills.' He bent over, putting his hands on his knees and catching his breath. 'Did I miss it?'

'Yeah, you did,' Luke said, staring over his father's shoulder into the distance.

'What did he say?'

Luke's hand tightened around Piper's. It hurt. 'He said they're going to stick needles all over me, suck out ten per cent of my bone marrow and I can't play in my match this week.'

Nick frowned. 'To hell with your match, this is about Jess.'

Luke's fingers were now crushing Piper's. 'Don't you dare tell me what it's about. What the hell would you know? You're hardly ever around, and when you are, you're either late or on the phone to your stupid fucking girlfriend, who can't seem to cross the road without you.'

Nick straightened and glared at him. 'Don't speak to me like that. I'm doing my best here. I'm trying to hold down a job so I can look after everyone. I'm the one who has to come up with the funds and I'm working my balls off. Why don't you give me a break and stop behaving like a child?'

Luke snorted. 'Yeah, you're a real contender for Dad of the Year.'

'Stop it, both of you,' Kate begged. 'None of this is helping Jess.'

Nick suddenly noticed Piper. 'Who's this?'

'My girlfriend,' Luke said.

'Oh, yes, Piper. Jess has told me lots about you.'

Piper didn't know what to say. She couldn't be rude, but she knew how much Luke hated his dad and what a rubbish father he had been. Still, she had to be polite. So she put out her hand and shook Nick's. 'Nice to meet you,' she said.

'You too. Thanks for being so good to Jess. She raves about you.'

Piper blushed. 'It's easy to be nice to Jess.'

Nick smiled. 'Yes, it is. She's a very special girl.'

'So special you barely saw her all year until she got sick,' Luke said.

Piper watched Nick's face darken. He was different from how she had imagined him. She'd thought he'd be tall, dark and handsome, a ladies' man. He was fit for his age, but average-looking: brown hair, greying at the sides, and blue eyes that seemed a bit too small for his face. He had deep black rings under them, which betrayed how tired he was.

Nick inhaled deeply. 'Luke, that's enough. I don't want to argue with you. I know it can't be easy having this procedure and I'm proud of you for stepping up for your sister.'

Piper felt Luke relax slightly beside her.

'Right. Let's go. I've to pick up Bobby,' Kate said, hustling Luke and Piper towards the car.

Later that day, on her way home from school, Piper was still thinking about Kate, what a good mother she was to Jess and how she wanted to be a good mother to her baby, when she heard Posy shout, 'Piper!'

'What?'

'I just asked you three times if I could borrow your leather jacket.'

'Oh, yeah, sure.'

'Are you okay?' Posy asked.

'What do you mean?'

'Well, you seem so distracted all the time.'

Piper pulled her schoolbag higher on her shoulder. 'I guess I am.'

'Is it because of Luke's sister?'

'Yes, and other stuff.'

'Like what?'

Piper shrugged. 'Just stuff.'

'Stuff to do with Luke?' Posy persisted.

'Yeah.'

'Are you and he breaking up?'

'No.'

'Do you think he fancies someone else?'

'No.'

'Do you think he's been with another girl?'

'No, Posy, it's nothing like that. Just forget it.' Piper cursed her stupidity. Posy would never let it go now that she was convinced something was wrong with Piper's relationship.

'OMG, did you find out he's gay?'

'Jesus, Posy, no!'

'Well, then, what's going on?'

'Nothing.'

'But you said – Ouch!' Posy squealed.

The twins had come up behind her and pulled her ponytail.

'Do you have any money?' Penny asked Piper.

'No, and you still owe me the tenner I lent you last week,' Piper reminded her.

'I'm starving.' Penny groaned.

'Stop moaning, we'll be home in ten minutes.' Piper had no patience for her sisters today. She wanted to lie down and sleep for a while in peace and quiet.

'Come on, Piper, you're our older sister. You're supposed to buy us stuff,' Poppy said.

'Sod off,' Piper snapped. 'I'm not in the mood.'

'God, you're so narky, these days,' Penny moaned. 'You used to be fun, but now we can't say anything without you biting our heads off.'

'Yeah, seriously, chill, Piper,' Poppy added. 'You've got so boring. I'm never going out with someone if it turns me into a granny like you.'

Penny laughed and started hobbling like an old woman. 'I'm Piper. I used to be fun but now I'm a boring girlfriend, who's always in a grump.'

Piper's blood boiled. 'I'm sick of the lot of you. All you ever think about is yourselves. Luke is donating his bone marrow to Jess and it's a big operation and I'm worried about it and him and Jess and everything. I hope I never get cancer because I know you'd never give me your bone marrow because you're so bloody selfish.' She burst into tears.

Her three sisters stopped walking and stared at her.

'I'll give you my bones if you get cancer, Piper, I promise.' Posy was upset.

'It's not your bones, you idiot, it's bone marrow,' Penny said. 'You can't give someone your bones. How could you walk if you gave Piper your leg bone?'

'I'd give Piper my leg bone if she wanted it,' Posy said. 'Piper, you can have any part of my body that you need.'

Piper tried to smile but grimaced instead.

'Jeez, Piper, I'm sorry if we upset you. We were just joking around,' Poppy said.

'I'd give my bone marrow if you needed it,' Penny said. 'As long as they gave me loads of painkillers so I was totally out of it.'

'We could give you half each,' Poppy noted. 'Then it wouldn't be so bad for either of us. Penny'd give you a bit and I'd give you a bit. A two-for-the-price-of-one deal.'

'Perfect.' Penny pulled her scarf over her face as a cold gust of winter wind blew across the park.

'So, you see, we're not selfish,' Posy said. 'We'd all help you.'

'Thanks,' Piper said, putting her arm around Posy. 'Sorry, I'm just tired, I guess.'

'Luke will be fine,' Penny assured her.

'Totally. He's as strong as Conor McGregor and he'll bounce back super-fast,' Poppy added.

'Yeah, he's like Superman,' Posy said.

Piper shivered. 'Come on, let's go home. It's freezing.'

The twins began to argue about which organ they'd be willing to donate to each other if they needed it.

Piper let their conversation wash over her as she prayed all would be well with Luke, the bone marrow and the baby growing inside her.

Bobby's Diary

Jess has Luke's fighter cells transplanted inside her now and they're going to kick all Jess's bad cells down and punch them and kill them, and Mummy said that hopefully now Jess will go from parshell remishen to complete remishen. And now Jess will get to come home and that is very good news for me. Someone to lissen to me at last!

Everyone is happy cos we ALL know that Luke's cells will make Jess better. When Mummy came home from the hospital with Luke after they took the fighter cells out of him, Granddad hugged Luke and he haded tears in his eyes. He kept saying, 'I'm proud of you, Luke, so proud.'

When Nathalie sawed Granddad with tears she got tears in her eyes. Nathalie never cries! She's super-tuff.

Granddad says that French women are tuff cookies but that they are also very forgiving cos they turn a blind eye to their husbands wanderings. I don't really understand Granddad sometimes, but he seems to think that the French women being blind in one eye and letting their husbands wander about is a good thing. I think it sounds dangerous. Besides, Nathalie has two normal eyes so I don't get it. Maybe French women go blind in one eye when they get married? But then why wood anyone want to get married?

Jess can come home soon wich is making everyone super-happy. Mummy is all smiley now and I hearded her singing in the shower yesterday.

Luke is super-happy too cos everyone keeps saying how great he is for helping Jess. Even Daddy said it!

He came over to Granddad's house and told Luke he was super-proud of him. Luke shrugged like he didn't care but I could tell he did cos his face went all red.

Granddad normally doesn't even speak to Daddy but he offered him a cup of coffee! Daddy said he'd love one but then his phone rang and he had to go. Jenny had some mergensy.

'She probably broke a nail,' Luke said, and me and Granddad and Mummy laughed. It was nice to see Mummy laughing. I felt all warm inside.

So, that's the good news. The bad news is that the play in school is a disaster and I don't want to be in it any more.

First of all it took Declan ages to say 'Are there any rooms free?' He got stuck on 'There' and T isn't even one of his bad letters! I think maybe he was nervous. Anyway, I decided to help him out so when we praktised the same lines again, I saw him begining to stuter on 'There', so I said: 'Don't bother asking for a room, Joseph. This inn is full.'

Declan got all grumpy and pushed me and said I was robbing his lines. Except it took him ages to say 'robbing', he got stuck on the R, which is one of his bad letters, so I said it for him but it made him even more crazy.

I know Mrs Lorgan said no one should finish Declan's words because it is important for him to speak for himself, but he was so red in his face I thawt he might have a heart attack so I was trying to help. I don't think Mrs Lorgan will be too happy if one of the kids in her class dies.

Declan pushed me really hard after I said 'robbing' and I banged my elbow on the side of a chair and it hurt. But Mrs Lorgan didn't even ask me if I was alrite. She said 'Let Declan say his lines and do not interupt.'

It's just so dum. Every time we practise the play, the first bit with Mary and the angel Gabriel takes about five minutes and then Declan/Joseph comes in and starts stutering and we all have to stand around and wait . . . and wait.

But Declan isn't the only problem. Tommy is being a total pain. He finaly agreed to be the donkey but today, every time I tried to say my lines he made a 'neigh neigh' sound really loud so no one could hear me.

Mrs Lorgan told him to stop but he said he was just getting into his part as the donkey. Mrs Lorgan was called out for a 'quik word' by the gym teacher and she told us to practise again. Tommy did the noise again. So I shouted at him to stop.

He shouted back, 'It's the same as you robbing Declan's lines.'

I had enuff of Tommy so I told him he was a rubbish donkey and that he was stupid becos a donkey says 'hee-haw' and a horse says 'neigh'.

Tommy said that knowing boring facts doesnt make me smart, it makes me weird. He said no one in the class is intrested in my stupid facts and that his Mum said I was 'special', like his brother with Down Sindrum.

'You're special needs,' Tommy said.

'I am not. I'm smart.'

'You're a weirdo,' Tommy said.

'Yeah,' Declan joined in, 'you're a d-d-d-d—'

'Dork?' Tommy tried to help Declan.

Declan shook his head. 'D-d—'

'Dickhead?' Tommy wispered.

Declan shook his head again. 'D-d—'

'Dumbass?' Tommy tried again.

'No!' Declan shouted. 'D-dweeb.'

I hate them all, even Mrs Lorgan, and I know it's bad to hate your teecher but I do.

I was so glad when school was over and Mummy came to collect me. I love when she comes to collect me. She used to all the time but since Jess got sick it's only some times. But when she does we have a chat on the walk home and she asks me things and it feels like everything isn't different and scary. I let

her hold my hand and I don't care who sees.
I like holding her hand. It makes me feel
safer.

When we got home, Mummy didn't rush off to
make phone calls or to go to the hospital. She
made me a hot choclate and sat down and talked
to me. She asked me about school and I was
going to tell her all about the play but then
Nathalie came in and said there was a man who
wanted to tell Mummy that the coffee was the
best he ever had. Mummy looked confused.

'Who is it?'

'I don't know. A hairy man who say you tell
him the coffee 'ere is fantastic and he agree
with you.'

Mummy went to peep out the door into the
café and then she did a big smile. I looked
out to see who she was smiling at.

She walked over to a man with a big beard
and crinkly eyes. They had a little chat and
then I heard her say about Jess and the remishen. The beardy man put his arms up in the
air and cheered and Mummy laughed.

'He is not perfect. *Un peu* caveman. But the
beard can be fixed and he has nice eyes and a
kind smile. He's not so bad,' Nathalie said.

I don't know what she was talking about. I
think maybe she's in love with the beardy
man. I was going to tell her about French
women getting married and going blind in one
eye and not knowing where there husbands
went wandering off to, but it's a bit confus-
ing so I'll let Granddad tell her.

23

Kate stood at the kitchen window, looking out over the small garden. There was nothing much to see on the cold December morning, but suddenly the bare tree looked beautiful, not bleak. She could hear birds twittering and a dog barking in the distance. It was as if a fog had been lifted from her. Kate couldn't remember seeing or hearing things clearly for months.

She felt lighter and younger. The constant headache had lifted and the tension in her neck was gone. Jess was in partial remission and Luke's bone marrow would get her into complete remission. Kate knew it was going to work. Jess looked better already. They had to wait four weeks until they could test to see if she was in complete remission, and Kate was determined to make those four weeks wonderful and distract them all from the waiting.

The fact that the weeks fell over the Christmas period was perfect. Another good sign that all would be well. It was a turning point. She could feel it in her bones. Their lives were going to get better. Jess would get well and they'd be happy again. She was even getting on well with Nick. Life was good right now. Kate was determined to grab the 'good' with both hands.

Recently her life had shrunk to home and hospital, but today she was taking Jess horse-riding. She was so happy that Jess was getting a chance to ride again. She knew it would give her a great lift.

Hazel had organized it. She said it was her Christmas present to Jess. She'd rung Kate and insisted on doing it.

'Chloë told me how much Jess loves riding, so please let me do this for her,' Hazel had said. 'We love Jess and we feel so helpless, so you'd be doing me a favour by letting me sort this out.'

It was amazing, really. Kate didn't know Hazel well. They had that mothers-of-kids-who-are-friends relationship – a little chat on the doorstep here and there, but that was it. They were different. Hazel lived a life of luxury, and Kate could barely pay her bills, so she felt they didn't have much in common, yet since Jess had been diagnosed, Hazel had been incredibly kind.

Aside from buying Jess clothes and treats that Chloë brought in on her visits, Hazel constantly texted Kate to check in with her. One particularly bad day during Jess's infection, Kate had come home to a big box of Jo Malone shower gels, candles and perfumes. There it was, sitting on the doorstep, with a big bow and a note that said, 'Thinking of you. Hazel.'

Kate had always liked Chloë, but she had worried that Chloë was a bit spoilt. How wrong she was. Chloë did have everything a girl could dream of, but it hadn't made her spoilt at all. In fact, she was the most generous, loyal friend Jess could possibly have had. Some of Jess's other friends had made an effort in the beginning, but they had gradually tailed off when Jess never returned to school.

Chloë, however, was ever-present. Kate had grown very fond of her. She bounded into the hospital in her bright clothes talking non-stop about things a twelve-year-old should be talking about – annoying classmates, boys, make-up, hairstyles, clothes . . . Kate loved seeing Jess giggling with Chloë about silly things. It made her worry less about Jess's childhood being stolen.

She heard footsteps and turned around. Luke opened the fridge and began pulling out mounds of food. Luke, her hero. Kate smiled at him. 'Morning.'

'Hey,' he croaked, and began to fry some eggs.

'Sit down, I'll do that for you.' Kate went over to the cooker. 'Four eggs? Seriously?'

Luke cut three big slices of granary bread. 'The coach is still saying I have to get my protein intake up. Besides, I finally feel hungry again so I'm going for it.'

'I'm really proud of you, Luke.'

'For making the team?' Luke grinned.

'Yes, and for helping to save your sister.'

Luke squirmed in his chair. 'I wish everyone would stop saying that, Mum. I didn't save her. She's not cured yet. I just helped.'

'Well, thank you.'

'Sure.'

Kate lifted the fried eggs onto a plate and handed it to Luke. 'So how are things with you? Is everything all right with school and Piper?'

Luke shovelled a full egg into his mouth and chewed. 'School is okay. Piper is good. She was so happy about Jess she cried for half an hour, like rivers of tears. We're going to catch a movie later.'

'She's lovely. I'm really glad you met her.'

Kate watched a smile spread across Luke's face. 'Yeah, she's pretty great. I'm lucky.'

'She's lucky too. You're pretty fantastic yourself.'

Luke flexed his arm. 'Yeah, I'm not bad.'

Kate coughed. 'So are you guys . . .'

Luke put his hand up. 'Stop. Don't even go there.'

'Luke, I need to know that if you're having sex you're being careful.'

Luke put down his slice of bread. 'You're ruining my appetite. Please stop talking.'

'Luke? I need to know.'

'Oh, God.' Luke looked down at his food, blushing. 'Yes, Mum, we are careful.'

'Good.'

The door opened and Jess came in. 'Morning,' she said, beaming.

Kate jumped up. 'Morning, sweetheart. How did you sleep? How do you feel? Sit down and I'll get you something to eat.'

Jess shook her head. 'I'm fine, Mum. I'll get my own breakfast. I'd like to. Let me make you a cup of coffee.'

'Don't be silly. Sit down and save your energy.'

'Mum!' Luke caught her eye. 'Let Jess do it. She wants to.'

Kate did as she was told. It felt very strange to be sitting still while Jess made her coffee. She wanted to jump up and carry the kettle for her. Jess's arms were like two little twigs and Kate was worried she'd drop the kettle or burn herself when she poured the hot water into the coffee cup, or trip or stumble or . . . Breathe, she told herself. Breathe and let Jess do this.

It was very difficult, but Kate managed to stay seated and not jump up, although she almost did when Jess made a little 'oof' sound, as she picked up the heavy kettle. As she moved to help her, Luke reached out and grabbed her hand. 'Don't, Mum,' he whispered. 'She wants to feel normal again. Stop fussing.'

Jess came over with a cup of coffee and placed it in front of her. 'There you go, Mum.' She was smiling from ear to ear.

Kate took a sip. 'Well, that's the nicest cup of coffee I ever tasted.'

Jess rolled her eyes. 'You don't have to say that.'

'It is, though, Jess, because you made it.'

'Favourite child!' Luke exclaimed. 'I always knew it.'

'I don't think so, Golden Boy,' Jess retorted.

'Yeah, right.' Luke swatted his sister with his hand, grinning. 'It's always been "Jess is so helpful", "Jess is so thoughtful", "Jess is so perfect".'

'That's such rubbish. It's all "Luke is so great at rugby", "Luke is so handsome", "Luke is such a good example to the other two".'

'Well, I am.' Brother and sister laughed.

Watching her two children bantering back and forth, laughing together, looking so happy made Kate want to jump up and down and shout, '*Yeeeeees!*' Life was almost back to normal, and it felt so good. She took out her phone and texted Maggie: *Good news! All going well with Jess. Get yourself over here later if you can. I'm opening the pink champagne tonight!* x

Kate drove towards a huge house, then followed the signs for 'Stables' around the back and down a laneway that led into a large yard.

'Wow,' Jess said. 'This is incredible. Look at that horse, Mum! It's so beautiful.'

Kate watched as it was led out of the stables. It looked like a thoroughbred racehorse, the kind you'd see at the races.

Hazel had said something about a friend of theirs who had horses and would be delighted to have Jess up for a ride. This was like a professional riding stable. Kate could see at least ten horses peeping out from their boxes.

A huge black Range Rover pulled up beside them and Chloë waved out of the window.

Kate and Jess got out of the car. Kate wrapped Jess's scarf around her neck. 'Are you sure you're warm enough?'

'Oh, Mum – yes!' Jess wriggled away from her and ran over to Chloë. The two girls hugged.

Kate joined Hazel, who was wearing a long fur coat that must have taken many animals to make.

'Hi,' Hazel said warmly, and hugged Kate, then Jess.

'Your coat is so soft,' Jess said.

'She's a murderer,' Chloë said. 'It's rabbit. Real rabbit fur. Hundreds of poor bunnies died so Mum could wear that coat.'

Hazel stroked it. 'Darling, there are far too many rabbits in the world. They're not exactly an endangered species.'

'They will be if you keep buying coats like that,' Chloë reprimanded.

'Kate and Jess didn't come here to listen to a save-the-rabbits speech. Now, come on, Julian's waiting for us.'

Julian turned out to be the stable manager. He was lovely with the girls. He introduced Jess to all the horses and told her he'd picked a very special one for her to ride.

'This place is amazing,' Kate said. 'Thanks so much for arranging it.'

'My friend Louise got it in the divorce settlement.'

'Some settlement,' Kate noted.

Hazel dropped her voice. 'She found her husband in bed with one of the stable boys – I know it sounds like a Jilly Cooper novel, but it actually happened.'

Kate giggled.

'He didn't want anyone to know, so he gave her everything she wanted in the divorce.'

'Is she here? I'd like to thank her.'

'No, she hates horses. She spends all of her time at her house in Turks and Caicos.'

Kate was incredulous. 'Why did she want the stables if she hates horses?'

Hazel raised an eyebrow. 'Because she didn't want him to have them. I'd be the same if my Keith cheated on me, I'd take the house in Portugal even though it's on a golf course and I hate golf. You've got to get them where they hurt.'

Nick didn't have anything for me to take, Kate thought. All he had were debts.

Jess and Chloë came out riding two gorgeous brown horses with shiny manes.

'Mum, my horse is called Jess!' Jess said.

'She's the best we have.' Julian winked.

Kate went over to have a word with him. 'Is she a calm horse? Jess cannot fall off – it would be a disaster.'

'Don't worry,' Julian said. 'Hazel filled me in. Jess is going to have a great time and be completely safe. If it's any comfort at all, my niece had leukaemia when she was a kid. She's twenty-seven now, got married last week.'

Kate wanted to kiss him. 'That's a huge comfort, thank you. I love hearing stories like that.'

'Come on, Julian, let's go!' Jess called out.

'Jess, don't be rude.'

'She's not rude, just keen. We like that. All right, let's go to the indoor arena and have some fun.'

To Hazel and Kate, he said, 'Ladies, I'll get one of the lads to make coffee for you. He'll bring it into the arena. It'll keep you warm while you're watching. What would you like?'

'I'll have a decaf skinny latte, please,' Hazel asked.

'Can you do lattes?' Kate was amazed.

'We have the best coffee machine in town. Louise gave it to us last Christmas.' Julian smiled.

'Wow! I'd love a cappuccino.'

Indoor arenas, coffee delivered to you by stable-hands . . . This was the life, Kate thought. She should have married a millionaire.

As she walked to the arena with Hazel, she muttered, 'I married for love the first time, but if I ever get married again, it'll be for money. I could get used to this.'

Hazel laughed. 'It's nice, all right. Not having to worry about money is a huge thing. Believe me, I know. My dad died when I was four and Mum brought me and my three brothers up on very little money. As Keith always says, "You weren't born to money, Hazel, but you certainly got used to it very quickly."'

They both cracked up laughing.

'The thing is, though, when you look at Jess and what's happened, you realize that money means nothing, really,' Hazel said. 'Health is wealth, right?'

'Yes,' Kate said. Her mother used to say that. 'It really is. It's strange, I never thought about the kids getting sick. I always worried about them being in car crashes, or drowning in swimming pools or falling out of trees, but never, ever cancer.'

'I know what you mean. When I think cancer I think older people, breast cancer or prostate, never a young girl,' Hazel agreed.

A stable boy arrived with their coffee and a plate of chocolate biscuits. They thanked him.

Kate took a sip: the coffee was delicious. She watched Jess as Julian guided her carefully over a small jump and praised her. Jess beamed.

She looked so much smaller than Chloë now. She was so thin and frail. Beside her, Chloë was a picture of health. Jess's stick-like legs clung to the saddle in jodhpurs that were once almost too small for her but now flapped about her thighs like flags.

'She's a great kid, Kate, and you're a brilliant mum. I don't know how you do it. I can barely cope with Chloë. I'd have liked more kids but . . . well . . .'

'What happened?' Kate asked gently.

'I had really bad haemorrhaging after Chloë was born and they had to do a hysterectomy.'

'I'm sorry.'

'Yeah, me too. I'd have liked her to have siblings. We thought about adopting, but Keith wasn't keen on social workers poking their noses into our lives and our finances. So we agreed that we'd stick with Chloë and give her the best life possible.'

'Well, you're certainly doing that.'

Hazel nodded, and Kate saw that her eyes were full of tears. Suddenly they had gone from idle chit-chat on the doorstep to a very intense personal conversation. It happened to Kate all the time now. Whenever she bumped into someone there was no small-talk about the weather or how the café was doing, people told her really personal things. She didn't know why. Maybe it was because her life was so serious now and they wanted to relate to her somehow by telling her their stories of struggle. Or maybe they wanted to have proper conversations about real issues but hadn't known how to do it before. Whatever the reason, in the last few months Kate had found out more about people than she ever had before Jess became ill.

Chloë cantered towards a small jump, but pulled up her horse in front of it. 'I can't do it.'

Jess cried, 'Come on, Chloë, if I can do it with cancer, you can too.'

'Maybe cancer makes you braver,' Chloë replied.

Jess looked thoughtful. 'Maybe it does. I guess when you face dying, nothing else seems very scary.'

'You see? It's easier for you,' Chloë said.

Hazel stood up to scold her, but Kate pulled her down. 'Don't. Please. It's good for Jess to talk freely about her cancer. I've never heard her do it before so she's obviously feeling very relaxed. It's great that Chloë isn't tiptoeing around her.'

Jess squeezed her horse with her legs and soared easily over the jump. 'See? It's not hard.'

Julian, tactfully saying nothing, pulled Chloë's horse back around.

'When I get close, I panic. What do you do when you're just in front of the jump?' Chloë asked Jess.

Jess patted her horse's neck. 'I close my eyes and trust the horse. A horse won't let you down if you trust it. They have to feel like you're their friend. When I jump, I feel like I'm flying. I feel like nothing can touch me or hurt me. Like I'm free from . . . well, everything, like pain and cancer.'

Kate gripped her hands together. While it was lovely to hear Jess talking freely about cancer, it was also incredibly difficult. She hated her daughter having these thoughts, that her grasp of life's cruellest lessons had been forced on her so young.

'She's amazing,' Hazel said quietly. 'She's so mature and brave.'

'I know,' Kate agreed. 'I just wish to God she didn't have to be. I wish her life was normal and carefree. Life gets so complicated when you're older. Kids should just be kids. She shouldn't have to deal with chemo and bone-marrow transplants and infections. She should just be horse-riding and going to school and having fun.'

Hazel put down her coffee cup. 'You're right. It's completely crap. But, you know, when she comes through this, Jess'll be even more extraordinary than she already is. The very first time I met Jess I said to Chloë, "There's something special about her. It's like she's been here before. She's got an old soul."'

'My mother used to say that about her,' Kate said. 'As well as that thing about health being wealth.' She felt a sudden pain in her heart. She wished her mother was there now.

She'd know what to do and say and how to reassure Kate that it was going to be okay. She'd tell her not to worry about the cancer coming back, to take the good news about the remission and trust it. She would have swept away Kate's nagging worry that it wasn't over yet.

She tried to remember the mindfulness teacher's advice: breathe and live in the moment. She focused on Jess's beaming face, not on her emaciated body. She concentrated on her daughter being in her happiest place, on the back of a horse, feeling free. She fought against the negative fears that were always there, crowded at the edge of her mind.

Please let it be over, she thought.

24

Nick handed Jenny a tissue and tried to be sympathetic. He was going to be late to pick up Jess now. Damn.

'I just feel so alone, Nick. You're always at work or visiting Jess, and I know she's sick and you need to spend time with her, but I seem to be the last person on your list of priorities. I miss you, and Jaden misses you too. I want you to have a good relationship with him. I want you to be best friends.'

Nick stiffened. 'My relationship with Jaden is fine. He's a baby, Jenny. All he wants is to eat and sleep.'

Jenny sniffled. 'You just don't get it, Nick. You form a bond with your baby from the minute they're born. It says so in all the books. You need to spend more time with Jaden and me. I hate being stuck in this apartment all day. When you do come home, you're always tired and narky.'

Nick tried to remain calm. He knew if he upset her he'd never get away. 'Look, Jenny, I know you're finding it all a bit difficult but I'm working my arse off to pay for everything for both families and I'm trying to be there for my daughter, who has cancer, and, yes, I am tired all the time. I'm tired and worried and really stressed about Jess.'

Jenny started crying. 'I just want it to be back to the way it was when we had fun and you looked after me and made me feel so special. I don't like this life. I don't think I'm made to be a mother. My own mother was shit at it and maybe I'm no good either. I find it really hard and scary. I keep panicking and thinking Jaden's going to get cancer and die, or something else terrible is going to happen to him. What if the cancer's genetic?'

Nick glanced at the clock. Damn. He was twenty minutes late. 'It's not genetic. Jaden's fine. Please, Jenny, you need to calm down. You're a great mother and Jaden is a really happy kid. Look, Jess's treatment will be over in a few months and she'll be well again, and we can all go back to normal.' He hoped he sounded more confident than he felt. Every time he looked at Jess he felt as if he was being punched in the chest. She was so sick.

He leant over and gave Jenny a hug. 'I've got to go. I promised Jess I'd pick her up. I'll come back tonight and cook you dinner and we'll open a bottle of wine. How about that?'

Jenny nodded. 'Sounds good. But be home by six. I want you to play with Jaden before he goes to bed. My dad was never around, and I want Jaden and you to be really close.'

Nick rushed out of the apartment and drove like a maniac to collect Jess. She was waiting at the front door for him, wrapped up in her winter coat.

'Sorry!' Nick said, as he hugged her. 'I'm really sorry. Did you text Larry to say we were running late?'

'Yes, it's fine. It's not like he's going anywhere,' Jess said, but she didn't smile.

'He'll be okay. He's a tough kid.'

Jess put on her seatbelt and looked out of the window. 'Not everyone gets better, Dad,' she said quietly.

Nick gripped the steering-wheel. 'But you will. Luke's bone marrow will cure you.'

Jess sighed. 'I wish everyone would stop telling me that. It might not. Some of the cancer is still in there. Luke's bone marrow may not cure me, Dad. Larry could die and so could I. That's a fact. Larry and Nathalie are the only people who actually let me say it.'

Nick slammed on the brakes to stop the car crashing into the one in front. The palms of his hands were damp with sweat. 'Please don't say that, Jess. We all just want you to get better and have the great life you deserve.'

'I want to get better too, but there's no guarantee. I can't make myself better. I'm trying, Dad, doing my best. I'm taking all the horrible drugs and praying and hoping and, well, I'm doing my best.' Jess began to cry.

Nick pulled into the car park and leant over to hug her. 'Oh, Jessie, I know you're trying, sweetheart. It's awful for you. I wish I could rip the cancer out of your body. But Luke's cells are going to cure you, I just know they are. Look at him – he's the fittest guy I know.' He tried not to get upset: he had to be strong for her. Jess's bird-like body trembled as she cried into his shoulder.

She pulled back and he handed her a tissue. Jess looked at herself in the mirror. 'I don't want Larry to know I've been crying.' She fished around in her bag and took out some make-up. Nick didn't like her wearing it – she seemed too young – but he wasn't going to stop her now.

Jess examined herself in the mirror. 'For a bald girl with cancer, I look okay.'

'You're beautiful, the most stunning girl in the world.'

She rolled her eyes. 'You have to say that. You're my dad.'

Nick smiled. 'True, but I mean it. I'm so proud of you, Jess, the way you're fighting this cancer. You've been so strong. We Higginses are warriors, and you get that from me. I know you'll be fine because you're not going to give up. None of us is going to give up until you're cured.'

Jess remained quiet. Nick was worried that maybe he'd come on too strong. But he wanted her to know that he was behind her and that it was vital she keep on fighting.

'Dad, can we go now?'

'Sure, of course.'

They walked into the hospital in silence, each lost in thought. Nick went with Jess to Haematology and Oncology and popped in to say hi to Larry. He seemed like a nice kid, but Nick didn't know him and didn't have time to get involved with any more kids. He made Jess laugh, though, and she seemed to like him so Nick was fine with that. He wanted Larry to get better, but he seemed to be getting worse. Nick didn't want Jess upset. He worried about the damage it would do to her morale if anything happened to Larry.

When Larry saw Jess his whole face lit up. 'Better late than never, I guess.' He grinned.

'Dad's fault,' Jess said.

'Sorry, I was late picking her up.'

''S okay. She's here now. So, what news from the outside world?'

Jess sat down on the side of his bed. 'I went horse-riding.'

'Did you fall off?'

'No! I was brilliant. I even did some jumps.'

'Bet it felt good.'

'Amazing. I didn't feel sick when I was riding. I was me again.'

'That's the best feeling. The longer you're sick, the harder it gets to forget.'

'I can see that. So how are you?'

'Not feeling too good. I think this chemo's going to kill me. It's the worst.'

'Yeah, but it'll make you better,' Nick said automatically. 'Stay positive.'

They both turned to face him.

'Seriously?' Larry raised an eyebrow.

Jess giggled. 'I know, they're all the same.'

'What?' Nick asked. 'I'm just trying to help. A positive attitude is important in all aspects of life.'

'It's also important to be able to be honest,' Larry said. 'I'm sorry, Mr H, but sometimes, after yet another day of puking your guts up into a bowl, feeling positive just isn't an option.'

Nick shuffled about uncomfortably. 'No, right – I mean, I get that. But in general it's good to stay focused and upbeat.'

'Is that for you or for us?' Larry looked directly at him.

'Well – I – for everyone,' Nick stuttered, unable to meet Larry's eye.

The door opened and a man came in. He handed Larry a bottle of water. 'Hi, Jess.'

'Hi, Mr Wilkinson. How are you?'

'Better for seeing you, thanks. You've come to visit?'

'Yep, can't keep me away.'

'You're some girl.' He smiled. Then, seeing Nick, he proffered a hand. 'Hi, I'm Norman, Larry's dad.'

'Nick, Jess's dad. Nice to meet you.' Nick moved towards the door, glad of the interruption and the opportunity to escape. 'I'll leave you guys to it. Is an hour enough time, Jess? I have to get back to the office for three.'

'Thanks, Dad.' Jess smiled.

Nick walked out, followed by Norman.

'She's a wonderful girl,' Norman said. 'It'll mean the world to Larry that she's come to visit.'

'Larry's a great kid. Jess is very fond of him.'

Norman smiled sadly. 'Yeah, he is. He can be a handful at times, but he's our pride and joy. He was a great footballer.'

'Really?' Nick said.

'Yep. Striker. We had every club in Dublin trying to poach him.'

'Wow. Well, I'm sure it'll take him a while to get back to form, but when he gets better he can go back to football.'

Norman shook his head. 'No, he's been out for eighteen months. His muscles are wasted. It'd take him years to get back to fitness and that's if . . . He's been in remission three times. We left here thinking it was over, but each time it came back. It gets harder to keep your hopes up.'

Nick didn't want to hear this. He wanted to hear the good stuff. He wanted to talk to the parents of kids who went into remission and stayed in remission. Kids who never came back. Kids who were back playing football and scoring goals. That was why he avoided the other parents on the ward. He didn't want to hear the bad stories. It was difficult enough to keep positive without hearing about other patients getting worse.

'Well, I'm sure he'll pull through. He seems like a tough boy.' He tried to move away.

'He is, Nick, but there are some things that, no matter how hard you try, you can't beat.'

'Well, hopefully he'll get a break this time. Kids are amazingly resilient. They're stronger than we think.'

'But not invincible.'

Fucking hell! Would this guy ever shove off? Nick did not want to listen to any negative talk. He refused to believe the worst could happen, no way. It was unthinkable.

'Well, I'm going to make a few work calls. Nice to meet you, Norman.'

'You, too, and you should be very proud of your lovely daughter.'

'I am, I really am.' Nick was choking up so he began to walk away. He *was* proud of Jess. So proud. She was his precious girl and he was damned if he was going to lose her.

25

Piper pulled at the waistband on her skirt. It wasn't going to close, no matter what. She rummaged around for a safety-pin.

There was a thump on the door.

'What the hell, Piper? I need to get my lip-gloss,' Penny shouted.

'Go away,' Piper snapped. She was in no mood for her sisters. Shit, shit, shit. Her stomach was beginning to grow and she still hadn't told Luke. She began to sweat as she imagined his face when she dropped the bombshell.

She pushed aside the twins' mounds of cheap make-up and found nothing. No safety-pin, no needle and thread, nothing to hold up her skirt. What the hell was she going to do?

'*Muuuuuum!* Piper's hogging the bathroom,' Penny roared.

'Open up, Piper. I need my hair spray.' Poppy shook the door handle.

God, this bloody house! You couldn't get a second's peace! Piper pulled her jumper down over her open skirt and flung the door open.

'There you go, you rude, ignorant pigs.' She stormed past her sisters.

'Jeez, relax,' Penny said.

'Yeah, seriously, who bit you in the arse?' Poppy said, and the twins giggled.

Piper went into her bedroom and slammed the door. Pauline was sitting up in bed with her laptop open on her knees. Piper began flinging drawers open and slamming them shut.

'What are you looking for? Maybe I can help before you tear the house down,' Pauline said.

'Don't you start! I just need a fucking safety-pin.' Piper kicked the bottom drawer of her bedside locker shut and sat down heavily on her bed.

Pauline opened her drawer and pulled out a little box of safety-pins, which she silently handed to her sister.

Piper muttered thanks and turned sideways to pin her skirt closed.

'I know,' Pauline said quietly.

'Know what?' Piper said, as she tried to close the safety-pin.

'I know why your skirt won't close.'

Piper stabbed herself with the pin. 'Ouch.' She was too distracted to pay attention to her sister's comment.

'Piper?'

'What? Jesus, I'm trying to concentrate here.' Piper snapped the safety-pin shut and breathed a sigh of relief.

Pauline got out of bed, went to the bedroom door and locked it.

'What are you doing?' Piper asked, picking up her schoolbag.

Pauline stared at her sister. 'Piper, I know.'

Piper froze. 'Know what?'

Pauline pointed to her stomach. 'I know you're pregnant.'

Piper's heart skipped a beat. 'What are you talking about?'

Pauline sat down on her bed opposite her sister. 'Piper, you can talk to me. I've known for a while, but I was waiting for you to tell me or Mum and Dad but you still haven't and you're going to start showing soon. How long are you planning on keeping it a secret?'

Piper sank down on her bed. 'I haven't told Luke yet.'

'Why not?' Pauline was clearly shocked.

'There's never a good time. Every time I go to tell him, something happens with Jess or rugby or – or – I dunno, life.' Piper pulled at a stray thread on her duvet cover. 'How did you guess?'

'Come on, we share a bedroom. I hear you tossing and turning at night and crying. I also heard you throwing up a couple of times and you keep touching your stomach.'

'Do you think anyone else has guessed?' Piper asked, her heart pounding.

Pauline laughed. 'You must be joking. The twins are far too self-obsessed, Posy is too young, Mum is too preoccupied with college and Dad probably thinks you're still a virgin.'

Piper winced. 'He's the one I'm dreading telling the most. He's going to be so disappointed in me.' She began to cry.

'I imagine he will be, very,' Pauline agreed.

'Thanks, Pauline, kick me while I'm down.' She sniffed.

'But he'll get over it. You've always been his favourite.'

Piper blew her nose. 'No, I'm not. Dad loves us all the same.'

Pauline snorted. 'No, he doesn't. He thinks the twins are vacuous, he likes Posy but finds her immature, and he doesn't get me at all. I'm far too serious for him.'

Piper felt uncomfortable because she knew Pauline was right. Piper was her dad's favourite and always had been.

Her mother was more subtle about which child she pre-ferred – Piper could see it was Posy, but Olivia was better at pretending she loved them all equally.

'How did it happen? You're a smart girl. Why didn't you use protection?'

'We were drunk and we didn't have any condoms and I thought a one-off would be okay if we were careful. I'm so stupid.' Piper covered her face with her hands and began to sob. Talking about it made it all so real. Suddenly it wasn't a little secret that she could ignore sometimes. It was real life. Piper was going to have a baby. She was going to be a teenage mother. Her life would never be the same. How the hell would she cope with a baby?

Pauline patted her awkwardly on the knee. Affection was not her sister's strong point so Piper appreciated the effort.

'Look, we all make mistakes. Well, some of us do. Anyway, the point is, what are you going to do? Do you want to have the baby? You don't have to, you know. If you want to go to London and have an abortion, I'll come with you.'

'Would you?' Piper was astounded.

Pauline nodded. 'Absolutely. Having a baby at eighteen could ruin your life, Piper. You've got to think very carefully about it. What if Luke doesn't want to know? What if you break up and you have to raise it on your own? How are you going to support it?'

Piper rubbed her eyes. She felt so weary. 'At first I was going to have an abortion, but now I don't want to. I kind of love the baby. I know I'm only about thirteen weeks gone but I feel protective of it. I can't get rid of it, I just can't.'

Pauline sighed. 'Think very carefully before making a final decision. You'll be this child's mother for the rest of your life. You may not be able to go to college or travel, like you wanted to, or have a successful career.'

'Come on, Pauline, lots of successful women have kids.'

'Not at eighteen they don't.'

'Well, I'm sure some of them do.'

Pauline stood up. 'All I'm saying is, deciding to have the baby will change your life for ever. So think carefully.'

Piper nodded. She thought about it all the time, but when it came down to getting rid of the baby or keeping it, her heart said, 'Keep it.'

'The thing is, Pauline, I saw Jess nearly die and it made me realize how precious life is. I can't get rid of this baby. I know it's going to change everything, I know Luke might break up with me, but I just can't have an abortion, even though I probably should.' Piper began to cry again.

There was a thump on the door. 'Hey, come on, narky head, you're going to be late for school. It's the Christmas carols today and I want to be on time,' Poppy called out.

Pauline went over to unlock the door. 'Before you make a final decision, Piper, you have to tell Luke. It's his baby, too. He should have a say in what happens, and at least you'll know where you stand with him. He might not react well. You need to be prepared for that.'

I am, Piper thought. I think he'll freak.

Luke hummed as he ate a huge bowl of egg noodles with chicken. Piper tried not to retch. The smell of chicken was one of her triggers. She was hoping the morning sickness would wear off soon.

'So where is everyone?' she asked.

'Mum's taken Jess and Bobby to get shoes and Granddad's working. So we have the place to ourselves for a while.' Luke grinned at Piper. 'When I've finished this, we could go to my room and hang out.'

Sex was the last thing on Piper's mind. Her stomach was twisting and turning. Now, she shouted inwardly, tell him now.

'So, uhm, Luke, there's something I need to talk to you about.'

Luke's phone pinged. He picked it up and laughed. 'Check out the photo Gavin just sent me.' He held his phone up so

Piper could see some lame photo of a donkey with a stupid sign on it. She wanted to get the phone and throw it across the room.

'So, anyway, as I was saying, I need to –'

Luke's phone rang. 'Hey, Gavin, hilarious pic, man,' he said, and began chatting about the upcoming rugby match. After missing the last one, he was hyped up about performing well this time.

Piper drummed her nails on the kitchen table and tried to resist the urge to turn the bowl of noodles upside-down on Luke's head. Yes, he was excited about the match, but what about the fact that she was sitting right in front of him, being ignored?

'Yeah, he was . . . He's a beast. Did you see the weights he was pumping? . . . I know . . . Savage session . . . I'm up for it, though. Bring on the match – we'll stuff those guys . . . No, they haven't a hope. They're not good upfront. Our forwards will kill them . . . Yeah . . . Yeah . . . I agree with you there . . .'

Piper's breathing was coming hard and fast. She'd had enough. Was Luke stupid, selfish or just immature? She'd told him she wanted to talk to him about something and he wasn't remotely interested or focused on her. Maybe he wasn't a great guy. Maybe Pauline was right – maybe he'd run a mile when he found out about the baby. Piper stared at her boyfriend. He was sitting in his school shirt and tie and he looked young. Too young to be a dad. Too young to have the responsibility of a baby.

'Dude, I know, he's class. Did you see his try last week? He was unstoppable . . . With Rocco on form, we're unbeatable . . . Yeah . . .'

Piper was wrong. She couldn't have this baby. They were kids themselves. How the hell could they possibly raise a child? They were still in school. What was she thinking? She should have had the abortion ages ago. Oh, God, it was a disaster. She must be mad thinking she could be a mum. Luke would dump her and she'd be living with her parents for the rest of her life – if they didn't kick her out when they found out she was up the pole at eighteen.

Piper stood up and rushed towards the door.

'Hey!' Luke called out.

Piper went to open the door but Luke grabbed her arm. 'Gotta go, Gavin,' he said into the phone, and threw his phone onto the countertop. 'Where are you going?' he asked.

'I have to get out of here.' Piper tugged at the door but Luke stopped her.

'What's wrong?'

'Nothing. Get out of my bloody way.'

Luke put his hands on her shoulders and made her turn to face him. 'Hey, Piper, what's going on? Talk to me.'

She looked down. She had no words. How do you tell your boyfriend that he's going to be a dad or else have to help pay for an abortion?

'Did something happen?' Luke's blue eyes were full of concern. 'Tell me. I'll fix it or help or whatever. Come on, Piper, it's me – you can tell me anything.'

Piper looked over his shoulder and tried to summon the courage and the words. Taking a deep breath she opened her mouth. 'It's –'

'Fuck, are you breaking up with me?' Luke moved away from her. 'That's it, isn't it?' Luke glared at her. 'Thanks a lot, Piper, thanks a fucking lot.'

Piper's blood pressure went through the roof. What the hell was wrong with Luke? Why couldn't he let her speak? 'WILL YOU SHUT UP AND LISTEN!' she screamed.

She had his attention now. Piper walked past him and stood at the opposite end of the room. 'I have to tell you something and I don't really know how to do it so I'm just going to blurt it out.'

'You cheated on me. Oh, Jesus, who with?' Luke's face darkened. 'Was it Harry? It'd better not be him.'

'Jesus, Luke, will you shut the fuck up!' Piper roared. 'I didn't cheat on you. I'm pregnant.'

Luke stared at Piper, his mouth hanging open like a fish's. She'd never seen anyone look so shocked. She'd wanted to tell him in a calm way, but he'd ruined it. She stood still and waited.

'Are you serious?' he eventually said.

'I can promise you this is no joke.'

'Like, how, when, what?' Luke's brow creased as he struggled to process the information.

Piper pulled out a chair and sat down. She felt exhausted. 'I guess it must have happened that night after you'd had the terrible dinner with your dad and we got drunk and you wanted to have sex but we didn't have any condoms.'

Luke sat down opposite her. 'But that was ages ago. I mean, what . . .'

'I think I'm about thirteen weeks pregnant,' she said.

'Why the hell didn't you tell me?'

Piper sighed. 'I tried. I tried to a million times, but something always happened, like Jess got the infection or you got dropped from the team or you had to donate bone marrow . . . Every single time I went to tell you, something got in the way.'

'Jesus, Piper, you should have just pulled me aside and told me. We see each other all the time. *Thirteen weeks?* You've known for all that time?'

Piper said nothing.

Luke chewed his thumbnail. 'A baby? What are we going to do? I mean, we're eighteen. We can't have a kid, can we? How can I tell Mum I've knocked you up when she's got so much shit to deal with? I can't do that to her. I just . . . What do you . . . What the hell are we going to do?'

Piper felt his fear and worry land heavily on her shoulders. She had to be calm and try to stay level-headed. She wished Luke would wrap his arms around her and tell her not to worry, that he'd fix it all or make it go away. But how could he? There was no magic wand for this.

'God, your dad! He'll kill me.' Luke's mind was racing.

Piper didn't care about her dad right now. She cared about what they were going to do. Luke hadn't mentioned abortion yet. She'd have to bring it up. Maybe he was afraid to.

'Well, my dad doesn't necessarily need to know. No one does.'

Luke stared across the table at her. Piper could almost see his mind working overtime. Biting his lip he said, 'Is that something you . . . I mean, is that what you want?'

Piper felt her throat closing over with stress and anxiety. 'I don't know what I want,' she croaked. 'I'm so confused and worried. I feel so alone.'

Luke came over and sat beside her. He held her hands. 'I'm here for you, babe. You're not alone. I'll do whatever you want to do.'

'Can we really bring up a baby?' Piper asked him.

Luke shrugged. 'I dunno. I guess technically we could, but . . . well, it would change everything. We'd be like parents and have to get jobs and an apartment and stuff.'

Piper was crying now. 'I don't want to give up my life, but I don't want to get rid of the baby either. It feels wrong.'

'It isn't, though. I mean, if we did go for an abortion, it would just be a decision. It's not wrong or bad or anything.'

'I know that, Luke, but I can feel the baby inside me. Maybe I'm imagining it, but I think I can. I'd feel so bad if I got rid of it.'

Luke rubbed her index finger. 'Well, then, we'll have it and just work it out. I can get a job and maybe study for a sport and performance degree at night.'

'What am I going to do? Sit in a tiny apartment all day with a baby?' Piper asked. She knew she was being unreasonable. Luke was just trying to figure things out, but suddenly she saw herself stuck at home, alone with a baby.

'No, you could work and study too. The baby could go to a nanny or crèche or something.'

'Do you have any idea how much that costs? Crèches and nannies are really expensive.'

'Piper, I'm trying here. Maybe your mum could mind the baby.'

'Why should she? She's busy.'

Luke was incredulous. 'Well, my mum can't. She's already looking after a sick child. There's no way we can dump a baby on her.'

Piper pulled her hands away. 'Well, you're not dumping this kid on my family to raise. It's your baby, too, and if you hadn't been so bloody insistent on having unprotected sex, I wouldn't be bloody well pregnant.'

Luke glared at her. 'Oh, so it's my fault. I don't remember you telling me to back off or pushing me away, Piper. I seem to remember you enjoying it.'

'I'm not saying it's your fault,' Piper said. 'I'm just . . . I'm scared, Luke.'

'Look, we don't need to have this stress in our lives. I can call Maggie. She'd help us, I know she would. And she wouldn't be judgemental. She'd find a clinic in London that could do the abortion, a good place, and we could stay with her for a few days. I could pretend to Mum that we'd just decided to go to London to visit Maggie. No one would find out.'

Piper paused. Now that she had told Luke, the reality of having a baby and raising it was hitting her hard. How could she bring up a baby when she was still living with her parents in an already cramped house? There was so much she wanted to do and see and experience. A baby would ruin all her plans. What if she broke up with Luke? It was possible: a baby would put their relationship under huge pressure.

Luke would get to walk away, but she'd be stuck with the baby. The woman always was. She could end up as a single mother, sitting in a bedsit all day long, living on welfare. Her stomach lurched. She didn't want that. She wanted a life full of adventure and excitement.

Maybe Luke was right. If Maggie could sort it out, then no one would have to find out and they could just do it and move on. Forget it had ever happened.

'Call Maggie. Let's see if she'll help and then we'll make a decision,' Piper said.

Luke picked up his phone, dialled Maggie's number and put the phone on loudspeaker.

She picked up after one ring. 'Is everything okay?' she asked, sounding worried.

'Everything's fine. Jess is good.'

'Oh, thank God! When I saw your number I almost had a heart attack.'

'Sorry, didn't mean to stress you out,' Luke said. 'Actually, Maggie, do you have a minute? I'm here with Piper and we need to talk to you about something.'

'Of course. Hi, Piper.'

'Hi, Maggie.' Piper twisted her fingers nervously as Luke took a deep breath and filled Maggie in on their situation. Maggie let him talk and said nothing until Luke finished. 'So we don't know what to do, but we think maybe we'll have an abortion, but we're not sure.'

'Well, I certainly wasn't expecting that. No pun intended,' she said.

Luke and Piper laughed weakly.

'Look, guys, this is a very serious decision. Luke, you've only just found out. You need to think about it for a few days. Taking some time to process the situation is important. Whatever decision you make, you must both be happy with it. If you have this baby, you will be parents to it for the rest of your lives. You don't get to walk away or change your mind. If you have an abortion, that decision will stay with you, too, but you will move on and it certainly gives you more options for your future. You are very young, and having a baby is a huge responsibility. Think very carefully about it all. But whatever you decide to do, I'll help you. I can arrange for you to be seen at a very good clinic over here, or if you decide to keep the baby I'll help you financially. But just remember, a baby is for life.'

Luke and Piper nodded. 'Thanks, Maggie,' Luke said. 'You're brilliant.'

'I'm here for you, Luke. You're the closest thing to family I have, so anything you need, just call. Now, can I talk to Piper privately, please?'

Luke raised an eyebrow. 'Uhm, sure.' He handed the phone to Piper.

He left the room. Piper switched the phone off loudspeaker and held it to her ear. 'Maggie?'

'Are you alone?'

'Yes.'

'Right, here's the deal. I'm going to be blunt with you because you seem like a great girl and I want the best for you and for Luke, who I adore. As the mother, you are going to be landed with bringing up this baby. Maybe you and Luke will make it. Maybe you'll get married and have other kids and things will work out great. But there is a big chance they might not. You need to think about that. You also need to think about your future and what you want to do with your life. Do you really want to be tied down at eighteen?'

Piper's head was spinning. Everything Maggie was saying she had thought about. It seemed that, suddenly, they were all leaning towards an abortion and it made sense. It made sense in every way but one: Piper loved this baby.

'Just put yourself first and think about it,' Maggie was saying. 'This is your choice, ultimately. Call me in a few days and let me know your decision. I'll do everything I can to help.'

'Thank you, Maggie. I really appreciate it.'

'No problem. I've gotta fly to a meeting now. Call me when you know what you want to do.'

Piper ended the call as Luke walked back into the kitchen. They stared at each other in silence. She knew he was wondering what her decision would be, and she was wondering what conclusion he'd reach. It was like that game she'd played as a kid, where someone thought of a number and you had to guess what it was. She was trying to read his mind. But this wasn't a game, and she wasn't a kid any more. This was possibly the biggest decision she would ever make in her life.

26

Chloë held Jess's hand as she led her into the classroom. Jess was shaking. Her legs felt like jelly. Mrs Fingleton had heard she was out of hospital and had invited her to come into school for a couple of hours, if she felt well enough.

Jess hadn't really wanted to go. She knew everyone would be staring at her and that it would feel weird. But then again, she did want to go because she wanted to feel normal again and going to school was what she would normally be doing.

When she'd tried on her uniform the night before, the skirt had literally slid to the floor and her shirt was like a tent. 'Try it on with this belt,' Mum had said.

But even with the belt, the skirt looked ridiculous. Her mother had turned around, pretending to look for socks, but Jess knew she was upset. Seeing herself in her uniform, with no hair and so skinny, was frightening. It was a punch in the face. The reality of what she had been through physically was plain to see. She was a different person now. The old Jess, who had filled out the uniform and sat in school with her thick hair in a ponytail, was gone.

'Just wear what you want, pet. Mrs Fingleton will understand. I'll text her tonight to explain,' her mother said.

Jess was relieved. At least now she could wear something that fitted her and she could hide her skinny arms under the cool sweatshirt that Chloë's mum had bought her.

Her mum had even let Jess put on a little bit of make-up. Just some foundation and some lip-gloss, but it had made her feel better. She knew she was as pale as a ghost and she didn't want everyone feeling sorry for her. She wore the black beanie hat with the diamanté and a pair of silver hoop earrings that her dad had bought her. She hated being bald, but the hat and the earrings were a distraction. She looked as good as she could under the circumstances. She did the breathing Mum had taught her from her mindfulness course and tried to calm her fluttering nerves.

She fiddled with the mask her mother wanted her to wear. She had promised to wear it to protect herself from germs but there was no way she was walking into that classroom with it over her mouth.

Chloë chatted away beside her. '. . . and Denise is, like, pretending she's your best friend ever. She keeps saying how much she misses you and how she's on WhatsApp to you all the time. Like, hello? I'm your best friend and Denise is just, like, a drama queen, attention-seeker. It makes me sick. Judy just sits there and agrees with everything she says. That girl has no personality, honestly. She's like Denise's lapdog. It's pathetic.' Chloë bounced along the corridor, pulling Jess with her.

Jess loved being with Chloë, who always cheered her up, but today she found her exhausting. She was so full of energy, life and chat that after the ten minutes they'd been together Jess wanted to lie down and sleep. She was wishing for the quiet of her house, sitting with Mum and just talking quietly or reading or watching movies together. She didn't want to be here. She didn't want to have to make small-talk with the girls in her class. She wanted to turn around and run.

She let go of Chloë's hand. 'Chloë, I can't . . . I just . . .'

Chloë grabbed her shoulders. 'Hey, I get it. You're worried it's going to be way too full-on with everyone crowding you and asking you about the cancer. Don't worry, Mrs Fingleton told everyone to leave you alone and just be normal.' Chloë snorted. 'Like any of *them* could be normal! Anyway, I'm your bodyguard today and I'll tell anyone who's annoying to piss off. I can be a bitch and they'll still be nice to me because of Dad being loaded. They all want to swim in my pool and play tennis and stuff.'

Jess grinned. 'Thanks.'

'By the way, how's Larry? Still "just friends".'

Jess smiled. 'Yes, Chloë, we are just friends. He's okay. He's had a tough few weeks, but he sounded stronger yesterday. I'll see him in three days when I go back in for chemo.'

Chloë stopped outside the classroom. 'I'd say he's a super-hottie with hair. It's such a pain that you have to go back to hospital. I wish the stupid cancer would just disappear. I really miss you, Jess.'

'Me too,' Jess said.

'Are you ready?'

Jess nodded. With Chloë by her side, she'd be fine.

Jess saw her mum standing in the car park, waiting anxiously to see how she'd got on. She ran over and hugged her.

'Was it awful?' Kate asked.

'No ... Well, kind of ... It was just weird. I felt like an outsider.'

Jess had felt like an alien. Everyone had been very nice and welcoming, but no one had known what to say to her so she'd had to do all the chatting. Trying to be 'normal' was exhausting. She'd even cracked a joke about cancer that Larry had sent her the night before. He'd said it would break the ice if things were awkward.

'Doctor, Doctor, my hair keeps falling out, can you give me anything to keep it in?'

'Yes, here's a paper bag!'

When Larry had told her the joke, they had laughed for five minutes. Jess had laughed so much her stomach ached.

But when she told it in class, everyone was embarrassed. Well, everyone except Chloë, who laughed loudly, but it was a fake friend-helping-a-friend-out laugh, which was almost worse. Jess had wanted the floor to open up and swallow her. Then Freda had asked her how long it would take for her hair to grow back.

Chloë had stood between Jess and Freda, and hissed, 'It'll take as long as it takes, and when it does grow back it'll be beautiful, not like your fuzzy mop.'

When Laura asked her if chemo was really awful, Chloë had once again jumped in: 'What the hell kind of question is that? Of course it's awful. She's being pumped full of chemicals that make her puke all the time.'

Thankfully, it had been time to go after that. Jess had never been so grateful to get out of school.

Her mother hugged her. 'Come on, let's get you home. Maybe it wasn't such a good idea for you to go in. I'm sorry, pet. I thought it would be nice for you to see your pals and catch up for an hour this morning.'

Jess didn't want her to feel bad. 'It's fine, Mum. I'm sure after a few days it'll feel okay, but I'll need to get my energy back up before I go back to school.'

Her mother patted her arm and started the car. 'Of course you will. Please God, this next round of chemo will be the last and we can build you back up. Now, what do you fancy for your lunch?'

Jess just wanted to lie down and rest for a bit. She felt wiped out from the effort of being upbeat and chatting to everyone. But she knew if she said she didn't want to eat, her mum would worry. 'Can I have some crackers and maybe some ice cream?'

'I could make you a roast-chicken roll?'

'No, thanks, Mum. I'm not super-hungry.'

Her mother looked disappointed. 'Okay, crackers it is.'

When they got home, Jess sank gratefully into the chair and picked at some crackers. Her mum went to help serve lunch in the café. Granddad popped his head into the kitchen to see how she was.

'I'm okay, just a bit tired.'

'Not surprised, all those girls pecking about, asking you hundreds of questions, no doubt. You look worn out. Have a lie-down and rest. I've made your favourite shepherd's pie for dinner. We'll have it about six when Luke gets back from training.' George opened the fridge and pulled out some whipped cream. As he was heading back into the café, he said, 'By the way, has he said anything to you about being dropped or not playing well? He's in a fierce mood these last few days and he's not eating much, which means something must be wrong.'

Luke hadn't said anything to her but Granddad was right: he had been in a really bad mood. He had barely spoken to her, and when she'd gone in to say goodnight to him yesterday, he'd almost jumped out of his skin. She could see writing on his notepad. There were two columns and the title of one said 'Keep it'. She didn't see the other because Luke had slammed it face-down.

Jess had no idea what it meant, but she thought maybe he was fighting with Piper because she hadn't been around. 'Maybe he's having problems with Piper,' Jess said.

'That's what it is.' George waved a finger at her. 'You're a little genius. It makes sense – he's off his food and moping about. God, I hope she doesn't break up with him. He needs to be in good form and focused for the big game on Saturday. Besides, she's a nice girl, and I'd be sorry to see her go.'

A piece of cracker stuck in Jess's throat. She drank some water. She'd hate Luke and Piper to break up. 'Please, God, don't let them,' she prayed.

There was a knock on the back door. Granddad went to open it. Her dad was standing outside. 'Hi, I was passing and I thought I'd pop in to see Jess.'

Although Jess longed to go to bed she was glad to see him – she hadn't seen him all week.

'Come on in,' Granddad said, letting him past. 'I'll leave you to it. I've a big crowd in for lunch. Help yourself to tea, coffee and whatever,' he said, as he left the room.

Dad gave Jess a big hug, then went to put the kettle on and make himself a coffee. 'How are you, Jessie?'

She shrugged. 'Okay. A bit tired.'

He peered at her closely. 'You look it. You must be doing too much. You need to rest, Jess. It's not good for you to overdo it.'

'I'm not, Dad.' Jess didn't want to get into another argument with him about overdoing it. He was obsessed with her resting. If he had his way, she'd be in bed all day long and never allowed to move. He was just being protective, but it was still annoying. She needed to have a life. She was twelve! She was supposed to be running around having fun, not stuck inside, bald, with cancer.

'Were you out this morning?' he asked.

Her mother came in to say hello as Jess was finishing telling him about the school visit.

He glared at her. 'What the hell is she doing, going into a school full of germs and infections? For Christ's sake, Kate, she could have caught anything. Her bloody immune system is shot! What were you thinking? First horse-riding and now this! She needs to be kept indoors with minimal visitors. A good mother would know that.'

Jess winced as her mother thumped her hand on the kitchen table.

'A good mother? How dare you accuse me of not being a good mother? Don't waltz in here and start throwing your weight around. Jess went to school for one hour. It's important that she sees her pals and gets out a bit. She's been cooped up for weeks.'

He wasn't backing down. 'If she gets an infection it'll set her back again, and I'll blame you entirely.'

Jess's stomach twisted.

Her mother laughed bitterly. 'Well, no surprise there. You're like a child – you always blame everyone else.'

'I want Jess to be kept away from any risk of infection.'

'She wore a bloody mask! She'll be fine!'

Jess felt in her pocket. The mask was still there. She'd taken it off before she'd gone into school. She looked enough of a freak without it. She'd lied and told her mum she'd worn it. Now she started panicking. What if she did get another infection? Dad would blame Mum and it would actually be Jess's fault. What if she died because she was too vain to wear the mask? And what if Dad never spoke to Mum again because of her? She felt sick.

Calm down, breathe, she told herself desperately. She wouldn't get an infection. No one had been sick. No one had come close enough to infect her with anything. The only person she'd touched in school was Chloë. Everyone else had just huddled around, close but not close enough to come into contact with her. She'd hugged Denise, but it had been a fake hug and their faces hadn't touched. In fact, they were probably all scared of being infected with her cancer, rather than the other way round. I'll be fine, she told herself, and her stomach unclenched.

'. . . I'm with her every day. I know what she can handle.' Mum had her hands on her hips and her cheeks were red.

'Well, she looks wrecked,' Dad snapped.

Jess had had enough. 'I'm going to lie down.'

Dad pointed a finger at Mum. 'See? I told you she was tired.'

Jess spun around, eyes blazing. 'Yes, I am tired. I'm tired of you two fighting all the time. Just stop it. I'm sick of it.' She ran out of the kitchen, slamming the door behind her.

Jess was tucked up in bed reading *The Hunger Games* for the zillionth time. She wished she was strong like Katniss, not weak and sick. She loved the books: they took her away from the real world of cancer and hospital and needles, drugs, doctors and nurses and off into the world of Panem, fighting and alliances, love, danger and victory. It was all so exciting and urgent, so different from her boring life stuck in bed.

There was a gentle knock on the door.

'Come in,' Jess said.

Her mum and dad came in and stood at the end of her bed, looking guilty.

'We're sorry, pet,' Mum said, clearly upset.

'Yes, we didn't mean to argue in front of you,' Dad agreed.

'We're just worried about you and it's not fair to you to have to listen to us bickering about silly things. We just want the best for you, darling. We love you so much.' Mum came over and kissed Jess's forehead.

Dad sat down and held her hand. 'Sorry, Jess, I'm probably being overprotective, I just don't want anything to go wrong. We need to do everything we can to help you get better. I do think that, from now on, you need to stay away from crowded places, though. If you want to see your friends, they can come and visit one by one. Or maybe you can just leave seeing them until you're better. FaceTime them instead. Going to school wasn't the best idea.'

'Nick . . .'

'I'm just saying.'

'You said it already.'

He ignored her. 'I just think that for the –'

Jess held up her hands. The last thing she needed was a lecture from Dad. 'Okay, I get it.'

His mouth was set in an obstinate line. 'We all want the same thing,' he said. 'That's what's important. Even if your mother and I have different ideas about how to achieve it.'

Jess saw her mother's whole body stiffen as she didn't say all the things she so plainly wanted to yell at him. He was staring straight at Jess, not giving her mother a glance. The tension between them was unbearable.

'Everyone just wants you to be well again,' Mum said tightly. 'We're all on the same page.'

Dad nodded curtly. 'You will get better,' he said emphatically. 'It's non-negotiable. I won't let it be other–'

Jess cut across him. 'I said I get it, Dad. Now can I please be left alone to rest?'

They went out of the room, and Jess heard the harsh whispers of them arguing the whole way down the stairs.

She went back to her book to block out them and all the dark thoughts in her head.

Bobby's Diary

The Christmas play was a disaster. Mrs Lorgan is foorious with me and Tommy but not with Declan, wich is unfair as he was the kause of it.

Mummy and Luke and Jess and Granddad came to see it. Daddy was supposed to come but he didn't until it was nearly over and then he just sawed the fight.

Declan came out and asked me if I had a room. But he got stuk on a word he didn't get stuk on the day before at all. He said it perfektly. But maybe he got stage scared or something but he got stuk. He said r . . . r . . . r . . . r . . . and there was silence and I could feel all the parents staring at him and he was getting all red in the face and sweting and he looked all stresed so I saided, 'Sorry no room here.'

Then the donkey Tommy shouted, 'Mrs Lorgan said not to say his lines for him, you're a thick' and I got really cross so I told him to shut up and mind his own bizness that I was just trying to help.

Mrs Lorgan was hissing like a snake from the side of the stage to 'move on with the play'. So I stared at Declan and waited for him to say his next line but he just said,

'I hate you Bobby' and he didn't stuter one bit even though B is one of his bad letters. Then Tommy pushed me.

I saw Luke standing up like he was going to protect me so I did what he would do and I pushed Tommy back but he was wearing these clumpy shoes that were supposed to look like a donkey's hooves but they just looked really dum like they were his dad's shoes and so he wobbled and then fell over.

Mrs Lorgan shouted at me to 'behave and get on with the play'. So I went over to help Tommy to get up and he put out his hand like he wanted help and then he pulled me down and started wresling me.

Declan was shouting, 'Kill him Tommy, kill him' and he didn't stuter and K is one of his REALLY bad letters so it just shows you that aktualy he isn't such a bad stuterer when he wants to be.

Tommy punched me in my stomak wich hurts all the time since Jess got sick and I was nearly crying but I saw Dad standing at the back of the room staring up and I saided to myself to be strong.

Tommy's brother with the Down Sindrum was jumping up and down in front of the stage saying 'Go Tommy, go.' He doesn't seem sick at all, just a bit mad and obvioosly into fighting. Tommy's whole family are agro.

It all happened in about one second and then Mrs Lorgan came onto the stage and pulled Tommy off me and dragged us both off the stage.

It didn't actually matter cos our parts were over anyway. Mrs Lorgan blamed me for starting the hole thing cos I stole Declan's lines and so as usual I'm the bad guy.

But when it was over and we did our bows and everyone claped, Daddy and Mummy and Luke and Granddad and Jess came over to me and said well done. Luke said I was great and that Mrs Lorgan should have given me the best part cos I could act and the others were all 'losers'.

I told them I was in big trouble with Mrs Lorgan. Daddy saided that it was a 'farse giving a kid with a stuter the lead role' which I agreed with. But unfortunately Declan's Mummy was standing behind Daddy and hearded him say it and she got all angry and said that her son was a 'brave solider who was dealing with a disability with kourage'.

Daddy said a stuter was not a disability that it was a speech impediment and that he shouldn't get special treatment and that we all had 'shit going on' and that a kid shouldn't get a role just because it took him ten minutes to say his name.

Declan's Mummy said that Daddy was a 'very rude man with a hart of stone' and that he had no idea how dificult it was for Declan to deal with life with a stuter and that I was a 'mean boy and a bully'.

Mummy said, 'Excuse me but Bobby is a lovely boy and has a hart of gold. He was just trying to help Declan.'

Declan's Mummy said that everyone with half a brain knew that you did not finish words for stuterers.

Mummy said 'May I remind you that Bobby is seven.'

Then Tommy's Daddy came over with his brother and said that I was a 'nasty piece of work' for nocking his Tommy down.

Mummy reminded him that Tommy had pushed me first and I was just defending myself.

'He's a violent bully' Tommy's Dad said. He said that Tommy is a 'kind-harted boy who looks after his brother' and that life wasn't easy.

Daddy putted his hand on my shoulder and said that he saw the way Tommy punched me and that the only violent person was his son.

I was so happy that Daddy was on my side. It was brilliant.

Tommy's Daddy said Tommy was a lamb who minded his little brother who had chalinges.

He was going to say more but Luke throwed his hands in the air and shouted, 'Can everyone just shut the hell up. Bobby was trying to help the dude with the stuter, Tommy stuck his nose in where it didn't belong and got violent. Bobby is dealing with a sister who has cancer and nearly died a few weeks ago, so you can take your stuterers and your Down Sindrum kids and shove them where the sun doesn't shine. Bobby is the nicest kid in the world so if ever I hear

anyone call him a bully again I sware to God
I will lose it.'

Luke looked so big and tall and strong,
like a warior.

'Luke!' Mummy was shocked but she was kind
of smiling too.

Tommy's Daddy and Declan's Mummy just went
quiet and looked shoked. Granddad said, 'Time
to go' and rushed us all out of the school
before any more fighting could happen. I was
so proud that Luke was my brother. I told him
thanks and he said, 'no worries dude, don't
let anyone push you around and if they do, let
me know.'

Jess was quiet. I heard Mummy ask her if
she was alrite. Jess nodded but I could see she
had tears in her eyes. I don't know why.
Maybe she wished she had a stuter or Down
Sindrum instead of cancer.

So I asked her and she did a sad smile and
said 'A stuter maybe but not Down Sindrum
because you can't be cured.'

I thought Down Sindrum just meant you were
agro but obvioosly it's worser than that. I
feel a bit bad for Tommy's brother now and
for Tommy. A bit . . . but not loads cos he
punched my sore stomak.

27

Kate washed her hands with one of the sanitizers that were all over the house and in every bag and coat pocket she owned.

Bobby watched her from his bed. He was wearing his dinosaur pyjamas and looked very sweet and young. Kate went over and hugged him. 'What's that for?' he asked.

'It's for being a great boy.'

'Did you think I was a great boy when I ruined the Christmas play?' Bobby asked.

'Of course I did, and you didn't ruin it. It was Mrs Lorgan's silly casting of the wrong boys in the wrong roles. You were wonderful.'

'Mummy,' Bobby asked, his little forehead wrinkling, 'why does chemotherapy make you so sick?'

Kate paused. 'Well, it makes you sick but better at the same time.'

'Why can't they make a medicine that cures cancer without making you sick and bald?'

'I wish they could, Bobby, and when you grow up, maybe you can invent a chemotherapy that makes patients feel good instead of awful.'

'I will, Mummy. I'll invent that and then we can be rich and I can buy you a house and you won't have to wait for Daddy to pay you money to get us things, and I'll buy Jess a pony all of her own, and I'll buy Luke his own rugby pitch to practise on.'

'What about Daddy and Jaden and Jenny?' Kate asked. She wanted to try to get Bobby to like his half-brother at least a little. It worried her how much he disliked him.

Bobby frowned. 'I'll buy them a small house, but I'm not spending loads of money on them. I'm keeping it for us.'

'You know that when Jaden gets older he's going to look up to you like you look up to Luke?' She tried to appeal to his ego.

Bobby looked surprised. 'Will he?'

'Yes. You'll be his cool big brother and he'll want to be like you and spend time with you.'

Bobby closed his book of facts. 'But he's only my half-brother, not like me and Luke. He's not really our family, Mum. He's Daddy's family, and he's kind of stinky and stupid.'

Kate took Bobby's hand in hers. 'Listen to me. Jaden is your family and you must try to be nice to him. When he's a bit older, you can teach him your facts. He'd love that.'

'Would he? He seems dumb to me. All he does is cry.'

'That's because he's a baby, Bobby. Babies cry. When he's talking and walking you'll be able to teach him things and help him to be as smart as you are.'

Bobby seemed doubtful. 'We'll see about that. Anyway, he has Daddy to teach him stuff. Daddy's always with him.'

'Daddy's been popping in more often lately to see you.'

Bobby's big brown eyes looked up at her. 'He's been coming to see Jess, not me or Luke. Daddy cares about Jess and Jaden and Jenny. Maybe if my name started with a J he'd care about me too.'

Kate felt so sad for her little son. He was so in need of a proper father who paid him attention. It broke her heart. 'Daddy loves you and Luke just as much as Jess. He's obviously paying more attention to Jess at the moment because she's sick. He came to your play and he stood up for you. That was nice, wasn't it?'

'He was late and he missed my lines. Anyway, Luke was the one who really stood up for me.'

'Oh, Bobby . . .' Kate hugged him. 'Your dad loves you and I love you enough for a million mums and dads.'

Bobby snuggled his head into her shoulder. 'I know, Mummy, and I love you too, so don't get cancer and die. I want you here.'

Kate held him tighter. 'I'm not going anywhere and nor is Jess. We're all going to grow old together.'

Bobby wriggled out from her embrace. 'You're kind of suffocating me now.'

Kate laughed and pulled back.

'It's not funny, Mummy. Since 2000, the number of child suffocations per year has risen in the US from less than eight hundred to more than a thousand.'

Kate stopped laughing and tried to look serious. 'I doubt many of those are from mothers hugging their children.'

'Well, I don't want to be the first. Is Luke home yet?'

'No. He said he was going to study at Piper's.'

'Why is he grumpy all the time? I went into his room yesterday and he was on his computer and when I asked him what he was looking at he snapped it shut and shouted at me to get lost and pushed me out.'

Kate had noticed that Luke was short-tempered. 'He has a lot on his plate. His finals are coming up in six months, he's training really hard to stay on the team and he's worried about Jess, too.'

'So am I, you know, and I don't go around pushing people.' Kate looked at him and Bobby went red. 'Well, not unless they push me first.'

Kate leant over and put his book on the bedside locker. She kissed his forehead and tried not to mind when she saw him rubbing it off. Switching off the light, she said goodnight.

As she was leaving the room she heard Bobby's tired voice say, 'I'm really glad you're my mummy.'

'And I'm thrilled you're my little boy.' Kate smiled into the darkness and quietly made her way down to the kitchen.

She glanced at the clock. She was supposed to be at her mindfulness course but she really wasn't in the mood. She was planning on Skyping Maggie and having a drink and a chat with her instead. She was pouring herself a glass of wine when she heard a knock on the back door. She pulled it open. Liam was standing there with snowflakes on his hair and beard.

'Hi.' Kate was surprised to see him.

'Sorry,' he said, 'I didn't mean to disturb you but there doesn't seem to be anyone doing mindfulness tonight. The room is empty and I wondered if it was cancelled because of the weather.'

Kate hadn't realized it was snowing. She'd left the door unlocked for the teacher and the class before putting Bobby to bed. 'Gosh, it really is pelting down. Come on in.'

Liam hesitated. 'I don't want to come on top of your family.'

'Don't be silly. I'm here on my own. Dad's in the shop sampling the new wines that have just come in with his friend Bill. Bobby's in bed, so is Jess, and Luke is out.'

'Well, just for a minute.'

Kate offered him a glass of wine. Liam shrugged off his coat and accepted it.

'The class must be cancelled – she's never been late before. Mind you, she should have sent a text if it is.' Kate took a sip of her wine.

At that moment Liam's phone buzzed. He looked down. 'Ah! She's apologizing for cancelling at the last minute but her car won't start.'

'I wasn't going tonight anyway. Just didn't feel like it.'

Liam smiled. 'Neither did I, but my daughter called in to make sure I went. I think she knew that after the first three my enthusiasm was waning.'

'Do you think it's just us?' Kate asked. 'The others seem to really get into it. I just can't switch my mind off and the swaying to music just makes me want to laugh.'

Liam grinned. 'It's very awkward for a fella like me who has two left feet and no balance.'

Kate giggled. 'I noticed that when you knocked me over in the first class.'

'I'm still mortified.' He chuckled.

They sipped their wine companionably. He was nice in a big-bear sort of way, Kate thought. Maggie had asked her if she fancied him when she'd told her about him coming to the coffee shop and being so nice about Jess. But she didn't fancy him. He was too . . . well, hairy and squidgy. The opposite of Nick, who waxed his back and shaved every day and was fit and toned. At least, he had been before his life became one long stressful problem. He probably got very little time to work out now. Just like me, she thought ruefully.

Kate knew she should try to fall for someone like Liam, who was kind and wouldn't cheat on you, but you can't make yourself like someone when there's no chemistry. She liked him as a man friend. She wasn't remotely embarrassed about Liam seeing her tonight in her slippers with no make-up on and wearing an old baggy sweatshirt. She felt comfortable with him, and it was nice.

'So how's Jess?' he asked.

Kate put down her glass. 'She's been doing really well since the bone-marrow transplant so things are better. I'm feeling really hopeful. I'm just so glad the chemo and transplant are over. It's been so hard on her little body.'

Liam shook his head. 'It's a terrible thing. My wife was so sick on chemo – I can't imagine how awful it must be for a child.'

'I just don't understand why, with all the money and funding that is put into cancer research, they haven't come up with something less aggressive to cure it.'

'June's oncologist used to say you have to fight fire with fire. Sometimes I wanted to punch him when he said it.'

'Sometimes I want to punch everyone,' Kate said.

'It's very hard on you as the mum, with two other children to worry about. My kids were all adults when June was diagnosed. They still suffered terribly but at least they were able to look after themselves and stay with her in the hospital when I needed to go home.'

Kate nodded. 'Still awful, though.'

'Yes, it was,' Liam said quietly.

'Do you miss her?'

'Yes. It's the quietness of the house. It's been nearly three years and I still can't get used to it. I think the hardest part is when something happens, like when Grace got engaged and I wanted to talk to June about it and celebrate together, but it was just me and the dog.'

'I miss that, too. I miss sitting on the couch and talking to Nick about the kids or what happened that day. In fairness, I don't miss it right now because he's driving me crazy, but in the beginning I did.'

'I don't think humans are built to be alone,' Liam said.

Kate agreed. Before Jess had got sick and her mind had filled with tests, research and terror, she used to wonder what would happen to her when the kids left home. She was afraid of turning into a sad old lady, with cats, who lived alone, watched daytime TV and got fatter by the hour. Maggie told her she was being ridiculous, that empty-nest syndrome was rubbish, and she'd have the time of her life, that she could come and live with Maggie and shag handsome younger men, get a job and have a ball.

Kate couldn't see herself living Maggie's life, though. She didn't want to sleep with younger men: she wanted to meet a Nick who didn't cheat.

'Anyway, it's great news about Jess, with the transplant going well, I'm really pleased for you.' Liam fished about in his pocket and pulled out a small plastic pouch with something silver in it. 'I hope you don't mind, but I wanted to give you this.' He handed it to her.

'What is it?'

'It's a medal of St Peregrine, the patron saint of healing for those who suffer with cancer and other life-threatening illnesses. I thought Jess might like to keep it beside her bed or under her pillow.'

Kate looked down at the medal, tried to hold back tears and failed. It was such a kind and thoughtful gesture. She stood up and hugged him. 'Thank you.'

Liam patted her on the back. 'It's nothing really but . . . well, every little thing helps, I suppose.'

Kate pulled away and wiped her cheeks. 'Sorry, I'm a wreck. I'm counting the days and holding my breath until she has the tests to see if the bone marrow worked. I shouldn't drink alcohol at all – it makes me weepy. I'd better have a coffee.'

Liam jumped up. 'I'll make it for you. Sit down and rest.'

Kate did so. It was nice to have someone doing things for her. Liam made them both a coffee and sat opposite her. He raised his cup. 'Here's to good health and complete remission in 2016.'

Kate clinked her cup against his. 'I can't believe Christmas is only days away. I've done nothing. I'll be glad to see the back of this year, that's for sure. I'm scared, though. It's funny, you think when something awful happens that you'll assume this is your bad card in life. But now I just think, Why wouldn't I get more bad cards? Who's to say more bad luck isn't on its way?'

Liam reached over and squeezed her hand. 'It's normal to feel like that, but I really think you've had your fill. I'll light a candle for Jess on Christmas Eve and one for you.'

Kate squeezed back. 'Thank you. It's silly, we barely know each other and yet I feel as if I've known you all my life.'

Liam smiled broadly. 'I know what you mean.'

The door opened. Luke came in and threw his kitbag onto the floor. He stopped dead when he saw Kate holding hands with Liam. Kate yanked her hand back. Oh, God! It looked like something it wasn't.

Luke glared at her. 'What the hell?'

Liam stood up and took charge. He took Luke's hand and shook it. 'Hi, Luke, I'm Liam. I met your mum at the mindfulness course but we decided to skip it tonight. Nice to meet you. I hear you're a great rugby player – best of luck in the cup. Right, I'd best be off. Good luck, Kate, and thanks for the coffee.'

Luke didn't have time to react.

Kate walked Liam to the back door. 'Thanks for dropping by, I really enjoyed that,' she said quietly.

'Me too. We should skip the mindfulness class more often.'

Kate grinned. 'I agree.'

'See you in January. If we decide to mitch off, we could go for a walk, if the weather permits.'

'Sounds great. Happy Christmas.'

Liam bent down and kissed her cheek. 'You too.' Then, looking over her shoulder, he said, 'Bye, Luke.'

'Uh, yeah . . . bye,' he muttered.

Kate watched Liam go. He turned when he reached the end of the garden path and waved at her.

'Can you close the fucking door? It's freezing,' Luke snapped.

Kate spun around. 'Watch your language.'

'So who's the dude? When did you get a boyfriend?'

'He's not my boyfriend. He's a friend, a very nice man.'

'Oh, yeah? Well, if he's just a friend, how come you were holding hands when I came in?'

'He was holding my hand to comfort me, Luke. I was feeling a bit down. That's all.'

Luke shrugged. 'I don't care if you're seeing him. He seems all right, but I don't need another dad. So, if you want to go out with him, fine, but he's not to start hanging around me or telling me what to do.'

Kate stood up and washed the coffee cups. 'For the last time, I'm not going out with him and I know you don't need another dad.'

'Fine, whatever.'

'Have you eaten?'

'No.'

'Do you want me to cook you something?'

'I'm not seven. I can cook for myself,' Luke said angrily.

'Fine. Sorry for asking and being concerned.'

'Jesus, I wish everyone would get off my back.' He slammed the fridge door.

'No one's on your back,' Kate said, eyeing him. 'What's wrong, Luke? You've been really grumpy this last week.'

'Nothing. I just want to eat in peace.'

'Are you sure it's nothing? Is everything okay with school and Piper?'

Luke hesitated. 'There's actually –'

Kate heard a scream. It was Jess. She left Luke and took the stairs two at a time, her heart beating wildly. At the top she skidded left and burst through the door into the bedroom.

'What's wrong?' Kate cried, terrified of the answer.

Jess was holding her phone, sobbing. 'It's La-Larry.'

28

Her mother handed her another tissue. Jess hadn't known she had so many tears. Larry was gone. Her person, her friend, the only one who understood exactly how she felt, was dead and she couldn't come to terms with it.

'There is no God,' she said, sobbing into Whiskey's soft face.

'Jess, don't say that.'

'No, Mum, there isn't. I don't believe in God any more or Mary or saints or miracles or any of it. It was nice of your friend Liam to give me that medal, but I don't want it.' Jess handed it to her.

Her mother put it into her pocket. 'Larry was just really sick and really unlucky.'

Jess stared at her, big eyes full of tears. 'He was a good person, a great person. He didn't deserve to die. There is no God and no justice. I hate this – I hate this life, this stupid bloody cancer! I hate it!' Jess was racked with sobs.

Her mother climbed onto the bed and held her. 'I hate it too,' she said. 'But you're going to be okay.'

Jess sniffled into her shoulder. 'What if I'm not, Mum? Larry was in remission three times and it came back and he's dead. He was my best friend. He made me laugh on the really bad days.'

'I know, sweetheart, I know.' She stroked Jess's bald head.

That felt nice. Jess loved it when she did that. It reminded her of being little, when her mum used to stroke her hair before she went to sleep.

Life seemed so bleak. She felt like a black cloud was descending on her, suffocating her. Everything was dark and depressing and pointless and frightening, and her heart ached. She felt so sick and exhausted and fed up and just . . . just sad. So, so, so, so sad.

If Larry could die, so could she. No one was safe from cancer. It didn't matter about the statistics or Luke's bone marrow or chemo or anything: cancer could come back or never go away and you could die.

Jess didn't want to die. She wanted to live and become a famous horse-rider and win a gold Olympic medal at show-jumping or dressage and have a gorgeous boyfriend and be happy and healthy and never, ever see a hospital again. Why had cancer come into her life? She hated it.

Larry said you had to stop asking why and accept it. He said acceptance was the only way to stop your head melting. He said that you couldn't fight having cancer: you could only fight the cancer itself. He said you had to keep all of your energy on that fight, good against evil. You against cancer. And he had tried, he had tried so hard, to fight and be posi-tive and not let it win. But it did. It bloody well did. Cancer had won and now Larry was gone.

As her mother gently stroked her head, Jess thought about their pact: how Larry had promised to send a sign if there was an afterlife. How she'd do the same if she'd died first. But she hadn't. Larry was dead and here she was, sick and broken. But she knew Larry would do it if he could, so she'd wait for the sign.

It had been only a few days but every morning she woke up and stared out of the window for a robin on her window-sill or rainbows or white feathers or something, but there had been nothing so far. When Jess had said that if she died first she'd send a white butterfly to sit on his shoulder, Larry had got cross and said that was silly. You couldn't be so spe-cific, he said, because they didn't know what it was like on the other side and it might be complicated to get a sign to someone, so it was best not to be too detailed.

Jess had seen a magpie on her windowsill yesterday but Larry had hated magpies – he'd said they were a sorry excuse for a bird – so she'd known that wasn't his sign.

Her mother shifted slightly on the bed. 'You have to be strong and get well for Larry,' she said. 'He'd want you to get better and live a brilliant life.'

Jess nodded, wiping her eyes.

'It's awful to lose a friend like Larry, but don't let it knock you back. Use the sadness and anger to drive yourself forward.'

'I'll try, Mum. I'm just so tired and sad.'

'I know, pet. Will you try to sleep now?'

'Yes. I'll see you later.'

'Are you sure? I'm happy to stay with you.'

'Yes. I'm okay, Mum.'

She watched her mother walk across her room and out of the door, closing it gently behind her. Once she was alone, Jess started to cry, the kind of heartbroken tears that fill your ears and make the bedsheets wet and leave you feeling emptied out and raw. She was about as far from okay as it was possible to get.

The next morning Jess was gazing out of the window, desperately praying for a sign from Larry, when she heard a knock on her door.

'Jess, are you awake? Larry's dad's called in to see you,' her mother said.

Jess sat bolt upright.

A moment later, Larry's father popped his head around the bedroom door. 'Sorry to disturb you, Jess, but I have something for you.'

He had aged ten years and looked awful. His eyes were red and bloodshot and the skin on his face was saggy. He reminded Jess of a Basset hound.

'Hi, Mr Wilkinson,' Jess said. 'I'm glad to see you. I'm so sorry about Larry. He was such an amazing person. I . . . I'm just so sorry.'

Mr Wilkinson nodded sadly and handed her an envelope. 'Larry made me promise that if anything happened to him I'd give you this.'

'Thank you so much,' Jess croaked.

With trembling hands she opened it. Inside she found a card with a picture of a dandelion on it. She began to cry. That was his sign.

Inside was a quotation. She read it out: '"What I need is the dandelion in the spring. The bright yellow that means rebirth instead of destruction. The promise that life can go on, no matter how bad our losses. That it can be good again."'

Jess, now sobbing, looked up at Larry's father who was crying too. 'It's our favourite part of *The Hunger Games*.'

'He loved that film. He loved you, too, Jess. Thanks for being his friend and making his time in hospital less awful.'

Jess couldn't speak.

'We're praying for you and hoping that you'll get well and live a full and happy life.'

'Thank you,' she whispered. 'I'm so, so sorry about Larry.'

'Me, too,' he said, and shuffled out of the room.

Jess sat staring at the card, laughing and crying. Eventually she turned to the window and said, 'Thank you, Larry. Dandelions will remind me of you for ever. I miss you.'

She kissed the card and, holding it to her chest, lay back and fell into a deep sleep.

29

Piper tried to sneak past the twins' room without being seen, but they shouted, 'Piper! We need help – please, Piper.'

She went in reluctantly. They were sitting at the end of Penny's bed wearing Santa hats and really cheesy Christmas jumpers.

'Penny's trying to film us with her phone propped up on top of the drawers, but it looks crap. We need the camera to move around a bit. Can you do it?' Poppy begged.

The last thing Piper wanted to do right now was film her two silly sisters but she knew they'd hound her until she agreed, so she said, 'You've got ten minutes and that's it.'

'Fine,' Penny said, and she and Poppy sat on the bed.

Piper held the phone up and began to record them.

'Hi, everyone.' They waved and smiled fake smiles.

'It's the two Ps here, wishing you a very merry Christmas Eve. With only one more sleep until the big day, we wanted to talk about Christmas.'

'If you're old and you're watching this, do not buy your kids or grandkids pyjamas or socks or crappy jumpers for Christmas. They don't want them,' Penny said.

'Yeah, totally. Just give them vouchers for cool shops. Vouchers are good because then the person can buy what they actually want and not have to pretend to like the purple jumper or the pyjamas with, like, reindeer on them,' Poppy agreed.

'Don't buy vouchers for Marks & Spencer's or shops like that, buy them for, like, H&M or River Island.'

'Or Superdry.'

'Or for ASOS.'

'Do ASOS do vouchers?' Poppy asked.

'I dunno. I think so.'

'You can't say you don't know. We're supposed to be telling people what to do,' Poppy remonstrated.

'Well, you don't know either, so don't give out to me.'

'You're rubbish at this, Penny.'

'Oh, for God's sake, just take that bit out.'

'Fine. Just leave it at Superdry,' Poppy said.

'Moving on to other Christmas things,' Penny said, 'you have to give me my present and I'll give you yours and be all, like, "Wow, that's so cool," like Zoella does with her friend.'

'What did you get me?' Poppy asked.

'It's supposed to be a surprise.'

'It'd better not be rubbish, then.'

'Who cares? It's just about looking happy and pretending,' Penny huffed.

Posy had come out of her box room and was standing behind Piper. 'You can't be fake,' she said. 'People will see through you. Zoella isn't fake, which is why everyone loves her.'

'Obviously we won't look fake. We can act, Posy,' Poppy said.

'Yeah, how hard is it to look excited anyway?' Penny agreed.

'Don't underestimate your viewers. We can tell fake from real,' Posy said.

'Piss off, Posy, we're trying to film here. When we're zillionaire YouTube stars you'll get nothing because you're just being negative.'

Piper put the phone down. 'You can argue on your own time. I'm going.'

'*No!* Wait, we have to do the presents and then we're finished,' Poppy said.

'When I give the present to Poppy, you need to zoom in on her opening it,' Penny said. 'Poppy, you need to say how amazing the wrapping is and all that too.'

Piper pressed record again and Penny handed Poppy a present wrapped in silver paper with a crooked red bow.

'Wow, Penny!' Poppy said, eyes wide. 'This is amazing! I'm super-excited. The wrapping paper is so cool, where did you get it?'

Penny fake-smiled. 'It's actually tinfoil, which I used to save money and the planet.'

Piper tried not to laugh. The planet? Was Penny serious? Could she be that clueless?

'Wow, it looks like designer paper. And the bow is so awesome! It's perfect!'

Posy snorted.

Penny glared at her. 'I spent ages getting it just right. I think a nicely wrapped present is so much better than one that's thrown together, don't you?'

'Oh, yes.' Poppy opened the present – an empty St Tropez fake-tan bottle.

'Seriously?'

Penny frowned at her. 'Isn't it fab?'

'It's *my* fake tan *and* it's empty.'

'For God's sake, they can't see that. Pretend it's full and you're happy. Jesus, Poppy, you're so bad at this.'

'You can see it's been used because it has brown streaks down the side,' Posy said.

'You are so scabby. I can't believe you're giving me my own fake tan as a present.' Poppy was furious.

'We're just pretending, you freak! It's not real!' Penny shouted.

'Zoella is real. She never pretends,' said Posy.

'Can you just shut the hell up and stop banging on about Zoella?' Penny hissed.

'I thought you wanted to be like her,' Posy said, thoroughly enjoying herself now. 'You're the opposite of her. You're like the fake Zoella twins.'

'The bogus twins,' Piper said, as Posy giggled.

Poppy wasn't letting the bad present go. 'I actually bought you something with my own money and I wrapped it in actual wrapping paper, not bloody tinfoil.'

'What is it?' Penny asked.

'It's a really cool T-shirt from H&M and I'm not giving it to you.' Poppy reached behind her to grab the present and waved it under her sister's nose.

'You have to! It's for the show, for our future.'

'No way. I'm going to do this on my own without you bossing me about.' Poppy held the gift tightly.

'You can't give yourself a present, you moron.'

'Oh, yeah? Watch me.' Turning to the phone camera, Poppy said, 'So how about this? How about you treat yourself to a gift at Christmas? We all spend so much time buying things for other people and get so many rubbish presents, especially from our scabby sisters. Why don't we buy ourselves something that we actually want?'

'That's ridiculous, Poppy,' Penny said. 'The entire point of Christmas is that you give presents to others! Isn't that right, everyone?'

'Yes, but not when you know for a fact that the other person isn't going to give you one. In that case you're perfectly entitled to spend the money you were going to spend on them on yourself.'

'That makes you Scrooge.'

Poppy grinned. 'No. You're Scrooge, because you're tight, scabby and mean.'

'I am not.' Penny shoved Poppy over.

'Yes, you bloody are.' Poppy shoved her back and they began to wrestle.

'OMG, they're so lame,' Posy said.

'Somehow I don't see a big future for them on YouTube.' Piper grinned.

'No one who is actually sane would want to watch this,' Posy agreed.

They left the room with the twins still fighting.

Piper went into her bedroom and flopped down on the bed. Her head ached. They'd phoned Maggie that morning and told her their decision. She'd been very nice about it and said she'd help them.

Piper heard her mother coming through the front door, shouting, 'Merry almost Christmas,' up the stairs. Two minutes later she called them all downstairs. It was a family tradition that they sat around the tree, eating mince pies and listening to carols on Christmas Eve. Even though they all moaned and groaned about it, they secretly liked it. Piper heard the twins thundering down the stairs, followed by Posy's lighter steps. She heard Pauline coming in from college – the only student in the world who studied on Christmas Eve.

She hauled herself up and took a very deep breath. This Christmas Eve was going to be very different for her. For all of them, in fact.

Seamus put on his favourite first, Bing Crosby singing 'White Christmas'. Everyone got to choose a song and that was his. Olivia passed around the mince pies and cream.

'Yum. These are really good, Mum,' Poppy said.

'Marks & Spencer's,' Olivia told her.

'Not exactly baked with love, are they?' Poppy said, then took a bite.

'So, girls, another year gone. Where does the time go?' Olivia wondered. 'Next year Pauline will be in her second year at med school, Piper will be in college, you two rascals will be in transition year and Posy will be in second. You're all growing up too quickly. I feel as if it was only yesterday when you were babies.'

'I wouldn't go back to the nappies and the sleepless nights if you paid me,' Seamus said, polishing off his second mince pie. 'I prefer them at this age – less work.'

'Oh, I loved the baby stage – they were adorable.'

'Jesus, Olivia, we were nearly divorced over lack of sleep and dirty nappies.'

Olivia smiled. 'I don't remember that. I just remember the chubby thighs and the little white teeth poking out from pink gums, the first words and the sound of babies laughing.'

Piper watched her mother's face light up as she remembered those days. It made her want to weep.

'I bet I was the cutest,' Penny said.

'You were in your arse,' Seamus said. 'A nightmare, that's what you were. You never bloody slept. Up all night. I never saw a child with so much energy.'

'Who was the best baby?' Poppy asked.

'Posy,' Seamus and Olivia said at the same time.

'I would have thought she'd be the worst because it was your last chance to have a boy and then it was a girl and you were devastated,' Poppy said.

'Thanks a lot, Poppy, I actually have feelings, you know.' Posy's cheeks were red.

'We weren't a bit disappointed. Don't mind her. You were the sweetest baby ever,' Olivia said.

'A little dote,' Seamus agreed.

'What was I like?' Piper asked, suddenly desperate to know.

Olivia and Seamus looked at each other.

'Good.'

'Yes, easy enough.'

'You don't remember, do you?' Piper said.

'It's kind of a blur. You only remember the really bad ones and the last one,' Seamus admitted.

'Thanks a lot.' Piper felt furious.

'You were lovely, darling, a lovely baby, a lovely girl and a lovely teenager too.' Olivia tried to reassure her.

Piper knew it was unreasonable, but she was raging. She wanted to know. She needed to know. What kind of a baby was she? Was she good? Did she sleep? Was she sweet? Was she . . . Oh, God, what was she doing?

She felt a cool hand on her arm. It was Pauline's. 'Breathe,' she whispered.

Everyone was distracted by Penny and Poppy arguing over their choice of songs.

'Do you want a glass of water?' Pauline asked quietly.

'No, I'm fine.'

'Have you made up your mind?'

Piper nodded.

'Are you sure?'

Piper nodded again. 'As sure as I can be.'

'No way am I listening to Mariah Carey! For God's sake, Penny, choose something else.'

'I like it and it's my choice.'

'I hate that song.'

'So do I.' Posy groaned.

The doorbell rang. Piper jumped up and went to open it. Luke was standing in the rain, soaking wet. 'What are you –'

'I can't sleep. I can't concentrate. We need to tell our parents. I know we said we'd wait until after Christmas, but it's wrecking my head. Mum knows something's wrong with me, I'm so jumpy all the time. I just can't keep it in. It's too big, it's too important. We can do this, Piper. You and me, together, we can do it. I love you.'

'I love you too.' Piper kissed him as relief flooded her body.

They laughed. It was the first time they'd laughed since she'd told him about the baby. They hugged again and kissed.

'Get a room,' Penny shouted, peeping around the door.

Luke grinned. 'Go away. I want one more kiss.'

Penny ducked back into the room.

'Now we have to tell our families,' Luke said.

'Will we do it now?'

'Let's get it over with. There's never going to be a good time. They'll be shocked, no matter what. May as well have it out there now.'

They walked into the living room where 'All I Want For Christmas' was booming out of the speakers.

Piper went over to her mother and, into her ear, said, 'Mum, Luke and I need to talk to you and Dad in the kitchen.'

Olivia's eyes widened. She shook Seamus's arm and told him to follow her.

'Where are you going?' Poppy asked.

'We just want a quick word with Mum and Dad,' Piper shouted, over the music.

'*Oooooh!* Are you engaged?' Poppy exclaimed.

'Are you getting married?' Posy asked.

Piper's heart sank. They'd be so shocked when they found out.

'Shut up and leave them alone.' Pauline closed the living-room door.

Seamus stood leaning against the cooker. 'So, what's going on?'

Luke's face was bright red. 'I, that is, we have some news and it's . . . well . . . it's . . .'

Olivia looked right into Piper's eyes. She knew. Piper could tell. Olivia's eyes filled with tears and Piper couldn't stand it any longer: she had to say it out loud. The secret had to come out – it was suffocating her.

'I'm pregnant.'

'What the hell?' Seamus looked as if he'd been shot.

Luke stared at the floor.

It was worse than Piper had imagined. Her mother was crying silently and her father's mouth was opening and closing, like a goldfish's.

'I promise I'll look after Piper and the baby,' Luke said.

'You're only kids,' Olivia whispered.

'How the hell did this happen?' Seamus asked. He shook his head and, in a voice thick with disappointment, said, 'Piper, you're my sensible one.'

Olivia recovered. 'How far gone are you?'

'About fourteen weeks.'

'Oh, my God.' Seamus sat down heavily on a chair.

'Have you thought about your options?' Olivia asked.

'Yes, we've thought and thought and thought, and we've decided to keep it.' Piper was firm. Keeping it had always felt right to her. She knew that having an abortion seemed like the sensible thing to do – she could get on with her life and all of that – but she was having this baby and nothing would change her mind.

'But your future,' Seamus said, sounding strangled. 'You'll be tied down, you'll have no choices, you'll never do the

267

things we wanted for you. Piper, you've your whole life ahead of you. How could you let this happen? How could you be so foolish?'

Piper's lip wobbled. She didn't want to cry. She wanted to be strong, but seeing her father so devastated was hard.

'It's my fault, sir. I'm the one to blame,' Luke said. 'It was my mistake and I can't tell you how sorry I am. But I love Piper and I promise to look after her.'

Seamus shook a trembling finger at Luke. 'You stupid son-of-a-bitch. You're eighteen, you have no idea what the hell you're talking about. Having a child is a lifetime commitment. You're kids. You know nothing about life. You're still in school, for God's sake. How the hell are you going to support my daughter and a baby?'

'I'll get a job and we'll rent a small flat and –'

'Oh, Jesus, son, you really are clueless. Both of you are clueless and stupid, so bloody stupid.'

Olivia placed a hand on her husband's arm. 'Look, you're both very young and a bit naïve. Piper is a bright, clever girl who deserves to achieve all of her goals and dreams, as do you, Luke. If you're determined to have this baby, you'll need support from us and from your family, too, and we'll help you, but ultimately you'll be tied down with this child for life. It's a huge commitment, much bigger than you can imagine.'

'We know, Mum. We've thought about nothing else and we've made up our minds that we're keeping it. We love each other, and I know we're young and I know we're naïve, but we're willing to make sacrifices to look after the baby.'

Seamus put his head into his hands. 'Why, Piper? Why did you have to be so stupid? Your life is not your own any more. And as for you,' he looked up at Luke, 'you'd better stand by her side day and night, and if I ever hear that you're not pulling your weight, I'll hunt you down and wring your neck. Piper is my pride and joy and you've ruined her bright future.'

'Stop it, Dad.' Piper began to cry now – she couldn't hold in the tears. 'It's not Luke's fault, and my future isn't ruined. It's just different.'

Luke stood up and put his hands on Piper's shoulders. 'I truly am sorry, but I've been through a lot over the last few years and I know how important it is to be a good father and to be there for your kids. I will not let Piper or our baby down.'

Olivia reached over and wiped her daughter's tears. 'It's all right. We're here for you and we'll support you, no matter what. We're just a bit shocked – we need a few days to process the news.'

Piper gave her mother a faint smile. It was a relief to hear her say she'd support her because she'd need every bit of support she could get. Now that they had told her parents, it was frighteningly real. Her heart was thumping. She knew it was the right decision but it was very scary. She couldn't bear to see her father so angry and upset. It was awful to think she'd done this to him. 'I'm sorry, Dad, I know I've let you down.' She was sobbing again.

Seamus buried his face in his hands.

'Get off me, Pauline! You're a freak.' Penny burst through the kitchen door with her eldest sister hot on her heels, Posy and Poppy right behind them.

'We want to know what's going on and . . . Oh!' She stopped when she saw her father and sister crying.

'Is Jess dead?' Posy gasped.

'No,' Luke said. 'It's not that.'

'What is it?' Poppy asked. 'Why do you all look so upset?'

Piper stood up. 'I've got something to tell you. I was stupid and I didn't protect myself properly and I'm pregnant.'

269

'*What?*' Penny squealed.

'Oh!' Poppy's eyes almost popped out of her head.

'Poor you.' Posy came over to give her a hug.

'It's okay. Luke and I are just going to be very young parents.' Piper tried to keep calm and not fall apart again.

'You'll be great, Piper,' Pauline said. 'You've always helped with this lot – you'll be a much better mother than I ever could be.'

Piper wanted to kiss Pauline. She had never expected her sister to be so supportive, but she had been brilliant. A total rock. She mouthed, 'Thank you,' to her.

'But you're only –'

'It'll be nice to have a baby in the house again,' Pauline cut across Penny. 'And we can all help babysit.'

'Yes, I'll help you loads, Piper, I promise. I love babies,' Posy said.

'I'll do it too, but you'll have to pay me,' Poppy said.

'Don't be so mean!' Posy was shocked.

As her sisters bickered over childcare, Piper held Luke's hand and prayed that it would all work out. It would be a long and lonely road, but she had her family, mad as they were, and she knew they'd be there for her through thick and thin. She was lucky, she knew that. Very lucky.

30

Jaden crawled across the living room, which was strewn with Christmas wrapping paper, gurgling happily as Jenny filmed him. Nick reckoned she must have caught every second of the baby's life on camera. She sent him at least three videos a day when he was at work.

Still, at least she was in better form, not panicking and crying all the time. She still freaked out a lot, but it was definitely better. Whatever the GP had said to her had calmed her down. Nick was glad he'd made her go. It was the best sixty euros he'd spent. She was still very different from the fun, sexy girl he'd fallen for, but at least she was less down. Maybe, with a bit more time, she'd get back to her old self.

Nick glanced at his watch. He'd promised Kate he'd be there for Christmas pudding at six. He'd have to leave now to make it on time. He was hoping the silver and diamond necklace he couldn't really afford would make Jenny less grumpy about him leaving.

He leant over and kissed her neck. 'So, babe, I have to pop in to the kids now and give them their presents.'

Jenny stiffened. 'How long will you be?'

'An hour, tops. That necklace looks so good on you.'

Jenny fingered the diamond. 'I love it. Okay, go and see the kids and say hi for me. I hope Jess likes the mini iPad.'

'She'll love it. It was a great idea. I'll tell her you thought of it.'

'Go and hurry back. I don't want to be on my own for long.'

'Sure.' Nick grabbed his jacket and ran out.

When he arrived at the back door of George's house, he could hear loud voices chatting and laughing. He peered in. They were all sitting around the kitchen table. Maggie was there too. God, he hoped she wasn't going to give him a hard time. She was all Team Kate, and he didn't want any hassle today. Even the French waitress was there – Kate had invited all the strays in town. Typical, he thought. She was always nice to everyone. It looked like fun, the way Christmas should be, lots of people and food and wine and chat. Nick missed the Christmases they used to have. Kate had always made a huge fuss and turned the house into Santa's grotto. Jenny had barely put up a tree: she'd said she didn't feel Christmassy and she was too tired.

He saw Jess, even frailer than she had been the other day, sitting in the middle, spinning the food around her plate, but clearly happy. He took a deep breath and plastered on a cheery smile as he pushed open the door. 'Hi, guys, Merry Christmas.'

'Dad!' Jess beamed up at him. The others muttered hello. At least someone was happy to see him.

'Hi, sweetie.' He went over and kissed her.

'Did you bring presents, Daddy?' Bobby asked.

'And a merry Christmas to you too,' Nick said, squeezing Bobby's nose in what he thought was a playful way but his son pulled back and said, 'Ouch.'

'Sit down here,' Kate said, pulling a chair over for him beside Jess. 'You have to taste Dad's Christmas pudding. He's surpassed himself this year.' She handed him a bottle of anti-bacterial sanitizer.

Nick doused his hands, then sat down gratefully. He pulled his presents out of his bag and handed them out to Jess, Luke and Bobby.

'OMG!' Jess squealed. 'A mini iPad! Wow, Dad, thanks so much.' She threw her stick-like arms around his neck.

'You're welcome, Jess. You deserve it.' He held her tightly. 'It was Jenny's idea. She said to send you her love.'

Jess nodded.

'What did you get, Bobby?' Kate asked.

'A football and a book about birds,' Bobby said, as he yanked off the wrapping, seeming decidedly unimpressed.

Obviously got it wrong again, Nick thought. 'It's to encourage you to play football, Bobby. I think, if you prac- tise, you might get into it. And you like facts, so I thought the book on bird facts would be up your alley.'

'That's great, Nick. Isn't it, Bobby?' Kate said, faking enthusiasm.

'I don't like football or birds.' Bobby kicked the edge of his chair. 'Jess is so lucky.'

Nick wanted to shout, *She has fucking cancer. Exactly how lucky is that?* He bit his lip and said nothing.

'Thanks,' Luke muttered, shoving his sweatshirt back into the bag.

Nick took a bite of the pudding. It was delicious. 'This is great, George, really delicious.'

'Glad you like it,' George said.

'I'm surprised you're eating it. I thought your body was a temple,' Maggie drawled.

'I let myself go sometimes, Maggie.'

'Oh, I know you do.' Maggie smirked.

Nick willed himself not to react. Maggie had never liked him. She'd always thought he wasn't good enough for Kate. She was one of those career types, a rampant feminist. She was all 'down with men' and 'let's break glass ceilings'. Nick found her hard to take. 'So, how's work, Maggie?' He decided to play nice.

'Good, thanks. The company is expanding and turnover is up.'

'Great.'

'You?'

'Things are on the up again,' Nick said. 'It was a tough few years.'

'It certainly was, more for some than others.' Maggie glared at him.

He couldn't win with her. Nick turned to Jess, who had barely touched her pudding. 'Hey, sweetie, try to eat a little more.'

'I'm not hungry, Dad. I feel a bit queasy.'

'Okay,' he said, rubbing her back.

'I think Jess might hit the hay soon,' Kate said, 'but you're very welcome to stay as long as you like, Nick.'

He nodded at her. 'Thanks. I have to go back, though. I'll enjoy this fantastic pudding and see Jess off to bed, but then I'll leave you all to your evening.' He felt a tiny stab of emotion, knowing that his place was no longer there. He didn't dare look at it closely enough to find out what exact emotion it was. He had to accept the new set-up and work with it, not go backwards.

They chatted about their presents and laughed about the pieces of coal George had left on Bobby's bedside locker as a joke. Kate asked politely about Jenny and Jaden and their first Christmas, but Nick knew no one was interested in hearing about that. When he saw Jess yawning, he stood up, intending to help her up to bed and then go home. Luke stopped him.

'Can you sit down, Dad, before you head off? There's something I need to tell you all.'

Nick turned to his son. His face was almost grey – as if he was about to puke. What was going on? He sat down again

274

and looked at Kate, who frowned and shrugged. Clearly she was in the dark too.

Luke clasped his hands together and took a deep breath. 'There is no easy way and no good time to say this, so I'll just say it. Piper's pregnant.'

Nick's mouth fell open. Beside him, Jess gasped, Kate put her hand over her mouth, and everyone else looked stunned.

Nick felt the blood run cold through his body. 'What the hell!'

'Sweet Jesus,' George muttered.

'Congratulations, Luke. You'll be a cool young dad and Piper will be a great mum,' the French waitress said.

Was she stupid? A cool young dad? Jesus Christ, this was a disaster. Nick turned to Kate again, but she seemed to have frozen solid, unmoving, unspeaking.

'There's nothing cool about having a kid at eighteen,' Nick snapped.

'Well, you had me at twenty-seven, and that didn't work out so well either,' Luke retorted.

'Don't cheek me after announcing that you've got your girlfriend pregnant. How could you be so stupid?'

'Don't you dare call me stupid!' Luke's face was bright red.

'Stop. Fighting isn't going to resolve anything,' Maggie said.

'Oh, Luke.' Tears welled in Kate's eyes.

'I'm sorry, Mum.' Luke was getting upset now.

'Don't cry, Luke,' Jess said. 'It'll be okay, won't it, Dad?'

Nick felt his temples throb. The stupidity of it. The bloody-minded stupidity of it. There was only one solution to this problem. 'You need to deal with it, Luke, and fast. You're too young to have a kid. You need to go to London.'

'We are not going to London,' Luke snapped.

'Yes, you are. You're not throwing your life away because of one stupid night.'

'What's in London?' Bobby asked.

'Nick, I don't think –' Kate began, but Luke shouted across her.

'I love Piper and we've decided to have the baby and I'm going to be a good father, one who shows up every day.'

Nick felt the sting. 'Yeah? Good luck with that. Don't come crying to me when you realize your mistake six months after the kid is born when your friends are in college and you're working in some dead-end job to support it.'

'I wouldn't come to you for anything,' Luke spat.

'Luke, your dad is right,' Kate said gently. 'This is a big decision and you need to take a moment and think about all of your options before making a final choice.'

'We have, Mum. We've thought about nothing else and we're not going to London. We've decided to keep it.'

'What's in London?' Bobby asked again.

'But how are you going to support it, Luke? You're both so young,' Kate reminded him, twisting her napkin into a knot in her fingers.

'Maggie's going to help.'

'What?' Kate looked like she'd been slapped in the face. Her cheeks had two spots of red as she turned to her friend. 'You knew about this?'

Maggie nodded slowly. 'Luke called me to ask for help. He didn't want to burden you as you have so much going on with Jess. I advised him to consider London as an option, but they decided against it. So I said they could have my little apartment here. I'll get rid of my tenants. They can still go to college and pay me whatever rent they can afford.'

'WHAT'S IN LONDON?' Bobby shouted.

'Nothing,' George said. 'Nothing for you to worry about. This conversation shouldn't be happening in front of the kids. Bobby and Jess, away upstairs with you.'

'I want to stay,' Jess said.

Nick shook his head. 'George is right. This is grown-up stuff.'

'Please, Jess, would you take Bobby to watch TV?' Kate asked.

Jess reluctantly got up and ushered Bobby out of the room.

'How could you not tell me?' Kate asked Maggie.

'I'm sorry, Kate. I didn't want to upset you, not with the way things are. I told Luke that when they had made their decision he had to tell you straight away. I guess I was trying to protect you.' She gazed pleadingly at Kate, who continued to stare at her in disbelief.

'How could you?' Kate said. 'Leaving me to find out like this. Keeping it a secret. I never thought you'd –'

'Stop, Mum,' Luke said. 'Don't be angry with Maggie. She's been a rock. Her offer to give us the apartment at a low rent means we can go to college and work part-time. I think we can do it all, Mum, I really do. Maggie just did what we asked, but she also said we had to tell you as soon as possible.'

Maggie reached over and put her hand over Kate's. 'It was a difficult situation and, on top of Jess, I had to do what I thought was best. I'm so sorry.'

Kate took a deep breath. 'Luke's right. You supported them. I shouldn't be upset with you. Sorry.'

Nick was staring at his eldest son, unable to believe what Luke was willingly walking into. God, he was so naive! As if love was ever enough! Luke hadn't a clue what lay ahead of him. Having a baby with no money, while trying to study and hold down a part-time job, was going to be a living nightmare. Christ knew it was hard enough when you were forty-five and had a decent job. The plain fact was that Luke was going to ruin his life, and Nick didn't want that. He wanted Luke to have the life he himself hadn't had – to go to college, travel, work in London or New York, meet people and have wonderful experiences.

Nick had gone straight to work from school, then got married young and had kids. He'd sold houses to guys who'd gone to college and spent twenty years on Wall Street making a fortune. They'd decide to come back to Ireland to raise their kids and buy big houses with barely any mortgage because they'd made so much money on bonuses and fat salaries.

Nick wanted that for Luke. He wanted his son to be the guy buying the big house, not the guy selling it to him. He wanted Luke to have it all. Getting tied down with a baby at eighteen years of age would ruin his life choices. It was a mess. He had to try to persuade him, to make him see sense.

'Luke, please listen to me. Don't do this. You have your whole life ahead of you. Don't blow it by making a stupid decision. I'll talk to your girlfriend – I'll make her see what a bad idea this is.'

Luke bent over the table and shoved his finger in Nick's face. 'You stay away from Piper. She's the best thing in my life. We've decided together to keep the baby and no one is going to change our minds, least of all you.'

'You're making a huge mistake,' Nick said.

'He hasn't taken this decision lightly, Nick. He's really thought about it,' Maggie said.

'Does her father know?' Nick asked. 'I'm sure he'll want her to go to London.'

'We told them yesterday,' Luke said, glaring at his father. 'Yes, they are shocked, but they're offering us their support.'

'Are you absolutely sure about your decision, Luke?' Kate asked.

He nodded. 'Yes, Mum. Look, I'm sorry, I know this is the last thing you need right now. I never meant it to happen but it did and . . . well, I'm sorry, Mum.' He wiped the tears from his eyes.

Kate got up and went over to put her arms around him. 'It's okay, Luke, it's okay. We'll work it out. We'll all help you and we'll muddle through, like we always do. I love you and I don't want you to blame yourself or feel bad.'

Luke sank into her arms and buried his head in her shoulder. Nick felt a pang of jealousy. Kate was so good with the kids. He wished he could connect with them like she did. He'd have to make more effort. Kids really were hard work. Luke had no idea what he was in for. No idea at all.

31

Kate finished filling Liam in and took a sip of her hot chocolate. She had been dying to tell him. She'd just known he'd understand and be sympathetic. He was the one person she wanted to confide in when anything happened, these days.

'Wow! Never a dull moment in your house,' he said.

'I'm forty-two, and I'm going to be a grandmother.' Kate laughed bitterly.

'Not ideal, I grant you that. But if I could try to point out some positives? At least you like Piper, her parents are on board to help out, Maggie's chipping in as well, and Luke's standing up and being a responsible young man. That's something to be very proud of, you know.'

Kate raised an eyebrow. 'It's a pity he couldn't have been more responsible when he was having sex. Then he wouldn't be in this mess.'

She was sick with anxiety about it. As if worrying about Jess wasn't bad enough, now she had to worry about Luke. The awkward meeting with Piper's parents on St Stephen's Day had been made less awful than she'd expected because Piper's parents were lovely. Well, the mother was lovely. The father was quiet, clearly angry and devastated.

Luke hadn't told Nick about the meeting and had begged Kate not to. He said he didn't want Nick ruining it by trying to force them to have an abortion in front of Piper's parents.

Thankfully, it quickly became apparent that Piper's parents were fully on board to help out and be supportive, a huge relief to Kate. She promised them that Luke would be a good father and would not renege on his duties, no matter what happened between him and Piper.

Every time Kate saw Luke, she wanted to cry. He'd had such a bright future and now it was going to be a mess. Maggie kept saying it would be okay, that they'd work it out so he could go to college, but Kate still worried. It was a mammoth responsibility on young shoulders.

'Come on, Kate, we were all young once, and were we responsible all the time? I doubt it. Luke was unlucky, very unlucky, but it doesn't mean his life is over. With both families and their friends supporting them, they'll be fine. They sound like a lovely pair of young people,' Liam said.

Kate leant forward, so Nathalie, who was clearing up, couldn't hear her. 'Is it awful to wish they'd had an abortion and put it behind them?'

Liam shook his head. 'No, it's human nature to want the best for your kids and to protect them from struggles. But this may not be the worst thing in the world. We both have kids and we love them. Would we change a hair on their heads? No. Is there ever really a right time to have children?'

'After school would be a good start!'

Liam grinned. 'You have a point there. Will she be able to sit her exams?'

'Yes. Her due date is early July, but the poor thing will be doing them hugely pregnant.'

'Tough, but not impossible.'

Kate looked at his kind, open face. 'Are you always this optimistic?'

He smiled. 'Only when faced with someone desperate to see light at the end of a dark tunnel. You've had a huge amount to deal with, but you're strong. You've raised wonderful kids. It'll all work out.'

Kate smiled and squeezed his hand. 'Thank you for listening and for making me feel better. Thank God I went to the mindfulness class. I hated it but I met you.'

Liam blushed and focused on sipping his cappuccino.

Nathalie came over. 'I am finished with the cleaning. Are you okay for drinks? Would you not prefer to 'ave a glass of wine?'

'I think if I open a bottle I may never stop,' Kate said.

'Poor Kate.' Nathalie patted her shoulder. 'She is 'aving the very stressful time. Why Luke could not put on the condom? I understand Piper not taking the pill, it make girls fat. I say *non* to the pill, but I always use the condom.'

'If only all young people were as sensible as you,' Liam said, winking at Kate.

'It's not sensible. It's fear. I never want to be 'aving the children. I 'ate babies – crying, sheeting and doing the *pipi* everywhere. *Non, merci.* I like nice clothes and beautiful rugs and books not ruined by chocolate hands or the snotty nose.'

Liam threw his head back and laughed, a kind of joyful hooting. Kate found it infectious and soon joined in.

Liam wiped tears from his eyes. 'Nathalie, you are too much. Babies do more than just secrete all over the place. They're great fun too.'

Nathalie shrugged in her nonchalant French way. 'Maybe fun for you, but for me a nightmare.'

'I won't put you down for babysitting duties then,' Kate said.

'When the baby can go to the toilet and wash their own 'ands, I am 'appy to 'elp.'

'So, about fourteen if it's a boy, then!' Liam chuckled.

Even Nathalie laughed. 'Yes, and two if it's a girl, *non*?'

Liam nodded. 'Yes.'

Nathalie studied Liam's face. 'You know, if you cut this beard short or maybe shave it off, you could be quite good-looking.'

Liam put his hand on his heart. 'From you, Nathalie, that backhanded compliment means a lot.'

'Seriously, you should cut it and put on a shirt that 'as been ironed. This look as if your dog sleep on it.'

Liam laughed again. 'He probably did.'

'Well, if you want to impress a lady,' Nathalie grinned, 'you need to be a bit better with the grooming and the fashion.'

It was Kate's turn to blush. 'Thanks, Nathalie. That's enough advice for one evening.'

As she was leaving, Nathalie said to Kate, 'I like this one. 'Airy, but funny and kind.'

When she'd gone, Kate looked down at her cup. 'Sorry, she can be a bit too free and easy with her advice.'

Liam stroked his beard. 'You know, she's right, I should do better with "the grooming and the fashion".'

Kate laughed. 'You're fine the way you are.'

'I'd like to be more than fine.' Liam stared straight at her.

'I didn't mean it like that. You're great.'

Liam beamed. 'You're pretty great yourself.'

Kate wasn't comfortable with the way the conversation was going so she changed the subject. She really liked Liam. In the short time she'd known him he had become someone she trusted and whose company she enjoyed, but she just didn't find him attractive and, in any case, she had no space for any kind of romance. She could barely breathe with all that was going on.

'So, how's work?'

'Work is fine. I've got some very intense students eager to get firsts. It's amazing how much more focused kids are, these days. When I started out teaching Spanish, the lectures were only ever half full on a good day. Now, every lecture is almost eighty per cent full and the kids are killing themselves studying. I don't know if it's better or worse. More importantly, how's Jess?'

Kate poked at a small marshmallow that was stuck to the bottom of her hot chocolate cup. She'd have to stop drinking it or she'd put on the weight she'd lost due to stress. 'To be honest, I'm worried about her. Larry dying has really set her back. She's heartbroken, and he was so good at cheering her up and making the days less long. It's just awful that he's gone. She'll miss him so much. He was so young and a really lovely boy. It really scared me. He'd been in remission three times, but it came back and . . . Well, he's gone now. I'm trying really hard not to think about it. I'm just focusing on the fact that, in two days' time, Jess is having the tests done to see if the bone-marrow transplant has put her into complete remission. I'm sick with nerves.'

'I'll pray it all goes well. How does she seem?'

Kate tried to swallow the fear that rose in her throat every time she thought about it. Jess didn't look well. She was constantly exhausted and slept a lot. Kate didn't even want to allow herself to think about it, but Jess had seemed worse in the last ten days. The results had to be good. They just had to. 'I don't know, really. She looks so frail. I'm a bit worried, to be honest.'

Liam put his cup down. 'I know it's frightening for you. Look, I'm here day or night, so just call me. I remember nights being the worst time, when you wake up and it's four a.m., and you know you're not going to get back to sleep and you start thinking very dark thoughts. Honestly, call me anytime. I'm not a great sleeper anyway – chances are I'll be awake, reading.'

He got it, Kate thought. Only someone who had been through this could understand. That was exactly how she felt when she woke up – terrified. She often wished she could talk to someone to calm herself down. One night, in complete desperation, she'd called Nick. Jaden had been woken by the noise of the phone ringing and Jenny had gone mad. Nick had tried to be nice to her, but had hung up after a minute because Jenny was shouting at him.

She smiled at Liam. 'You may regret that offer.'

He smiled back. 'I won't.'

Kate glanced at the clock on the wall. 'Shoot! I have to go. I had no idea it was so late. I want to try to get Jess to eat something.'

'Good luck and keep me posted. I'm crossing all fingers for good news.'

Liam leant down and gave Kate a bear hug. She kissed the side of his scratchy beard and said goodbye.

32

Kate tucked Bobby into his bed and turned out the light. She went in to Jess, who was lying on her side with her eyes closed, quietly changed into her pyjamas and lay down beside her daughter in the double bed. Looking at the dandelion card on the bedside table, she said a prayer to Larry: 'Wherever you are, please help her. Please may the results be good. Please may she be in complete remission. Please, Larry, please.'

Jess had barely touched her food at dinner. She'd said she was feeling tired and had gone to bed at eight. Kate had wanted to weep. This was not a good sign. She didn't look like someone who was getting better. All of the hope was draining right out of Kate's bones.

'Mum, will you read to me?' Jess said, startling her.

'Of course I will. I thought you were asleep.'

Jess rolled over to face her. 'No, just resting.'

'How do you feel?'

'Same.'

'Would you eat any little thing now? I bought you chocolate milk. Luke said it's great for energy.'

'Gross,' Jess said.

'How about a scone? Or a muffin? Or a yoghurt?'

Jess shook her head. 'Sorry, but no. I don't feel hungry.'

Kate studied her daughter's pinched face and scrawny arms and tried not to worry. 'Will I continue with *Jane Eyre*?'

'Yes, I like the crazy woman. I want to know who she is.'

Kate cuddled Jess to her and began to read. She inhaled the smell of her daughter, the essence of her. Jess snuggled into her mother's shoulder.

As Kate was about to start a new chapter, a little voice said, 'I miss him.'

Kate put down her Kindle and held her daughter to her. She's like a broken sparrow, she thought. A tiny broken sparrow. 'I'm so sorry, sweetie. I wish it hadn't happened.'

'Me too,' Jess whispered. 'If I die, I'll send you a sign, I promise. I told Larry if I died first, I'd send him a white butterfly. I'll do the same for you.'

Kate squeezed her eyes tightly shut. She didn't want to hear that. She didn't want Jess ever to say the word 'die'. 'You don't need to think about signs or any of that, darling. You're not going anywhere.' She held her tighter. 'Please don't talk like that. I won't let you go, ever. You're going to get better. You must believe it.'

Jess sighed. 'Okay, Mum.'

'I love you so much, Jess. I just can't bear to hear you talk about signs. You can buy me a white butterfly for my birthday and give it to me. Okay?'

'Sure.'

Kate switched on her Kindle.

'Mum?'

'Yes?'

'I think it's nice Luke's having a baby. I know he's young, but it's what life's about, really, isn't it? Finding someone you love and having kids.'

'Well, I suppose so, yes. Children are the best thing in life. I just wish Luke and Piper weren't so young.'

'It'll be the cutest baby ever. Luke and Piper are so gorgeous. It'll have amazing blue eyes like them and really thick shiny brown hair. Chloë said she bets it'll look like Megan Fox if it's a girl and Zac Efron if it's a boy.'

Kate had no idea who those people were but she nodded. 'Gorgeous.'

'I wish I had blue eyes.'

'Jess,' Kate said, looking into her daughter's eyes, 'you have the most beautiful melt-your-heart brown ones I've ever seen.'

'You always say I'm beautiful, even when I look terrible, like right now.'

Kate held Jess's small face in her hands and smiled. 'You are the most wonderful, stunning creature on this earth and always will be.'

Jess giggled. 'Yeah, right! I look like crap.'

'No, you don't. You look incredible, considering what you've been through. We just need to feed you up.'

Jess laid her bald head on Kate's chest. 'Tell me about the day I was born again.'

Kate kissed it. 'There was a huge thunderstorm and a bolt of lightning struck as you were being born. I knew then that you'd be invincible. Your dad wanted to call you Storm, but I said no. Jess was always my favourite name. I stood my ground on that one. The doctor said, "This girl will be extraordinary." He'd never seen a child being born on the strike of lightning. We knew then that you were special, really, truly special, and you are, Jess. You're so special.'

Kate looked down. Jess was fast asleep. She held her daughter and prayed to the god of thunder and lightning to give Jess strength and help her beat cancer for good.

33

Dr Kennedy took off his glasses. Kate stopped breathing. If they take off their glasses, you're screwed. She knew this from all the hospital TV shows she'd watched. Whenever the doctor removes his glasses, it's inevitably bad news.

'I'm very sorry, but the bone-marrow transplant has not been successful ... The test results showed a relapse ... Most unfortunate.'

'Relapse' was the word Kate heard through the fog. Such an ordinary little word, but it had the ability to destroy you. She'd known. In her heart she'd known Jess wasn't getting better. In the first two weeks after the transplant she'd been full of hope, but after Christmas she'd watched Jess go downhill. She'd barely eaten, slept all the time, shrunk physically before Kate's eyes. She'd known, but she hadn't let herself know.

Oh, Jess, my beautiful Jess. Why hadn't Luke's bone marrow worked? He was so strong and healthy. They'd all been so sure it would save her. Kate had allowed herself to hope. Why? Why? Why?

Her head felt as if it was being crushed. What did this really mean? Was Jess going to die? No, no way. They'd fix her – they'd find a way. There had to be more treatment. They'd only tried one bone-marrow transplant – they could do another. Maybe with donor marrow. This was only the beginning. But Jess was so weak: could she take any more treatment? What about infections? Kate bent over and clutched her stomach. The pain was searing. There had to be light – there had to be some kind of light at the end of this dark tunnel. Please, God.

'Okay, so it didn't work, which is – is a setback. So what do we do now?' Nick snapped. 'More chemo? Another transplant? How do we fix this? How do we make her better? What's the plan?'

Dr Kennedy explained that there were some options. He said that approximately thirty per cent of children with AML experienced relapse. He spoke of re-induction regimens . . . high-dose cytarabine . . . anthracycline . . . depending on cardiac function . . . fludarabine . . . clofarabine . . . Kate's head spun. She couldn't take it in, couldn't begin to fathom what all those words meant.

Nick banged his hand on the desk. 'Can you just give it to us in plain English, please? What can we do now?'

Dr Kennedy clasped his hands together. 'I would suggest that we could try one course of chemotherapy using novel agents. I have to warn you that it is aggressive and there are risks involved. Jess is weak, and infections would be a concern. But if she reacted well, it could certainly help to get her back into remission, partial or otherwise.'

Nick stood up. 'Right, let's do it. When do we start?'

Aggressive chemotherapy? When was it not aggressive? If Dr Kennedy was saying it was going to be aggressive, it must be horrendous, Kate thought, with a shudder. Jess was so weak – could she take it? Would it kill her? Kate's head was spinning with fear and questions and worry and terror.

'Can she start tomorrow?' Nick asked.

'Wait, hold on,' Kate said, raising her head. 'Can she take it? Should we wait until she's a bit stronger? Should we build her up? Is it safe?'

'She's not getting stronger,' Nick snapped. 'For Christ's sake, Kate, she's getting worse. We have to act now.'

Kate pressed her fingers to her temples to try to help her think straight. This was Jess's life they were talking about. They had to be sure it was the right decision. It felt so rushed. At one second you're told the treatment hasn't worked, and the next you're discussing new options, aggressive options . . . There was no time to process it all. She had to be absolutely sure.

Kate eyeballed Dr Kennedy. 'If it was your daughter, would you do this?'

He looked her straight in the eye. 'I think it's worth trying.'

Kate breathed deeply. 'Then let's do it.'

'We need to discuss it with Jess. Would you rather do it or would you like me to?' Dr Kennedy asked.

'I think she needs to hear it from you. You can explain it better,' Nick said.

Kate bit her lip so hard, she drew blood.

Dr Kennedy stood up and went to call Jess in. She was sitting outside, reading a magazine.

Kate patted the empty chair beside her. Jess was searching her eyes for answers. Kate blinked back tears. Jess's face fell. She knew. Kate reached out to hold her hand. Jess closed her eyes and breathed deeply.

'How are you feeling, Jess?' Dr Kennedy said quietly.

'Not great,' Jess whispered.

As clearly as he could, Dr Kennedy explained that the treatment hadn't worked, and that they were going to try another round of more radical chemo. It was torture watching Jess's face as she took in the news. Nick put his hand on her shoulder and squeezed it tightly.

'Do you understand what I've said to you, Jess?' the doctor asked.

'Yes, I do. I knew it hadn't worked,' she said quietly.

Kate wanted to throw her arms around her, to take away her pain, but she was useless in the face of this stupid, horrible, cruel disease.

'So, you think this new chemo could help?' Jess asked.

'I think it's worth trying.'

'Is it going to be worse than the other chemo?'

'It's going to be a bit more aggressive.'

'Oh.'

Kate reached out and put her arms around her daughter, but Jess shrugged her off. She moved away from Nick too.

'We're only going to do one course,' Dr Kennedy said.

'It's only about six days and then it'll be done. It's worth it, Jess,' Nick said.

Jess glared at him. 'It's not your body, Dad. It's not you who has to have poison put into you that makes you so sick you want to die.'

Nick flinched. 'I know, Jessie. I know it's awful, but it'll make you better. What's a week against a lifetime?'

'*Might* make me better, Dad,' Jess corrected.

Kate laid her hand gently on Jess's arm. 'Why don't you have some time to think about it? It's a lot to take in.'

'There's nothing to think about,' Nick barked. 'She's doing it, starting ASAP.'

Kate frowned at him. 'Give her time, Nick.'

'We don't have time!'

Dr Kennedy stood up. 'Jess, take a day or two to think it over and discuss it with your parents. When you've made your decision you can call me and we'll take it from there.'

Nick shook a finger in his face. 'There's no taking a few days to think it over. She's doing it. Set it up.'

Dr Kennedy regarded him coldly. 'It's important for Jess to have time to consider the option I've set out before her.

Take a day or two to process it. Let me know when you've made a decision.' He showed them out.

They walked down the corridor in shattered silence. Kate looked at Nick, pleading with her eyes for him to let it drop for now. But Nick was like a man possessed. He arranged his face into an awkward smile and moved close to Jess. 'You have to start as soon as possible, Jess. We don't have a minute to waste. We need to get on with it.'

'Stop hassling me, Dad!'

'Leave her, Nick,' Kate said. 'She's had a shock.'

Nick rubbed his eyes. 'Look, I'm not hassling you, Jess. I just want to make you better.'

'It might not work, though, and it's going to be awful.' Jess began to cry. 'I hate this. I hate it so much.'

'Oh, Jess, it will work – it has to.' Nick's voice cracked as he bent down to hug her.

Kate watched them, and let her own tears flow. If she could have taken Jess's place, she'd have done it in a heartbeat, without a thought. She'd welcome physical pain: it would be a relief from the constant emotional torture. But she couldn't do anything. She was useless. Utterly useless. The cancer was doing whatever it wanted, rampaging around her daughter's body, and she hadn't a single weapon to use against it. The first instinct of motherhood was to protect. That was her duty. And she couldn't fulfil it. She felt a grief that took her breath away – grief for her beautiful Jess and grief for her inability to help her. Looking at Nick, she knew it was killing him too. They were failures.

Jess peered up and saw her mother crying. She held out her arm. Kate went over and the three of them held each other, each praying for a miracle, each praying for an end to the hell they were in.

34

Jess was trying not to hyperventilate. She looked in the hand mirror for the zillionth time. Piper reached over and took it from her.

'You're gorgeous.'

'Totally fab,' Chloë agreed. 'Piper did, like, an awesome job on your make-up.'

Jess smiled nervously. 'Is he definitely coming? Like, definitely?'

'Yes.' Chloë grinned. 'I've told you a zillion times. Mum told Dad that we needed to cheer you up because you were about to start the new horrible chemo. So Dad called his friend, who knows Drago's agent, and he phoned the agent and he said Drago was in Dublin for a week and he'd come to see you. The fact that he's here the week of your chemo is, like, Fate. You could be destined for each other.'

Jess giggled. Chloë was mad but in the best way. This had been such a brilliant distraction from the hell she was facing tomorrow. She was so happy to have this visit to take her mind off the chemo. She was dreading it more than anything and felt panicky every time she thought about it.

But today ... Drago Jackson was coming to hospital to visit her! The coolest singer ever. She couldn't believe it. Since Chloë had FaceTimed her, screaming, two days ago to tell her, she'd barely slept. Drago Jackson! It was unbelievable.

She worshipped him. 'Never Let Me Go' was her favourite song ever. Larry used to make fun of her obsession and tell her she was a freak, that he was just a sixteen-year-old geek and couldn't sing, that it was all backing tracks and lip-synching. But Jess hadn't believed him: she thought Drago was the best singer ever. His voice was amazing.

'Do you know if the baby's a boy or a girl?' Chloë asked Piper.

'No. We've decided to wait. We want it to be a surprise.'

'That's cool. Are you excited?'

Piper instinctively put her hand to her stomach. 'Yes. Now that everyone knows and is being so supportive, I feel calmer and excited. Nervous, too, though.'

'You'll be such a cool mum,' Chloë said. 'I'd love to have you and Luke as my parents.'

Piper laughed. 'I'm not so sure about that, but thanks.'

'And me as their aunt,' Jess said, applying lip-gloss for the tenth time.

'Totally,' Chloë agreed. 'You'll be such a brilliant auntie, and I can be like a nearly aunt, can't I?'

'Of course you can,' Piper said.

'Your mum's like my fairy godmother,' Jess told Chloë. 'I still can't believe she organized this for me. I'm so happy.'

Chloë flicked back her long blonde hair. 'You know she adores you. She's, like, "Jess is the sweetest girl ever" *all* the time. If you weren't my BF and I didn't love you so much, it would be really annoying.'

Jess and Piper laughed. Chloë peered out of the hospital room's door. 'Here comes your mum.'

Kate came rushing in. 'He's here! Hazel just texted. They're on the way up.'

Chloë and Jess started screaming. Kate covered her ears. 'Girls, calm down, you'll scare him.'

'He's well used to screaming girls,' Piper assured her. 'It's what his career's based on.'

'OMG! It's him.' Chloë ducked back into the room and ran around flapping her arms, grinning wildly at Jess.

Jess's mouth was dry. She thought she might faint. Her mother went over and held her hand. 'Breathe, darling. He's just a boy who can sing.'

She didn't get it. Drago wasn't a boy who could sing, he was the coolest, most divine person on this earth. Jess hadn't felt this alive or excited since . . . She didn't know how long, but definitely since she'd got cancer. It was the *best* day. She'd love Hazel for ever.

Just as Jess started seeing double and was about to pass out, he came through the door.

'Ta-dah!' Hazel said. 'Jess, this is Drago. Drago, this is the wonderful Jess.'

Drago was shorter than Jess had expected. He was only a tiny bit taller than Chloë. He was gorgeous, though. Chloë was staring at him with her mouth open.

'Goldfish, Chloë,' Hazel said.

Chloë automatically closed her mouth but continued to stare.

'This is my daughter, Chloë. She'll stop staring in a minute.' Hazel nudged Drago towards Jess's bed.

'Hey, what's up?' he said, in his gorgeous American accent.

'Hi,' was all Jess could say. She felt so dumb, but she couldn't think of anything to say to him.

There was an awkward silence. Drago shuffled his feet.

'Jess is a big fan.' Piper broke the silence. 'What's your favourite song, Jess?'

'It's "Never Let Me Go". I love that one.' Jess blushed.

'Cool,' Drago said.

'What's the song about?' Kate asked.

Drago shrugged. 'You know, just about, like, never letting go and stuff.'

'My favourite is "I'm Hot And I Know It",' Chloë said, her eyes never leaving Drago's face. 'It's such a cool dance song.'

'Cool,' Drago said, nodding.

'What's that about, then?' Hazel asked, cracking up.

'It's about being hot.' Drago didn't get the sarcasm.

Jess didn't want them making fun of Drago. 'Are you working on a new album?' she asked.

'Yeah, totally.'

'Is it true you're dating Katie Ryan?' Chloë asked.

'Nah, we're just friends.'

'Are you dating anyone?' Chloë looked hopeful.

'Kinda, not really,' Drago said.

Jess wished she wasn't bald and skinny and sick. Maybe if she was healthy and had her hair back, he might look at her. But she had no chance now. Still, it was nice to dream. She wished she could think of something clever to ask. She racked her brains. 'Are you in Ireland for a break?' she asked.

Drago took the fingernail he was biting out of his mouth. 'I'm hooking up with a songwriter here to check out some tunes.'

'Do you like the songs?'

Drago crinkled his nose. 'I guess so.'

'Oh, for the love of Jesus,' Hazel muttered. 'Why don't you sing us something?' she asked him.

Drago looked shocked. 'No way, man. No one told me I'd have to sing. They said just come and say hi.'

Hazel's face darkened. 'Can I have a word?' she asked, dragging him outside by the arm.

They watched as Hazel yanked him out of the room and closed the door. Through the window onto the corridor, they could see her shouting at him. Jess winced as she heard her say, 'What the hell is wrong with you? There is a very sick girl in there and I've paid a bloody fortune for you to come and visit her. You're a fucking singer, so sing something, you moron.'

Chloë and Jess exchanged a horrified look. Hazel was going to mess it all up. He'd walk out of there without a backward glance.

'Dude, my manager said I was to come and say hi to the sick kid and, like, talk for a bit and then I was done.'

'Your manager is a dickhead because that was not the deal. I am telling you now, get your skinny arse in there and sing something. I don't care what you sing and I don't care if it's out of tune, just open your goddamn mouth and sing. In fact, sing her that song she likes and then you can go back to La La Land and snort your millions up your nose, for all I care. But you are not going to let that girl down, okay?'

'Jeez, I did not sign up for this. I'm gonna kill Nikki.'

'Yeah, well, Nikki isn't here. He's back in the hotel charging me a fortune to put him up in that suite. So stop moaning and get in there.'

Chloë shook her head. 'My mum is so embarrassing. I am never going to get over the mortification of this. Did you hear her cursing at him? She just shouted at Drago Jackson to sing!'

Jess giggled. 'It's kind of funny.' She was disappointed that Drago wasn't nicer, but she still loved him.

The door opened. Hazel and Drago came back in.

'Drago is going to sing you that song you like. Aren't you, Drago?'

'Yeah, whatever, but, like, I don't have a track to sing to and my throat is dry, so it might not sound too good.'

'You don't have to sing if you don't want to.' Jess didn't want him to feel bad. This was hard for him. Stuck in a hospital room with five women staring at him. She felt sorry for him. It was a lot of pressure.

Hazel raised her hand. 'Drago is going to sing now.' She handed him a glass of water. 'Drink this for your dry throat and get on with it.'

Chloë was standing beside Jess. 'OMG, she is *so* bossy,' she whispered.

Drago cleared his throat. Jess clasped her hands together and waited for her favourite song.

> *My girl needs to love me the way I deserve,*
> *Else I'm gonna go.*
> *She ain't giving me what I need.*
> *I said I'm leavin' but she says, 'Never let me go . . .'*

Drago's voice was off key in parts. It sounded different – not in a good way – from the actual song. His throat must be very dry, Jess thought . . . or Larry was right, and it is all backing tracks.

He sang another verse, then stopped.

'Is that it?' Hazel barked. 'Is that the whole song?'

'No, there's more,' Chloë said.

'Sing on,' Hazel commanded.

'Dude, I can't. My voice is hurting, and I have to preserve it for my performance next week.'

'Listen here –'

'Hazel, it's okay.' Jess didn't want Hazel to force Drago to sing on. He was going to hate Jess for being the cause of all this. 'It was lovely of Drago to sing for me. I'm so grateful, but I understand he has to mind his voice.' To Drago she said, 'That was amazing. Thank you.'

'Yeah, well, you're welcome. I, like, hope you feel better soon.'

'Thanks.'

He asked Hazel, 'Can I go now?'

'Don't you have something to give her?' Hazel flared at him.

'Oh, yeah.' Drago fished around in his jacket pocket and handed Jess a signed CD of his latest album. It said, 'To Jessie, get beter soon, Drago, xx'.

'OMG! He misspelt better.' Chloë clamped a hand over her mouth.

Jess shushed her. 'Thank you so much.'

'Cool, so I'm gonna go now.' Drago scurried towards the door, followed by Hazel.

They heard her mutter, 'Thirty grand for five minutes and you can't sing.'

There was silence in the room, until Chloë said, 'Who knew Drago Jackson can't sing or spell?' and burst out laughing.

Jess looked down at the CD and began to laugh too. Then Kate and Piper joined in. They laughed until tears rolled down their faces.

When Hazel arrived back, they were still laughing. Her harassed face broke into a smile. 'Jesus, I'm glad you're all laughing – I was afraid you'd be crying. Useless, overindulged eejit of a boy.'

Jess wiped tears from her eyes. 'Thank you, Hazel. It was the best morning ever.'

'I'm sorry he was such a disappointment,' Hazel said.

'He wasn't,' Jess protested. 'I loved him, and I kind of feel sorry for him. I used to want to be famous, but now I'm not sure. It's a lot of pressure.'

'Pressure, my arse,' Hazel exclaimed. 'Pressure is having cancer, not singing out of tune.'

They all laughed again.

'Wait until I tell everyone that my mum forced Drago to sing and shouted at him. You're mad, Mum, but I love you.'

Hazel threw her arms around Chloë and kissed the top of her head. 'Well, to see Jess laughing and hear you say you love me, it was worth every penny.'

35

Kate and Olivia stood at the side of the bed, their faces turned towards the scanner. On the screen they could see Piper's baby clearly. As the sonographer moved the probe around, clicking images and measuring the child, they stood shoulder to shoulder, watching in silence.

Seeing the baby on the screen made it all very real in a new way. Kate could feel herself getting emotional. Her baby's baby. Her firstborn's child. It was insane, yet here they were, staring at this tiny new life.

She glanced at Luke, who was squeezing Piper's hand and shaking his head in amazement. They looked so young. Kate caught Olivia's eye – she was welling up too. Kate knew she was thinking the same thing: they were too young for all this responsibility. But they had made their decision and their families had to respect it and try to help.

If there was one thing Jess's cancer had taught Kate it was that you never knew what was around the corner. You could make all the plans you wanted for your children, but life would slam you in the face at any second and turn your world upside-down.

Who knew? Maybe they'd be great parents and it would all work out. Kate just had to hope for the best. She smiled encouragingly at Olivia, and Olivia raised her eyebrows and sighed. From what she'd seen of her so far, Kate really liked Olivia. She seemed down-to-earth and forthright. You knew where you stood with someone like Olivia. It would be a great help to the whole situation if the two grannies got on well. Kate winced. Granny! It was crazy.

She looked back at the screen. The baby floated around before them, oblivious to them in its dark world. It really was a miracle to think that inside Piper's stomach a child was being formed. It was what life was about, Kate thought. Life creating life. Motherhood was her *raison d'être*. She vowed to be a good grandmother and love this child as much as she did her own three.

The sonographer began talking to Luke and Piper, and showing them the measurements. Olivia leant against Kate and said quietly, 'They're so young.'

'That's just what I was thinking. God, I hope they'll be all right.'

'I think we're going to have to do a lot of minding and helping out,' Olivia whispered.

'I agree. They have no idea what's ahead.'

'None,' Olivia said. 'I hope it works out.'

'Me too.' Kate took Olivia's hand and squeezed it.

'I'm so glad you're on board, Kate. I was worried before we met that you'd want nothing to do with it all.'

'Gosh, no! I want to help as much as I can,' Kate assured her. 'This is Luke's responsibility and my grandchild. I'll be there every step of the way.'

'I really appreciate it. I know you have your hands full at the moment with Jess. We're all praying for her. Piper's so fond of her.'

'Thank you. Jess adores Piper – she's so lovely to her. She's a credit to you.'

Olivia's eyes filled again. 'She's a great girl. I just wish her father would come around – he's heartbroken. He can't handle it at all.'

'Fathers can be difficult.' Kate sighed. Nick had called her ten times to try to get her to force Luke and Piper into having an abortion. He was driving her mad. She knew he only wanted the best for Luke, but he needed to bloody well accept the baby instead of fighting it. He had chosen the path of most aggression – with the doctors, with cancer, and now with an unborn baby. It was unhelpful and bloody exhausting.

'I think Luke's going to be a great dad,' Olivia said. 'He's a really genuine boy. You've raised him well.'

'I hope so. It hasn't been easy for him with Nick leaving and all that, but he's been such a rock to me. I think he's probably more responsible than most eighteen-year-olds – he's had to be.'

'Maybe they'll make it,' Olivia said.

'We have to hope so,' Kate said.

Luke came over to them. 'I have to go. I've got rugby training.'

'I can give you a lift – I've a seminar to get to now,' Olivia said.

'You guys go ahead. I'll drop Piper home,' Kate offered.

'Are you sure?' Olivia asked.

'Absolutely.'

'Cool. Thanks, Mum.' Luke leant over to kiss her cheek. 'I'll be in to see Jess later. And thanks for being here today, Mum.'

'The baby's beautiful, Luke.'

He grinned. 'I know. It's incredible to see it growing.'

Kate watched them go as Piper wiped the gel off her stomach and pulled up her tracksuit bottoms.

She waddled over to Kate. 'Thanks for dropping me home.'

'I'm happy to. It was lovely to see the baby. It was a great distraction. Thanks for asking me to come.'

'I really wanted you to see it. I wanted my mum and dad to see it too. Dad said no, though.' Piper's cheeks flushed.

'Give him time. Nick hasn't totally come around either. Fathers can take longer to accept things.'

'I hope you're right. He seems so disappointed in me. It's hard to . . . to . . .' Piper began to sob.

Kate steered her to a row of chairs in the reception area and sat down beside her. It was the first time they had been alone together, and the first time Kate saw how hard the poor girl was struggling. 'Hey, now. I know it's hard for you, but your dad loves you and nothing can change that.'

'That's what Mum says. I'm sorry, Kate, I didn't mean to cry. I'm so emotional all the time. I just feel so bad for upsetting everyone. I know this must be hard for you. I mean, you've got so much stress with Jess – you really didn't need your son's stupid girlfriend getting pregnant.'

Kate patted Piper's hand. 'Don't you go blaming yourself. It takes two to tango. You were both careless, but it happens. The important thing is that you stay strong for each other and your baby.'

'I will, I promise. I know I'm a mess now, but I'm strong and I love Luke. I really do. He's so amazing. You all are. Jess is the bravest girl I know, and Bobby's so cute, and I'm so lucky to be part of your family. I'd never do anything to hurt you and I just want you to know that I'm sorry.' More tears ran down Piper's face.

Kate put her arm around Piper's shoulders. 'Stop apologizing. We're the lucky ones. You've been so lovely to Jess and I'll never be able to thank you enough for that. You're like the sister she always wished for. And I know you love Luke – I can see it. He loves you too. You've been a rock to him, and I'm so glad he has you, Piper. You're a fantastic girl.'

Piper pulled a tissue out of her coat pocket. 'Don't be nice to me or I'll never stop crying. I never knew you could be happy and terrified at the same time.'

Kate laughed. 'Welcome to the world of motherhood. You'll spend the rest of your life happy and terrified for your children. We mothers adore our kids, but we worry about them all the time, too. That's normal. The important thing for you to know is that we're all here for you. You're not alone, Piper. You have a wonderful family who love you and a new family who love you too.'

Piper threw her arms around Kate and buried her face in her neck. 'You have no idea how much that means to me. You're such a brilliant mother. I want to be just like you.'

I sincerely hope you have a less bumpy road, Kate thought, as she stroked Piper's hair.

That evening, Kate was sitting in hospital reading aloud when Jess began to cough. It got worse. Kate stood up and leant over her, patting her back gently. 'Take it easy – try to catch your breath.'

Jess was gasping for breath. '*Ooooooooh*.' She groaned as she coughed again. Blood splattered all over the sheets and Kate.

'Help me,' Jess wheezed, and vomited more blood. Her breath was ragged, and her eyes were wild with panic.

'Oh, my God!' Kate held her and screamed for help. Don't let her die, she prayed, please don't let her die.

A couple of seconds passed, which felt like hours, and panic gripped her. She felt sick with fear. Where were they? She didn't want to let Jess go, but she needed back-up. She sprinted to the door and onto the corridor, looking around wildly.

'Help,' she cried. 'It's Jess. Quickly!' She heard running feet and swivelled around.

Aideen, Jess's favourite nurse, was racing towards her. 'What's happened?' she called.

Kate didn't stop to talk, she dashed back into the room and grasped Jess by the shoulders, holding her upright.

Aideen burst in, then stopped short when she saw all the blood. She turned and barked instructions to a passing nurse, the urgency and concern clear in her voice. Then she walked quickly to the bed. 'It's okay, Jess, I'm here,' she said calmly.

Please, God, don't take her, Kate begged. Don't take my baby, please, please.

A moment later Kate was ushered out of the room while doctors and nurses dashed about, trying to control Jess's bleeding. After what seemed like an eternity, Dr Kennedy came out of the room. 'She's stable and sleeping now, Kate. But I'm afraid Jess has developed another infection, which is most unfortunate. We've put her on an antibiotic drip and we're going to run some tests to see if we can find the source. Often in these cases we don't discover it but the infection is dealt with nonetheless by the antibiotics. Her white blood count will hopefully reach a level soon where it will allow her to fight the infection on her own. She's very weak right now. She needs rest. I'll be back later to check on her. It's another unfortunate setback.'

Kate nodded. She felt more tired than she'd ever thought possible. It was one step forwards and three steps back. Over and over again. Why couldn't Jess catch a break? Why couldn't she just get better, come home and be herself again?

Kate sank into a chair and put her head into her hands. Why, God, why are you doing this to us, to her, to the sweetest girl in the world? Why are you punishing her? She sobbed, for Jess, for herself, for Luke, for Bobby, for her father, for the unborn baby . . . for everyone. Kate wanted to sleep and sleep and wake up when all of this was over. When life was good and kind again. When the nightmare was over once and for all.

36

Piper shuffled into the kitchen in her slippers and dressing-gown. She'd slept badly and was tired and hungry.

Her father was sitting at the kitchen table with the twins and Pauline, reading his newspaper and doing his best to ignore them.

'Morning, Dad,' Piper said, trying to sound more cheerful than she felt.

'Morning,' he said curtly.

'How are you?' Piper asked.

'Fine.'

Piper tried not to let it bother her. Ever since she'd told her parents about the pregnancy, her father had been distant and, frankly, cold. She knew he was disappointed, she knew he was upset, but she'd hoped that after six weeks of knowing, he'd have thawed a little. She missed their conversations. She missed how he'd roll his eyes across the table at her when the twins were being annoying. She missed how his face used to light up when he saw her. Now he avoided eye contact or just looked angry when he saw her.

Her mother said he'd come around, that she needed to give him time. But Piper wondered how much time. She was beginning to think he'd never forgive her for 'messing her life up'. It really hurt. 'Would you like a coffee?' she asked him.

'No, I've had one.'

'Toast?'

'No.'

'Okay, then.' Piper filled the kettle and busied herself making toast, hiding her disappointment from him.

As her toast popped up, her father stood up and left the room, not addressing a word or even a glance in her direction. Piper buttered her toast and tried not to get upset.

Pauline put her plate into the dishwasher and said quietly, 'He still loves you. He just can't show it right now.'

Piper smiled at her sister. 'Thanks.'

One of the best things about being pregnant was how close she'd got to Pauline. She'd been amazing. So calm and measured and sensible and kind. Piper felt really bad for ever thinking Pauline was selfish. She realized now that her sister had a very big heart and was just a serious, focused person. Olivia said that from the first day Pauline had gone to school in Junior Infants, her goal was to be top of the class and nothing else mattered. She had no interest in sport or playing games or art.

But underneath her ambition and single-mindedness lay a compassionate soul. Piper hoped she could repay her sister's kindness some day. She'd already decided to ask Pauline to be the baby's godmother. No one deserved it more.

Pauline left to go to the college library and study in peace. Piper was left with the twins, who were bickering about whether Liam Hemsworth was hotter than his brother, Chris. She sat down and ate her toast.

Penny turned her attention to her older sister. 'Are you and Luke still having sex?'

Piper almost choked on her toast. 'What?'

'Are you having sex?'

'That is none of your business, you cheeky cow!'

'If you are, you'd better use protection,' Poppy warned her.

'Bit late for that,' Penny said, and they roared with laughter.

'Shut up, you freaks,' Piper hissed.

'Seriously, though, is it safe to have sex when you have a baby in your stomach?' Poppy asked.

'Why wouldn't it be?' Penny said.

'Wouldn't it poke the baby?'

'Urgh, gross! I never thought about that.'

Poppy turned to Piper. 'You need to stop having sex. You're poking your baby. You could poke it in the eye and blind it.'

'OMG, could you?'

'Yes, totally.'

'Do you think that's why Janine Oliver has a wonky eye?' Penny asked.

'Oh, my God, yes. Her dad's willy must have poked her.'

'*Grooooss*,' they both squealed.

Piper put her toast down. 'It never ceases to amaze me what idiots you are.'

'If you have sex just after getting pregnant, can you have twins?' Poppy wondered.

'Duh, of course not,' Penny said.

'How do you know?'

'Because twins are conceived the same day,' Penny said.

'I read about this woman who had twins three weeks apart. They obviously weren't conceived the same day.'

'Maybe she just had one early and one on time,' Penny said.

'Do you think Piper could be having twins? Apparently it's genetic, and if your mum had twins, you could have twins.'

'She had a scan and it was just one baby,' Penny said, talking as if Piper wasn't in the room.

'Yeah, but sometimes the twin can be hiding behind the other baby.'

'It would be so cool if she had twins.'

It would be so not cool if I had twins, Piper thought. Thank God the obstetrician had confirmed only one baby, which was quite enough of a prospect to deal with.

'Piper, are you sure it's not twins?' Penny asked her.

'Yes, positive, thank God,' Piper said.

'No need to be so rude. You'd be lucky to have twins like us.' Penny was unimpressed.

'I'd shoot myself if I had twins like you,' Piper muttered.

'You're so narky. You should be careful. If you're this narky to Luke, he might dump you.'

Piper took a bite of her toast. 'Thanks, Penny, that's just what I need to hear.'

'You should also watch what you eat,' Poppy said, pointing to the toast. 'One slice is plenty, Piper. You're not actually eating for two. Some women stuff their faces the whole way through their pregnancies and are like whales and it takes them ages to lose the baby weight. Some of them never lose it and are just fat for ever.'

Piper stood up and threw the rest of her toast into the bin. 'Thanks for making me lose my appetite and for the great advice.' She slammed the door hard on her way out.

Piper lay on her bed and tried to do calming breathing exercises, inhale for five and exhale for five. She shouldn't let her sisters wind her up, but they were so annoying. They were clueless about life. She rolled onto her side. She was due to meet Luke in an hour for coffee. She'd eat with him – at least he wouldn't comment on how much she ate. Mind you, maybe she should watch what she was eating. She had been eating way more than usual. She didn't want to be a big whale. What if she was one of the women who couldn't lose the weight? Luke would dump her for a fit girl.

*

Piper sat in the café staring out of the window. Luke was late. She was nervous: he had barely been in touch in the last four days. He'd said things with Jess were bad and he'd meet her when he could. Piper had tried not to hound him, but she was desperate for news. Two days ago, she'd even called Maggie, who'd said she'd fill her in when she could but had never called back.

Piper watched Luke walking towards the café and her heart sank. She knew by the way his head was down that something was wrong. She knew Jess had been very slow to recover from the infection and was due more test results. Maybe they weren't good.

Luke sank into the chair opposite her.

'What's going on?' Piper asked. 'What did they say?'

Luke began to cry. Oh, God. Piper reached out and held his hands. He pulled one back to wipe his tears with a napkin.

'It's bad. Really bad. The cancer is worse. Way worse. The chemo's not working and it's the strongest they can give her without killing her.'

'Oh, Luke.' Piper bit her lip, trying to hold back the tears.

'It's . . . it's . . . over, Piper. She's not going to make it.' He covered his face with the napkin and sobbed.

Piper was so shocked that she was numb. Over? How could this happen? They had all believed one hundred per cent that Jess would get better. She had to – she was twelve, for God's sake. Jess couldn't die – she just couldn't. It was crazy to say that could happen.

'There must be something,' Piper said desperately. 'Maybe she needs to go to America. They have more cutting-edge treatments over there. I can research it. We can go with her, we'll figure it out.'

Luke pulled the napkin from his face. 'We've spent the last three days with Maggie and Hazel and everyone we know looking at options. Hazel offered to charter a plane to fly us to America. Maggie got on to the best paediatric oncologist in the top cancer hospital in Boston. He looked at the test results and said the same thing. So she found the second best one, in Philadelphia, same answer, same with Cincinnati. She got the top guy at Great Ormond Street in London to talk to us. Same answer. She's dying, Piper. My little sister is dying. How can there be a God? My stupid fucking bone marrow didn't help her. I can't deal with this and Mum is . . . she's . . . she's broken.'

Piper's body was cold, as if ice was running through her veins. She was shaking. 'Does Jess know?'

Luke shook his head. 'She knows the cancer is worse, but they haven't told her yet how bad it is. But they'll tell her soon – I'd say she knows anyway. She's just so sick.'

'Look, this might not be the right thing to say, but miracles do happen.'

'Don't,' Luke snapped. 'Don't do that. I don't want false hope. Dad keeps banging on about miracles and trying more risky treatment. He read about some dodgy experimental treatment they're testing in India and he wants to take Jess there. But when Mum mentioned it, the American doctors were, like, "no way". They said it would be a really bad idea and that she would die in India, away from home and those she loved. They said the best thing to do was to try to keep Jess as comfortable as possible and make the next few months really special.'

'What did your dad say?'

'He's going crazy, shouting at everyone that they're not trying hard enough, telling them all to think outside the box, telling Mum she's quitting on her own child, shouting at

Maggie to do more, cursing, punching walls and generally having a total fucking meltdown.'

Piper wouldn't say so to Luke, but she felt really sorry for Nick. Whatever about his failings as a father to Luke and Bobby, he loved Jess madly. He'd spent as much time as he could with her in hospital, playing cards and watching goofy YouTube videos. He could probably have tried to spend more time with her – Kate was the one who was there seventy per cent of the time – but every time he came to see Jess his phone would start ringing, either Jenny or work. Jenny always seemed to need him for some drama or other or else work did . . . He always seemed stressed. Every time she saw him, and his pale, tight face, Piper worried he might have a heart attack.

Luke rubbed his exhausted eyes. 'I haven't slept in four nights. We've been up all night researching, calling people and going over and over the options.'

'What are you going to do?'

'The doctors hold out no hope. They said Jess's cancer was incredibly aggressive and unlucky and unfortunate, and all those words you just don't want to hear. They were all very sorry not to be able to give us better news or more hope.'

Piper was lost for words. What do you say to the boy you love when he's just told you his sister is dying? 'Sorry' seems so lame. But she was sorry, desperately sorry, and sad and heartbroken.

She adored Jess. She was an amazing girl. She was so brave and never complained. She'd been through so much in her short life – her parents breaking up, Larry dying, getting cancer . . . It was just so unfair. Why was life so cruel to her? Jess deserved to grow up and have boyfriends, a husband and a family and happiness and joy. She deserved more time.

Lots more time. How come bad people got to live and good people, really, really good people, like Jess, didn't? It wasn't right. It was all wrong. Everything was wrong. Piper felt physically sick. She looked at Luke's devastated face and held his hand.

Over and over again she said one little word, 'Sorry, sorry, sorry . . .'

37

Kate sat very still and tried to take in the words.

'Bacterial and fungal infection,' Dr Kennedy said. 'Her heart function has been adversely affected . . . the chemotherapy was unsuccessful . . .'

It took Dr Kennedy three minutes to tell them that Jess was going to die. Three minutes for Kate's world to be crushed by the wrecking ball of the unthinkable and be destroyed. Three minutes for her heart to be shattered into a thousand jagged pieces.

'I'm afraid the prognosis is now bad. I'm so very sorry,' he said.

Kate felt as if she was swimming under water, the words blurred. Bad? Did he say bad? 'Bad' in medical terms meant 'fatal'. She gasped for air. Her mouth was dry, her lungs wouldn't work. No air. She wheezed . . . Still no air.

'Kate?' She could hear someone calling her name, but they seemed far away, back at the shore, while she was far out to sea, sinking fast. 'Kate?'

Bad prognosis? Bad . . . bad . . . bad.

No air. Can't breathe. She tried to suck in, nothing. Breathe, Kate, she told herself. Breathe!

She sucked in air . . . Yes, air. In and out, in and out.

He said again that he was 'very sorry' . . . Oh, God.

Her chest moved up and down. She could hear now. It was Nick. He was shouting. She opened her eyes.

'Did you say *bad* prognosis?'

Dr Kennedy nodded sadly. 'The drugs have damaged her heart. Her cardiac function has been compromised. The risk of heart failure and further distressing infections is very high. The odds are stacked against her, I'm afraid. I'm so very sorry.'

Nick was stomping around the room, shouting. 'There has to be something you can do! For Christ's sake, she's twelve years old – you can't give up. There must be something, some new treatment, some miracle cure.'

'I promise you that we have exhausted every avenue and looked at every possible option. No stone has been left unturned,' Dr Kennedy assured him quietly.

'No!' Nick shook his fist in the doctor's face. 'No way. Not my Jess, not her.' His voice broke and he punched the wall violently. Kate heard a crunch. He'd broken something. It probably felt good. Maybe she should punch something too.

One word comes into your life: cancer. One two-syllable word that splits your heart down the middle. Broken. You can't fix it.

'There has to be something you can do,' Nick raged. 'There's always a solution. What about a full body blood transfusion?'

Dr Kennedy hesitated. 'We tried new agents with this round of chemotherapy and unfortunately we were unsuccessful. This treatment was aggressive. She is very weak.'

'I don't care what you think. We'll try another round of it. Let's get her signed up.'

'I would be concerned that Jess wouldn't survive any further treatment, and that her quality of life during treatment would be even worse than it is now.'

'Jess is a fighter. You don't know her. She's stronger than she looks. She's the bravest kid . . .' Nick broke down.

'I don't think her heart could take it,' Dr Kennedy said gently.

'How long does she have?' Kate somehow managed to ask.

'It's very difficult to say.'

'Try.'

'Weeks.'

'How many?'

'Four, perhaps six, possibly a few more. Children are extraordinary.'

Kate shoved her fist into her mouth to stop herself screaming. Weeks? She only had precious weeks left with her beautiful Jess. She bent over as the pain hit her again.

'You have to do something, for Christ's sake. You have to save her!' Nick yelled, his face twisted in anger and grief. Kate watched as he threw a chair against the wall, then kicked and punched it until he wore himself out. He eventually collapsed on the floor, sobbing. 'Not Jess, not my baby girl.'

Kate knelt beside him and held him. They held each other and cried. Jess wasn't going to make it. She wasn't going to grow up, she wasn't going to have the life Kate wished for her. She was going to be taken from them. Ripped away when her life was only beginning. Their Jess was going to die, and they were powerless to stop it.

Kate stood on the seafront and looked around. Where the hell was he?

A man waved at her and rushed towards her, his arms open wide. She walked towards him. When she reached him, he pulled her into a bear hug, holding her tight.

She pulled back. 'Is it really you?'

'Sorry, I should have warned you I'd shaved the beard off.'

'Liam, you look completely different, younger and...' Kate trailed off. He looked ten years younger, and handsome. Under all that hair was a lovely face.

'I can't tell you how sorry I am,' Liam said, his face full of concern and kindness. 'I'm not going to ask you how you are, but I am going to bring you somewhere I used to come to shout at the world. It helped a little.'

Kate followed him up a steep path and across a forested area to a clearing. She'd never been there before and it was only ten miles from her house. 'How did you know about this place?' she asked, out of breath from climbing.

'A colleague told me about it when June was sick and suggested I come here for walks to clear my head. I don't think he meant for me to come and shout my head off.' He smiled. 'It's just over here.'

They came to the edge of a cliff. The sea spread out in front of them. You could see nothing but sea and sky and, far in the distance, the faint line where they met.

'Now, I'm going to walk away and I want you to shout, Kate. Scream your head off and tell God and the universe exactly what you think of them. I promise it will help you. You must get some of the pain out or it'll kill you.'

Kate waited until he'd walked away and then she turned to the ocean. Watching seagulls dipping and diving, she thought about Jess and how she was being robbed of a future and her beautiful little family was being robbed of a daughter, a sister and a granddaughter, and now an auntie as well.

Grief and rage rose in her chest and she began to shout. She shouted louder than she'd thought possible. She screamed until she thought the veins in her neck would burst. She wanted them to – she wanted them to burst. She wanted to throw herself off the cliff and for her body to smash into pieces below. She wanted to die. She should be the one dying. Her, the mother, not the child, never, ever the child.

Kate shouted and screamed until her voice ran out. She collapsed onto her knees. Liam appeared beside her.

'Are you okay?'

'Yes,' she croaked.

'You gave it socks. Well done. All that anger will eat you up inside. I recommend you come here once a week, if not more.'

'Thank you, Doctor.' Kate gave him a half-smile, her heart breaking.

Liam put his arm around her. 'Now I'm taking you for a lemon and honey tea, fix up that throat. There's a little tea shop in the village I think you'll like.'

Kate laid her head on his shoulder. 'Why is this happening?'

'Don't ask why. It will torment you and there is no answer. You have to focus now on making these last weeks the best of Jess's life. If I can help in any way, please just ask.'

Kate looked up at him. 'You already are.' She kissed his smooth cheek. It was lovely and soft. 'You really do look so different.'

He grinned. 'Nathalie told me that no self-respecting man would go around looking like *un hobo*. She insisted on bringing me to a barber her ex-boyfriend used to go to, and before I knew it, I was clean-shaven. I've had a beard for thirty years. It took me a while to get used to it myself.'

'I like it,' Kate said.

'Good.' He smiled down at her.

A little later they sat in the little tea shop, Liam drinking coffee and Kate sipping the lemon and honey tea he'd ordered to soothe her throat. They shared a slice of chocolate cake. It was the first time Kate had been able to taste anything since Jess's diagnosis.

Most of the time she forgot to eat, and when she did, everything tasted like chalk or cardboard. But she could taste that cake.

'Penny for your thoughts?' Liam asked.

'I was just thinking that when I'm with you I feel calmer. Most of the time I either think I'm going to have a heart attack or I feel numb. But today is the first day I feel in any way calmer. It's the first time I've stopped shaking too.'

'Much as I'd like to take credit, I think letting go of some of your anger helped.'

'Yes, but don't underestimate your positive influence. I'm sorry for calling you at all hours all the time. I just need someone to get me through the nights and you're the person I want to talk to.'

Liam smiled at her. 'It's my pleasure. What you're going through is unbearable. I want to help in any way I can. I wish I could do more.'

Kate sighed. 'No one can. It's just a nightmare that I have to go through and I have no idea how to do it. How do you watch your daughter die? How do you watch her fade away, suffer and die? There's no manual for that. No *Dummy's Guide to Losing a Child*.' Her croaky voice broke and she began to cry, head bent low, shoulders shuddering.

Liam handed her a handkerchief. A proper linen one from his pocket.

'I'll ruin it,' Kate said.

'That's what it's there for.'

She blew her nose. Typical Liam to have a handkerchief on him. He was an old-fashioned gent. Kate folded it and put it into her pocket. 'Sorry.'

'How are the boys?'

'Luke is throwing himself into rugby. His big final is on Sunday. He's quiet and doesn't say much. I'm glad he has

Piper. Bobby is Bobby. Angry, kicking everything, arguing with his teacher and generally furious with the world. The poor child just doesn't understand.'

'Hard to process so much at the tender age of seven. How's your dad?'

Kate began to cry again. 'He's heartbroken. He's aged ten years. He just can't believe it. Seeing him so crushed is unbearable. He keeps saying, "It should be me, not her."'

'Poor man. He's right, too.'

Kate pushed the cake away, her appetite gone again. 'I'd better go. Maggie's back from her work trip to New York to sort us all out, as she says. She's a wonder.'

'I'm glad you have such a good friend to rely on.'

Kate took his hand in hers. 'I have another good one right here.'

Liam reddened. 'I'm glad you think so. I'll be cheering for Luke on Sunday. I hope they win. Give him a bit of a boost.'

'Thanks. It'll be a welcome distraction anyway.'

They hugged, and Kate rushed off to her car, thanking God for sending Liam to her just when she needed someone. He was so kind, so unobtrusive and undemanding, but there whenever he was needed. He really was like a gift, and she felt very grateful to have met him.

When she got home, she found Maggie sitting at the table talking to Bobby. She stood to the side of the door and watched them.

'So what you're saying is that when you grow up you're going to find the cure for stinky cancer?' Maggie said.

'Yes.'

'High five,' Maggie said. 'And, by the way, I think you're the very person who will do it because you're smart, single-minded and determined.'

'What does single-minded mean? It sounds like I only have one mind, but I don't, I have lots of minds. One for facts, one for maths, one for spelling –'

'No, it doesn't mean only one mind,' Maggie cut across him. 'It means focused, which is a good thing, vital if you want to cure cancer.'

'Well, I do. I never want other families to feel like this. It's the worst. I hate cancer. I want to kill it and smash it into pieces.'

'Me, too,' Maggie agreed, her eyes shining with tears. 'Hey, let's get something and crush it to make ourselves feel better.' She looked around and saw some bread dough on the counter. She went over, picked it up and brought it over to the table. She pushed it up into a big mound. 'Now, Bobby, smash it with your fists. Go for it. Pretend it's cancer.'

Bobby stood up and, leaning over the table, he walloped the dough. He beat it over and over again.

'Go on,' Maggie shouted. 'Punch its lights out.'

Kate watched Bobby's little hands flying at the dough, like a boxer's. His face was red with exertion, but he kept punching. Eventually he fell back into his chair, puffing.

'Good boy. Do you feel better?'

He nodded.

Kate smiled to herself. Shouting at the sea for her, punching dough for Bobby. Who knew that such simple things would help get rid of some of the agony of grief?

Maggie sat down again opposite Bobby. 'I know this sucks. No kid should have a sister who is dying. I'm really sorry this is happening to you, Bobby, and you know that Mum and Dad and Granddad and I would do anything to stop it, but we can't. I know you're sad and angry and it's important that you get the anger out. Otherwise it'll make your stomach hurt and your chest too.'

'Could I get cancer?' Bobby's eyes were wide.

'No, God, no.' Maggie went over to hug him. 'Nothing like that. It's just that worry and sadness and anger can make your stomach ache.'

Bobby twisted Maggie's long silver chain around in his little fingers. 'My stomach hurts all the time.'

Kate felt sick. Her poor little boy. He was hurting so much. She walked into the kitchen, picked him up and hugged him tight. 'I'm sorry, Bobby. I'm sorry about your stomach. I'm sorry about everything. You're such a great boy.'

Bobby hugged her back fiercely. 'It's okay, Mummy. I didn't tell you cos I didn't want you to have any more worries.'

Kate cried into his hair. 'I'm your mum. You should tell me when anything hurts. I wish none of this was happening. I hate that you're sad. I love you, and I'm sorry I've been so distracted with everything and haven't had more time for you.'

Bobby stroked her hair. 'It's all right, Mummy. When Jess is gone you'll have more time.' He jerked backwards, his hand flew up to his mouth. 'I didn't mean it like that, I swear. I didn't mean it.'

Kate hugged him closer. 'I know, angel, I know.'

For the first time since Jess's diagnosis, the long months of worry and the awful final news, Bobby cried. His little body let out all of his pain. He shook and quivered as he wept huge tears, crying with his whole body.

Maggie couldn't hold back her own any longer. She hid her face in her hands, shoulders sagging.

Kate held tight to Bobby and said over and over, 'Let it out, let it all out. I'm here for you. I'm here for you.'

Maggie silently left the room. Kate saw her punch the dough as she passed it.

38

Jess looked at the dandelion card. 'Wherever you are, Larry, I'm coming too,' she whispered. She felt awful, really awful. The chemo had been horrendous and then the infection . . . It had been terrifying. She'd thought she was going to choke to death on her own blood. She wasn't going to die like that, no way. It wasn't how she was going to leave this world. Thank God the antibiotics had cleared up the infection. At least that was some small mercy. She was hoping to go home in a few days.

Nick had just left her room, striding out in frustration. She knew he was upset with her, but she couldn't give him what he wanted. He was insisting she tried some new treatment, but Dr Kennedy said she was too weak for it.

'Come on, Jess, what harm can it do to give it a go?' he'd wheedled. 'This is a chance, a real chance. We've got to take it.'

Jess shook her head. 'I'm sorry, Dad, I can't.'

'Why not?' he said impatiently. 'You're stronger than you think, I know it.'

She shook her head again. 'Not any more. I can't do it. I feel so sick, Dad. I don't want any more drugs or pain. I can't. I just want to go home.'

Nick raked his fingers through his hair. 'Jessie, please, for me,' he implored. 'I can't be without you. What they're saying . . . we have to try.'

He was so intense, and she knew it came from love, which was what hurt most of all.

'Daddy, I need you to start letting me go,' she said quietly, looking directly into his eyes.

Nick's head was shaking, but no sound was coming from his open mouth. Jess reached over and put her hand on his, willing him to understand.

'No.' His voice trembled. 'No, Jess. I will never, ever let you go. Do you hear me? Never.'

Jess remembered Larry saying he wanted his parents to hate him, to make it easier on them when he died. She had told him it wouldn't work that way, and it wouldn't work for her and her parents either. But she could feel death upon her and she had to try to make them understand that it was coming, and they couldn't stop it.

'Dad, you have to start letting me go. I love you, and I know it's really hard for you,' her voice caught in her throat, 'but I'm not going to get better and I want to go home. I don't want to die in here. I need you to hear me, Dad, and I need you to help me.' She watched his face carefully. 'And if the pain gets unbearable maybe you could help it stop. When it gets too much for me, maybe someone could make it all go away.'

Nick stood up with a jolt, as if a bolt of electricity had shot through him. He was staring at her in horror, blinking rapidly. 'Jesus Christ, Jess, what are you saying? If you think . . .'

She knew he understood, and she also knew that he was incapable of helping. She should have known he'd react like that. Her strong, fight-to-the-end father would not help her.

'I'll never give up on you,' he said roughly. 'Never. I'm going to keep fighting until we fix this.'

Jess sank back tiredly onto her pillow. 'Okay, Dad.'

After that, there had been nothing to say. Nick gazed at her reproachfully, as if he thought she was quitting on him and life. But he had no idea how awful it was. It wasn't his fault. No one could imagine this physical hell unless they were in it. In the end, to put them both out of their misery, Jess had told him she wanted to sleep. He'd held her tight and told her to keep strong and then, thankfully, he'd left her alone.

Silent tears seeped out of Jess's tightly shut eyes. She had tried. She had given it everything, but the cancer was too strong. She didn't have anything left in her. Her dad didn't understand, no one did. It was so hard, so painful, so awful. There had to be an end to it, one way or another, because she couldn't carry on like this.

Jess loved her dad, but he was wearing her out. His constant talk of miracles made her want to scream. She was only twelve, but even she knew there were no miracles. If there were, Larry wouldn't have died.

The truth was, Jess wasn't afraid of death. She was sick of feeling ill. She watched as everyone around her suffered too, everyone she loved and wanted to protect. Her cancer was ruining their lives, too. They all looked older and sadder, exhausted and heartbroken. Cancer hadn't just destroyed Jess's life, it had destroyed theirs, too, and that was as hard to bear as her own suffering.

Everyone was worn out. Cancer had controlled her life for long enough, and Jess knew what she had to do. She was going to take control. She lay back in her bed and stared at the ceiling. 'I'm going to do this my way, Cancer, you bastard, not yours.'

It was Sunday afternoon and Jess was woken by the sense of someone moving around her room. She slowly opened her eyes, and as she blinked, Piper and Chloë came into focus, smiling down at her.

'Hi,' she said, trying to sit up but her arms were too weak. Chloë and Piper instinctively bent to help her.

'What are you guys doing here?'

Chloë and Piper smiled at each other. 'We're breaking you out.'

'What?'

'Look!' Chloë opened the door and pulled in a wheelchair.

Piper smiled at Jess's surprised face. 'I know the doctors said you couldn't go to Luke's final because you're still on IV antibiotics, but we spoke to Dr Kennedy this morning and we told him we'd look after you and bring the IV drip and put you in a wheelchair and make sure your mask was on to prevent infection and wrap you up warmly and keep you away from the crowds and all that . . . so he said yes!' Piper beamed at her.

'Piper was, like, OMG, amazing. She would not take no for an answer.' Chloë danced around the room.

'You were pretty great too. Chloë said she wasn't leaving until he said yes.'

Jess's heart jumped. 'Seriously? I can go?' She wanted to punch the air. She had been crushed when they said she couldn't go to Luke's match. It was his big day, his big final. She wanted to be there so badly. Her dad had said he'd come and watch it with her on the TV in her room, but she really wanted to see it live, and now she was going to.

'I love you, guys! I'll never forget this.'

'Stop!' Chloë exclaimed. 'I'm not crying – it took me ages to do my eye make-up.'

Nathalie strode through the door, carrying blankets, followed by Aideen, who had a mask for Jess. Aideen took Jess's temperature, then her blood pressure and checked her thoroughly before she let the others take her away. 'You have a wonderful time, pet. You deserve it. I'll be cheering Luke's team on from here. See you later.' She kissed Jess's head. Turning to the three girls, she said sternly, 'You're to mind her carefully, all right, and if it's too much or she shows any signs of deteriorating, you bring her straight back here. Is that clear?'

They nodded solemnly. Aideen winked at Jess and left them to get her ready.

They helped her to get dressed. Chloë did her eye make-up, and Piper tucked the blankets around her. Then Nathalie produced Luke's school hat and scarf. 'Luke said you 'ad to wear these for the good luck.' She gently placed the hat on Jess's head and wrapped the scarf around her neck.

'He thinks you're watching the match in here with your dad. He's going to be so happy when he sees you,' Piper said. She adjusted the hat and fixed the blankets one last time. 'Now you're perfect.'

'Fab,' Chloë agreed.

'Not too bad,' Nathalie said.

Jess was impatient to go. 'Get me out of here,' she said.

They wheeled her out of the hospital, and Jess's heart soared as she got out into the fresh air. Her mum usually took her out for a few minutes every day, but lately Jess hadn't had the energy. Now she felt wiped out from the effort of getting dressed and ready for the match, but elated from excitement too.

Granddad was waiting for them in his car. He jumped out when he saw them. Bowing, he said, 'Your carriage awaits, m'lady,' and kissed Jess's cheek.

They lifted her into the front seat and put the wheelchair in the boot.

'Does Mum know I'm coming?' Jess asked.

'It's a surprise for her and Luke,' Piper said.

Granddad drove slowly, taking great care not to hit any potholes or bumps in the road. Eventually Chloë leant forward. 'I don't mean to be rude, George, but you need to step on it or we'll be late.'

'Yes, George, why are you driving like the old man?' Nathalie asked.

'Possibly because I am an old man,' Granddad reminded her. 'I'm driving carefully so Jess won't get jostled about.'

Jess patted his arm. 'You can go a bit faster.'

He nodded and put his foot on the accelerator. They arrived with five minutes to go before the starting whistle.

As they wheeled Jess into the grounds, she could see the teams warming up. Luke was passing a ball to Rocco. He looked so strong and handsome that Jess wanted to stand up and shout, 'That's my brother.'

Chloë ran ahead to where Jess's mother and Bobby were standing beside the pitch. Bobby was swinging on the bar that ran around it. Chloë tapped Kate on the shoulder. 'Turn around, we have a surprise.'

She turned to look. 'Oh, my God . . . How?' Kate squeaked. 'She shouldn't be . . .'

'It's fine.' Piper was straight over to reassure her. 'We squared it with Dr Kennedy and Aideen checked her just before we left. They said it's okay. We just didn't want her to miss it.'

Mum threw her arms around Piper, then Chloë, Nathalie and Granddad. Finally she crouched down and hugged Jess. 'Do you feel all right?'

Jess nodded. 'Yes. The adrenalin will keep me going. I'm so happy to be here, Mum. Please don't worry, let's just enjoy it.'

Her mother kissed her. 'I'm so glad you're here.'

Bobby shouted to Luke, 'Look, Luke! Look who's here!'

Luke turned, and when he saw Jess, his whole face lit up. He ran over. 'Jess? I can't believe it.'

'I came. Piper and Chloë and Nathalie busted me out.'

Luke looked at Piper, and Jess saw the love in his eyes. 'We couldn't let her miss it.' Piper grinned at him.

'We have to win now, for you, Jess.' Luke began to choke up.

'Off with you,' Granddad said. 'You need to focus on the game.'

Luke ran onto the pitch, but turned back one last time and gave Jess the thumbs-up. She did the same back.

'Hello, gang.' They turned to see Maggie walking towards them, with Hazel.

'You made it.' Kate hugged her friend.

'I almost didn't. Couldn't get a taxi at the airport for love or money – the queue was a mile long, all the bloody tourists over for St Patrick's weekend, but Hazel here saved the day. She came out to the airport and picked me up.'

Hazel looked at Jess. 'You're a bit cold, darling. Put this over you and you'll be toasty.' Hazel took off her fur coat and wrapped it around Jess.

It felt soft and warm. Jess smiled up at her. 'Thank you, Hazel, but won't you be cold?'

'Don't you worry about me, I'll be fine.'

Nathalie gave Hazel her hat, Chloë gave her her scarf, Piper gave her her gloves and Granddad offered her his jacket.

'Stop, I'm fine,' Hazel said, shivering.

'I insist.' Granddad wrapped it around her.

'You're a gentleman, George, thank you.'

Nathalie pointed to a man in the stand behind them. 'It's Liam.'

They looked round. Jess peered to see him. Luke had told her about Liam: he'd said he was a hairy yoke and he didn't think there was anything going on with Kate, they were just pals, but this man wasn't hairy: he was clean-shaven and had a nice, kind face.

'Don't you think he looks so much more 'andsome now without the beard?' Nathalie said to Kate.

She nodded awkwardly.

'So that's Liam,' Maggie said, grinning. 'Not the older hairy hobo you described, but a very attractive man.'

'Who's Liam?' Hazel asked.

'A friend of Kate's,' Granddad said.

' 'E is a lovely man. I like this one,' Nathalie said.

'A good friend?' Hazel winked at Kate.

'A friend,' she said firmly.

Nathalie waved up at him. Liam spotted them and waved enthusiastically back.

Jess noticed her mum flushing and smiling, which made her smile too.

Chloë nudged her friend. 'She likes him.'

'I had no idea he was coming,' Kate muttered to Maggie.

'He isn't here for Luke,' Maggie drawled.

Nathalie indicated for Liam to come down. He shook his head. Then, to Kate, he mouthed, 'Good luck.'

Jess watched her mum smiling again, then Jess waved at Liam. He waved back, beaming at her.

'Who are we waving at?' Nick asked, as he joined them, rubbing his hands together against the cold.

'No one,' Kate said quickly.

'A friend of Kate's,' Maggie said, just as quickly.

'Do I know him?' Nick peered up into the stand.

'No,' Kate said firmly, giving Maggie a warning look. 'Now, come on, let's watch the match.'

Jess tugged her mum's coat. Kate bent down. 'He looks nice, Mum.'

'He's a friend, Jess.'

'I know, but he looks like a nice one.'

'He is,' she agreed. 'Now, enough about that.'

Nick came over and hugged Jess. 'You look good, Jess. I was thrilled when Piper texted me to tell me she'd broken you out for the game. Are you feeling stronger?'

Jess looked into her father's hopeful eyes and decided to lie, just for today. 'A bit, Dad, yes.'

'Brilliant,' Nick said. 'That's my girl.'

The whistle blew and the match started. It was very close. The teams were well matched. Just before half-time, Luke missed a tackle and the other team scored to go ahead by five points. Luke's head hung down as the coach gave them their team talk.

They couldn't hear what he was saying, but Jess saw him pointing his finger at Luke, and it didn't look like he was praising him.

'Poor Luke.' Piper was upset. 'He'll never forgive himself if they lose because of that try.'

'He'll come back fighting,' George comforted her.

'Of course he will, he's brilliant,' Maggie said, putting a protective arm around Piper.

'Luke's the best,' Bobby said.

Jess stared up at a passing cloud. 'Larry, if you're up there, help Luke play well,' she prayed.

Beside Jess, Kate was jumping from one foot to the other. Nick went over to her. 'Hey, calm down, you'll have a heart attack. Luke will come through, mark my words. Our son is tough. He'll bounce back.'

'I just couldn't bear it if they lost and he felt it was his fault,' she said.

'Stay calm. This is Iron Will Luke we're talking about,' he told her.

She smiled at the use of their old nickname for him. Nick had christened him that when he was about three years old – a solid lump of toddler determination, climbing on every stick of furniture and never heeding any warnings. She'd almost forgotten it – Iron Will Luke. She nodded. 'You're right,' she said. 'He'll come back out and kick up murder.'

Nick had indeed been right: Luke came out in the second half and tackled everyone and every ball. He was like a man possessed.

'I think the rugby is so violent. I prefer the tennis.' Nathalie sighed as they watched Lorcan being smashed to the ground by the opposition. 'All this running and pushing each other down in the mud is ridiculous.'

George shook his head. 'It's a very skilful game, Nathalie. One that your lot are actually pretty good at.'

'Pfff! What is skilful about 'olding another boy's legs so he fall over? Or 'ugging in a big group and trying to push the other team back? It make no sense.'

'The scrum is an integral part of the game.' George slapped his forehead.

'Integral, why? Because I think maybe they like to 'ug each other, maybe they are 'omosexual but too afraid to say.'

'Sweet Mother of Jesus, will you stop talking rubbish? They are not gay, they are just playing a game of rugby.'

'Don't wind him up, Nathalie,' Kate warned her. 'We don't need his blood pressure going any higher.'

Dad's phone rang. It was Jenny. Jess was delighted when he ignored it and put his phone on silent.

With five minutes to go, Luke's team were three points down. Their little group was quiet. Jess could hear her father muttering under his breath, 'Come on, Luke, you can do it. Give us a try.'

With two minutes to go they passed the ball to Rocco, star of the team. He came thundering down the line towards them. They all cheered and shouted – even Nathalie was screaming, 'Go, go, go.'

As Rocco got closer to the try line he glanced around. Luke was beside him. Rocco looked ahead: he could have dived and scored, but he passed it to Luke. The ball soared into the air. Luke caught it and dived to the ground. Try!

The place erupted. Jess sat in her wheelchair grinning as everyone danced, jumped, cheered, hugged and cried.

Luke hugged Rocco, then pulled him across the field to where his family was waiting. 'That was for you, sis.' Then he pushed a bashful Rocco in front of her. 'This man is a legend,' he declared, as Rocco blushed and laughed. 'He let me take the try,' Luke said, choking up with all the emotion.

'Just teamwork,' Rocco said, smiling at Jess. 'I knew it meant the world to him.' She nodded at him gratefully. 'I hope you're feeling better soon,' he said. 'I'm sorry you've been so sick.'

Jess nodded again, unable to speak, and watched as Rocco and Luke ran back to their teammates. Rocco took the kick and put it over to add two more points. Then the referee blew the whistle and the whole place erupted again. Jess was crying, laughing and cheering all at once. It felt so good to be part of normal life, of all these people happy together. She felt so happy herself.

Her mother held her hand and smiled through her tears. 'Wasn't he amazing?' she said.

'Absolutely,' Jess said.

Behind Kate, she saw Liam approaching. He gently tapped her mother on the shoulder. 'I'm so happy for you. What a try,' he said. 'I'll talk to you soon.' He turned to leave, but she pulled him back.

'Liam, wait, I want you to meet Jess.'

She introduced them. Jess shook his hand.

'I'm very pleased to meet you, Jess. I've heard so much about you. You must be very proud of your brother today.'

'Yes, I am. I'm happy to meet you too.' Jess looked into his blue eyes. They were full of kindness. 'I know you've been a good friend to Mum through all this. I'm glad about that.'

'It's been a very hard time for you all,' he said, looking straight at her. Jess felt he understood and smiled at him. 'Well, I won't keep you. You've a lot to celebrate. I'll be off.'

'Hang on there! I'm Maggie, and I want to say hello too.'

Liam stuck out his hand. 'Great to meet you, Maggie. I've heard you're the fantastic best friend.'

Maggie smiled. 'Charming to boot. You really are the whole package.'

Liam laughed and shook a finger at her. 'Kate said you were a live wire. She was right.'

Maggie threw back her head and laughed. '*Touché.*'

George came over then and introduced himself, followed by Hazel and Chloë, and finally Bobby. Liam seemed a bit overwhelmed, but he handled it with grace and good humour.

Bobby peered up at him. 'Did you used to be all hairy?'

'Yes, I did, until Nathalie here very kindly told me I looked like a hobo and to shave it off.'

'I sawed you in the café once when you were hairy. You look much better now. You were a bit scary before.'

'Well, I'm very pleased to hear that. I don't want to scare people off.'

Jess watched her mother closely. She was standing close to Liam. They weren't touching, but it was as if they were. Her father clicked his phone shut. He had been talking into it at speed for the last five minutes.

'Let's go, guys,' he said. Then, noticing Liam, he said, 'Oh, hi, I'm Nick.'

'Liam.'

They shook hands.

'Are you one of the other parents?' Nick asked.

'No.' Maggie was grinning. 'He's a friend of Kate's.'

Nick did a double-take. 'Oh, really?'

'Yes,' Maggie said. 'And we're all getting on like a house on fire.'

Jess saw that her mother was getting uncomfortable.

Liam had obviously noticed, too, because he cut in before she had a chance to. 'Well, very nice to meet you all and well done again. Luke was the star of the show today. Bye now.'

He turned to go but Kate walked to the side with him. Jess heard her say, 'Thanks so much for coming.'

'I wouldn't have missed it. Go back to your family. I'll call you.'

'Tonight. Call me tonight,' she whispered.

Jess felt warm inside. She was happy her mum had a friend or boyfriend or whatever he was. He was nice, and Jess could see that he was mad about her. It was what Mum needed most, someone to love her. It would make things easier in the future, Jess knew, and that made her feel good.

Liam left and Nick came over to Kate. 'Who's your friend?' he asked.

'Liam.'

'Yeah, I know, but who is he? How long have you been together?'

'We're not together. He's a friend who has been really supportive to me over these past months.'

'So you've never –'

'It's none of your business.'

'No need to bite my head off. I think I'm allowed to know if you're seeing someone.'

'No, you're not. You lost that privilege when you left me.'

Nick regarded her for a moment, then he nodded. 'That's fair enough,' he said quietly. 'I'm glad if you've found someone.'

Kate blinked, momentarily lost for words. She saw Maggie make an exaggerated shocked face behind Nick's back and had to suppress a giggle.

'Thanks,' she said at last. 'That means a lot to me.'

'I've got to go,' Nick said. He held up his phone. 'You can guess why.'

'No problem,' Kate said. 'We'll get Jess back to the hospital now.'

Aideen came in to check her blood pressure and smiled at Jess, lying tucked up in her bed.

'Today has wrecked you, hasn't it, sweetheart?' Aideen said. 'You're done in.'

Jess nodded. 'Yeah, I'm really tired. But I'm really happy too.'

'Well, that's all that matters,' Aideen said, stroking her forehead. 'Happy trumps tired every time. It was worth it, so.'

'It really was,' Jess said, thinking back over the day and being with everyone again. It had been wonderful.

'Hey, sis.'

Aideen and Jess turned to see Luke standing there, holding the cup. He grinned at them. 'I know you must be wiped

339

out, but I wanted to show you the cup. I won't stay long, Aideen, I promise.'

'You certainly won't,' Aideen said briskly. Then her face broke into a smile. 'Come in! Come in and show us what you won. Aren't you brilliant? Look at that, Jess. Isn't he fantastic?'

'He really is,' Jess said, gazing up at him.

She didn't have the energy to sit up, so Luke placed the cup on her stomach and she wrapped her hands around the sides. 'Wow, Luke, it's gorgeous.'

He beamed. 'I know. What a day.'

'You were amazing, the hero of the match.'

'Right, hero,' Aideen said. 'I'm going for my tea break and you'll have to skedaddle when I get back. Otherwise you'll get me in trouble.'

'I'll go the moment you say,' Luke said.

'Good man,' Aideen said, heading for the door. 'I'll be back in fifteen minutes to settle you for the night, Jess.'

Luke took the trophy and placed it on the floor. 'Rocco was very generous to give me that pass.'

'It was Fate, your moment to take.'

'Yeah, I guess it was.' Luke looked down at his hands. 'I'm so glad you were there, Jess. It meant the world to me.'

Jess swallowed hard. 'It was the best day ever.'

'You're an amazing kid, you know that?'

'No, I'm not.'

'You are, Jess. You're so bloody brave. I just wish . . . I wish my bone marrow had saved you. I'm sorry it didn't. I feel I let you down.'

Jess felt tears rolling down her cheeks. 'Luke, you did everything you could and more. You've been my rock, always. When Mum and Dad split up, you were there for me and

Bobby. You've been there for Mum, too. It's been hardest on you because you're the eldest.'

'I've let her down too, you know, with the baby and all.'

Jess was angry now. 'Stop it, Luke. Stop blaming yourself. You didn't mean to have a baby so young but you took responsibility, like you always do. You stand up to things and for things and you protect people. You're going to be a great dad. That baby is so lucky to have you and Piper as its parents. It's all going to be fine, Luke.'

Luke wiped away a tear. 'How did you get to be so nice? I think all of Mum's genes went into you, and me and Bobby got a mixture of both.'

'Don't be too hard on Dad. He's trying.'

Luke sat back in the chair. 'I know, but he's never going to be Dad of the Year. He's just fundamentally a selfish person. You bring out the best in him, though.'

'It's only because I'm a girl. I think he feels he has to be harder on you and Bobby because you're boys.'

'Maybe. Poor Bobby, though – he doesn't really get a look in.'

'Since Jaden came along, the bit of attention he used to get is gone. You need to keep an eye on him, Luke. He needs you.'

'I need you, Jess. We all do. You're the glue in the family. You're the link to Dad. You're . . . you're the – the ham in the sandwich.'

Jess grinned. 'If I'm the ham, you're the bread that wraps around us.'

'What does that make Bobby?'

'Mustard?' Jess suggested, and they laughed.

'Yes, hot and spicy.'

'Spiky.' Jess giggled.

'Do you think he'll still be kicking things when he's my age?'

'Probably. He didn't lick it off a stone. Dad's kicked and punched the walls in here a lot,' Jess said.

'Well, that's different. I've punched a few walls over your cancer, too.'

'I'm sorry,' Jess said quietly. 'I'm sorry my stupid cancer's caused so much grief.'

Luke grabbed her arm. It hurt, but she didn't say anything. 'Don't you dare apologize. You're an innocent victim. This should never have happened. It's so unfair. I don't understand it, Jess. Why? Why you?' He loosened his grip.

'Don't ask yourself why, Luke. I did, and it doesn't get you anywhere. I've accepted it now and it's so much better that way. It's the only way to deal with it. When Larry died I was so angry with the world. But it didn't help. I have to accept that this is life. There is no why. There is just the life you're given and the cards you're dealt. These are my cards.'

Luke shook his head. 'I don't want you to die, Jess. I just can't handle it. You deserve a long, happy life. It's just not fair.'

'I know, Luke, but I'm going to die and you have to accept it. I'm tired. I'm tired of treatment, I'm tired of feeling like crap all the time, I'm tired of hospitals and doctors and needles and drugs and rashes and vomiting and X-rays and bone-marrow transfusions and false hope. Most of all I'm tired of that. The hope. There are no miracles. This is it and I'm okay with it. Please try to be too.'

Luke rubbed his wet eyes with the back of his shirt sleeve. 'I'll try, Jess.'

Aideen popped her head around the door. 'Time to go home, hero,' she said.

Luke bent down and kissed Jess, then pressed his forehead against hers for a few seconds. 'I love you, Jess.'

'I love you, Luke.'

She watched him leave, then closed her eyes and let sleep take her away from the pain.

39

Kate was making herbal tea in the kitchen when her phone beeped. It was a message from Nick: *I'm outside. Need to talk. Can I come in?*

Kate looked at the clock. It was almost eleven p.m. How had he managed to get out of his apartment? She felt bone tired. The last thing she wanted was to have a conversation with an overwrought Nick, but if he needed to talk, she couldn't turn him away. She went to the front door and opened it. He was sitting in his car at the kerb. She raised her hand to beckon him in.

'Would you like tea?' she asked, as they walked into the kitchen.

'No, I'm fine,' Nick said.

Kate sat down heavily on a chair, but Nick paced up and down, up and down, the nervous energy sparking off him. He was wound up and she felt exhausted just by his physical presence.

'Sit down, Nick,' she said. 'You're making me dizzy with all that striding about.'

For a second he seemed about to argue. Then he took a deep breath and sat down across from her. He began to drum his fingers on the table. Kate massaged her temples. 'What is it, Nick? What do you need to talk about?'

'She has to try it,' he said. 'She can't give up. Come on, Kate. We need to be united on this. It's the only way to get her to agree.'

Kate looked at the bags under his eyes, his pale face, his twitchy body, and she felt sorry for him. But she also felt the weight of his blind hope, like an anchor pulling them all down. How could she counter him? 'She's too weak, Nick. Any more treatment will kill her. She's begged us both to stop. She can't take any more.'

'She has to,' he said urgently, leaning forward. 'She can't give up. We can't give up. I won't, Kate, I bloody won't. She has to fight. We're not quitters, we're fighters.'

'It's not a war, Nick. Jess isn't a soldier fighting the enemy. She's a little girl with cancer,' Kate said, pleading with him to understand. 'You have to stop pressurizing her. She's so frail and weak and sick.'

'I can't, Kate.' His face crumpled. 'I can't let her go. We have to give it one more shot. It might work.'

'Nick, all the experts have told us it will cause her more pain and will probably kill her.' Kate sighed. 'You can't force her to do something she doesn't want to do. It's her body. We have to respect her wishes, Nick.'

He glared at her, the anger seeping out of him, filling the room. 'She's a child, Kate, we're the adults. She doesn't know what she wants. She told me she wanted to die. She said . . .' his voice cracked '. . . she said, "Please, Dad, I just want the pain to stop and for it to be over." I mean, Jesus Christ, Kate,' he was shaking now, as if his body was cold, 'she doesn't know what she's saying. The drugs are messing with her mind. She asked me to . . . well, she kind of suggested I or someone else help her stop the pain. She'll probably say the same to you. I told her no way. We are her parents. We are the ones who have to keep her alive and make her do treatment to save her.'

Tears ran down Kate's cheeks. 'She's not a child when it comes to cancer and pain. She knows far more about it than we do. And only she knows how much she can take. I know it's awful, I hate it too, but there comes a point when –'

'I will *not* give up on her, Kate, and you're a bad mother if you do. We have to do everything possible to save her. Even if it's only a one per cent chance, we have to seize it. I will not let her go. I need you to stand with me on this. For God's sake, Kate, this is our daughter's life we're talking about here.'

Kate could feel her own anger rising. She was struggling to remain composed. Yes, she felt for him, but why was he being wilfully blind to reality? 'Do you honestly think I want to let her go? Jesus, Nick, I love her as much as you do. She's my baby. This is killing me. I want her to try more treatment, too, but I also don't want her last weeks to be full of pain and suffering.'

'She's going to suffer anyway!' Nick shouted. 'She either dies without trying more treatment or she tries and maybe, just maybe, it works. It's a no-brainer! She has to do it! Jesus, Kate, why don't you get it? We have to try everything, and I mean *everything*, to keep Jess alive. That's our bloody job, Kate, to protect her and keep her safe and alive.'

'Keep your voice down! The last thing I need is the boys to hear you.' She steadied her breathing again. 'Please, Nick. We can't force her. It's ultimately her choice.'

'Bullshit! We're her parents. *We* make the decisions. She's just tired and feeling low. Of course she doesn't want any more treatment, but in a few days, when she's feeling better, she'll change her mind and she'll be glad we persuaded her to do it.'

'She has begged us not to, Nick,' Kate reminded him. Nick closed his eyes, as if trying to block out her words, block out their reality, but this was it. It was happening now and she had to make him see. 'All of the professionals we've spoken to said that more treatment will be incredibly aggressive and most likely kill her, Nick. I'd never forgive myself if that happened after she begged us not to do it. I won't do that to her. I can't.'

Nick opened his eyes and stared at her. 'You're being weak, Kate,' he said coldly. 'You need to grow some balls and step up to your responsibilities here.'

That was it. Kate felt a white-hot streak in her brain and lost the battle to stay calm.

'Don't you dare call me weak!' she said, her jaw clenched tight, her hands balled into fists. 'I've been there every single day, holding Jess's hand and watching her suffer, while you breeze in and out whenever you manage to get off the leash Jenny has you on.'

Nick slammed his hand on the table. 'That's crap! I've been there as much as possible. I've got more ties than you, that's all. I have to work and I have to see Jaden and Jenny, too.'

'Oh, poor you, Nick. I have such an easy life. I'm only raising Luke and Bobby basically alone, and helping Dad in the café every spare minute I have. You're no busier than me, I can assure you.'

'Spare me the martyr act, Kate, you're not raising them alone.'

'Really, Nick? How much time have you spent with your sons in the last six months?'

'Here we go! I'm the bad father again. I've seen the boys as much as I could. No matter what I do, someone's pissed off with me. I can't win.'

'Maybe if you hadn't cheated on me your life would be a lot simpler.' Kate sat back, arms folded, cheeks flushed. In a way, the fight was almost a relief. She needed to lash out and she'd gladly punch someone too. Nick wouldn't stand a chance against her. She felt like she could pick him up and break him in two. She was fearless – and that felt good in its own way.

'Don't start with that shit now, Kate. I know I messed things up royally. Believe me, I'm the one who's paying for it.'

'Poor you,' Kate snapped.

'Jesus, Kate, can we please not argue about Jenny now? I've paid for my mistake and, yes, I know you did, too, and the kids and, yes, I know I'm a selfish prick and all the other names you've called me, but please can we just focus on Jess right now? I don't have the energy for anything else. Please.'

Kate's anger began to slide away. Looking at him, she saw he was a broken man already. There was nothing she could do to him that could hurt him more. Jess had only weeks to live: that was the reality they were both facing and trying to deal with. Nick could be an idiot, but he was still Jess's father and he adored her. And Kate had loved him, too, once. When Jess was born, those were really happy times. She felt a stab of guilt at ever thinking she wanted to hurt him. What was wrong with her? This whole situation was making her crazy.

She looked across the table at her ex-lover, her ex-husband, Jess's father, and she knew the only way through this was together.

'Do you remember the day Jess was born, with the big thunderstorms?'

Nick was clearly surprised by her change of tack. Then his face softened. 'Of course I do, like it was yesterday. I knew then she'd be special.'

'Me too.'

'And she is, isn't she, Kate?' he said sadly.

'Yes, Nick, she is.'

He sighed deeply. 'I know I'm not a great father to the boys, I know I need to try harder, but with Jess I feel I did a good job.' He pulled at the bandage wrapped around the finger he'd broken, punching the wall in the hospital. 'Mind you, it wasn't hard. She was always the sweetest thing.'

Kate smiled. 'Yes, she was – she still is. She's the glue in our family. She's the one who worries about everyone and tries to fix things.'

Nick nodded. 'Your mum used to say she was an old soul, and she was absolutely right. Jess has always been mature beyond her years.'

'That's true,' Kate agreed. 'There's just something different about Jess, something special.'

They sat in the kitchen and reminisced. It was nice, sitting together, talking about Jess the way only parents can, boasting, proud, over-exaggerating her achievements, talents and all-round incredibleness.

Nick talked and talked, crying in parts, laughing in others. Kate held his hand and listened, joining in, jogging his memory, laughing and crying with him.

Finally, Nick looked up at the clock. 'God,' he said, rubbing his hand across his face. 'Sorry, I've kept you up late.'

'I wouldn't be sleeping anyway,' Kate said. 'Will you get into trouble?'

'Yes,' Nick said, with a half-smile. 'But that's nothing new.'

'It's hard on Jenny, too,' Kate said. 'She's probably feeling very left out and low down in the pecking order in your life.'

Nick nodded wearily. 'I do know. But it's just . . . times like this . . .'

Kate understood. 'Times like this, you need to talk to me?'

He nodded again. 'We're her mother and father, only we feel this same pain.'

'I know,' Kate said. 'But that's hard on Jenny, too. Even though it's just the way things are.'

'Thanks for letting me come in,' Nick said, standing up.

'Sorry I got so thick with you earlier,' Kate said.

'Me too. It's all just so . . . impossible,' he said, his shoulders sagging again.

He walked over and held Kate in a long hug. In that moment Kate realized they could be friends. With things about to get really awful, with the loss of their beautiful Jess, they'd need each other to lean on. When it came to the children, love went deeper than everything else.

Spring

40

Piper stood sideways in front of the bathroom mirror in her bra and pants. She was really showing now. At almost seven months, her bump was really growing. It was hard being in school with it. She felt like a freak. Thank God it was her final year. Once the exams were over, she'd be free of her stupid uniform and the constraints of school.

It was so kind of Maggie to offer them her apartment. She called it her pension fund. It was small but perfect and close enough to both families, but not too close. It was a one-bedroom on the ground floor, with a tiny garden.

'That means you can sit out with the baby in the summer and not be stuck indoors,' Maggie had said, when she'd shown it to them. 'Now, look, I'm not taking any rent for the first six months and that's final. After that, when you get settled in college and work out part-time jobs and childcare, we can talk about it. But for the first six months it's on me. Consider it my baby-shower present.'

Piper felt bad about Maggie being so generous, but Maggie had insisted. 'Luke is the closest thing to a child I'll ever have and I love him. I want the best for him and you. Kate needs to focus on Jess, so I'm happy to take this on. There will be no more discussion about it and no more thank-yous. It's my pleasure to do this.'

Piper's mum wasn't sure about the arrangement at first, but she'd met Maggie, and Maggie had explained she was Luke's honorary aunt, had no kids and it was a gift. She said she thought it best for Luke and Piper to be together when the baby was born and to figure it all out between them. Also, Luke might feel left out if Piper was living at home: it was his baby, his responsibility, and he wanted to be involved from the get-go. This was a way of letting him do that.

Maggie had been very persuasive and Olivia had come around to the idea. But she told Piper that if she preferred to stay at home, Luke could move in when the baby came. It would mean Pauline would have to sleep with the twins or else they'd put bunk-beds in Posy's tiny box room. Piper was grateful to her for offering, but she knew it would be a complete nightmare. Especially with her dad still barely speaking to her. She was so glad Maggie was there to save the day.

The door burst open and the twins came in. 'Oh, my God!' Penny squealed.

'Argh.' Poppy covered her eyes.

'Put some clothes on! You look like a freak,' Penny said.

'It's like there's an alien in there,' Poppy said.

'Your stomach's all stretched and gross.'

'It'll never be the same,' Poppy assured her. 'They say after you have a baby, the skin on your stomach never goes back to the way it was.'

Penny frowned. 'I dunno, Poppy. Look at Nicole Richie, she's, like, super-slim and so is Kourtney Kardashian.'

'Yeah, but they probably had a tummy tuck when they were having their babies. That's what all the celebs do.'

Penny turned to Piper. 'You should definitely do that. You don't want to be all saggy and flabby after the baby comes out. Luke is hot – you need to look good to keep him.'

'Definitely,' Poppy agreed. 'He'll totally go off with some-one else if you turn into a fat lump.'

'Thanks a lot, girls. You really know how to cheer me up.' Piper pulled on her dressing-gown.

Penny picked up her mascara wand and began coating her eyelashes. 'What's wrong? We're just helping you, Piper. We're trying to make sure you don't end up a single mum pushing a buggy around the park in a saggy tracksuit all day.'

'Everyone knows that if you look like crap, you'll feel like crap,' Poppy, the mothering expert, said.

'Totally,' Penny agreed. 'Kim Kardashian was, like, totally miserable when she had her baby because she whacked on so much weight. But she knew she had to lose it or Kanye would be humping one of his backing singers or whatever, so she focused like mad and got her figure back and started wearing all sexy clothes and everything was fine.'

Piper put her hands up. 'I can't listen to another word of this drivel.' She pushed past them.

'Oh, Piper,' Penny called after her, 'seeing as you're kind of a whale now and can't fit into any normal clothes, can I borrow your skinny black jeans?'

'No way. I love those jeans and I plan to wear them again when I'm not a whale, after my tummy tuck,' Piper snapped.

'Are you going to get a tummy tuck?' Posy asked, coming out of her bedroom in her school uniform with her bag on her back.

'Of course not. Those two are just telling me what a heifer I am and that I need one.'

Posy's eyes widened. 'They're so mean. You look beautiful, Piper. All glowy and healthy.'

Piper smiled at her youngest sister. 'Thanks, Posy. I know I do look a bit like a whale, but it's sweet of you to say so.'

'They can be right cows. As you always say to me, Piper, just ignore them.'

'Don't worry, I will.'

'Will I wait for you?' Posy asked.

'No, go ahead. I'm going to take my time today. I'll just make you late for school.'

'See you later.' Posy skipped down the stairs, followed by the twins, who were arguing over a lipstick.

Piper lay down on her bed, enjoying the peace and quiet. She wasn't feeling well and her stomach was cramping. She must have eaten her breakfast too quickly. She closed her eyes and waited for the cramps to pass. But they didn't.

A moment later she felt something trickle down between her legs. She sat up and looked. Blood. Oh, no. Please, no. She began to shake. She stood up on wobbly legs and stumbled to the bathroom. More blood ran down her thighs.

Her mother had gone to college early with Pauline. She knew she should call Luke, but he had his Irish oral exam this morning and she didn't want to ruin that for him. Oh, God. There was only one person in the house.

Piper pulled on tracksuit bottoms and a hoodie. Clinging to the banisters, she made her way carefully down the stairs. She went through the kitchen, out of the back door and across the garden to her father's shed. She could see him typing furiously on his laptop.

She knocked on the door. He frowned, stood up and opened it. 'What?'

'Help,' Piper gasped, holding her stomach as another cramp doubled her over.

'Jesus, Piper! Is it the baby?' Seamus held her up.

'I need to go to hospital, Dad.'

'Of course. Come on, we'll get you there.'

Seamus half carried her to the car, helped her into the front seat and buckled her seatbelt. He then hopped in and drove like a maniac towards the hospital.

Piper sat crouched in the front seat. Please, God, don't take my baby away. Please, she prayed.

'You're going to be all right, love,' Seamus kept saying. 'It'll be okay.'

He screeched to a halt outside A&E and ran in, shouting, 'My daughter needs help! She's pregnant and she's bleeding! Help! HELP!'

A nurse came out and helped Piper into a wheelchair. While her father went to move the car, Piper was wheeled into the waiting room where her details were logged into a computer. Then she was taken for an ultrasound.

As the gel was being applied to her stomach her dad rushed in, pulling back the curtain. 'Is she okay? Is my girl okay? Is the baby all right?'

'We're just checking now. We need you both to be calm.'

The sonographer moved the scanner probe over Piper's stomach and stopped. Piper held her breath. She loved this baby. She wanted this baby. This baby was part of her. She couldn't bear for anything to happen to it.

Then she heard it, the beautiful sound. The sound of a horse's hoofs, galloping galloping . . . Her baby's heartbeat.

'The baby's fine.' The sonographer smiled. 'Everything looks good. Sometimes bleeding can happen when pregnancy hormones cause you to develop more sensitive, expanded blood vessels. But the baby is fine and the placenta looks perfectly healthy, too, so please don't worry.'

Piper burst into tears. Beside her, her father, holding her hand and staring at his grandchild on the scanner, wiped away a tear. 'Will you look at that?' he said, amazed.

The sonographer smiled at him. 'I take it you're Granddad,' she said.

Seamus nodded.

'And this is your first time to see the baby?'

He nodded silently again, never taking his eyes off the screen.

'It's a pretty special moment,' the sonographer said, running the probe over again, so they could see the baby *in utero* from every angle. 'It won't be long now before you're holding this little one in your arms.'

'Jesus,' said Seamus, utterly gobsmacked.

'You'll need to take it easy for a few days,' the sonographer told Piper. 'It's important to get some rest after a bleed. You need to put your feet up and tell this man here to wait on you.'

Piper nodded, unable to speak. She felt suddenly exhausted after the whole drama.

Seamus patted her shoulder. She glanced up at him. He was gazing at her intently. 'We'll make sure she relaxes, Doctor.'

'Good. She needs it. She looks tired.'

'Sure the poor girl is worn out,' Seamus said. 'Between studying for her exams and the stress of the baby, and her boyfriend's sister is very sick too. Piper's always the one who helps everyone. The most selfless girl you could meet.'

The sonographer smiled as she wiped the gel from Piper's stomach. 'Your dad clearly thinks very highly of you.'

'I used to think so,' Piper said quietly.

The sonographer shot her a look. 'Okay, folks, you're free to go,' she said. 'We're here if you have any worries at all, Piper.'

They stepped outside the room and Seamus suddenly grabbed her in a tight hug. 'I'm sorry, pet,' he said. 'I've been all caught up in myself. I was just worried about you being so young and having a baby and your future and all of that. But it doesn't matter. We'll all help you. And I'm proud of you, Piper, more proud than I can say. Sure you're the light of my life.'

Piper buried her face in her father's woolly jumper and bawled. Tears that had been buried deep came gushing up. She'd been so hurt by his coldness and disappointment, and it was a huge relief to know he still loved her and would support her.

'Now listen to me,' Seamus said sternly. 'I want you to rest. Enough running around doing things for Luke and his sister and everyone else. You are coming home with me and I'm tucking you up in bed. Then you're going to sleep and relax. No studying today either. You must mind yourself, pet, for yourself and the baby.'

Seamus put his arm around her as they walked slowly out of the hospital. In the car, Piper leant her head back and smiled to herself. She'd thought her father would be angry with her for ever. She was so glad he'd changed his mind. She felt as if a huge weight had been lifted off her chest and she could breathe again.

When they got home, Seamus ordered her into bed, then brought her up a cup of tea and a plate of chocolate biscuits. 'Now, I'm going to work in the kitchen today, and if I hear you move, I'll be up like a shot to get you back into that bed. You're exhausted, pet. You need a good sleep.' He closed the curtains and kissed her forehead.

'Thanks, Dad,' she said, feeling like a kid again and enjoying it immensely. It was lovely to be looked after.

'Right, I'll leave you to it. Sleep well, and if you need anything, just shout.' As he was leaving the room, he said softly, without turning around, 'I love you, Piper.'

'I love you too, Dad.' She saw him smile as he closed the door.

Piper snuggled down in the bed and took out her phone to call Luke. But then she stopped. He didn't need to know. Everything was fine. The baby was perfect. He had enough worries. Piper closed her eyes and savoured the feeling of warmth spreading through her body and her heart. She had her dad back and it felt wonderful. Knowing he still loved her made everything so much better.

41

Jess began to cry, jerky sobs that shook her tiny body. 'It hurts, Mum, it really hurts.' The pain was getting worse by the day, and the intravenous morphine drip wasn't enough any more.

Her mother called Aideen, who appeared, like an angel, at the door. An angel of mercy, Jess thought. 'She needs more morphine. There isn't enough pain relief in the drip,' Mum said.

'No problem. We'll give the poor dote a booster.' Aideen came over and adjusted the drip. Jess closed her eyes and welcomed the relief. 'Is there anything else I can get you?' she asked.

Jess shook her head.

'All right. You try and get some sleep now.' She watched as Jess's eyes fluttered, then closed. To Kate, she said, 'She'll be more comfortable now. I'll pop back in to check on her in a bit.'

Fighting the sleep that was overwhelming her, Jess opened her eyes and looked at her mother, who was exhausted. Jess hated what her cancer had done to her whole family. It was enough, it was time. She had to tell her mother now, before it got worse.

'Mum,' she said.

'Yes, love?' She leant over, putting her ear close to Jess's mouth.

'I need to ask you to do something.'

'Anything, my darling.'

Jess took a deep breath. She'd gone over this speech in her mind a thousand times. She had to get it right. She glanced up at the dandelion card and felt Larry's presence. 'Mum, I know I'm going to die and I've accepted it. Over the last eight months I've had no control over anything. But I can control this. I can control how I leave this world. I don't want to die on a day when I get an infection and I'm vomiting blood and can't breathe. I don't want to die like that, when I'm not expecting it. I want to go when I decide to. I can't fight any more, Mum. I just don't have the energy. I've tried, I've really tried, but it's beaten me. I need you to help me, Mum. I need you to help me die.'

Jess watched her mother's face. Kate didn't move. She was completely still, bent over her daughter's body, her ear close to Jess's mouth, catching every unbelievable syllable. Jess saw the pain and sorrow in her eyes. Please say yes, she prayed. Please, Mum.

Her mother tried to compose herself, but tears streamed down her face. Jess hated seeing her so upset, but she needed this. She would not let cancer dictate to her any more. This was the one decision she could make, and she was going to make it.

The light from the lamp on the bedside locker framed her mother in silhouette. She was a blend of light and shadow, like the line between night and day. Between life and death.

'I know it's a terrible thing to ask,' Jess whispered, 'but if you love me, Mum, if you really love me, you'll help me. I know you will. I want to die in my own way. Everything has been stripped away from me. I'm just a shell, Mum. I have no life. I can't stand the pain any more. I hate it. I hate what I've become. I'm not me. This isn't Jess.' She began to cry again. Damn, she'd promised herself she'd remain calm and in control.

Her mother breathed out, and slowly found the ability to move again. She put her arms around Jess. 'But you are. You are you. You're still the wonderful, beautiful, amazing Jess we all adore. We love you, Jess. We want every second that we can get with you. I can't cut your life short. I need you, Jess. Every minute I have with you is a gift. I can't cut that short.'

Jess stopped crying and pulled herself together. She had to make her mother see. She had to make her understand that by helping her die she was doing the best and kindest thing she could do. 'Mum, please, listen. I know it's going to be hard for you, but I'm begging you. There is nothing better that you can do for me. It's what I want more than anything in the world, Mum. Please do this for me. You've always been there for me. You can do this, Mum. I know you love me enough to do it. You're the only person who can. No one loves me the way you do. That's why I have to ask you to do this. I'm sorry, but I want this more than anything. I'm ready.'

Jess waited while her mother struggled to find words. Finally she said, 'I understand why you want to do this. You've had such a terrible time. And I want to help you more than anything in the world, but, Jess, how can I let you go when the thought of it just rips me apart?' She covered her face with her hands. 'Your dad said you mentioned this to him and he flipped out,' she whispered. 'How can I possibly say yes?'

Jess shook her head. 'I said it to him to see his reaction. I knew he'd freak out. But I just wanted to plant the seed in his mind. I know he can't do it. You're the only one who can because you're the one who loves me the most.'

'Yes, I do love you the most, which is why I'm the last person who can do this. You're my only daughter, Jess. You're my baby girl. I . . . You don't understand . . . to lose a child. Jess, what you're asking, it's too much.'

Jess dug deep. She dug down to her toes. She had to be strong. 'Mum, it's only going to get worse. I'm going to be in more pain and sleeping all the time and slipping in and out of consciousness. And it's going to happen anyway, no matter what we do. I want to control this one last thing. I know I could possibly live for another month or so, but I can't do it, Mum. It's not a life. This isn't living. This is dying all the time, and I want to do it my way. Please, Mum, please do this for me. It's the right thing, I promise you.'

Her mother was crying now. 'But what if . . .'

'. . . a miracle happens and I get better?' Jess was getting angry. 'I'm not getting better. There is no cure. It's over and we all know it. Even Dad knows it deep down. I'm begging you, Mum, help me.' Jess's strength began to fade and she turned her head to cry into her pillow.

Her mother came over and lay down beside her, holding her, stroking her face, kissing her cheek. 'Don't get upset, sweetheart, please don't cry. You've taken me by surprise. I need time to process this. I need to think about it. Can you give me a day or two? It's such a huge decision. Can you give me some time?'

Jess nodded. 'Okay, but please don't take long, Mum. I need to know. I need to know this will soon be over. You're the best mum in the world. I know you can do this.'

As her mother's tears landed on her cheek, Jess felt herself drifting as the morphine took over her body and mind. Jess prayed as sleep crept up on her: Help me, Mum . . . If you love me, help me die.

42

Kate left the hospital, walking quickly down the quiet corridors. She went straight to her car, sat inside and bent her head to the steering-wheel. She waited for the tears to come, but they didn't. She felt emptied out, hollowed. She had moved beyond tears into some kind of shocked space where she simply couldn't believe that this was her life.

How the hell was she going to make the decision?

She picked up her phone and stared at it. She couldn't ring Nick: he'd come straight here and scream blue murder at her. He'd be disgusted with her for even considering it. A part of her wanted to hear her father's voice, but she knew this was too big to confide in him. It would be a huge burden to put on someone else, to ask them to share the decision with her. There was only one person she trusted absolutely one hundred per cent.

The phone rang at the other end and Kate held her breath.

'You've reached Maggie O'Neill. I'm not available to take your call, but please leave a message.'

'Damn,' Kate breathed. Maggie's phone beeped. 'Em . . . oh, hi, it's just me. Nothing important. Everything's okay here. Was just ringing for a chat. I'll try you tomorrow.'

She threw her phone onto the passenger seat and her stomach churned, as if she was going to be sick. She stared up at the hospital, counting the windows across on the third floor to the one she knew was Jess's. Up there her daughter lay dying. The grief of that was fathoms deep, and now Jess wanted to die early, to go sooner – and Kate was the one she'd turned to for help to do that. How can this be happening? Kate thought, her head aching. It was a nightmare there was no waking up from.

She had a sudden idea and knew where she wanted to be. She buckled up her seatbelt, turned the key in the ignition, put the car into gear and drove away from her daughter, turning onto the motorway as the stars came out and the moon rose higher in the sky.

She didn't remember any of the journey, other than the vague impression of lampposts forming a tunnel down which she drove. She drove on automatic pilot, hearing Jess's voice over and over again: 'I know you can do this . . . You love me the most . . .'

Eventually, she reached the turn-off and followed it to the little car park. Everything was silent. There wasn't a soul about. She locked the car and made for the steep path, walking fast up it, enjoying the sensation of her lungs burning with effort. She didn't stop once, just pushed on across the forested area and then to the clearing. Below the cliff's edge, the waves crashed against the rock. The grass was springy and tough beneath her feet as she walked to the edge. The moon was high enough to provide some light, but the shapes around her were still only half formed, made mostly of darkness.

Kate sat down and watched and listened, taking in the sounds and smells of the night. She breathed deeply, slowing her racing heartbeat, trying to be in the moment as the mindfulness teacher had shown them. She felt she needed to be calm now, to think clearly so that she could make the right choice.

What had really struck her about Jess was how serious and determined she had looked – it was the face of someone who had thought long and hard about their decision. She had said, 'I'm ready,' and Kate had to admit that she had looked ready. There had been no fear in her eyes, no hesitation in her voice. She had never seemed more grown-up than in that moment. She had known exactly what she was asking and why.

Kate could understand her desire to take control now. She really could. When your life is reduced to constant pain and suffering, who wouldn't want to say, 'Enough'? So was it because of Jess's age that she had been so shocked by what she had said? That was probably some of it, yes. How could a twelve-year-old be so sure they wanted to leave this world? But, then, Jess was no ordinary twelve-year-old.

It hurt, though – it really hurt that Jess was ready to give up and leave them all. When she had said she was ready to die, she was also saying she was ready to leave her family. That part Kate couldn't bear.

But was it fair? None of them could feel her physical pain. It always seemed impossible from the outside that someone could want to die, but if you were living in a body racked with pain, it was probably the case that you reached a point of acceptance and the desire to end it. And, by God, Jess had suffered. Kate had watched her go through hell, her poor body battered and bruised, pushed to the limits of pain. Who could blame her for wanting it to stop?

Kate shifted about, then lay down to be more comfortable. She gazed up at the stars.

'My daughter is going to die,' she said out loud. It was the first time she'd spoken those words. She felt the weight of them, even if they didn't feel quite real yet. Her mind kept resisting them, blocking them, arguing with them, telling her it couldn't be true. 'It's true,' she said to the stars. 'My daughter is going to die.'

But could she help her to die, hasten her death? She felt a cold lump in the bottom of her stomach at the thought of it. No matter the motive, it was still killing. Kate hadn't done an illegal or wrong thing in her life. It wasn't the way she was made. She wouldn't hurt anyone, wouldn't want to, but now her own child wanted her to kill her. That was the truth of it – and if anyone ever discovered what had happened, that was how the police would see it. Kate would be a murderer in the eyes of the law, pure and simple. Could she risk that? What about Luke and Bobby? What if she got caught? In order to fulfil Jess's last wish, she could be setting up a lifetime of pain for her sons. Was that fair?

Her phone buzzed in her pocket. She looked at it. It was 2.05 a.m., the bright screen told her. How had it got so late so quickly? The message was from Maggie: *Probably too late, but I'm here now if you need me.*

Kate stared at the words. Did she need her? Yes, it would be great to talk it over with her, but it really was too big a thing to ask of Maggie. It would implicate her as well. Kate put her phone away and tried to think of what Maggie's advice would be. She'd be shocked – the idea of a twelve-year-old begging to die was shocking – but she felt that once she'd got over that, Maggie would probably say that Jess should be allowed to choose her own way to die. She'd probably tell Kate that the grief would be the same whether it happened tomorrow or in a month, so why not allow Jess to make the call?

That's true, Kate thought. It won't actually change the aftermath for everyone else – they'll be devastated no matter what. Yes, it will be different for me, living with the knowledge of what I did, but I'll also be living with the knowledge that I did exactly what Jess wanted. I mean, if I were old and sick and asked my children to help me go, I'd be asking because I really wanted to do it. And I'd be hoping against hope that they'd have the guts to do it for me.

Kate curled up on her side, smelling the grass and the soil and the salty air. She tried to put herself into Jess's shoes, think herself out of her own body. If I were lying in a hospital bed, day after day, with tubes in my arms, vomiting, bleeding, soiling the bed, losing all my hair, the pain of mouth ulcers, watching my loved ones suffer over me, and the doctors told me death was now inevitable, how would I feel? What would I want? In her heart, Kate knew she would think just as Jess was thinking. She knew she would want to be allowed to die with dignity, by choice and before the bitter end.

She felt her mind move towards 'Yes', but just as quickly it snapped shut again, screaming, 'No!' The thought of being without Jess, of her not being in the world . . . It hurt with a jagged, searing pain that made her hunch her shoulders and curl up as if she'd been stabbed. It just hurt so much. The prospect of burying her Jess, and soon, made her want to throw herself off the cliff. She didn't want to be here if Jess wasn't. It would be unbearable. But then . . . but then . . . but then . . . it was going to happen anyway. It was now inevitable. That was what the doctors had told them. She was going to have to find a way of living without Jess. Find a way of being a mother to Bobby and Luke and of being a grandmother to the new little one. Life would go on, no matter what.

Kate rolled over onto her stomach and her whole body shook as she cried, gulping for air. She balled her hands into fists and hit the hard brown earth over and over again. Jess was going to die. She was going to be buried in this soil. She would be gone. Kate couldn't change that.

When she finally sat up, shivering with cold, her eyes sore from crying, limbs stiff from being so tensely held, she turned to face the sea and saw the dawn beginning to spread across the horizon. She watched, numb in mind and body, as the peachy pink colours became stronger, pinker. It was as if the whole heaving sea was holding its breath, waiting for the sun to come up above the horizon. Kate wrapped her arms tightly around her body and waited too.

Her tired eyes saw the moment when the rim of the sun curved above the horizon line, the sudden shot of gold, bright and hot against the pinkish wash. She was on the edge of the world, wishing she could drop over the side.

But she couldn't. She was a mother, which meant you never got to give up. It was a relentless love that wouldn't ever let you rest. She had to be a mother to Jess now, and to Bobby and Luke. And she had to help Piper be a mother in the years to come. Kate had to play her part. She couldn't step back from it. That wasn't an option.

The sun rose higher, and Kate's mind went back and forth, back and forth. I can do it. I can't do it. Pros and cons, she said to herself wearily. Let's do it that way. Okay, cons: Jess dies; maybe someone figures it out and I go to prison. Her mind drew a blank. That was it. Okay, pros: I give Jess her dying wish, which makes her die happy, with dignity and safe in the knowledge that I love her more than life itself.

Kate bowed her head and squeezed her eyes shut. She had thought about it for hours but, really, she'd known deep inside all along that there was only one option. She was Jess's mother, and her daughter needed this to make her happy, to take away her pain, to let her feel in control of her own life. Jess had asked her to love her by letting her go, and that was what Kate had to do.

She stood up and stretched out her stiff body. The seagulls were wheeling across the sky now, screeching to each other, looking for food. The day had begun.

Kate slowly retraced her steps, back through the forest, down the steep path, to the car. She reversed out of the car park, drove back to the exit onto the motorway, quiet in the early morning. Eventually she went through the gates of the hospital and parked the car. She walked slowly back inside, nodding good morning to the nurse at Reception. She went down the corridors she had passed through just hours before, feeling like a different person. She already felt like a culprit, as if they'd see it written on her face, what she was going to do. She reached Jess's room and stopped outside, took a few deep breaths, rubbed her eyes, then pushed back her shoulders and went in.

She sat on the side of the bed and watched as Jess came back from sleep. The first noise she made, before she'd even opened her eyes, was a whimper of pain. Her eyes opened and she saw Kate. She smiled at her. 'Mum.'

'I'm here,' Kate said.

'What time is it?' Jess asked.

'About six,' Kate replied. 'Early. I've been up all night, thinking.'

Hope filled the beautiful brown eyes. 'And?'

'I love you, Jess,' Kate said. 'I love you more than anyone else in the world. From the day you were conceived I felt connected to you in a way no one could understand. The day you were born was the happiest day of my life. You were so longed for and so perfect. I love you in a way that has always scared me because, even before you got sick, I knew that level of love could mean the same level of hurt one day. But I never in my wildest dreams imagined I'd be losing you.' She smiled weakly. 'It's unimaginable for a mother to lose a child.'

Jess bit her lip as tears came into her eyes. She couldn't speak. Her eyes were trained on Kate's, waiting, waiting.

'Because I love you like that,' Kate said, taking her hand, 'I'm going to do as you've asked. If you're absolutely, totally sure.'

Jess nodded, still unable to speak, but she squeezed Kate's hand.

'I'll help you die the way you want to,' Kate whispered. 'I'll figure it out, and you can tell me when.'

They sat there, unmoving, staring into each other's eyes. Kate felt a sense of exquisite understanding, as if they'd come full circle and Jess was part of her again, part of her body and mind, as she had been in the womb. It was a strange feeling, but it was as if Jess was coming home, and that home was her. For the first time, Kate felt a small sense of relief – that it was the right decision, even though it would condemn her to a lifetime of hurt and to a secret that would burden her for ever. But she was Jess's mother and that was her sacrifice, and she was going to make it because she loved her daughter enough to do it.

43

When her mother had left to go home for a few hours, Jess lay in her bed feeling a strange mix of emotions. She couldn't quite believe she had agreed. She'd felt there was a chance she would, but seeing Mum's face when she'd asked her had made her think that the chance was very small. But whatever had happened in her mind overnight, she had seen in her face that morning that she was now convinced by what Jess had said, that she would do it.

For Jess, it was a relief, but it was bittersweet at the same time. She wanted to go, and she didn't want to go. If she could live, she'd grab life with both hands and live for all she was worth. But she had accepted that death was now a fact, and she knew in her bones that this was the best way to handle it.

She asked Aideen to let Dr Kennedy know that she had made her decision, and after morning rounds, he came to see her.

'How are we this morning, Jess?'

'I'm good, thanks.'

'So you've discussed things with your parents and thought things over?'

Jess nodded. 'I don't want any more treatment. I can't take any more. I'd like to go home now and let whatever happens happen.'

Dr Kennedy nodded sadly at her. 'For what it's worth, I think you're right.' He smiled. 'You've got a very wise head on those young shoulders.'

'It's for the best all round,' Jess said.

'Jess . . . I'm so very sorry.' The poor man looked like he might cry, which was very unlike him. It made Jess feel a bit uncomfortable. 'I wish the treatment had been more successful.'

She felt for him. It must be awful to do a job where you had to watch people die all the time. Timidly, she reached out and touched his hand. 'Thank you for trying so hard,' she said. 'It's no one's fault. I've accepted that this is just the fate I've been dealt.'

He bent his head for a moment, then raised it again and smiled. 'That's the way it seems to work, unfortunately.' He stood up. 'I'll talk to Aideen and your parents, and we'll sort out palliative care for you at home. They'll make sure you're comfortable and pain-free at all times.'

'That's perfect. Thank you so much.'

Dr Kennedy left, and she lay back, staring up at the ceiling. Jess smiled. She was so happy to be going home. Her heart lifted at the thought that she'd be leaving this hospital never to return. Jess knew she'd made the right decision. It felt so right, and she loved her mother so much for helping her.

'Hello, beautiful.' Dad walked in, carrying a tall sunflower in a vase. 'Something to cheer up the room,' he said.

'Wow, that's gorgeous,' Jess said. 'It's huge. Aideen's going to kill you for bringing that in.'

Nick looked guiltily at her. 'Oh, crap, are flowers not allowed?'

Jess took a fit of laughing. 'You're actually scared of Aideen, aren't you?' she wheezed.

Nick grinned. 'Yes, and man enough to admit it too.'

'Don't worry, I'll tell her you'll take it home with you. You can share it with Jenny and Jaden.'

'Thanks,' Nick said, smiling. 'Was that Dr Kennedy I saw rushing down the corridor?'

Jess's heart sank at the sight of his hopeful face. 'Yes, it was. We were just confirming things.'

Nick sat down quickly on the edge of her bed. 'And what did you confirm?' he asked eagerly.

'I'm sorry, Dad,' Jess said. 'I know you want me to do it but I'm not doing the treatment. I'm going home.'

He stared at her for a long minute, then turned away. He bent over and Jess watched in shock as her father's body heaved with sobs. She had no idea what to do. She'd expected him to shout at her or punch the wall, but not this, not crumble in front of her. She reached out and patted his back gently, feeling awful that she had done this to him.

Nick cried and cried, shaking with grief. After some minutes the tears began to subside.

'I think you're wrong,' he said, when he could speak again. 'You're giving up too soon. We're fighters not quitters.'

'I'm sorry, Dad, but I just can't do it any more. I'm ready to go home. It's over, Dad.'

'Please, Jess.' His face was wretched. 'Just one more try.'

Jess wanted to scream at him to stop harassing her, but she held it together. She shook her head. 'No, Dad. I'm done.'

He began to cry again. 'I don't want you to die,' he sobbed.

She put her arm around him. 'Dad, I know that. And I don't want to die either. But we can't change what's inside me. The cancer is in there. At some point, we have to accept that.'

He looked up sharply at her and rubbed his eyes hard. 'And if your mother was standing here pleading with you to keep trying, would you say no to her?'

Jess was taken aback. 'I would say to her exactly what I'm saying to you,' she said.

'No. Kate has the power to make you change your mind. I know she does. If she'd just bloody well listen to me, I know she could persuade you.'

'No, Dad, she couldn't. No one can change my mind. Mum respects my decision. She'd love to change my mind, but she accepts she can't. She listens to me.'

Nick turned his body so that he was looking directly at her. His eyes narrowed as he watched her carefully. 'Your mother had better not be letting you make any foolish decisions, Jess. I want you here as long as possible. Every second with you counts. Do you understand? Every single second. Is precious.' He began to cry again.

Jess felt worried now. Her dad would go mad if he found out what Mum had agreed to do. What if he made trouble for her afterwards? What if he told Dr Kennedy? Or the police? She hadn't thought about that. She'd been so focused on persuading Mum to help her die that she hadn't thought about Dad causing trouble if he found out or even suspected. They'd have to be really careful. Jess's heart was beating wildly as her mind raced through the possibilities of her father's grief destroying everything. She breathed deeply and willed herself to be calm.

Nick held her gaze. She felt as if he was looking through her and could see all.

She muttered, 'Yes, Dad, of course, I know that,' and then, mercifully, his phone beeped. He cursed.

'Sorry, Jessie, but I have to go to work.' He looked at her again. 'Promise me you won't do anything silly? I want you for as long as I can have you.' His voice cracked as he leant down to kiss her cheek.

Jess swallowed. 'Okay, Dad, I love you,' she said, afraid to say anything else for fear of implicating herself or her mother.

He nodded – exhausted, and his day had barely begun. 'Take care. I'll pop in after work, okay?'

'Bye, Dad.'

Jess breathed a sigh of relief when he left. She went over their conversation in her mind again and again. She was worried now. She'd been so caught up in controlling her end that she hadn't given a thought to what might come afterwards. She had to make sure that Dad wouldn't cause any trouble for Mum.

When Aideen came on shift that afternoon, Jess asked her for a pen and paper.

44

Piper handed Luke half a cupcake.

'Should we be eating these before she arrives?' Luke asked.

'Your baby is starving and there are about five thousand more, so I think it's all right,' Piper said.

They watched Chloë and Bobby putting out the plates and napkins. Maggie was placing mountains of presents around the space where Jess would be sitting.

George and Nathalie were polishing glasses and cutlery. Hazel was shouting down the phone at someone. 'If you don't get here in the next thirty minutes, I'll come and burn your fucking place down.'

'Mum!' Chloë hissed.

Hazel's face was flushed. 'I apologize for my language. Sorry, Bobby. I'm just a bit stressed.'

Maggie handed her a glass of wine. 'Get that down your neck.'

Hazel smiled at her. 'Thanks, Maggie, you're a star.'

'That woman needs to calm down,' George grumbled to Luke. 'Turning my café into a party shop. I can't see a bloody thing with all these balloons.'

Luke and Piper grinned. When Hazel had offered to help decorate, they hadn't known she was going to hire a professional event organizer. The café was crammed full of balloon decorations, towers of cupcakes, three huge birthday cakes, a chocolate fountain surrounded by vast plates of marshmallows and strawberries. There was a tent in the corner full of dress-up clothes and Hazel had even ordered a photo booth for everyone to get their photo taken with Jess.

'Hazel's great, but everything is kind of super-sized,' Luke said quietly.

'I know, but it's kind of fabulous, too. Jess will love it,' Piper said.

Maggie came over and sat beside them. 'How are you feeling, Piper?'

'Good, thanks,' Piper said honestly. After the bleed, she'd rested for a few days and had really felt the benefit. Things with her father were great again, too, and she felt happier than she had in months.

'Doesn't she look gorgeous?' Luke said, and kissed her.

'Get a room . . . Oh, no, you already did.' Maggie grinned. They all laughed.

'Are you managing to study?' Maggie asked Luke. 'I know it must be so difficult right now with Jess being so unwell, but try to do some work – it'll help distract you.'

Luke stared at the floor. 'I know. It's hard, though, Maggie. She's so . . . so . . .'

Maggie's eyes welled. 'I know.'

'Before, I could believe she'd get better, but now she looks as if she's dying.' He wiped tears from his eyes.

Piper held his hand.

'I wish I could think of something comforting to say, but it's just so unfair. I wish there was something I could do, but I feel so useless. I'm a fixer, and I can't fix this.'

Piper leant over to hug Maggie. 'You've helped in so many ways. You've been amazing to me, Luke, Kate and everyone.'

'You're a rock, Maggie,' Luke agreed. 'A total rock.'

'Ah, stop, my make-up will be ruined. I'm glad Jess is coming home. It'll do her the world of good.'

'Yeah, it'll be really nice having her here with us,' Luke agreed. 'Dr Kennedy says we'll take it day by day, but he won't bring her back into hospital unless he has to.'

Bobby ran into the room. 'She's coming!'

Everyone got up and rushed to the front door. An ambulance was parked at the kerb, its back lowered to accommodate Jess's wheelchair. She was fixed up to a morphine drip and had a blanket tucked around her legs. The palliative-care nurse was by her side, supervising the transfer.

'Looks like some people are happy to see you, Jess,' she said, smiling at the little crowd gathered to greet them.

Chloë ran over and hugged her. 'You look gorge, Jess. Wait until you see the café! It's amazeballs.'

'I can't wait.' Jess grinned.

'Mum went totally over the top, but in a good way this time,' Chloë gushed.

Nick walked down and took charge of pushing the wheelchair. He was trying to smile, but it couldn't reach his eyes. Kate knew that while he was happy to see Jess at home, he was still cut up about her decision not to take further treatment. He looked as emptied out as she felt. It was as if he was dying, too, alongside Jess. But, still, he fixed his face into some form of a smile as he wheeled Jess up the path and into the house.

When she reached the kitchen, Kate grabbed her in a tight hug. 'Now close your eyes, darling,' she said, nodding at Nick to wheel Jess through the door and into the café.

Nick stopped just inside the door. 'Okay. You can open them,' he said.

'Oh, my God, it's *amazing*!' Jess cried, clapping her hands together with delight. 'I can't believe it.'

'It's all for you, darling. Happy nearly birthday,' Kate said.

'When is your birthday?' Nathalie asked.

'Second of July,' Jess said, 'but why wait when you can have an amazing birthday right now?'

'Amen to that,' Hazel said.

Piper went over to give Jess a kiss. 'Happy almost birthday.'

'Thanks! I'm so happy.'

She looked it, Piper thought. For the first time in ages, her cheeks were flushed with colour and her eyes were bright and shiny. She genuinely looked happy. 'You deserve it, Jess.'

'Can I feel the baby?' she asked.

'Of course.' Piper took Jess's hand, placed it on her stomach and pushed a little. The baby kicked back.

'*Oooooob!* I love when it does that!'

'Me too.' Luke grinned. 'I reckon there's a future football star in there.'

'I hope it's a boy like you, Luke,' Jess said.

'I hope it's a girl like you,' Luke replied.

'Hey, what about me?' Piper laughed.

'A mixture of Jess and you would be perfection,' Luke said.

'Okay, I'll take that.' Piper winked at Jess.

They sat down at the table. Piper tucked in, feeling ravenous. She hoped that she wouldn't end up being a whale, but right now she needed food. The baby was obviously having a growth spurt. To hell with Penny and Poppy and their fat-pregnant-women stories! Piper bit into her cupcake with relish.

Hazel, Chloë and Maggie were wonderful, keeping the conversation light and fun, making sure there were no silences for sadness to creep in. By sheer force of will, they pushed the grief out of the room for a few blissful hours.

When Piper got up to go to the toilet for the zillionth time, she heard a noise coming from the kitchen and peered around the door. George was sitting in a chair with his back to her, weeping into a tea-towel. Nathalie was standing behind him, hugging his neck. 'Let it out, George. You must let it out.'

'Why her? Why not me? That beautiful little girl had her whole life ahead of her. I've had my life and it was a good one. Why is this happening to her? I can barely look at Kate, she's so broken. It's just not right.'

'Kate is full of sadness, yes, but she is a strong woman. She will be okay. She 'as you and Luke and Bobby and her Maggie. And she 'as Liam now also. 'E is very kind.'

'No parent should see a child die. It's not right.'

Nathalie patted him on the back. 'George, life is not always 'appy. There is a lot of tragedy as well. But you 'ave to accept it or it will kill you. Look at Jess today, just focus on that. She is 'appy. Go and be with 'er. You can do this, George, you are a wonderful father and grandfather. They are lucky to 'ave you. Now, take the deep breath and you go back and be with Jess.'

George turned around and hugged her. 'Thank you for coming into our lives when we needed you, for being mad but in a good way, and for being a bloody decent human being.'

He walked out, and Piper saw Nathalie bury her face in the already tear-stained tea-towel.

When she got back to the table, Chloë was in the photo booth with Jess, the wheelchair squeezed in sideways. She was dressing Jess up in funny hats and glasses and feather boas and they were making goofy faces and being young and carefree. It was so lovely to see Jess having fun.

Chloë waited for the photos to print. She whooped when she saw them and showed them to Jess, laughing loudly. 'I have to show them to Piper,' she said, rushing over to her.

'Look, Piper, aren't they hilarious?' she said, as tears streamed down her cheeks. 'Don't let Jess see me cry,' she whispered.

'They're brilliant,' Piper said. 'Come and show them to Luke.' She brought Chloë to the other side of the room, where she shielded her from view while Chloë mopped her face.

'She looks so sick – she's like a little alien. Oh, Piper, she's my best friend. What am I going to do without her?'

'I know, sweetie, it's unbearable. But always remember you've been the best friend she could have wished for. You really have been brilliant, Chloë. You always cheer her up. Every time, no matter what.'

Chloë fought back more tears. 'That's my goal when I see her. I have to make her laugh as much as I can, and then I don't feel so bad. Mum said the most important thing I can do is cheer her up. I'm trying, Piper, I really am.'

Piper leant in and whispered, 'You're doing an amazing job, Chloë. Really amazing.'

Chloë plastered a smile on her face. 'Come on, Jess,' she called. 'One more funny one. Let's do the wigs now.'

Nick came over to her. Piper froze – he made her nervous. He seemed so on edge all the time.

'So, how's the pregnancy going?'

'Okay, thanks.'

He smiled. 'Better than Jenny's, I'd say. She moaned the whole way through.'

'Well, some women get very sick. I've felt fine, really, just tired.'

Nick nodded. 'Kate was like you – she just got on with it. So, I hear Maggie's offered you her place?'

'Yes, she's been so generous. I hope we can pay her back some day.'

Nick fiddled with his watch. 'I wish I could have helped more. I'm just stretched so thin, supporting two families.'

'Oh, gosh, no, it's fine, honestly. We wouldn't expect anything.'

Nick turned to watch Luke, who was showing Bobby how to do a press-up. 'Luke will be a great dad.'

Piper smiled. 'Yes, he will.'

'A lot better than I ever was.'

Piper didn't know what to say. She remained silent.

'Maybe I'll turn out to be a great granddad,' Nick went on. 'Who knows? Stranger things have happened.'

'I'm sure you will,' Piper said, trying to be polite.

'You're a nice girl, Piper. I really hope it works out for you both. Look after Luke – he pretends he's so strong and resilient, but he needs you. And he will continue to need you.'

'I will, I promise.'

Nick left her and went over to Jess and Chloë. He let them dress him up in ridiculous outfits and smiled for the photos.

Luke came over. 'What was Dad saying?'

'Just how great I am.' She grinned at him.

'Seriously?'

'Yes! No need to sound so surprised.'

Luke kissed her. 'You know I'm your number-one fan.'

'He was nice, actually, sweet.'

'Dad and the word "sweet" do not go hand in hand.'

'He's trying, Luke. At least give him credit for that.'

Luke stroked her hair. 'For you, anything.'

Hazel shouted over everyone, 'The final surprise for Jess is here – and about bloody time too.'

They looked out of the café door, and there was a horse on the street outside.

'It's Jess the pony, and Julian!' Jess squealed. 'Oh, Hazel.'

Nick picked Jess up and carried her outside to the horse. Kate followed, clutching a blanket for her, and the others streamed after them.

'It's so good to see you again, Julian,' Jess said. 'Thanks for bringing Jess. Can I ride her?'

Julian nodded. 'I'll sit behind you and hold you and the drip. If your dad can lift you, I reckon we can go for a short walk.'

'Mother of God, the neighbours are going to love this.' George shook his head.

Between them, Nick and Luke managed to hoist Jess into position, seated in front of Julian. Kate fussed around with the blanket, but Jess waved her away happily. Julian tapped the horse's sides lightly and, very slowly and carefully, the huge animal started to move. They watched as Jess and Julian walked slowly down the road, cars slowing as they saw them. Jess was smiling from ear to ear.

Piper looked around: every single person in their little group was crying.

45

Jess hugged Hazel. 'Thank you for the best party ever.'

'I'm glad you had a good time, sweetie.'

'You've been so amazing, Hazel. You have the biggest heart. I'm so grateful for everything.'

'There's plenty more fun to come, so you just stay strong.'

Chloë nudged her mother aside. 'Bye, Jess. I'll send you all the photos I took. Some of the ones with your dad are hilarious.'

Jess kissed Chloë's cheek. 'You're the best friend in the world. Thanks for always cheering me up, even on my worst days.'

Chloë blushed. 'That's what friends are for.'

'No,' Jess said. 'That's what really special friends do. I love you, Chloë, you're the best.'

'Stop! You'll make me cry!' Chloë said.

Hazel took her daughter by the arm. 'Right, let's get you home. Jess needs some rest. See you soon, sweetie.'

Jess watched them walk down the path. Hazel put her hand out and Chloë took it. Two very special people I was lucky to know, Jess thought.

She'd miss them. She wondered what Chloë would become. She reckoned she'd be famous in some way. Chloë had pizzazz and energy and so much charm, she'd probably end up taking over the world. Jess wished she could be there to see it.

Nathalie came up behind her. 'Did you enjoy the day?' she asked.

Jess nodded. 'It was brilliant. Thanks for all your help making it so special.'

Nathalie shrugged. 'It was my pleasure. To see you so 'appy with your eyes shining makes me 'appy.'

'It was the best party ever.'

Nathalie picked up some plates. 'You 'ave a fantastic family, Jess. They love you so much. It's beautiful to see this.'

'I know I'm a lucky girl.'

Nathalie smiled crookedly. 'Maybe not so lucky with the cancer, but with the family, yes.'

Jess laughed. 'Thanks for being so great with Granddad and so lovely to me and Bobby and everyone.'

Nathalie paused. 'For me, it has been a great experience. I am honoured to be part of this family's life. It can be a bit crazy sometimes but there is so much love, it's beautiful to see.'

Love, thought Jess. It was what life was all about. When you took away everything else, it all came down to love. That was what sustained you through the difficult times. It got you through the bad news, the pain, the suffering – love was the most powerful thing in the world.

'Anyway,' Nathalie interrupted Jess's thoughts, 'I 'ave to go. I 'ave a date.'

'Ooooh! Who with?'

'A man I met at a poetry reading.'

'What's this?' George asked.

'Nathalie has a date.' Jess filled him in. 'Is he nice?'

'We'll see. He doesn't drink, so at least I know he won't be falling down after ten o'clock.' Nathalie grinned.

'Is this the poet fella?' George seemed up-to-date.

'Yes.'

'Poets are a flaky lot. You should go out with a fella with a decent job who'll look after you, not some eejit who spends three years writing five lines of drivel,' George told her.

Nathalie laughed. 'Come on, George, you know me. I like the artistic men.'

'You deserve better,' George said.

'If I don't like him and 'e is – 'ow you say? – flaky, I just move on and find someone else. Don't worry about me, George. I am a strong French woman.'

'You can say that again.' George laughed. 'Most of my customers are afraid of you.'

Nathalie punched him playfully in the arm. 'I 'ave to go. See you tomorrow.' She hugged Jess.

'Thanks for everything, Nathalie. You've been like a sister and a friend all mixed together.'

Nathalie looked into Jess's eyes. She became very still and then she whispered, '*Au revoir*, my beautiful Jess.' Her eyes filled with tears as she turned to go.

Everyone finished tidying up, and then Kate said it was time for Jess to get some rest. As Nick and Maggie were putting on their jackets, the door opened. Jenny walked in, holding Jaden.

'Oh, no.' Bobby groaned.

'What the hell is she doing here?' Maggie muttered.

Jenny smiled awkwardly. 'I'm sorry to interrupt – I'm not staying. I just wanted to give Jess a present.' She went over to Jess and handed her a gift. 'I thought you might like to have it beside your bed. I'm sorry you're having such a terrible time,' she said.

Jess unwrapped it. It was a framed photo of her dad throwing her up in the air. She must have been about a year old in the photo and she was laughing hysterically. Nick was beaming up at her, so handsome and happy. Jess felt a well of emotion building up. She crushed it down. 'Thank you, Jenny, so much. I'll treasure it.'

'Oh, it's nothing, really, but I'm glad you like it.'

'It's beautiful, Jen.' Nick beamed at her.

'It was really thoughtful of you,' Kate said.

Bobby came bustling over. 'Jaden won't let go of my leg and he stinks.'

Jenny laughed. 'Oh, God, sorry. You're right, he needs to be changed. Anyway, I'll go.'

'I'll come with you. I was just leaving,' Nick said.

'Hey, let's get a photo of me with Jaden,' Jess said.

'Great idea!' Nick looked surprised and pleased.

Jess tried to ignore the smell of Jaden's dirty nappy. She held him and smiled as the photo booth flash went off. When it was finished, Jenny came over and picked him up off Jess's lap.

Nick turned to Jess and leant down to give her a hug. 'Thanks for doing that. See you tomorrow, Jessie.'

Jess clung to him and inhaled the scent of his aftershave. 'I love you, Dad,' she whispered into his ear.

'Oh, Jess, I love you too, more than you can imagine.'

They held each other for a minute, until Bobby said, 'Daddy, you have to go before Jaden stinks the whole house out.'

Everyone laughed, and Jess watched her father leave. As he got to the door, he turned and blew her a kiss.

Maggie helped Kate tuck Jess into bed, then sat with her after Kate had gone down to sort Bobby out.

'Good day?' Maggie asked.

'The best ever,' Jess said.

'You deserved it. You're an amazing girl, Jess, just like your mum.'

'I'm so glad she has you, Maggie. You're such a support to her, and to all of us.'

'You're like my family, kiddo. You're stuck with me. It's a pity your mum and I aren't gay – we'd make a great couple.'

Jess giggled. 'Now that would be funny.'

'Anyway, you look tired and I've got a conference call with the US. I'll pop in to see you in the morning before I fly back to London.' Maggie hugged her.

As she was leaving, Jess called out, 'Look after Mum, won't you, Maggie?'

'Always, Jess, you know I will.'

Watching everyone leave was draining Jess of the little energy she had, but she knew the worst goodbyes were to come. But, as awful as it was having to say goodbye to everyone without them even knowing it, she knew without a shadow of a doubt that this was the right thing to do. It was time to go. Cancer had controlled and ravaged her life. It had come into her body and destroyed it. It was destroying the happiness of her family and friends. Everyone was at the end of their tether, worn out, devastated and unable to take much more. Jess wanted out. It was time to do things her way.

Granddad, Piper, Luke and Bobby came in to say goodnight. Jess hugged them all in turn.

'I wish I could have an almost-birthday party like that,' Bobby said.

'Maybe we could organize one for you next year,' Piper said.

'Really?' Bobby's eyes lit up.

'Sure, but it wouldn't be quite the same. We don't have Hazel's bank account.' Luke grinned.

'I wouldn't want all the pink stuff, just the cakes and the people and the sweets.'

'I was pretty surprised to see Jenny arriving,' Luke said.

'The photo is beautiful,' Piper said, looking at it on the table beside Kate's double bed where Jess was lying.

'Jaden was obsessed with me,' Bobby said. 'He was stalking me and he kept grabbing my leg.'

'You used to do that to Luke.' Their mother came in, holding a cup of tea.

'Did I?' Bobby was surprised.

'I guess it's a younger-brother thing,' Luke said.

'Well, it wasn't fun cos he stinks,' Bobby grumbled.

'He can't help that,' Mum said.

'Does that mean you're not going to help change our baby's nappies, Bobby?' Piper asked.

'No way!' Bobby shouted.

Jess smiled. She'd miss this. The banter, the fun, the family time. Just her family being her crazy, beautiful family.

'Right, this poor child is worn out. Let her rest.' George kissed Jess goodnight.

'I love you, Granddad. Thanks for letting us come and live with you. It's been amazing.'

'I've loved having you, my little pet. Now sleep well.'

Piper kissed her. Jess pulled her close. 'Look after Luke. He needs you.'

Piper looked surprised at the urgency in Jess's voice. 'Of course I will. I promise.'

'He loves you so much.'

'I love him, too, sweetie, so don't worry. It's all going to work out,' Piper whispered. 'Now rest up and stop worrying about everyone else.'

'I love you, Piper.'

'I love you more.'

Luke walked Piper out and Bobby followed them. 'Hang on, Bobby, come here for a second,' Jess called out.

He came back in, reluctantly. 'What? I'm tired, Jess. I want to go to bed.'

'I just want you to give me a hug. Please?'

He rolled his eyes. 'Everyone's always hugging in this house.'

'Bobby,' his mother said sharply, 'give your sister a hug.' Then she got up and left the room.

'Okay, one hug cos it's your almost-birthday, but that's it.'

He threw an arm around her, then pulled back.

'Thanks, Bobby. You know I love you and I think you're just brilliant.'

'You always say that, Jess.'

'I mean it, though. Don't let anyone try to change you. You're perfect just the way you are. I think you're going to do something incredible with your life, I really do. There's something really special about you.'

'Are you joking now?'

'No.'

'Did Mummy tell you I want to cure cancer?'

Jess coughed to hide the sob that escaped from her throat. 'No.'

'Well, that's what I'm going to do, Jess. I'm going to cure it so no one has to suffer like you.'

'That would be amazing, and I bet you'll do it.'

'Can I go now?'

She smiled. 'Yes, love you.'

'I know. You said it already.' He bustled out of the room.

Jess lay back on the bed. Only Luke to go. He'd be the hardest. Apart from Mum, he knew her the best. She had to keep calm. She wanted this memory to be a good one for him.

'Penny for your thoughts?' Luke stood at the door, hands in his pockets.

Jess smiled. 'Hey, come in.' She patted the bed.

'Good day,' he said. 'Even Jenny didn't cause a scene.'

'It was sweet of her to do that.'

Luke wrinkled his nose. 'About bloody time she did something nice for you.'

'Come on, Luke, give her a break. It's not easy for her. She's the home-wrecker no one wants to see. It was brave and kind of her to come today.'

'All right, Mother Teresa, I admit it was a nice gesture. Maybe she's not all bad.'

Jess folded the bed cover over in her fingers. 'You'll be a great dad.'

'I hope so. I want to be, but it's kind of scary.'

'Yeah, I can imagine.'

'I just want to get the exams over, then focus on Piper and the baby and trying to figure it all out.'

'You'll be fine. You've got so many people looking out for you who want to help.'

Luke nodded. 'You're right. Even though our family's a bit mental and half the people in it aren't even related to us, they're a good bunch.'

'A great bunch.'

He bent his head. 'I wish I could fix it, Jess.'

Jess put out her hand and took Luke's. 'You can't. You tried, and I'm so grateful to you for your bone marrow, but you can't fix me, Luke. No one can. But it's okay, honestly. This is how things are, and I've accepted it now.'

'It's not okay. It's so unfair.'

Jess squeezed his hand. 'Luke, please listen to me. I've made peace with it. You have to try to do the same.'

'I'll never accept it,' he said, in a strangled voice. 'You're the nicest, bravest person I know. You don't deserve this.'

'No one does, but it happens all the time. Please, Luke, don't be angry. It'll eat you up.'

Luke rubbed his eyes. 'I'll try, Jess.'

Jess reached under the pillow and pulled out an envelope. 'I need you to give this to Dad when I die. It's important, Luke. Promise you won't forget.'

'What is it?'

'It's just something I need to say to him and it was easier to write it down.'

Luke took the envelope and stood up. 'I'll let you get some rest.'

Jess held up her arms for one final hug. 'I love you, Luke. You're the best older brother I could ever have wished for. Everything's going to be fine.'

Luke smiled. 'If you say so, Jess. Now get some sleep. Love you, sis.'

Jess watched her brother and her hero walk out of the room, and her life.

46

Kate looked down at the pills spread out on her bathroom shelf and counted: twenty-eight Xanax tablets and fourteen Tylex. This was what would kill Jess.

Agreeing to end her child's life was one thing. Planning it was another. At first, Kate had thought about stealing morphine from one of the palliative-care nurses or doctors who came every day to check Jess's morphine pump and up the dose as her pain got worse. But she quickly found that they were incredibly careful with their medications and never left any lying around.

They were very kind. They said it was important for Jess to be comfortable, but not knocked out by the morphine so she could still function 'normally'. Kate loved and hated them coming – loved them because they were so caring, hated them because of what they represented.

She'd thought about asking Dr Willis, their GP, who also called in regularly to see Jess, to get her some morphine. But she didn't want to implicate him in any wrongdoing. No, Kate was on her own. This was something no one could knowingly help her with, and no one could ever find out about. She had to be careful, really careful, or she'd end up in prison. Then Bobby and Luke would have a dead sister and a convict mother.

So Kate went to plan B: search the internet. She was shocked by what she found. If you wanted to know how to kill yourself or someone else, the internet would provide you with all the information you needed. She had spent hours trawling for ways to overdose. If anyone looked at her Google search history, she'd be locked away on that evidence alone. But she'd covered her steps as best she could, scrubbing out her search history again and again.

She had quickly found everything she needed to know. The information she'd gathered told her it would take a combination of medications to end Jess's life. She needed benzodiazepines and morphine. Benzos she could get in Xanax, and morphine by taking codeine, in Tylex tablets. It was far simpler than she'd thought it would be. A part of her actually wanted it to be harder, so she could stall and delay it, but the all-knowing internet spewed out everything in a morning.

Kate hated lying, but this was not a 'normal' situation and she was no longer afraid of anything. The worst possible thing was already happening to her: her daughter was dying. So she went to Dr Willis and told a few white lies. She said the stress of Jess's cancer was making her extremely anxious and she needed Xanax. He readily gave her a prescription. Then she said she was also having terrible migraines and needed dissolvable Tylex. She began to cry at this point because part of her wanted him to say no. Then she wouldn't be able to kill Jess.

But Dr Willis patted her hand sympathetically and said she was under terrible duress and he'd gladly give her Tylex, but that she must be careful not to take the two together. He said he'd pop into the house in a few days' time to see Jess and check on Kate.

Kate had cried harder then. If only he knew, she'd thought. If only he knew what I plan to do with these tablets. I'm a bad person. I'm a bad mother. I'm a murderer.

Her mind kept flip-flopping crazily from 'This is right, it will be okay' to 'I'm killing my own child. I'm a child-killer.

I'm immoral and unnatural.' She wanted to honour Jess's final wish, but felt like it might kill her too. She could never be the same after this act, an act of which she'd never have thought herself capable – until her daughter had looked her in the eye and begged her.

Luke was saying goodnight to Jess, not knowing he was saying goodbye. Kate leant her forehead against the cool glass of the bathroom mirror. Give me strength, Mum, she pleaded. Help me.

She stared down at the tablets spread out before her. Jess trusted her. She was waiting. She would be devastated if Kate changed her mind now.

Kate mixed the effervescent Tylex tablets in a glass of apple juice and scooped up the little Xanax tablets in her hand. She went in to Jess. Her eyes were closed. Whiskey, the cat, was tucked under her chin. She looked so peaceful and so young. Kate put the glass and the tablets on the bedside table, then lay beside her daughter and held her one last time.

A montage of memories floated through her mind: Jess's birth, her first day at school, swimming lessons, roller-skating with her bright pink helmet, smiling with no front teeth, shouting up the chimney on Christmas morning, 'I love you, Santa', laughing hysterically when Nick tickled her, hugging Whiskey in bed at night, smiling, happy, alive . . . so alive.

Kate lay holding her broken, emaciated, bald daughter, the one cancer had ravaged, and she remembered the good times, allowed herself to travel back there and take solace. She thanked God for giving her this incredible child, who had lit up her life every day for twelve years and 306 days.

Jess was a gift, a precious gift, and Kate knew she was lucky to have had her. Jess had been the light of all their lives.

Imagining a future without her was unbearable, unthinkable, yet here she was about to help her end it.

Love, Kate realized, was very complicated. She loved Jess so much that she was willing to help her die. True love meant putting your feelings aside. True love meant helping your loved one die with dignity. True love meant sacrificing your wishes for theirs. It hurt like hell, but it was love nonetheless.

Jess stirred and groaned. She opened her eyes. 'What time is it?' she asked.

'Almost one.'

'I know this is hard for you, Mum, but thank you.'

'I'm only going to ask you once more. Are you sure?'

Jess nodded. 'More sure than I've ever been. The pain is getting unbearable. Yesterday was amazing, though. I saw everyone I love. It's the perfect time to go.'

Kate pushed the tears down. There were things she needed to say. She didn't want to waste the time crying. 'I love you so much and I'm so proud of you. I can't believe that Dad and I made someone so perfect.'

Jess smiled. 'I'm proud to be your daughter. You're amazing, Mum. Through thick and thin, you've always been there for us.'

'You three kids are my life.' Kate couldn't help it, she began to cry.

Jess wiped the tears away with the palm of her hand. 'Don't cry, Mum. I'm happy to go now and, besides, Luke's baby will make it three again.'

'No one will ever replace you. I love you so much, Jess. From the very first moment they put you in my arms, such a tiny thing, I felt a surge of pure love. It's never gone away. I adore you. Every last little bit of you. You're such an amazing person.'

'I know you love me, Mum. You're going to be okay – you have so many people who love you and will be there for you. You're the best mother in the world. I love you. And I'm so sorry it has to be like this. I'm sorry that we have to say good-bye this way.'

Kate pulled her daughter's fragile body even closer, breathing in her scent, resting her lips against her cheek. 'Me too. You should have had a better life,' she whispered. 'But you must know that every second of the last almost thirteen years has been a privilege and a joy.' Kate pushed up on her elbow to look into her daughter's eyes. 'I will miss you every single day of my life.'

Jess nodded, tears starting to fall down her cheeks. 'I'm sorry I have to go,' she whispered back.

Kate pressed her forehead against Jess's. Around them, the house was silent with sleep. It was dark and warm in there, just the two of them.

'If I can I'll try to send you a sign. I told you before, remember?'

'Yes,' Kate said. 'Send me a sign so I know you're okay.'

'I'll send a white butterfly. Larry always said I'd better not die in winter or you'd be waiting a long time to see one.'

'Say hi to Larry for me, and to your granny. She'll be there to look after you,' Kate croaked.

'I will. Can you open the curtains and the window?' Jess asked.

Kate did so. It was still dark outside, but in a few hours light would begin to break its way through and another day would begin. Her first without Jess. Kate felt her resolve weaken, and fiercely ordered herself to be strong. All those wakings without Jess, one after another for the rest of her life, were going to be like little deaths every time she opened her eyes. She tried to push the thought away. Not now, she told herself.

From behind her Jess said gently, 'I'm ready now, Mum.'

Kate turned and picked up the tablets. Jess opened her mouth. Kate's hand was shaking. Sadness crashed through her, taking her breath away. 'I can't do it. I want more time with you,' she sobbed.

Jess grabbed her arm, and put Kate's hand up to her mouth. 'Please, Mum, you have to let me go.'

Kate gulped back tears and looked at Jess's determined little face, at the morphine drip, at her bald head, at her thin body. She wanted to be selfish, to hold on to Jess for every second she could, but that was what she wanted. It went against Jess's own wishes. She was going to have to find the purest love inside her and hold on to it to enable herself to do this. She focused on Jess's face, on Jess's need, and dissolved her own wishes to nothing. She could do this. She could do it for Jess.

'Sorry, sweetheart. It's okay.'

She placed the tablets in Jess's mouth and helped her swallow them with water. Then she handed her daughter the glass of apple juice containing the Tylex and Jess drank it straight down. No shaking hands, no hesitation.

Jess lay back on her pillow and sighed. Kate groaned and her legs went to jelly and she collapsed beside the bed, her knees sinking to the floor. 'What have I done?' she gasped. 'Oh, Jesus, Jess, what have I done?'

Jess took Kate's trembling hands in her small, bony ones. 'Look at me, Mum,' she ordered.

Kate raised her head and gazed into the beautiful brown eyes.

'Thank you. Thank you for saving me from any more pain. Thank you for letting me die my way. I'm happy, Mum. I'm ready to go. This is what I want. I love you so much.'

Kate looked deep into her daughter's eyes and knew she had done the right thing for Jess, but that didn't take into account how she herself was feeling. It wasn't simple for her. It was a crushing blow of emotions, all racing around her body making her feel panicked and grief-stricken. She had done the unthinkable – helped her own child to die.

She climbed into the bed, under the covers, and held Jess close. She stroked her cheek, her head, kissed her face over and over again. She told her how much she loved her, she told her how wonderful it felt to be her mother. Kate talked through life and on into death.

For four hours Kate held her precious girl and watched as her breathing got slower and slower. She breathed with her, she breathed for her. This is love, she thought. This is the ultimate act of love: letting someone go.

Never in her wildest dreams when she'd held that bonny, healthy baby girl for the first time almost thirteen years ago could she have imagined that she'd now be holding her as she took her last breath.

Kate keened and moaned, as she rocked Jess in her arms. The room steadily became brighter as the sun slipped above the horizon. Jess's breathing was very shallow now, more like gasping. She was peaceful, though, not struggling. Then there came a shuddering gasp, and she was still. Kate bent her head and kissed Jess's eyelids.

With the end of Jess's breathing, which Kate had been straining to listen to for so many hours, came other sounds she hadn't noticed before. The birds in the garden had taken up their chorus, which broke into her consciousness now. Morning song. Mourning song. They were singing the new day into being – Kate's first day without her daughter. It was over. Jess was gone.

47

Kate woke up with a start. Luke was shaking her.

'Wake up! Jess isn't breathing. Jesus, Mum, I think she's . . . I think . . .' He began to cry.

Kate pulled her arms from around her daughter's body. Jess lay still, her body still warm but her soul now far away. She wasn't there any more. The enormity of what she'd done hit Kate and she doubled over in pain.

'Is she dead, Mum? Is she?' Luke cried.

Kate nodded.

'Oh, God, *nooooooo* . . .' Luke covered his face with his hands and wept. 'Why, Mum? Why did it have to happen? I thought we had more time? Oh, God.'

Kate stroked Jess's face. What had she done? She'd cut her life short. What mother does that? She heard Jess's voice in her head: *If you love me, you'll do this.* Well, she did love her. She loved her more than anything in the world and she wanted her back. She wanted one more day, one more hour. Oh, Jess . . . what have I done? Kate began to sob uncontrollably.

Luke came over and put his arms around her. They cried together, each broken-hearted over the loss of their beloved Jess.

George came in and froze when he saw them crying. 'Oh, sweet Jesus,' he murmured. He came over to the bed and looked down at Jess. 'Oh, Jess, poor broken bird.' He put his arm around Kate. 'Come here, Katie, it's okay. At least she's at peace now. No more pain for the poor pet.'

He turned to hug Luke. 'She won't suffer any more, Luke. She was ready to go.'

Luke shook his head. 'But I'm not ready, Granddad,' he said, through his tears, and Kate's heart broke.

George patted him on the back. 'We're never ready to let go of the ones we love. There is no right time to say goodbye.'

Kate felt her throat closing. Jess, my beautiful Jess. I want you back, I need you, I can't believe I did this . . .

George bent down and forced Kate to look at him. 'Breathe, Kate. Come on now, look at me. Breathe.'

Bobby stumbled in in his pyjamas. 'What's going on? Why is everyone crying? Is Jess sicker?'

Luke went over to his little brother. 'Bobby, I'm really sorry to have to tell you this but . . . Jess died last night.'

Bobby frowned. 'Died? How could she die? She was all happy yesterday and smiling and taking photos and . . . and alive. I think she's just sleeping, Luke.'

Kate pulled herself together and gathered Bobby into her arms. 'She is sleeping, Bobby, but she's not going to wake up. She's gone to Heaven now.'

Bobby wriggled away from her. 'She is not in Heaven cos there is no Heaven,' he shouted. 'God is not real. If he was, he wouldn't have made Jess get stinky cancer and he would never, ever have made her die.' He kicked the bed violently. 'Ouch!' He began to cry.

The four of them stood around the bed, crying, each lost in their own thoughts. Finally, George wiped his eyes with his handkerchief and said, 'Kate, you have to tell Nick.'

Kate's heart sank. She was dreading it.

'I'll do it, if you like,' George offered.

'No, it should be me. I'll ring him now.'

Kate left the room and went down to the kitchen. She also had to phone Dr Willis and ask him to come over to sign the death certificate. There was no way Jess could have a post-mortem. If that happened, they'd find out what Kate had done.

Part of her would have welcomed being found out and sent to prison. She wanted to be punished for what she had done. She wanted to feel physical pain. She wanted someone to punch or hit her. She was a bad person, a bad mother. She had killed her baby. Oh, God . . .

Stop it, Mum. I wanted to die. Jess's voice sounded in her ears.

Kate pinched her arm, hard. The pain brought her back to her senses. Her sons needed her. She couldn't risk a post-mortem. She called Dr Willis.

'I'm so very sorry, Kate,' he said. 'The poor child was very sick. At least she's out of pain and at peace now. I'll be right over.'

Kate thanked him. She'd call the palliative-care team a little later. She wanted Dr Willis to get there first. Taking a long, deep breath, she dialled Nick's number. Her hands shook.

'Hi.' He sounded sleepy.

'Nick, it's Jess. She's . . .' Kate tried to get the word out '. . . she's . . .' She couldn't say it. How could she tell him? She knew that his heart would split in two and it would be irrevocable.

'What?' Nick sounded alert now. 'Is she in the hospital?'

'No, she's . . .'

'Oh, shit, is it another infection?'

'No, Nick. She's – she's dead,' Kate blurted. 'She passed away during the night.'

'*What?*' Nick shouted. 'What did you say?'

Kate began to cry. She'd done it now, she'd told him. His life would never be the same again. None of their lives would ever be the same. It would always be 'before this moment' and 'after this moment'. 'Before Jess' and 'after Jess'. There was no way to fix this or go back and change the outcome. Jess was dead. Gone. Never, ever coming back. They'd never see her smile again, never hear her voice, hold her, kiss her, love her. Kate slid down onto the kitchen floor and sobbed.

'*Nooooooo*, Kate, please. No, it can't be . . . Oh, Jesus Christ, no.' Nick broke down. Kate could hear Jenny beside him, asking him what was wrong.

'I'm sorry,' Kate said. 'I'm so sorry.' And then she hung up.

Dr Willis gently examined Jess's body. He listened for heart sounds, then for breathing sounds in the lungs and then checked Jess's pupils with a torch. Kate saw him give Jess's hand a little squeeze and heard him mutter, 'May you rest in peace, sweet girl.'

Turning to Kate, he said, 'I'm so very sorry. She went quickly in the end.'

Kate looked away from him. 'Yes, she did.'

'She was in a lot of pain, and it was only going to get worse. It's no comfort to you, but perhaps it was best that she went now and didn't suffer any more.'

Kate was afraid to speak. She wanted to tell him. She wanted to confess what she had done. It was eating her up inside. 'I killed her,' she wanted to shout. 'I'm an evil person. I cut my baby's life short.' She shook all over with guilt.

Dr Willis walked towards her, clearly concerned. 'Do you have the Xanax I prescribed? You might need to take one, Kate. Will I get one for you? Where are they?'

'*No!*' Kate gasped. 'No, I'm fine. I just need a minute.' The empty packets were tightly wrapped up in a bag in the bathroom bin.

'Well, sit down and put your head between your legs – it'll help with your breathing.' He guided her to the chair in the corner of the room.

As Kate concentrated on catching her breath, Nick crashed into the room. He ran to the bed and cried out his daughter's name over and over. He kissed her face and her hands and stroked her cheek, sobbing wildly.

Dr Willis whispered, 'I'll pop downstairs and see your dad,' then discreetly left the room.

Kate sat in the chair, silently watching Nick fall apart.

He turned to her, his eyes red and bloodshot. 'How could she go so soon? How could she just die like that? I thought we had more time.'

Kate didn't trust herself to speak.

'Our little girl. How can she be gone, Kate? How? It's not right. It's too soon.'

Kate felt her stomach twist.

'I didn't tell her I loved her.'

'You did, Nick.' Kate found her voice.

'Not enough. I should have told her more.'

'She knew you loved her.'

'How did it happen? Were you here? Was she alone?'

'I was with her. She just went to sleep and then she . . . Well, she . . . stopped breathing.'

'What did you do? Did you try to bring her back? Did you do CPR? Was the nurse here?'

'No, she'd gone home. I didn't do CPR. I just . . . well, I just knew she was gone.' Kate could feel herself blushing.

'Did she say anything? What were her last words? Do you think she knew?'

How could Kate tell him that Jess's last words were *Thank you for saving me. I'm happy, Mum, I'm ready to go*?

'She was happy, Nick. She loved the party yesterday and saw everyone and I think she was just ready to go.'

Nick knelt beside the bed, caressing Jess's arm. 'That's just it. She seemed so joyful yesterday. I said to Jenny on the way home, "I think maybe she'll get her strength up and be able to do more chemo." I honestly thought she might make it. I can't believe this has happened . . . It's all wrong. It's such a shock. I mean, I know she was really sick but I just can't take it in. Jess, my little girl . . .' He buried his face in the duvet and sobbed.

Kate went over and laid her hand on his shoulder. She felt as if she was made of glass and could shatter at any moment.

Nick looked up at her wild-eyed. He grabbed her arms. It hurt. 'Did you do something?'

She stared at him, unable to compose herself quickly enough. She shook her head. 'No,' she whispered. 'I didn't do anything.'

He stared hard at her, still gripping her arms. 'Because if you did anything to cut her life short,' he said quietly, 'I would never, ever forgive you. I want my Jess back. I don't want her to be gone. If you did anything at all, I promise you now, Kate, I'll bring you down.'

48

Nick sat in the corner of the café in a daze. People came and went, bringing food. So much food. There were cakes and buns and lasagnes and dinners on every surface. People he knew and didn't know shook his hand and told him they were sorry for his loss.

Loss. What a ridiculous word. He hadn't lost Jess, she'd been ripped from him. Fate had wrenched her from this life to the next. If she was lost, he'd be able to find her. There was no finding her now, no getting her back. He was bereft.

Bobby wandered around in circles, kicking the tables and chairs. Luke and Piper sat in the corner, holding hands. Maggie and Hazel moved around talking to everyone and making sure they all had food and something to drink. Chloë sat in a corner, staring at photos on her phone and crying quietly.

In the sitting room, in a closed coffin, lay Jess. His little girl, put inside a wooden box. Tomorrow, after the funeral, she'd be in the ground, buried six feet under. This was not how life should be. His head thumped with anger. It took huge effort not to jump up and scream, hurl the furniture through the windows and punch all of the well-meaning onlookers who were staring at the debris of his smashed-up life.

The French waitress made vats of coffee and tea and kept trying to get him to eat. 'You must keep the strength up,' she said, as she offered Nick yet another plate of food. But he couldn't eat. He felt constantly nauseous. How could people sit around drinking fucking coffee and eating cake? Jess was dead, for Christ's sake.

Kate kept wandering in and out, unable to sit still. Whenever she saw Bobby or Luke or George, she hugged them. Nick watched her, knowing she was as ripped apart inside as he was and marvelling at her ability to think of others still.

'Dad?'

Nick looked up. Luke was standing beside him, holding out an envelope.

'Jess asked me to give you this.'

'What?'

'The night she died, she told me to give this to you once she was gone.'

'My God.' Nick's hands were shaking as he took the envelope. 'Thank you, Luke.'

Luke nodded at him, then went back to Piper. Nick opened the envelope and pulled out the letter. It wasn't Jess's normal writing: it was sloping, jerky and much harder to read. It had clearly taken her enormous effort to write it. He squinted, deciphering the letters and the words one by one, a lump forming in his throat as he read her last words to him.

Dear Dad

By the time you read this letter, I'll be gone. I'll be in a place where I can be at peace. I'm not happy here any more. I can't take it any more, Dad. It's too much pain. I want to go. I'm happy to go – it's important you know that, even if it's hard to hear.

I know you wanted me to do more treatment, but I couldn't. I knew I was dying before the doctors told me. It was a feeling I had, hard to explain, but I just knew. I think I'd accepted it long before everyone else did. But I love you all so much for trying to keep me alive.

The strange thing is, I'm okay about dying. I guess I've had a while to get used to the idea. Until Larry died, I didn't even allow myself to think it was a possibility, but after he went I realized it could happen to me too.

I hoped it wouldn't, but I got sicker and here we are.

I tried, Dad, I tried really hard to beat it, but the cancer beat me. I tried to tell you I was ready to go, but you weren't ready to hear it. Dying this way, at home with dignity, is my final wish, Dad – let me go and don't blame anyone for my death. Please.

I want to die in my own way, on my own terms, just as I told you. I want to be in charge. That means everything to me. So please don't blame Mum. She only did what I begged her to do. She allowed me to leave this world with dignity. I asked her to help me die because I knew you couldn't. I made her say yes, I forced her to agree, and I love her so much for doing this.

You reacted so strongly when I mentioned wanting to let go and I understand why. You're a fighter and a warrior and someone who never gives up and wouldn't allow me to either. And I love that about you. But sometimes, Dad, sometimes you have to accept defeat and let go.

I've had a short life, but it's been a brilliant one. I have the best family in the world. I love you all so much. It was hard when you met Jenny and left, but I understand that life can be complicated and that you fell in love with her and that's okay. I want you to be happy. I want everyone to be happy. I know you worry about your relationship with the boys not being that good. But it can be, Dad. You can fix it so easily. Just spend more time with them. Luke needs you in his life. He pretends he doesn't but he really does.

Bobby looks up to you so much and he's jealous of Jaden only because he thinks he's taking you away. He's angry because he's confused and scared. Be patient with him, Dad. He's such a gorgeous boy. He just needs to know he's loved. Thanks for being a great dad to me. I love you so much. I'm so proud to be your daughter. You always made me feel like the most important girl in the world.

I'm sorry I caused everyone so much unhappiness. I wish cancer had never come into our lives but it did and I've accepted that my time is up. You need to accept it too. Remember the good times and try to look forward.

I'm sorry I'll miss Luke's baby being born, but I'll be watching. Wherever I am, I'll be watching. If you see a white butterfly, it'll be me, letting you know I'm okay. But even if you don't, please don't worry about me. I know I'll be fine.

I'm not scared, Dad. I'm not frightened of dying any more. I want to go.

Mum is letting me go, and you must too.

I love you always,
Jess

Nick's hands were shaking so much, he could barely read the last line. Rage welled up inside him. White hot, burning through him.

He stood up, unsteady on his feet, and stumbled forward. He had to find her. She wasn't in the café. He staggered into the kitchen. She was there, with Maggie. He grabbed her by the shoulder and spun her around to face him.

'You lying bitch,' he hissed, shaking the letter in her face.

Maggie stepped in. 'Jesus, Nick, calm down.'

'It's okay,' Kate said quickly.

'No, it isn't. He can't speak to you like that. She's heart-broken too, Nick.'

'You don't know what she is! She's a monster!' he spat.

'You need to calm down, Nick.' Maggie stood in front of Kate, protecting her from his venom.

'It's okay, Maggie, leave it.' Kate took hold of Nick's arm. 'Nick, come upstairs. We can talk about this in private.'

'So your dirty little secret doesn't get out?' he snapped.

Kate turned and strode out of the kitchen. Maggie looked shocked, but she let them go. Nick followed Kate into her bedroom and slammed the door.

'You bitch, you lying bitch! You killed her!' he shouted. 'It's here in black and white.'

Tears spilt down Kate's cheeks. 'Yes, I did help her die. I did it because she begged me, Nick. She wanted to die in her own way.'

'Her own way? She was twelve! She was a child. She didn't know what she was saying! She was sick. How could you do this? You cut her life short. You stole her from me, from us. Who the hell are you to decide when she should die? Who made you God?' He dug his finger into her chest.

Kate pushed his hand away. 'I didn't decide, you moron. Jess did. Do you think I wanted to do it? Do you think I wanted to cut her precious life short and lose one minute with her? She begged me, she pleaded with me – and you know what, Nick? She deserved to die her own way. She'd suffered so much. She desperately wanted that final control, and I let her have it.'

'She should have died when it was her time, not now, not before. She could have got better.'

Kate glared at him. 'No, she couldn't. She was terminally ill. You saw how weak she was.'

'Weak, yes. About to die, no. How could you do this? Why didn't you say no? What the hell is wrong with you?'

Kate sank down on the edge of the bed. 'I did say no. But she kept pleading with me. She wanted to go, Nick. She was tired of the pain and suffering. She couldn't take any more.'

'She was a child. You were supposed to talk her down, make her see that she had to live.'

'Jesus, don't you think I tried? Do you think I wanted to do this? It broke me in two, Nick. But she asked me and it was what she wanted. And Jess wasn't a kid, not really, she was a very old, wise soul.'

'She was twelve!' Nick roared, his hands balled into tight fists. 'You should have told me. How could you not tell me? I would have talked her out of it. I'd have made her see sense.'

'You told me that she did talk to you about it, remember? So you must know, in your heart, that she didn't want to be talked out of it. She wasn't going to change her mind. It wasn't a snap decision. She thought it through long and hard.'

'I'm her father, for Christ's sake! How could you decide this without me? I wanted more time with her. You stole that from me. You robbed me of that. You robbed all of us. Her brothers, George, everyone. How could you, Kate? You were her mother — how could a mother do that to her own child? I mean, Jesus Christ . . .'

Kate began to cry again. 'She said, "If you love me enough you'll help me." I didn't want to do it. Don't you get it? I wanted her to keep going but she couldn't. She just couldn't go on. I tried, Nick . . . I loved her so much — I never wanted this. I'm broken, destroyed.'

'You're destroyed? Oh, poor Kate. What about me? There were so many things I wanted to say to her, to do with her, to . . . to . . . just to be with her.'

'I'm sorry. I don't know what else to say. I did what Jess wanted. I know it was wrong, but for her it was right. She was happy. She'd had a wonderful day with everyone and she was happy to go.'

'Don't try to justify this.' Nick shook the letter in her face. 'If I hadn't read it, you'd never have told me and I'd never have known what a devious witch you are. I'd have had my suspicions, but you'd never have been straight with me, would you?'

'What does it say? What did Jess say?' Kate grabbed the letter and scanned it quickly. She read aloud: '*I made her say yes, I forced her to agree, and I love her so much for doing this*. You see? She tells you herself.'

'I don't care what this says. She was my daughter and you had no right to do this. I could go to the police.'

Kate stood up. 'Go ahead, Nick. I really don't care what happens to me. My heart is broken and I'd be happy to die right now because then I'd be with Jess. But just remember, if you put me in prison, you'll be raising the boys. It'll make a nice change from me raising them on my own.'

'Don't start with that crap.'

'It's true, though. In the last three years I've been pretty much on my own with the kids while you were tied up with Jenny and then Jaden. I'm not saying you weren't there for Jess when she got sick, but you weren't there much before-hand. I'm not shouting at you for being a rubbish dad. I never went to a lawyer when you were constantly late with maintenance cheques. I let you see the kids whenever you could fit them into your schedule. I picked up the pieces when you cancelled on them or just didn't turn up. I never spoke badly of you in front of them. I bent over backwards for you, Nick, even though you treated me very badly. So go ahead, sit on your high horse, put me in prison. Ruin the boys' lives. You can't hurt me more than life already has.'

Nick picked up a glass from the bedside locker and flung it against the wall. He needed to hear something smash. He was afraid he was going to hit Kate. She winced as the glass shattered and the pieces bounced onto the floor.

'I will never forgive you,' he said, his face red with fury. 'I will never forgive you for being a *murderer*. I might even go to the police. What kind of a monster are you? I could never have done that. Never.'

'That's because you didn't love her like I did.' She raised her hands. 'I'm not saying you didn't adore her, just that I loved her enough to give her what she most wanted, even though I knew it would destroy me. I made the ultimate sacrifice because I loved her. Can't you see?'

Nick walked towards the door. 'You can try to justify it any way you want, but you cut her life short and that is wrong, not to mention immoral and illegal and completely unforgivable.'

Kate's eyes were swollen from crying. 'It was love, Nick, pure love.'

Nick walked out of the room and closed the door on the woman he'd thought he knew, the stranger who had killed his daughter.

Bobby's Diary

Mummy made me wear a scrachy jaket to the funeral. I hated it. It made me all uncomfortable. The funeral was horrible. Daddy and Mummy didn't speek even one word and Daddy was giving Mummy dagger eyes the whole time, which is really mean cos she is hartbroken about Jess.

Luke said Daddy was just acting weird cos he's hartbroken too.

Jess died exaktly ten days ago and everyone is walking around like zombies. No one nows what to say. People still keep coming to the house with food which is ridikulus cos we own a café and we have tons of food.

Everyone cries now all the time. No one hides it or tries to pretend or put on a brave face. They all just cry out loud. Even Nathalie and she's a strong French woman. Nathalie has a new boyfriend who writes poems. He has long hair and is a bit smelly. Granddad said he's a useless 'bad word' and she needs to get rid of him.

Nathalie says he is a kreative soul and she loves his mind. Granddad said she'd have to love his mind cos his body stinks. He also said that the poet isn't getting any more free cofee or food and needs to pay his way like a real man.

Nathalie said Granddad has no soul. Granddad said his soul left him when Jess died. Nathalie looked sad then and hugged Granddad and said she loved him with or without a soul.

Piper comes over every morning and makes sure Luke is up and studying and not in bed crying. Piper is ginormous now. She looks like a normal person from the back but a big whale from the front.

Mummy sleeps a lot and cries a lot and goes out a lot with Liam to a place where she says she shouts. She said she'll take me there one day but I like punching doe. I showed Granddad how to do it and he thinks it's great. He does it all the time now.

Daddy came over and took me out yesterday. He still isn't speeking to Mummy and still gives her dagger eyes.

He brawt Jaden with him and we went to the playground in the park. Daddy sat on the bench with his sunglasses on and tried to hide that he was crying but I cud see the tears coming down his face.

Jaden was kind of annoying. He folowed me everywhere. He can't get enuff of me so I tryed to be nice to him. He calls me 'Dobby', which is kind of funny. He asked me to push him on the swing so I did.

When I feel my hart getting sad about Jess and there's no doe to punch, I go outside and kick the wall. Daddy found me kicking the wall out the back yesterday and he kicked it too. We kicked and kicked until our toes hurt and our shoes were all scrached. Daddy ruffled my hair and said I was a great boy and that he was proud of me. I didn't think kicking a wall was something a Dad would be proud of but whatever.

I miss Jess a lot. It's like there's a big hole in the house where she used to be. Maggie said for a small girl she had a huge presense and made a big and beootiful mark on life.

I keep looking for white buterflys cos when I was crying really hard one day, Luke told me that Jess said she would try to send a white buterfly to let us no she was okay. But I don't see any, ever.

I sleep with Whiskey now. Mummy said I cud. If I sniff him reelly hard he smells of Jess. Mrs Lorgan is being super-nice to me now Jess is dead. Even Tommy and Declan are being nice to me because having a dead sister is way worse than a stuter or a brother with Down Sindrum.

Mrs Lorgan said time will heal my sad hart, but so far it feels the same - reelly reelly sore.

49

Kate sat opposite her father and stared at her plate.

'Try to eat something, Katie,' George pleaded with her.

'I can't, Dad. Everything sticks in my throat and I think I'm going to choke.'

George patted her hand. 'I know that feeling. But you have to keep your strength up for the boys. They need you, Kate.'

She sighed and shovelled a forkful of lasagne into her mouth, then gagged and spat it into her paper napkin.

'Well, maybe tomorrow.' George took the plate away. 'Are you getting any sleep at all?'

Kate shook her head. 'Not really. I wish I could sleep more because when I do sometimes I dream of her. It's magical. She's right there beside me. I can see her, but when I go to touch her I wake up, and then I remember she's gone. It almost hurts as much as when she died.'

George handed her a tissue. 'I had those dreams after your mother died. It's wonderful and terrible at the same time.'

Kate wiped her eyes. 'I don't know how to do this, Dad. I just want to curl up in a ball and hide and only come out when the pain is over.'

'I know, pet, but life doesn't work like that. You have to get up and keep going. It feels like torture now, it's all so raw, but if you keep getting up and living, one day it won't be such an uphill struggle.'

'She was too young, Dad. Only twelve.'

'It's unspeakably cruel.' George's eyes welled up. 'No mother should bury her child.'

'Why her and not me or Nick?'

George slammed his fist on the kitchen countertop. 'It should have been me. I wish it had been me, not that beautiful little girl.' His chin wobbled and Kate watched as her father fell apart. He sobbed into the tea-towel he was holding.

She stood up and put her arms around him. 'I'm glad you're letting it out, Dad. You've been so brave for all of us, but I know how much you loved her.'

George nodded and Kate handed him a tissue. He had been getting up every morning, cooking breakfast for the boys, getting them off to school and collecting Bobby most days when Kate couldn't face it. He'd opened the café three days after the funeral and worked from dawn until dusk.

Kate was worried he'd drop dead from grief, overwork and exhaustion. It had been three weeks now and her father hadn't sat down for a second. She knew he was going to crash at some point and she was relieved that he was finally showing his grief.

He looked old and weary, she thought. He had aged. They all had. Even Luke and Bobby had creases under their eyes from crying and lack of sleep. Kate had Bobby in her bed most nights. He'd come in to her holding Whiskey and telling her he couldn't sleep. She liked having him beside her. Watching him sleep was soothing.

She was so glad Luke had Piper. She'd been a trouper. Calling in every day to make sure he was up, walking to school with him and studying with him in the evenings. Kate loved how affectionate Piper was with Luke, constantly holding his hand or rubbing his back or resting her head against his shoulder. She knew Luke was comforted by her presence.

Olivia sent over little gifts with Piper, not wishing to intrude but wanting Kate to know she was thinking of her. Piper had delivered soothing bath salts, scented candles and calming body lotions. Olivia had been quietly kind and supportive and Kate loved her for it.

Hazel rang every day to check in and left messages offering to pay for luxury holidays for Kate and the boys, spa days for Kate, a new car, prams and cots for Piper . . . Her generosity was endless.

'I know you probably wish I'd stop calling, but I'll keep leaving messages and suggestions. One day you might feel like going out and doing something. When you do, I'll be outside, ready to pick you up and whisk you off wherever you want to go. We miss her terribly. Chloë is bereft. We're thinking of you all.'

Kate liked Hazel's daily messages. Sometimes they even made her smile.

Nathalie came into the kitchen. 'Oh, sorry. I am interrupting,' she said, looking at George's tear-stained face.

He wiped his nose. 'It's fine. I'm fine. What do you need?'

'I'm sorry to be a pain in the ear, but that woman, Rosemary, is in the café again with more casserole for you. She says she wants to make sure you are eating and she won't leave until she sees that you are okay. She is very insistent. She like you, George.'

George threw his tissue into the bin. 'For the love of Jesus, I'm going to have to get a restraining order. She's stalking me. Right, Nathalie. You come with me – I need your protection.' George walked ahead into the café, with Nathalie following behind, patting him on the back and telling him to be nice to the casserole lady.

Kate laid her head on the table. It felt too heavy for her body. Everything was wrong. The world was twisted and upside-down. The pain of Jess being gone was worse than she could ever have imagined. It was a visceral pain, like nothing she'd ever known. Even breathing was a struggle. Some days she was tempted to kill herself so she could be with Jess again. She wouldn't do that to Luke and Bobby, though, she couldn't hurt them, but if she hadn't had them, she probably would have killed herself. Her yearning to be with Jess was so strong. To hold her one more time, to tell her she loved her once more, to feel her soft cheek against her own . . . It was a crippling pain.

Liam had been a lifeline. She called him at all times of the night and he was always there. Listening, understanding, being sympathetic. She went to the cliff with him almost daily to shout. He held her when the pain was too great and her legs buckled. She relied on him more each day. She honestly thought she would have gone mad or done something stupid without him there to hold her up and support her. He was such a good man.

The kitchen door opened and Maggie's face appeared. 'Hey, I was hoping I'd catch you.' She came in wheeling a suitcase behind her.

'Did you come straight from the airport?' Kate asked.

'Of course I did. I hated being away these last two weeks. As you know, I tried to cancel the stupid Asian trip.'

'I'm glad I insisted you go. Was it worth it?'

'We got the deal.'

'That's great, Maggie.' Kate tried to be enthusiastic.

'Thanks, but it means nothing in the scheme of things. Nothing really matters any more, does it?'

'Not to me, no.'

Maggie bent down and hugged her. 'How are you? I know it's a stupid question.'

'It's unbearable.' Kate was crying again.

Maggie sat down opposite her best friend and held her hand. Tears formed in her eyes. 'I was only her godmother and *I* can barely function with the pain of it. I don't know how you're managing.'

'I miss her so much,' Kate sobbed. 'I miss her smile, her voice, her laugh, her . . .' The pain of a memory flooded her body. It was Jess giggling as Luke danced around the kitchen in his boxer shorts singing into a wooden spoon. She could hear Jess's laugh, her wonderful laugh.

Maggie rubbed her back. 'Breathe, Kate, breathe.'

Kate felt her heart rate slowing. 'Jesus, Maggie, how do people do this? How do they go on? What am I going to do?'

'Live, survive, struggle on. I'm here for you, and so are George and Liam and Hazel and the boys. You are surrounded by people who love you and want to support you. We'll help you, Kate, I promise.'

Kate gave her friend a small smile. 'Thanks, Maggie.'

Maggie got up and opened the fridge. 'I need a drink.' She pulled out a bottle of wine and poured two glasses.

Kate picked hers up and swirled the wine around. 'I haven't drunk since it happened,' she said. 'I'm afraid to. I'm afraid of never being able to stop. The idea of diving into the abyss of alcohol is very tempting.'

'I can see why, but one glass won't kill you.' Maggie drank deeply from hers.

Kate took a sip. The wine rushed to her empty stomach. She noticed the effect almost immediately. Her head felt light and a bit woozy.

'How are the boys?' Maggie asked.

Kate sighed. 'Bobby walks around like a headless chicken. He's completely lost. He has nightmares most nights. He's kicking the walls a lot and not saying much. I can see his little mind trying to make sense of it all.'

'And Luke?'

'Thankfully he has Piper, who is holding him up. She's so loving and kind to him, it's really beautiful to see. If it wasn't for Piper and the baby, I think Luke would fall apart. He loved Jess so much – we all did.' Kate was crying.

Maggie squeezed her hand and cried with her. 'She was a very special girl.'

'I can't bear it, Maggie. I want her back. I just want her back,' Kate sobbed.

'I know you do. It's just so cruel.'

Kate wiped her eyes with the soggy tissue her father had given her. 'I go to the cliff to shout most days, but I've run out of expletives to yell at the universe.'

Maggie drained her wine. 'Keep shouting. If it gets you out of the house and gives you even the tiniest bit of relief, do it.'

'Liam brings me. He's been so kind. He just gets it, you know. He doesn't try to make me feel better or tell me Heaven needed another angel or any of that crap.'

Maggie smiled. 'I'm very glad he's there. He seems like a gem.'

'He's a good friend in a time of need, that's for sure.'

'I think he's more than that,' Maggie said gently.

Kate shrugged. 'Maybe. I don't know. I can't think straight, but I do know that I want him in my life. I need him.'

Maggie poured herself a second glass of wine while Kate took another small sip of hers.

'How's Piper? She must be big now. It must be hard in school. Can you imagine being hugely pregnant and trying to study for your final school exams? Not easy.'

'She's great,' Kate said, 'and getting bigger by the day. But she's studying hard and getting Luke to study too. It's funny,

I was so upset about the pregnancy but now it's the only ray of light in the midst of all this horror.'

'Hopefully it'll bring you all some badly needed joy.'

Kate nodded. 'We need it.'

'How's Nick?' Maggie asked.

'Not good.'

'What was that all about the day he screamed at you?' Maggie asked.

'What?' Kate pretended not to know what she was talking about.

Maggie raised an eyebrow. 'Come on, Kate, the day he called you a lying bitch and was shaking a letter in your face. What was going on?'

Kate's hands began to shake. 'Nothing. He was just being Nick.'

Maggie reached out and put a hand on Kate's arm. 'Hey, Kate, it's me. You can tell me anything. You know that.'

Kate felt her breath quickening. 'I can't, it's too shocking. You'd hate me.'

Maggie frowned. 'What could be so bad? Come on, Kate, talk to me. I'll never judge you.'

Kate looked at her friend's concerned face. It was Maggie, her dearest pal. Could she tell her the truth? Could she tell her that she'd murdered her own child? What if Maggie never forgave her, like Nick? Could she bear to lose another person in her life? No, she couldn't, but the desire to admit what she had done was too strong.

Kate picked up her glass of wine, drank it down in two big gulps and spluttered, 'I killed Jess.'

Maggie stared at her. 'What?'

'I gave her an overdose of drugs and I killed her.'

Maggie's eyes were huge now. 'Jesus Christ, Kate, why?'

Kate looked directly at her friend. It was a relief to say the words out loud. 'Because she asked me to. She begged me to.'

Maggie's eyes filled with tears. 'Because of the pain?'

'She couldn't stand it. She wanted to go out her own way, with dignity. She was terrified of dying alone, choking on her own blood in the middle of the night when we were asleep. She was so weak and sick. She wanted to decide when to say goodbye.'

Tears streamed down Maggie's face. 'Oh, God ... poor Jess. And poor you.'

'Poor me? I'm a murderer, Maggie. I killed the person I loved most in the world. I cut her life short. I deprived her loved ones of a few last weeks with her. I'm a monster.' Kate began to weep. 'I wish I hadn't done it. I want those weeks with her. I should never have agreed to it.'

Maggie grabbed her shoulders and shook her. 'You are not a monster! You allowed your daughter to leave this world the way she wanted to. She'd been through so much, it's no wonder she wanted it all to stop. The poor thing was shattered. You're not a monster! You're the bravest person I know.'

Kate was shocked. 'Brave? I'm weak. I should have talked her out of it. I should have said no. She pleaded with me – she wanted it so badly. But it was still wrong.'

'She asked you because she knew you were the only person who loved her enough to do it. She knew no one else could.'

Kate let the guilt and fear wash over her. She put her head on the table and wept.

'You poor thing, carrying around the weight of all this on top of your grief. I don't know how you're still standing upright. But you mustn't feel guilty. Jess was dying, and her last few weeks would have been awful. You did what she wanted. You granted her a last wish. I always thought it was amazing the way she died after that wonderful day we all spent here with her. When I left that night, I knew she was saying goodbye to me. I felt it. I remember going home and thinking, I'll never see her again. But she was happy, Kate, she was almost glowing that day. You did the right thing.'

'Nick doesn't feel that way. He hates me, and he said he might go to the police.'

Maggie's face went red. 'What? The bastard. How dare he say that? How dare he threaten you?'

'He has the right to be angry, Maggie. I didn't tell him, although he was suspicious because he knew Jess couldn't take any more. Jess wrote him a letter and told him it was her decision and he wasn't to blame me, but he does. Oh, God, he does. He's so angry he could do anything. What if he does go to the police? I could be in serious trouble.'

Maggie stood up and paced the kitchen floor. 'Nick won't go to the police because Jess begged you to do it, and he isn't going to get you into trouble when you have his two sons to look after. Besides, if he was going to do it, he would have acted by now. Of course I understand that he's angry, but he won't do anything stupid. He's not going to bring the police into it. He's just lashing out at you.'

'But what if he does?'

'He won't. Do you want me to talk to him?'

Kate shook her head. 'He'll go mad if he thinks I told any-one. I think it's best to say nothing and hope he eventually understands why I did it, although I don't think he ever will.'

Maggie sat down again and sighed. 'I suppose you'd be pretty angry if he'd done it and not told you.'

Kate smiled sadly. 'That's the thing. I'd probably never forgive him if he'd done it.'

'You didn't do anything wrong, Kate. You just loved Jess, literally to death.'

'"Loved her to death". Now that's a saying I never thought I'd truly understand.'

They smiled at each other and Maggie poured them both another drink.

'To you, Kate, a good mother, a brilliant mother, who loved her daughter enough to let her go.'

Kate drank the wine. She didn't feel like a good mother. She closed her eyes and pictured Jess's face. Wherever you are, Jess, she thought, know that I miss you every minute of every day. Know that I struggle to get up in the morning because the grief of losing you is so strong. But I promise to keep trying. One foot in front of the other. I'll keep going to the cliff with Liam and shouting. I'll keep being a mum to Luke and Bobby. I'll keep being a daughter to George and a friend to Maggie and Hazel. But, most of all, I'll keep being your mum, always and for ever.

50

Piper rolled out of bed and waddled to the bathroom. It was still dark outside. She glanced at her watch. Five a.m. She caught her reflection in the bathroom mirror. God, I do look like a whale, she thought, and I still have five weeks to go. How can my stomach possibly get any bigger?

She shuffled back to her bed and lay down on her side with a pillow between her legs. Her mother had told her to put it there and it had really helped her to find a comfortable position to lie in. Mind you, Piper wasn't getting much sleep, these days.

Since Jess had died she kept having nightmares that she was losing the baby. She'd wake up sweating and crying out. Pauline had been brilliant. She'd talk her through the dreams and calm her down. Piper was so glad she was sharing a bedroom with her elder sister. The thought of being on her own at the moment frightened her.

She was scared of everything now. She was worried the baby was going to die, that her parents were going to die, that Luke was going to dump her, that she was going to fail all of her exams, that she was going to end up alone, living in a bedsit, on welfare, with a screaming baby.

Pauline told her that the nightmares were caused by her mind being overloaded with stress and grief – that she was grieving the loss of Jess, full of baby hormones and also doing the most important exams of her life, so it was perfectly normal that she was freaking out. Pauline had helped her come up with a study plan and tested her every evening on what she'd been doing.

Piper was also really worried about Luke. He was so heart-broken about Jess, he could barely speak. She made sure he went to school and tried to study with him, but most of the time he was in a world of his own. She was worried he'd fail all of his exams and get even more depressed. He had to do well for the sake of his self-esteem and also for their future. They both needed to get into college, then get good jobs and support their baby.

Pauline said it didn't matter if Luke failed his exams. He could always get a part-time job, study at night and repeat the exams next year. But Piper didn't want that. She wanted him to go to college in September and have the life he'd always dreamed of. She didn't want his life to be ruined. She was afraid he'd blame her and the baby, get depressed, dump her and end up an alcoholic or a drug addict or something.

Pauline said it was the hormones making her crazy: she needed to calm down. Piper was trying really hard to do that, but she still worried all the time.

She gave up trying to sleep and went downstairs with her books to get a coffee and try to study. Her exams began next week and she was very nervous. She was praying the baby didn't come early. She had three weeks of exams and then, after that, about ten days before her due date. She really didn't want to go into labour during Maths Paper 1. It was bad enough being pregnant in school with everyone staring at her and talking about her, but to go into labour during an exam would be too awful.

Another thing to worry about, she thought wearily. She made herself a cup of coffee and sat down at the kitchen table. The door opened, which made her jump. It was Dad.

'Sorry, pet. Did I give you a fright?'

'Yes.'

'Couldn't sleep?'

Piper shook her head. 'Nope. You?'

'I heard you get up and I wanted to check on you.'

'Sorry, Dad. I didn't mean to wake you.'

'Ah, sure I like being up early.'

'No, you don't!'

He grinned. 'Well, not usually, but these are not usual circumstances. How are you, pet? You look exhausted.'

'I'm all right.'

'Your mother and I are worried about you. It's been a very hard time for you, and for Luke.'

Piper could feel a lump forming in her throat. Her father came over and kissed the top of her head. 'You're a great girl, Piper, and we'll support you no matter what happens. I don't want you to worry about anything.'

'Thanks, Dad,' she croaked.

'How's Luke doing?'

Piper wiped away a tear. 'He's not great. He's just so sad. He adored Jess, and they had such a brilliant relationship. It's just awful to see him so upset. He barely speaks these days and I'm trying to be supportive, I really am.'

'Of course you are. Isn't he lucky to have you? But you need to mind yourself as well, Piper. This has been hard on you too.'

Piper sniffed. 'I miss Jess, Dad. I loved her. She was an amazing girl.'

Seamus shook his head. 'It's a cruel world. You were so good to that child. Kate said you were the sister Jess never had. You're a really wonderful, kind person. I don't tell you that enough. I'm very proud of you.' Seamus's eyes filled with tears.

431

Piper stood up, threw her arms around his neck and sobbed into his shoulder.

Piper knocked on the kitchen door, opened it and found Bobby sitting at the table, punching a lump of dough.

'Hi.'

'Hi. Do you want to punch?'

'Sure.' Piper stuck her fist into the dough.

'It feels good, doesn't it?' Bobby said, pummelling hard with his little fists.

'Yes, it does. Is Luke up?'

'Nope. I looked into his bedroom and he's asleep in his clothes with his headphones on. Mummy's asleep too. She's holding Whiskey really tight so I couldn't bring him down with me. I gave him to her when I hearded her crying last night.'

'That was really kind of you, Bobby. Where's Granddad?'

'He had to go out to the shops to get stuff.'

'Have you had breakfast?'

'I'm not hungry.'

'Would you eat a little bit of something?'

'No, thank you.'

'If I made toast and put it on a plate, maybe you'd have a bite.'

'Maybe.'

Piper busied herself making toast.

'Piper?'

'Yes.'

'Do you believe in Heaven?'

Piper paused. 'Yes.'

'Do you think Jess is there?'

'Definitely. They're very lucky to have her too.'

'I hate God for taking Jess away.'

Piper buttered the toast. 'I know, Bobby. It's very hard to understand why.'

'Mrs Lorgan said Jess died because all the best people die young and become guardian angels. She said Jess is sitting on my shoulder now, looking after me. Tommy said that was rubbish because his granddad died and he was mean and drank too much beer and shouted at his granny.'

'What did Mrs Lorgan say?'

'She said she was talking about children dying, not old people. But then Suzie started crying and saying she was a good girl and she didn't want to die young and be a guardian angel. She wanted to be a pop star like Taylor Swift. Then Juliette started crying because she thought Suzie said Taylor Swift had died. She was, like, crying really hard and saying, "But I've got tickets for her concert." Then I got supercross because Taylor Swift isn't dead, and even if she was, we don't actually know her and my sister is dead and it's way worser.'

Piper tried not to smile. 'They sound like silly girls.'

Absentmindedly Bobby picked up a slice of toast and took a bite. 'They are. They just don't get it. No one does. Having your sister die is the baddest thing ever.'

'Yes, it is.'

'It's worse than your dad leaving and having another baby. Way worse. It's worse than your mum not getting up to bring you to school because she's too sad to get dressed. It's worse than your brother not speaking because he's too sad to speak. It's worse than – than anything.' Bobby began to bawl.

Piper rushed over and put her arms around him. 'Oh, Bobby, you poor, poor boy. It's just awful. I know how much you loved Jess and how much she loved you. You must miss her so much.'

'I do,' he sobbed. 'She was the one who listened to me about my facts. I know people find them boring, but Jess always made me feel as if they were interesting. She listened to me when I told her about school too. Mummy and Granddad and Daddy and Luke and everyone else, they always say, "Not now, Bobby," but Jess never said it, never. She was so nice and I wish she was still here. Everything is all upside-down and I want things to be back to normal the way they used to be, when we were happy and we laughed and had fun. It's so quiet now all the time.'

Piper handed him a tissue. She tried to find the right words to comfort the lost seven-year-old. 'It's really hard for you all. Everyone's missing Jess and trying to cope in their own way, but it will get better, Bobby. I promise. You won't stop missing Jess, but in a while you'll be able to remember her and talk about her without it hurting so much. You and your mum and Luke will stop being sad all the time and it'll be just some of the time and you'll be happy again. It will probably take a while, but things will get better. You must try to believe that, Bobby. And I'm here if you ever need to talk.'

Bobby hugged her, squeezing her bump. Then he pulled back suddenly. 'Something moved!'

Piper laughed. 'It was the baby kicking, saying hello to his or her uncle.'

Bobby's eyes were wide. 'Wow! I'm going to be an uncle!'

'Yes, you are, and it's a very important role. You'll have to teach the baby all the things you know. They'll look up to their uncle Bobby and come to you for advice and help.'

Bobby frowned. 'I'd better learn more stuff before they come out then. I need to know more facts to tell them.' He ran out of the door and up the stairs, shouting, 'I'm going to get my book.'

Luke came in, hair askew, deep creases under his eyes. 'What's up with him?'

Piper smiled. 'Nothing. We just had a little chat.'

Luke slumped down in a chair.

'Coffee?' Piper asked.

'Please.'

Piper made him a cup and set it in front of him. 'You look exhausted.'

Luke yawned. 'Bad night.'

'Nightmares?'

'No, memories. Every time I think of Jess and a memory comes back, I feel as if someone's punching me in the gut. It's ... I ... It's just so hard.' He was bereft, she knew.

Piper held his hand. 'You loved her so much. It's just awful.'

'I wish my bone marrow had saved her. I feel as if I let her down.' Tears streamed down his face.

Piper kissed his hand. 'You did everything you could, Luke. Nothing worked. The cancer was too aggressive. You tried and I was so proud of you, but it's not your fault. It's no one's fault. You have to stop blaming yourself.'

'I wish none of this had happened. Why did it have to happen, Piper? Why Jess? Why our family?'

Piper leant over and kissed his cheek. 'There are no answers, Luke. It's just cruel and awful, and I wish I could say something comforting to you. I'm sorry about the baby and dragging you down with all this responsibility and, well ... I'm sorry, I'm so sorry, Luke. I feel so useless.'

Luke looked up at her. 'Useless? Piper, you're amazing, you're the glue. Now Jess has gone, you're the glue in our family. Look at you talking to Bobby this morning and coming here every day to make sure I get up and go to school and study. You're the only thing that's keeping me going. And the baby! Don't you dare apologize! We both got into this and I want that baby. The baby is the one good thing in this whole nightmare. It'll give Mum something to focus on, and Granddad and Bobby and me and you. Piper, I'm so glad you're pregnant. I want our baby so much. More than ever. We need it – our family needs it.'

Piper stared at Luke. It was the most he'd said in weeks. She felt tension flood out of her. It was going to be okay. Luke still wanted the baby and he'd said she was the glue. The glue! Tears of relief flowed down her face. Luke held her and kissed her.

51

Nick sat with Jaden passed out on his shoulder. The poor kid had a rotten cold and couldn't sleep with his stuffy nose, so Nick had got up and walked him around the apartment until he'd finally dropped off. Little puffs of his breath tickled Nick's neck, comforting him. He held him close and inhaled his baby smell.

Since Jess had died, Nick hadn't been able to let go of Jaden. He needed him close all the time. When he cried at night, Nick jumped up to settle him. He liked having a baby to hold and look after. It distracted him, stopped him crying or wanting to punch the wall.

He'd gone back to work a week after the funeral. He was there in body, but not in mind. He had no interest in selling stupid houses to stupid people. When a woman complained that the house he was showing her was a bit small for her taste, he'd wanted to shout, *My daughter's dead, you stupid, shallow bitch*.

He spent a lot of time in the bathroom or his car, crying. It was like a tsunami of tears. He couldn't stop it. The pain of Jess's death was crushing. On top of that was the rage and hate he felt towards Kate for robbing him of time. Time with Jess was all they'd had. Every second was precious. How could she take that away? How could she? Every time Nick thought about it he wanted to scream. It was eating him up inside.

Jenny had booked him in to see a shrink. She said she was worried about him because he wasn't sleeping and he was so angry all the time. She didn't know why – he hadn't told anyone. How could he tell them that his ex-wife was a murderer? He'd wanted to tell the police. He'd wanted to make her pay. He'd even picked up the phone a few times to report her, but he couldn't do it. He couldn't do that to his boys. Their lives were messed up enough as it was.

Careful not to wake his sleeping son, Nick slowly and gently placed him back in his cot and tiptoed out of the room. He went into the kitchen and took out Jess's letter. He read it for the millionth time. *I couldn't take it any more ... too much pain ... begged her to do it ... I love her for doing this ...*

I love her for doing this. Nick looked out of the window into the dark night. He remembered Jess's face on the last day of her short life, how happy she'd been. She knew, he thought. She knew it was all going to be over that night. That was why she'd been so happy.

He thought back to her face when he'd tried to get her to do more chemo. How upset she'd been. Her thin, pale face crumpling and her eyes pleading, 'No more, Dad.'

But it still came back to Kate robbing him of time. Such precious time. Nick folded the letter and tucked it into the pocket of his suit jacket, which was hanging on the kitchen chair.

The sun would be up soon and he'd have to get dressed, go to work and pretend everything was fine. When he'd first gone back, most of his colleagues had avoided him. Some gave him sad smiles and a few asked him how he was doing. But soon everyone moved on. People began to talk to him about work – houses, rentals, sales, margins, mortgages. He'd sit there listening but not hearing and wonder at their ability to actually give a shit about such trivial nonsense.

My daughter's dead, was all he could think, over and over in his mind. *My daughter's dead.* He wanted to shout it out, he wanted to scream it in their faces. He wanted them to feel pain too. He wanted everyone to feel pain. Why Jess? Why her? Why his beautiful Jess? It wasn't right or fair or even human.

Jenny had been kind, gentle and caring, but she didn't get it. The only person who knew how much this hurt, how badly the pain of Jess's loss cut into his heart, was Kate.

Nick wanted to talk to Kate. He wanted to talk about Jess and tell stories and share memories, but he couldn't. He couldn't even look at her.

The words came back into his mind – *begged her to do it . . . I love her for doing this . . .*

Could he have done it? Could he have helped Jess put an end to her life? No. Why? Because he loved her too much. But Kate had said she'd done it because she loved her so much.

What was love? What did it mean? If you loved someone, you kept them close. If you loved someone, you didn't let them go. But what if they begged you? Nick's head throbbed. He laid it on his arms and closed his eyes. He couldn't go on like this. He had to see her. He had to speak to her and have it out with her. He had to understand how she could have done something so awful.

He picked up his phone and texted her: *Meet me in Café Cos tomorrow 9.30.*

She responded immediately: *I'll be there.*

Nick sat nursing his Americano, watching the door. He saw her come in. He barely recognized her: she looked old and hunched. Her hair was lank and her coat was too big for her. Her body bent forward, as if the weight of the world was pressing her down. She glanced around the café, then saw him. As she came towards him, he saw the deep black

439

pockets under her eyes. She looks even worse than me, he thought.

Kate sat down opposite him and closed her coat around her, shivering.

'Coffee?' he asked.

'No, thanks, I'm fine. I've had three already.'

'You look terrible,' Nick said.

Kate shrugged.

'Guilt will do that to you, I suppose,' he added.

'Yes, grief, too,' she said sadly.

Nick leant in. 'How could you do it, Kate? How could you?'

Kate's eyes were full of sorrow. 'Because she asked me to. I told you, Nick, she begged me. She didn't want to die alone, choking on her own blood. I was there the night she got the infection and vomited blood. It was horrifying. She was terrified. She was afraid of dying like that, and she didn't deserve to go that way. She deserved better.'

'She deserved to live!' Nick shouted.

The people at the table beside them turned to stare at them.

Kate leant closer. 'She deserved to choose how she died.'

'She was twelve,' Nick hissed. 'She didn't get to choose when to die.'

'She wasn't a normal twelve-year-old and you know it. She lived ten lives in the last few months. She was more mature than either of us. You said it yourself, Nick, that night in my kitchen. Remember? You said how my mum always called her an old soul, and you said that was right. That she was different from other kids her age, more mature. You know this, Nick, please. Jess knew she was dying before anyone else did. She knew the cancer was back. She was so broken, Nick, so frail and battered, she just couldn't take it any more.'

Nick gazed at her coldly, his whole body tense. 'Every day I wake up and feel like puking because the pain of her loss is so bad. Then I want to kill you. I actually want to kill you for what you did. I could have had a few more weeks with her. I could have told her –'

Kate cut across him. 'Told her what? That you loved her? She knew. She knew how much she meant to you. You know she did. I'm sorry you're angry, I understand why, but I did it for her, Nick. You have to believe me. I did it for Jess. Whatever you think about me, you know how much I loved her and you know I would have given my life for her.'

Nick looked down at his coffee. 'I want to know how you did it,' he said quietly.

Kate squeezed her eyes shut and took a deep breath. 'I drugged her.'

'With what?'

'Twenty-eight Xanax tablets and fourteen dissolvable Tylex.'

Bile rose in his throat. He struggled to keep his emotions in check. 'Jesus. How did you –'

'Internet.'

'You bought the drugs online?'

'No. I got them from my GP. I pretended they were for me.'

'Christ, Kate.'

'I know it sounds completely insane, but it was for Jess. I would have done anything to make her happy.'

'What was it like? What happened at the end?' Nick's voice shook. Part of him wanted to know about Jess's last hours but another part didn't.

Kate bit her lip. 'She went into a deep sleep and then, after about four hours, she stopped breathing. It was very peaceful.

Before she drifted into sleep she smiled up at me and said, "I'm happy, Mum, I'm ready to go."'

Nick cursed under his breath. 'How could you do it? I could never have done that. It's not right. You should have talked her out of it.'

'Nick, I tried, but Jess knew what she wanted. It was something she'd thought about a lot. She was determined to go out on her own terms. I know what I did was wrong and immoral and illegal. But I granted Jess her final wish and that matters more to me than anything.'

Nick ripped up a sugar pack and watched the grains bounce off the table. *You have to let me go, Dad.* Jess had said that. He could see her gaunt, sad face gazing up at him, her brown eyes pleading with him. She had wanted to go. She had wanted to do it her way.

Nick looked at Kate, who was crying quietly. She was heartbroken. She was a shell of her former self. There was nothing he could do to make her feel worse or to hurt her more. The rage he'd felt since the moment he'd read Jess's letter slowly began to subside.

'It's hell, isn't it?' he said.

Kate nodded.

'It just hurts so fucking much,' he said.

Kate sobbed into a tissue, unable to speak.

'People keep saying it'll get easier with time. I want to shout, "Good to know, because if it gets any harder, I'll die of pain."'

Kate smiled. 'I know. Or the people who say it was God's will or there's a reason for everything. Really? What possible reason could there be for a twelve-year-old girl to get cancer and die?'

'I really hate the people who say she's in a better place – to hell with you and your better place. With her family is where

442

she should be, right here, right now.' Nick banged the table with his fist, making the cup jump.

'She was the core of our family. It's so quiet and lonely without her.' Kate was crying again.

Nick wanted to reach out to her but he couldn't: the anger was still there. 'I hate that you did what you did,' he said, 'but I understand that it was what Jess wanted. I'm going to try to forgive you because the anger is eating me up inside. It's destroying me and that's not fair on Jaden and Jenny. I know you acted out of love, but it doesn't make it right. I don't think I'll ever get over it, but I will learn to live with it. And I won't tell anyone. I owe that to Bobby and Luke. I just wish . . . I just wish we'd had more time.' His voice broke.

'I'm sorry, Nick. If there was any other way of granting Jess her wish, I would have chosen a different path. It was a nightmare. I think about it every single day, but she was happy, I promise you that.'

Nick sighed. 'She was my little angel.'

'She really was special, wasn't she?'

'Yes.' Nick wiped away tears. 'We did something right. We created an exceptional human being.'

'We did. We really did.' Kate reached out to touch his arm.

Nick pulled back and stood up. 'I'm going now. I think I might be able to sleep for the first time in weeks. I'll text you about taking the boys out.'

Kate got to her feet and they walked towards the door. As she turned to go to her car, she said, 'I'm glad we talked, and I'm sorry.'

He knew she was. He was sorry too. Sorry that life had thrown them this awful fate. But what did sorry change? What did anger change? Nothing. Jess was gone and she wasn't coming back.

Nick walked to his car and took out the letter. He read his favourite line: *I love you so much and I'm so proud to be your daughter.*

Nick pressed the letter to his lips and kissed the words. 'I love you too, Jess. I hope you know how much,' he whispered into the silence.

Summer

52

The door of her bedroom burst open. Kate sat bolt upright. Luke was standing at the end of her bed holding his mobile phone, his mouth opening and closing but no words coming out.

'Oh, my God!' she exclaimed. 'Is it the baby?'

'Yes.' Luke finally found his voice.

Kate jumped up and pushed him into his bedroom. 'Get dressed – come on, quickly. Where's Piper?'

'Her mum's taking her to hospital right now.'

Kate rushed back into her room and pulled on a pair of jeans and a sweatshirt.

George came in, woken by the shouting. 'Is it the baby?' he asked sleepily.

'Yes! Piper's on her way to hospital. I'm going to bring Luke now.'

'I'll come with you,' George said.

'Me too.' Bobby appeared in his pyjamas.

'Okay. Hurry up and put some clothes on.'

A little later George swung dangerously into the car park outside the maternity hospital, jerking to a halt at the front entrance doors. Kate and Luke jumped out.

'Stay with Granddad while he parks,' Kate ordered Bobby. She wanted to find out what was going on before they all descended on poor Piper.

Luke ran ahead and Kate rushed to keep up with him. They were told which room Piper was in and took the lift up. Luke went to open the door, and Kate stood back.

'Mum, I want you here. Come on.' He pulled her in with him.

Olivia was standing beside the midwife, her face drawn and tense. Piper was lying in bed in a hospital gown, looking frightened.

Luke went straight over and bent down to gather her in a hug, kissing her face tenderly. 'Are you okay, babe?'

'I'm fine, but the baby's coming, Luke. I'm already six centimetres dilated.'

'Jesus, I can't believe it's actually happening.' Luke's breathing was ragged.

'I'm scared,' Piper said, in a small voice.

'Don't be. I'm here, babe.'

Kate went over to stand beside Olivia. 'Is everything okay?' she asked quietly.

'Yes. The baby's heartbeat is strong and the labour is coming along well, and fast.'

'Thank God,' Kate said. She needed this to go well. They all needed the baby to come out healthy. After so much sorrow, the family needed some joy.

Piper cried out in pain. Luke held her hand. The midwife told her to breathe.

Kate felt they should be alone. She tapped Luke on the shoulder and said she'd wait just outside. He nodded. Olivia followed her out. George and Bobby were there, along with Seamus and all of Piper's sisters.

Kate had met them at Jess's funeral, but it had been a blur. They reintroduced themselves, but she was sure she'd mix them up anyway – they were all so similar.

'So why *do* you all have names that start with P?' Bobby asked.

'Because our parents are losers,' Penny answered.

Bobby grinned. 'What name would you choose if you could? I'd be Dynamo.'

'Cool name,' Penny said. 'I'd be Taylor.'

'Like Taylor Swift?' Bobby asked.

'Kind of, but hotter obviously.'

'Jesus, Penny, he's seven, tone it down,' Seamus barked.

They heard Piper shouting. Kate saw Seamus wince. He was sweating profusely with stress.

'Is she all right? Should you not go in and see?' he asked Olivia.

'She's having a baby, Seamus. It hurts. I'd have thought you might remember that from the four labours I went through.'

'Piper isn't like you.'

'What's that supposed to mean?'

'She's more petite.'

'OMG, Dad! Do you have a death wish?' Poppy gasped.

'I was more petite before I had five kids,' Olivia snapped.

'What's petite?' Bobby asked.

'It's what every girl wants to be, skinny,' Poppy told him.

'I don't like skinny. When Jess was sick she got all skinny and she looked terrible.'

Kate felt everyone freeze at the mention of Jess's name. It happened all the time. She wondered if they'd ever be able to say it outside the family without people being uncomfortable. It made her furious: she wanted to talk about Jess all the time, but people didn't seem to know what to say when she did and usually tried to change the subject.

Liam said it was because they were afraid to say the wrong thing or be insensitive, so they steered the subject away from Jess. Or maybe they were trying to distract Kate with other topics of conversation.

As if Kate could be distracted from Jess. All she thought about all of her waking hours was Jess. Her face, her smile, her eyes, her . . . Just her. She watched old videos of her over and over again. She kissed photos of her, she smelt her clothes, she wore her lip-gloss – she ached to be close to her. A primal mother's yearning.

Inside the room, Piper let out a shriek, bringing Kate back to earth.

'Mother of Divine Christ, will you ever go in and see what the hell is going on?' Seamus nudged Olivia towards the room.

'I will if my fat hips can make it through the door.' Olivia shot him a look, then knocked quietly and went inside.

'Seriously, Dad, after twenty-six years of marriage do you not know what not to say?' Posy asked.

'I never said she had fat hips.'

'You implied it,' Pauline said.

'And that's as bad,' Poppy reminded him.

Seamus waved a hand at them. 'I'll never understand women.'

Bobby's eyes widened. 'How come? You've got so many of them living in your house, you should totally understand them.'

'It's not easy, Bobby,' George defended Seamus. 'Women are complicated.'

'We're not really,' Penny disagreed. 'All you have to do is tell us we're fabulous and buy us presents and we're happy.'

'Shallow women, that is,' Pauline said. To Bobby, she added, 'On the other hand, there are women who like to be told they're smart and interesting.'

'OMG, Pauline! You are never getting married, unless he's like one of those geeky professors with Asperger's,' Poppy said.

'Can you please behave for once?' Seamus asked wearily.

Olivia came out, her face flushed. 'Not long now. The baby's coming.'

They stood around the bed, all staring at the beautiful baby girl in Piper's arms. Luke sat on the edge of the bed beside her, gazing adoringly at his daughter.

The door burst open and Nick fell into the room, out of breath. 'Is it . . . Did I . . . Is everything okay?'

'It's a girl,' Luke said, holding up his baby.

'That's . . . well, wonderful.' Nick gazed at the tiny creature, his eyes welling. 'She's beautiful.'

'Yes, she is,' Kate agreed.

'Just like . . .' Nick said, looking at Kate and she nodded. Yes, she was beautiful just like Jess had been.

'Would you like to hold her?' Piper asked Kate.

Kate held out her hands and felt the little bundle in her arms. She snuggled the baby into her neck and inhaled the baby smell. She closed her eyes and remembered the same smell when Jess was born.

Life and death. So close together, so far apart. To have lost her baby girl and have another born eight weeks later . . . It was heartbreak and a miracle in one.

Kate gazed into her granddaughter's eyes, blue like the sky. She was beautiful. A precious gift in a time of such sorrow. A blessing. Kate kissed her tiny nose and closed her eyes as the baby wrapped her little fingers around her grandmother's thumb.

'What are you going to call her?' Bobby asked.

Luke and Piper looked at each other. Luke cleared his throat. 'Louise Jess Higgins.'

Kate smiled. 'Beautiful.'

'Perfect,' Nick said.

'Lovely,' Olivia agreed.

'I'm glad it's not another P name,' Bobby said, and they all laughed.

Luke came over to Kate. 'I just texted Maggie – look.'

Maggie's text back read: *Am now bawling in the middle of a meeting! Over the moon for you all. Will be in later today to see her and hold her.*

Kate smiled. 'I'm glad you told her. She's very much part of this.'

Luke nodded. 'She's been great.' Looking at his daughter, he asked sheepishly, 'Can I have her back? I just want to hold her again.'

'Of course.' Kate handed him his little girl.

Seamus asked for everyone's attention. 'I'd just like to make a little toast,' he said. He had smuggled in a bottle of Champagne and some plastic cups. Now he poured them all a thimbleful to 'wet the baby's head'.

'Mummy, look!' Bobby shouted.

'Not now, Bobby,' Kate said. 'Listen to Seamus.'

'DON'T YOU DARE SAY, "NOT NOW, BOBBY," TO ME!' he roared.

Everyone turned to look at him.

'Bobby!' Kate snapped. 'What's got into you?'

He grabbed her arm. 'Look! It's Jess. She came to see the baby.'

Kate's head whipped around. Outside, on the windowsill, was a white butterfly. It paused, fluttered its wings then slowly flew away.

Acknowledgements

No matter how many novels you have under your belt, writing a book is never straightforward. One thing I've learnt is that a writer never has it 'sussed'. You are never going to find it easy to write a novel. It's not supposed to be easy. It's supposed to challenge you and take you to places you haven't been before. This novel certainly did that for me. I sincerely hope you, the reader, enjoyed it.

Every book is a collaboration and there are always so many people to thank.

I had to do a lot of research into AML (acute myeloid leukaemia) for this book and I was helped greatly by my uncle, Michael Moriarty, oncologist supreme. Any and all mistakes are entirely my own.

A big thank-you to Paul Carroll for his help in researching the role of a GP. He was also a fount of information on medication and the GP's involvement and function after the death of a child at home.

Thanks to my godson, James Moriarty, for his insight into the world of rugby training.

Rachel Pierce, my editor, has such great insight and ideas. Rachel is a huge asset to my writing life.

Patricia Deevy, for always championing me and for her valuable input into all of my novels.

Michael McLoughlin, Cliona Lewis, Patricia McVeigh, Brian Walker and all the team at Penguin Ireland for their continued support and help.

To all in the Penguin UK office, especially Tom Weldon, Joanna Prior and the fantastic sales, marketing and creative teams.

To my agent Marianne Gunn O'Connor, for being a rock of support and so very kind and thoughtful.

To Vicki Satlow, for her support and tenacity on foreign rights.

To Hazel Orme, for her wonderful copy-editing and for being such a positive force.

To the wonderful people at the Tyrone Guthrie Centre at Annaghmakerrig, where I spent a magical five days finishing this novel.

To my fellow writers, thank you for your support and encouragement. It is a solitary life and those coffees, emails and phone calls are lifelines.

To Mum, who has had a very tough year: you are an amazing woman and have always been an inspiration to me.

To Sue and Mike who are always there for me, through thick and thin. Thanks for your unwavering love and support and for always being on the end of a phone.

To my amazing friends – your kindness, thoughtfulness and loyalty mean so much.

To Hugo, Geordy and Amy – quite simply the loves of my life.

And as always, the biggest thank-you goes to Troy, for being my rock in stormy waters.

Finally, this book is dedicated to my dad, who died very suddenly last year. We miss him.